TAYO TERSOO

AND THE

HUNTER OF SOULS

Other Books By Edward Allen Karr

*   *   *   *   *

SERIES: Fringes Of Infinity

Lin Finity And Her Mayhem Rising – Book One

Lin Finity In Holding On
(A Fringes Of Infinity Novella)

Lin Finity And The Words Unspoken – Book Two

Lin Finity And The Islands Of Time – Book Three

Lin Finity And The Flights To Forever – Book Four

*   *   *   *   *

SERIES: Thrills N Kills In The Hills

Dayzee Dazzle And The Kildare Killers – Book One

Dayzee Dazzle And Her Manic Mansion – Book Two

Dayzee Dazzle And The On-Set Onslaught – Book Three

*   *   *   *   *

TAYO TERSOO
AND THE
HUNTER OF SOULS

Fringes Of Infinity
Book Five

Edward Allen Karr

LAKESIDE
LETTERS, LLC

Lakeside Letters, LLC
30628 Detroit Road, #247
Westlake, OH 44145

Tayo Tersoo And The Hunter Of Souls
Fringes Of Infinity Book Five

First Edition, 2022
www.lakesideletters.com

Cover design by JD Smith Design
Back Cover Model: Kim Hendrickson as Lin Finity

ISBN-13: 978-1-950886-29-6

Tayo Tersoo: "She said the entity I must try to kill would appear somewhere in the world. And besides devising a way to destroy it, I had to locate it first."

Lee Ternity: "Yeah, that's right. Lin said she had no idea what it would be. Or where."

Where. Yes, Lee . . . where. Shall I tell you? How could I speak of it without also displaying the weakness and fear that will soon bury me?

Lee: "Tayo, did you find it?"

He glanced again in the small mirror that he held close to his face, giving him a view of his back in the larger mirror. Stifling an urge to scream, or to sob, or to run blindly in any direction, he looked upon his own back.

Tayo: "It has found me."

From Prologue – New Year's Eve

Dedication

This work is dedicated to:

Any and all,
Whose problems seem small,
And cause laughter behind their backs.

But you're brave and you're strong,
You've been fighting so long,
To survive the horrific attacks.

What they think is a mouse,
Is much larger than a house,
And swings a heavy sharp axe.

Table of Contents

Prologue – New Year's Eve

"Tayo, listen to me! You are too stubborn for your own good. You never should have left Nigeria."

"I never should have told you of that promise I made, Jenny. It's been six weeks and still, nothing has—"

"Only six weeks! How can you know that you will remain safe? You cannot!"

"No, that's certainly a true statement—I cannot know for sure. However, much time has passed since I last saw Lin, and that tends to assure me that—"

"Lin Finity has been nothing but trouble for you! And that cult you ran off to join. Nothing but trouble, Tayo!"

"Jenny, The Shield is not a cult. And besides, that organization has dissolved. Their purpose was good, even though they—"

"Good? You said they were good? Oh, Tayo . . . chasing after some mysterious Words of God. You're a wiser man than that."

Tayo Tersoo sat in the tiny, cramped living room of his modest apartment in Baltimore. The heater rattled but kept his home warm, perhaps too warm, so he wore only khakis and a white tank top. He'd just switched on the TV in anticipation of the New Year's Eve broadcast that would soon begin.

"I'm still wise, Jenny, and everything I do is for the good of mankind. How could I *not* try to learn the Words of God? Would knowing those Words not benefit all of humanity?"

"Well, how has that worked out for you, Tayo?'

He sighed and rubbed his face with one hand before answering.

"It hasn't worked out. That pursuit led to events in which I'd preferred to have had no involvement. Still, all of that allowed me to witness the wonder, the mystery of Lin Finity and how she could—"

"Again with Lin Finity! Tayo, you are far across the ocean and telling me of your fascination with another woman. I must question whether I believe you'd rather be there with her than here in Lagos with me."

"Jenny, I'm not with her. She has vanished. I must question whether she still lives on this Earth or not."

"Then, why do you not return?"

Jenny Oladayo had turned down the blankets on her bed and sat on the edge, staring out at the midnight lights of the city from her fifth-floor apartment, a steady number of them yielding to the night as she watched. She twirled one finger into her thick, wild black hair and kicked out one slender leg after the other. The conversation kept her from focusing entirely on the new high-heeled shoes she'd tried on before ending her day.

"I do not wish to alarm you in any way, but I—"

"You do not wish? Well, Tayo, you have certainly alarmed me many times already. You told me of shooting a rocket to destroy a cabin. With people inside!"

"It was either that or—"

"And somehow, some evil power knocked you from the tree, breaking many of your bones?"

"Lin's power is not evil. I'm unable to explain it, but she is in no way—"

"So you say. Oh, I interrupted you. I apologize. What were you saying? In what way will you alarm me next?"

"I began to say there is still a negligible possibility of my having to confront what I mentioned to you six weeks ago. I promised Lin that I'd apply myself to that task, and if it were to appear—which seems less likely with every passing day—then I don't wish for it to be near you."

"Oh, Tayo, you are a good man. I won't claim to understand you all of the time, but your heart is—"

A loud squeak rang out from somewhere in Tayo's apartment, loud enough to be heard over the TV and noisy heater. Tayo froze and stared at the wall near his front door.

"Tayo, what was that?"

"Oh, um, Jenny, I believe that heater is beginning a new phase of malfunctioning. I'll have to call the landlord as soon as—"

Two more loud squeaks emanated from the walls.

"Tayo, that's your heater? I've heard many of its noises since you've been in America, but never have I—"

A loud scratching drowned out all other sounds in his apartment and lingered for several long seconds.

"That was not a heater, Tayo. Tell me, what's going on?"

"Perhaps it has taken its troublesome nature to a new, higher level, Jenny?"

"You should not joke. Something is—"

A combination of loud squeaking and scratching began inside the wall near his door, and it circled around the room, gaining volume with each circuit. Tayo hit the mute button of his phone and waited.

The sounds paused and even though he felt the hairs on the back of his neck standing at attention, he resumed his call.

"Jenny, perhaps I should call you back. It's late there anyway, isn't it?"

"Yes, it's late, but, Tayo, what's going on? Tell me you're safe, okay?"

"I'll be fine. You need not worry."

She began saying, "I'll decide whether to worry or not, and you—" just as the walls erupted with more squeaks and scratches.

"Jenny, I must go. Happy New Year. I'll call you soon."

He tapped off his phone and stared at each of his walls in turn.

* * *

As each squeak or scratch erupted, he snapped his head to see, swaying his short black dreadlocks from side to side, his big black eyes staring through his heavy black eyeglasses. But the walls told him nothing.

He wiped a hand across his forehead and lowered it, seeing it covered in sweat. A quick glance at the large thermometer on the wall told him that the temperature had not changed. After half a minute of sounds from alternating walls, the squeaks and scratches cried out from every wall surrounding him, so he quit trying to learn what caused them. Instead, he sat quietly on his beige couch, closed his eyes, and took deep, measured breaths.

Discipline. I must remain diligent. I don't know what this is, but I do know that I must remain balanced. Perhaps it's as I suggested to Jenny: only mechanical systems malfunctioning in new and unexpected ways.

He flinched when every noise halted, even the rattling of the heater. The TV went silent, though it still showed the start of the holiday celebrations, then it, too, went blank.

Tayo stood up from the couch, controlling his breaths, fighting the voice inside that screamed for him to run out of there. Even standing on his cold porch, wearing only a thin tank top, pants, and shoes, would be preferable, he knew.

But he stood in silence, looking at each of the quiet walls as he slowly turned his head toward each.

I've made a promise. If I'm being visited by whatever Lin Finity foretold, I won't run. What she described has convinced me that it's a noble cause.

A small squeak ripped loose from the lowest part of the wall behind him, from somewhere behind his couch.

Perhaps it's nothing. Still, I'll demonstrate to whatever elements of creation observe me that I don't submit to fear.

A scratch called out from the wall directly in front of him. He gazed at it without blinking.

It's a hunter, Lin had said. Something that's neither alive nor dead, yet still, it hunts. It hunts our souls.

A squeak from his left at the same time as a scratch from his right.

I won't run. I can't anyway. Where would I go? If it's indeed here, it has come for me. Lin has succeeded in bringing it to our world. Will I succeed at my task?

The squeaking and scratching began high along every wall around him. He took a deep breath, let it out, and closed his eyes.

Dedication. Diligence. Striving for the benefit of humanity.

The volume of whatever hid in his walls increased.

I will not falter. Though my eyes are closed, I'm not hiding, and I won't back down. Not from a promise to Lin. Never for Lin, with her glowing green eyes.

The sounds began low in the walls, too, adding to those still calling out from near the ceiling. The four walls were alive with whatever had come for him.

Though I hold my eyes closed, it's not from weakness. Or fear. It's only because what I face cannot be seen.

He focused on his breathing as the strange sounds grew louder.

I must remember to be steadfast. I must remain devoted to my mission. I won't feel fear or grow weak.

The sounds started a steady increase, growing loud enough to rattle small photos and African artworks hanging on the walls. It approached a deafening level, and the silent scream inside Tayo, alone in a hot apartment in Baltimore, keeping a promise to Lin Finity, who had long ago disappeared and perhaps had died, rose just as high.

I am strong! I have a good heart! I will not be—"

The squeaks and scratches became so loud that Tayo could no longer think of anything except covering his ears but only until his arms moved on their own.

Ah! No, it cannot be!

He opened his eyes as his stiff body fell forward and when he found he could not enlist his arms to break his fall, he closed his eyes, prayed that he might survive the impact, and held in his mind the image he'd seen from high in the tree near her cabin: Lin Finity, standing far away on a porch, her eyes burning like two green suns.

* * *

Tayo awoke to a silent but still warm room. He felt the wood floor cool against his cheek as he lay along the couch with his arms at his sides.

He remembered falling and when he initiated a check for damage, before ever moving, he found that his head felt fine as if he'd never hit it against the floor.

I remember now that I fell at a rate not dictated by gravity. Was I lowered somehow? How could that be?

He felt fine everywhere else, too, except for his back . . . that was on fire.

Oh, what can that possibly be? I'm relieved that the odd sounds have departed, but what has happened to my back?

He struggled to bring his hands up near his shoulders but when he tried to push himself up off of the floor, he found that he didn't have enough strength.

And his back was in flames.

I don't understand this, but I don't need to. My strength will carry me through. I'll remain diligent, and if this is somehow what Lin—Ah!"

Sharp pains, too many to count and all over his back, pinned him to the floor. There was more than one fire on his back, and they were moving.

My back! What has happened to my back?

He felt pieces of burning material sliding and scraping, dragging across the smooth skin of his back. He opened his mouth for a scream, but he would not permit it. His breaths came quick and shallow.

Is it on fire? Will I burst into flames? Am I already in flames?

He tried again to move and found that he couldn't pick himself up. He knew that even if he could run, there was nowhere left to go. He did manage to retrieve his phone from his pants pocket, and he called Lin's number.

With his tormented back nearly bringing him to tears, he listened to the greeting from Lin, as pleasant sounding as it had been the several times he'd tried, unsuccessfully, to speak with her the last six weeks.

A sigh that carried a small sob leaked out of him as he returned the phone to his pocket. He listened for sounds from the walls, heard nothing, and focused again on his back. Whatever had found his back felt like shards of burning glass, and they weren't happy with their present locations. They seemed to be searching, gouging and burning, intent only on making themselves comfortable with no regard to the man suffering quietly, facedown on his apartment floor.

Discipline. My heart is good. I can survive this. I will survive this.

He closed his eyes and fought to concentrate on his breaths, slowing them as well as he could, as his agony reached levels he'd believed could be possible only in Hell.

There was no longer any way to sense time passing. There was only eternal misery for the man with a good heart, focused and dedicated like no other, as the Hunter of Souls made him its home.

I made . . . a promise . . . to Lin. I will not . . . I will never . . ."

The pain never left, but it had been shrouded by a thick layer of night that carried Tayo to a place where his consciousness would not have to face the weakness and fear taking root inside him.

* * *

Before opening his eyes, he heard first the rattling of his heater beneath the window. Nearby, the TV once again transmitted the celebrations from Times Square. He groaned at the sound of a male voice proclaiming that it would surely be a happy year.

I must try again to stand, now that the fiery wounding of my back has ceased.

He pushed against the floor and found that his strength had returned. A cloud of dread approached when he noted that the pain in his back had been replaced by an ominous numbness. He could feel nothing from his shoulders to his waist and from one side to the other.

Standing next to his couch, he took a deep breath and looked around the room at the walls which had contained the source of the unexplained noises.

It's a relief that my back is no longer engulfed with flames, but there should be at least some sensation, not an expanse with no indication that it's still a part of me. Do I dare look at it?

He knew that he had to see, so he walked into his bedroom and stood before the large mirror above his dresser. Remembering that a small hand mirror was kept in one of the drawers, he retrieved it, turned his back to the dresser, and let out a deep breath.

Holding up his small mirror to see his back, he reached up with his other hand to grab the top of the shirt, and he began pulling it up.

The hand holding the mirror shook, but he kept removing the shirt, revealing what had been done to him. Finally, the shirt was bunched around his neck, and he stared at his back in the small mirror, reflected by the larger mirror above his dresser.

Oh no, that cannot be. What manner of madness is this?

* * *

After removing his shirt completely, Tayo struggled to calm his quickened breaths. He once again got out his phone but accepting that Lin might never be found again, he dialed someone else that he believed might be able to help.

"This is Lee."

"Lee, this is Tayo Tersoo. Do you have a moment to converse?"

Through the open doorway to his bedroom, he studied his living room area, which presented no evidence that anything unusual had happened. The radiator under the window still rattled, and the TV, which he had muted and sat surrounded by piles of books and journals, still showed scenes of the approaching midnight celebration in Times Square.

"Sure. What's going on?"

What's going on? I wish only to scream to you! If I were to scream, though, how would you understand what has happened to me?

"Nothing good. I need you."

"Look, I never should have done that with you."

He thought back to their encounter at the restaurant in Allentown—the last time he had seen Lin. His leg was in a cast, still recovering from Lin toppling him from the tree from which he'd launched a missile. And somehow, Lee had healed him. All he remembered was some kind of pleasant satisfaction and after that, his broken bones were no longer broken.

"I only meant to heal your injuries. It was fun, but—"

"Yes, that was exceedingly enjoyable. But I'm not telephoning about that. It's something else."

"What?"

What? you ask. I do not know! How could anyone know what this is?

"I've called Lin many times, but she hasn't responded. You're my only hope."

"Lin is gone, Tayo. She's just . . . gone. What's wrong?"

He took a deep breath and let it out slowly, knowing that he wished more than anything to speak with Lin but that that might never again be possible.

"She said the entity I must try to kill would appear somewhere in the world. And besides devising a way to destroy it, I had to locate it first."

"Yeah, that's right. Lin said she had no idea what it would be. Or where."

Where. Yes, Lee . . . where. Shall I tell you? How could I speak of it without also displaying the weakness and fear that will soon bury me?

"Tayo, did you find it?"

He glanced again in the small mirror that he held close to his face, giving him a view of his back in the larger mirror. Stifling an urge to scream, or to sob, or to run blindly in any direction, he looked upon his own back.

What had been smooth, perfect skin was now completely covered with raised welts forming unrecognizable symbols. Each one was small, and rows and columns of them bunched together and covered all of his back, from his shoulders to his waist and across the width.

He took another deep breath while listening to the heater rattling and feeling the once comforting heat in his small, lonely apartment in Baltimore on New Year's Eve.

"It has found me."

Chapter 1 – Are You Looking At Me?

Lee almost dropped her box of baklava, but she managed to set it on a small table on her backyard deck. Still looking up at the stars in the midnight sky above her in Jacksonville, she shook her head slowly at Tayo's revelation.

"You're serious? That thing Lin talked about, it's in the world somewhere?"

Tayo fought to get his shirt back on while holding his phone against his ear. He stood in front of his dresser mirror, turning to try to study the affliction that had invaded his back.

"I did not say that it was somewhere. It's here. It has found *me*."

"It's in your apartment?"

I cannot speak of it yet. I am teetering at the edge of an abyss and to speak of it, I must look into the deepest part of that pit. No, I don't have the strength.

"Yes, Lee. It's very near."

"What is it?"

"I don't know."

"But you can see it, right?"

"Yes. It's visible."

"Alright, then what is—hang on, Tayo."

The phone went silent and since Tayo had finished dressing, he again viewed his back with his small hand mirror. He reached it over his shoulder and tapped his back in several places.

"Sorry. I'm back. It was just Alessa. She was—"

"Your child?"

"Yeah, my daughter. I shouldn't have let her stay up this late, but it *is* New Year's Eve. Anyway, she wanted me to come watch the show. She's just kind of odd sometimes."

"I believe many children would want their parents to welcome the new year together."

"Oh yeah, nothing odd about that. She's just odd. So, what were you saying? That thing is there with you? What does it look like?"

"I cannot describe it, Lee."

"Come on, Tayo. It must have some kind of appearance. What does it—"

"I could select descriptive words to relate what I see. The problem is that my acceptance of my situation hasn't yet appeared. It might not ever."

"I have no idea what you're talking about. Lin would know."

"Yes, she might. But I fear she's dead."

"We don't know that. She . . . changed. Something happened to her. But that doesn't mean she won't ever come back. Gabriel thinks she will."

Tayo let out a shallow sigh.

"There's some relief and hope in that thought. Gabriel appears to be wise."

"Hang on again, alright? That kid of mine . . ."

She's a problem? Would you like to trade for my new companion?

Tayo laughed out loud just once.

Ah!

An axe, feeling heavy and sharp, struck high behind his left shoulder. He stifled a scream long enough to mute his phone, then one loud yell filled his bedroom and rolled into every other room.

He fell to his hands and knees, still holding the phone, and twisted his back from side to side, snapping his head to see. With breaths racing in and out, he fell flat out, facedown, moving only his head while he looked at the phone in his left hand and fought to not cry out again.

The axe withdrew, leaving his back numb like before. While panting and remembering that he'd have to speak again into the device in his hand, he watched it slip out of that hand and flop over onto the thick area rug between his bed and dresser. He stared with big eyes at his hand as he rotated it back and forth.

I cannot move my fingers now?

He stood, held up his right hand, and wiggled those fingers all around, then he reached up to touch his left hand. He poked a finger into it at several different locations, and he felt nothing.

Perhaps it's some sort of repetitive stress, but it has arisen as a delayed reaction of some type. Could that be? No, that's an unreasonable conclusion based on fear and the lunacy of my plight. Something from my back stabbed me, then it took up residence in my hand. That's a more plausible explanation.

With his right hand, he retrieved his phone, listened, and heard nothing. He walked the short distance to his small but very clean kitchen and sat at the table with his left arm laid out on the tablecloth.

"Tayo? Are you still there?"

"I'm here, Lee. Is everything okay?"

"Yeah, it's fine. I just put Alessa to bed. So, what are you—"

"Lee, my left hand is now completely numb and doesn't respond to commands."

"Why is that?"

"I don't know. It's only the left hand, not the right."

"Sounds like a circulation problem. Maybe you should—"

"Ah!"

Lee's questions arrived to Tayo's right ear in a continuous stream, but his eyes could only watch as the very end of his little finger, the one on his uncooperative hand, began to crack open. That crack fed itself into four more, equally spaced all around, and those red crevices started tracing jagged paths toward the base of his finger.

"Lee, I—"

Her voice became more urgent, but Tayo had more reasons to ignore her. Along each split, the blood began to flow, though he felt no pain at all. He'd forgotten to breathe as he watched the four sections peeling away like unseen pliers held the ends and dragged them down, leaving only the raw flesh below.

One of the strips of skin dangled a slimy nail on its end.

When they'd been ripped halfway down his finger, Tayo said, "Lee, my finger . . . something is taking my finger!"

"What do you mean, 'taking?'"

"What I mean is, taking it 'apart!'"

"Tayo, I really don't understand. How could—"

"Lee, this is beyond understanding. I fear watching it happen, though I feel nothing. Still, I fear not observing it even more."

"It's breaking off in pieces?"

"No, Lee, it's being peeled like a ripe banana. A gruesome, gory, bloody—"

"Alright, hang on a second. How far is it peeled back?"

"It's now about one half of the entire finger. Still, it progresses."

"I hate to even say this, Tayo, but do you think it will stop with the finger?"

"I hate that you said that too! No, I have no reason to believe that it will stop there. The hand will be next. Then, I can only pray that my arm will go numb before that is stripped of skin as well. Where will it end? Am I being skinned alive?"

"Tayo, you have to try to stop it. You know what I mean. Do it while there's still time."

"You're suggesting that I cut off that finger? What's left of that finger?"

"Yes, and I'll get there as soon as I can. You know that I can heal that, right?"

"You can restore parts that have been removed? Are you sure?"

"Well, pretty sure."

"What?" he said in a much higher pitch.

Tayo couldn't blink, and his breaths rushed in and out as he watched his finger undressing itself, attached to a hand that felt nothing, above an expanding pool of blood on his kitchen table.

"What other options do you have?"

"None. I'll mute the phone. Please. Please, don't hang up."

"I won't."

I do not wish for you to hear me scream. And though I don't expect pain from this operation, I still have every reason to cry. No one should ever hear that.

Grateful that his kitchen was small, Tayo managed to keep his dripping hand above its puddle as he reached for a drawer and brought out a steak knife. He sat and held it in his shaking right hand.

He located the serrated edge to the very base of the finger, then he rattled the knife onto the table, outside of the growing red puddle, and unmuted the phone.

"Lee, I must go. You will come?"

"Did you do it?"

"No. No, I have not. That's not an action on which a quick decision can be—"

"Tayo, you don't have time! Do it before it's too late!"

She's right. Indecision at this moment is due only to weakness. Why would I entertain the idea that I have a choice in this matter?

"You're right, of course. I eagerly await your arrival, and I will go now!"

He tapped with his thumb to end the call and set the phone down. The knife's edge, already wetted with his blood, again rested against the soft flesh of this finger, and he paused to watch in fascination and fear at the advancing flaps of flesh curling closer to where he knew he must cut.

Lin Finity . . . I gave you my word.

Watching in disgust and regret over the self-destruction, he held a vision of Lin's eyes lit up like blazing green stars as he began sawing, watching his nearly skinless finger roll with the cuts like a stubborn hot dog on a plate.

* * *

Oh, this cannot be!

Tayo had cut completely through the finger, finding that he needed a surprising amount of force to sever the bone, and he clattered the knife with a splash, releasing the instrument as quickly as he could.

And he found that the feeling had just then returned to his hand.

And the freed finger began wiggling its way through the puddle, onto the still-dry tabletop surface, and tracing a meandering, crimson path toward the edge.

I wish to scream, but I must capture my own finger too? What to do first? Can I do both? I never imagined I'd ever be asking myself such questions!

With a deep throbbing where he'd cut and a steady flow of blood from the open wound, which he strove to maintain above the puddle, he reached for the escaping finger with his good hand.

Even now, I seek to minimize the mess? Perhaps I was already insane when I began this horrible adventure? Perhaps I'm achieving a new level of insanity now?

Still dripping from a short distance above the table, he felt a knot develop in his stomach at the sensation of his own finger feeling like a piece of wet, shredded meat.

Ice? If Lee is to return it to my hand, should I immerse it in ice? At least, things are resolved and once I dress the wound, I can—

"Ah! No, that cannot happen!"

The bone of the sawed-off finger in his hand began to twist around, drilling into his palm. He gasped and let it flop into the puddle, where it continued to snake around, the tip rising up out of the fluid and circling around until it pointed at him. Then, it stopped.

No! Are you looking at me? What next? Please don't prove to me that you can fly as well!

Still bleeding and still stifling a scream, Tayo scanned along his countertop, and his eyes rested on the new bank checks that had arrived in the mail the day before. Ignoring the dripping, he stepped toward it, leaving a dashed red line across the linoleum, and grabbed the box. He lifted off the top, spilled the contents, and hurried back to the table.

Oh, you are still studying me? Does that bring you satisfaction?

He set the box down, winced as he snatched up the staring finger, and closed it up with the finger inside and the box top covering the bottom.

Well, now I can—oh, you're trying to escape?

He tapped the box a few times, and the scratching sounds ceased.

Yes, you need to cooperate. Do not forget that I own you.

He looked at the ceiling and instead of letting out his scream, he only laughed and shook his head.

"Finally, I can find some sort of first aid for this and then, before Lee arrives," he said aloud, "I must clean up some of—"

The agitated scratching inside the box started again, and the container was lurching around, moving closer to the blood. Tayo let out a deep breath, made a bigger mess by going to the cabinet for a heavy can of soup, and placed it on the box.

I truly hope that's the end of that. What madness am I living now, where I use food to aid in the confinement of my finger?

He let out a deep sigh and closed his eyes.

They snapped back open at the sound of squeaking in every wall of his kitchen. He also heard his finger's attempts at escape. His entire left hand throbbed.

Oh, Lin, I don't know about this . . .

He crossed his arms on the table, still careful to keep the damaged one near the slick red pool, and laid himself down with his cheek resting on the back of his right hand.

I'll rest only a minute.

The squeaking in the walls continued.

His finger fought against its thin cardboard prison.

A sloppy circle of raw meat kept adding to the puddle.

When I'm cleaned up, I'll call Anna. She has helped before, and maybe she . . . perhaps she can be convinced to . . . to . . .

With one low sob, Tayo couldn't fight the darkness that engulfed him.

Chapter 2 – This Can't Be

"You're really going to keep dressing like that? Copying that Lin Finity style?"

"Yes, Daria. As frightening as she was, her fashion knowledge cannot be debated."

"Well, the short skirt and heels do look good—way better than how you dressed when working with The Shield."

Anna Kelgina paused to brush back her shoulder-length brown hair on each side before continuing.

"I am even enjoying the lenses for my eyes too."

"You look good. I like how it made Lin jealous every time she saw you."

"I did sense some of that but mostly, I noticed anger. She is not a good person to make angry. You are wearing that camouflage dress today? With tall black boots?"

Daria looked down at her boots with a grin, causing her thick black hair to fall forward past her shoulders. She looked again at her mother while snapping it all back with both hands.

"Crazy, huh? For some reason, I felt like trying this on again today. What do you think?"

Anna shook her head and grinned.

"I have just now understood this: when either of us considers fashions, our questions to ourselves should be, 'what would Lin do?'"

"That's kind of brilliant, Mom. She'd say shorten the dress, I bet."

"Yes, that is likely accurate. She might also suggest that high boots hide too much of one's legs. She rarely hid hers."

"I think you're right. About all of that. Alright, I have a solid plan: lose the boots and shorten the dress."

"Still, all of this only reminds me of all that happened more than six weeks ago. Down in that tunnel with the Words of God, then being convinced to assist Tayo in St. Simons Island. Daria, I am glad we are done with all of that."

"Mom, we should just get the hell out of here already. Maybe not Russia, though. But why are we still hanging around Baltimore?"

"Daria, there are no longer any disastrous situations to attack us. And our lease has time on it still. You remember that Jack sent me a comforting text six weeks ago too."

"Yeah, I remember. About Lin being gone. Still, what if she comes back?"

"She will not be back. I observed the tone of Jack's voice—he was very despondent. I believe she is dead."

"If anyone that evil can really die," Daria said with a smirk.

"I do not believe she was evil. There were many times that she allowed us to live, did she not?"

"See? That whole idea is wrong. Who is she to 'decide' that we can live?"

"She was frighteningly powerful in unknown ways. That is how."

"Not powerful enough, it seems. I'm glad she's—"

Daria's phone vibrated in her hand and when she tapped to see who had sent her a text message, her face went blank, and her wide-open eyes stared at it. She finally looked at her mother.

"Mom, this can't be."

* * *

"What cannot be, Daria?"

"Um, nothing. Just a text from someone I thought I'd never hear from again."

"Someone like who?"

"Nobody. Look, I'm going out for a while."

Anna reached down to pick up her little black dog, Ozzy, before continuing.

"It is after midnight, and you are now going out? Who is your mystery person?"

"Oh, that. Um, no, I just need to get out and get some air. You won't be needing the car, will you?"

"I do not suppose so. I wish to sit with a glass of vodka and contemplate the beginning of a new year, one without the horrible, terrifying Lin—"

"Mom, you need to get over her. She's gone. And besides, did she ever really hurt you? No. Enjoy your vodka and the peace and quiet. I'll be back soon."

Anna watched her daughter slip on a wool coat, lengthy enough to cover the tops of her boots, and she donned a furry black hat. After grabbing the car keys, she paused at the door, blew a kiss her way, and slammed the door behind her.

A fresh bottle needed to be opened, then poured in a large, clear tumbler, and Anna sat on the couch in her quiet apartment on the outskirts of Baltimore, a drowsy Ozzy on her lap, sipping and telling herself that all of that madness had gone, never to return.

*　*　*

Daria parked in the street and while walking along the cold sidewalk toward a tall brick apartment building, near the former headquarters of The Shield, she blew warm air into her hands and cussed under her breath.

She climbed the dozen or so steps, grateful for boots that had tread enough to keep her upright on the icy patches. A quick series of raps with her bare knuckles ended with her jamming that hand deep into a pocket. A glance down the street showed no one about, the only company being the trash that was light enough to travel along with the cool wind.

The door opened, and a familiar face appeared against a backdrop of complete darkness. He was as she knew him when working with The Shield: short, military-style brown hair, intense eyes, and lean, angular features. His tight t-shirt only confirmed that he'd been keeping himself in good shape.

She felt a continuous wave of hot air pouring out, which felt good and alarmed her at the same time.

"This can't be. Benson, I shot you."

"Thanks for that."

"You mean, I really did, right? In that alley over by the headquarters?"

"Oh yeah, you sure did."

He offered a grim smile, showing clean but not completely white teeth in the faint light of a lamppost.

"You're not mad?"

"Nah, I don't blame you. You thought I'd rat you out to your mom, right? Because you were screwing around, wanting to take a picture of that priest?"

"You could tell? Hell yeah, I did think that."

"Smart move. Good aim too."

She shook her head, staring at the man she thought she'd killed, and stamped her feet.

"You're cold. Come on in."

He stepped aside and swung the door farther in, and Daria took a step into a tropical room that caused her to instantly unbutton her coat and flap it around, seeking a cooler current if she could find it.

"What the hell? Hot enough, Benson?"

"Hell? Not quite. It's only about ninety. Damn furnace."

She stared at him as he shut the door carefully and bolted it.

"How about a light? Unless you're afraid I might shoot you again."

"That's funny, Daria. Nope, not worried at all."

He flipped on a dim light, and she looked around a room that was mostly empty except for a few pieces of clean furniture. Nothing adorned the walls, and only the one lamp resided on a small table.

"Nice place."

He looked around and said, "You bring some life to it. Please, have a seat."

Before accepting a place on the couch, she wiggled out of her coat and laid it to one side. Right away, she felt the warmth of the couch soaking its way through her dress as if she were sitting on a park bench that had baked in the sun.

"Why so damn hot, Benson? You sick or something?"

"That's not the most important question on your mind."

She stared for a moment, then said, "Um, no, you're right."

"So, ask."

"I'm a good shot. I might not have been the most dedicated agent The Shield ever hired, but I can handle a pistol. I was sure I shot you right in your heart."

"So, you thought I was dead, and you left me in that alley?"

"Not like I had anywhere to bury you," she said with a grin.

"I suppose not. You could have kicked some trash over me, though. That would have been decent of you."

"Tell you what," she said with a smirk. "Next time I think I killed someone in an alley, I'll lay a newspaper over his head. How's that?"

"You really are a smartass," he said with the same unenthusiastic smile before he looked down at her thighs. "No complaints about those legs, though."

She took a deep breath before answering with a faint grin.

"They do look good in camo, don't they?"

He looked back up into her eyes and said, "Even better without. Probably that ass of yours too."

She shook her head a couple of times and looked at the ceiling with a smile before looking him in the eye.

"I always did kind of turn you on, didn't I?"

He leaned a bit closer to her from his seat on the other end of the couch and said, "It's New Year's Eve. Showing you is way better than telling you."

"Show and tell, huh?"

She leaned toward him, and their lips met but only briefly.

"God, you're freezing! Are you sick? That's why it's so hot in here?"

"I feel better than I ever have. Don't let the cold scare you."

She gave him another kiss, longer than the first, then stood.

When she reached down for a boot, he said, "Uh-uh. The boots are good."

"Let me guess: no camo, though?"

"Yep."

*　*　*

Anna finished her glass and gave herself a generous refill. She nudged the dog off to one side, stood, and walked to the bathroom, set her drink on the vanity, and chuckled while turning the knobs to fill the tub.

She wondered why she began to think of Lancaster Wolfe, the destroyed, demonic former leader of The Shield, while she undressed herself. But she didn't block the memories. She did lock the door, though, to keep Ozzy out.

Instead, she focused on one in particular, her favorite over the last few days: alone with him in his car, outside the entrance to The Shield's underground base. How he'd treated her like a pet. Seduced her. Then squeezed her throat in an iron grip, preventing any breath. She knew that she'd only stared at him, wondering if he'd kill her but hoping he'd have better plans.

He had, and as she dropped her underwear down around her ankles, kicked it off to the side, then set her drink on the edge of the tub, she blocked the rest of the recollection until she'd sunk down below the surface, up to her neck, feeling the heat caressing her everywhere.

Then, she let the memory roll on, allowing every intense detail to unfold. He'd spoken with such control as if there were no possibility of her denying his demands. He'd made so damn clear what he wanted her to do.

She'd felt his strong hand nodding her head in agreement. She'd been a toy in his hands, nothing more. A willing toy. A toy that loved not being able to say no.

Both hands slipped below the surface, eager to help her relive how freeing it had been to be helpless in his hands.

* * *

Daria soon stood near Benson, seated on the couch, wearing only her boots and underwear. She'd already tossed her bra across the room, smiling at seeing his eyes staring before looking up into hers.

"Nice contrast: camo covering some sweet lace. Don't stop."

"Enjoying the show, Benson?"

"Beats getting shot."

She sighed and grabbed the elastic strap hugging her hips, then she pulled it down along her thighs and shifted around until it got hung up on her boots. She leaned forward to free it, and he reached out to hold one of her breasts.

She paused to grin at him, and he found the other.

"Cold hands, Benson."

"Yep."

She shook her head and stretched the thin cloth over the tops of her boots, then pulled her legs free.

Looking down on him with her hands on her hips, wearing only her boots, she shook back her long, wavy black hair, and it tickled across her bare back. She watched as he unbuckled, unzipped, then slid his khakis down and off, leaving only his t-shirt.

"You seem to like what you see, Benson."

"Yep. What did I tell you when you had clothes on? Oh, yeah. Have a seat. That's what it was."

She shook her head with a grin and accepted his offer, a knee on each side of him. Before she'd taken him completely, she held his shoulders and said, "God, Benson, you're cold everywhere!"

"Blame it on the damn furnace."

"No, seriously," she said and began a slow, steady motion on his lap.

"How does cold feel? Something new, huh?"

She sighed and got a grip on his t-shirt with both hands as she sped up her motions.

"Yeah, new, for sure. Not bad either. I could get used to that."

"I bet. Just don't stop."

"I don't think I could. It's been a while for me."

"Time to make up for it."

She let out a low moan but never slowed.

"Just tell me when you're getting close."

She nodded but stayed quiet, and she rose and fell repeatedly, bouncing down onto his thighs and shaking her breasts gently with every motion.

"Oh . . . that was quick. Yeah, I'm getting close."

"That does feel good. I sure wanted you at least once before I died."

"Well, happy New Year to you. You got me naked on your lap to start the year."

"Tell me when you think you couldn't stop for any reason."

"Oh, Benson, I'm already there. I wouldn't stop this for anything."

She ground herself into him and shook from side to side for his staring eyes.

"You're sure?"

"God yeah, I'm sure."

"'Hell yeah' is a better choice of words."

She laughed softly, never slowed, and said, "Hell yeah. No way in hell I'm going to stop."

"Good, because I have something to tell you."

Between rapid breaths, while she bounced on him over and over, she managed to whisper, "What?"

He looked into her eyes, which showed the rapture that was just about to break loose for her, and said, "You *are* a good shot. I'm dead."

Daria gasped and quickly rose up but before she could free herself entirely, he'd grabbed high on her thighs, with both hands, keeping her there.

"Look into my eyes," he said.

She did and after a few seconds, her frown softened, and she lowered herself back to sitting still on his lap.

"Good. You like that I'm dead. There's no shame in admitting it."

She nodded, and her lips moved without her speaking.

"Say it."

She hesitated only a second, then said, in a monotone, "I like that you're dead. It's a turn-on."

He grinned and held her waist, his arms riding along with her steady motions.

"Good girl. Enjoy what you've always fantasized about: stripping yourself naked and satisfying yourself with a man after you murdered him."

With his cold hands on her warm thighs, Daria rose up as high as she could and looked down at him.

"God, this is—"

"Hell."

"Yeah. Hell, this is so good."

"Do it. Use a dead man for your perverse pleasure."

With a loud groan, Daria hesitated high up.

"You can't stop yourself."

She moaned as she dropped herself down all the way, and she only shifted her hips from there, finishing the act in a hot apartment with Benson's cold body.

Chapter 3 – A Tangled Mess

The intense throbbing in his left hand jarred Tayo awake, and then, what was left of that hand felt the sticky puddle in which it rested. Before opening his eyes, he listened for any noises coming from the walls and at hearing nothing, he let a deep breath seep out.

Sitting upright at his kitchen table, he looked down at the drying pool on the vinyl tablecloth, then at the ragged cuts he'd made to rid his hand of the finger that had been taken.

I will dress my self-imposed wound first and address the mess after that. And I'll pray that no more fingers, or any other parts of my anatomy, decide to rebel.

He stood and found his first-aid kit in the cabinet above the refrigerator, and he frowned at the inadequacy of it. Then, he shook his head and chuckled.

Yes, I should be prepared for situations such as this. Of course, I should. Every rational man would.

After treating the crusty damage, he wrapped it as well as he could with the supplies he had, then he rolled up the tablecloth and left it in the sink to drain and dry. After he'd finished, he stretched his arms out while checking the time.

Only one hour into the new year, and I live amidst a disaster that I can't explain, though I did volunteer for it. Perhaps this is the end of it?

A short walk into the bedroom, a lifting of his shirt, and the proper aligning of mirrors showed him that most likely, his challenges had only just begun. Nothing had changed on his back.

He looked more closely and saw that near his left shoulder, where he remembered feeling the strike of a cleaver, the skin appeared more uniform. Whatever had been written there had been erased, and the skin sagged in its absence.

No, I wasn't struck with an actual axe, but something has changed. The markings in that corner region appear to be gone.

He looked all around his entire back and sighed, then he let the shirt drop to cover it all.

There's a correlation—there must be. A portion of what has invaded my body is gone, and it probably occurred in relation to my finger desiring to escape its skin.

He pulled the shirt back up for a quick look, then let it drop again.

There is much to come. But I have the strength to do this. I'm dedicated, and that's why Lin Finity petitioned me to assist. It's for the good of all humanity.

Another look at the clock showed that only several more minutes had crawled past.

It's only 7:00 in Lagos. Jenny sleeps until 8:00. I'll try to wait because calling her now would raise concerns that there's an emergency. She must not know.

Still, he took out his phone, hit a few numbers, and listened to Anna's recorded greeting.

"Anna, this is Tayo. I hope the new year finds you well and healthy. Please return this call at your convenience."

Seated again at the table, he closed his eyes and listened to the walls. They remained silent, so he crossed his arms and laid his head down, with the intention of resting until he could call Jenny.

*   *   *

Half-drunk and beginning to shrivel from lounging in the hot tub, Anna heard her phone ringing in the other room. She opened her eyes and stretched her arms out, then she stood, stepped out, dripped all over the floor, and began to dry off.

Wrapped in a soft robe, she took a quick look around the apartment and saw that her daughter had not yet returned. She saw also that Ozzy waited on the couch.

That must be a special mystery date, she thought. *Good. She deserves some harmless, innocent fun after all we have been through.*

She poured a half-glass of vodka and curled up under a blanket on the couch, covering most of Ozzy too. While watching the front door, expecting her daughter to return any minute, the hot bath and vodka conspired to whisk her into a dreamless sleep.

* * *

Standing up and getting dressed, Daria looked down on Benson, still seated on the couch, grinning and with his hands behind his head.

"God, even that was cold. Whatever you have, you really do need that furnace cranked up."

"Again with God?"

"Oh, right. Hell."

"But you were right. I do need some heat."

"I will admit that that was a fun kind of fantasy thing, though. I never thought I'd buy into something that kinky. What a weird night."

"Me being dead?"

She laughed and said, "Yeah, that. I did like that."

"Not just dead. Murdered. You murdered me. How sweet is that?"

"You're a sick man, Benson," she said with a grin.

She'd finished with her dress, and she brushed back her hair with both hands. She shook her head and let out a deep breath.

"I gotta go. I told my mom that—"

"Oh yeah—Anna. Do you suppose *she* likes sleeping with guys after she's killed them?"

"You're a funny guy, Benson. No, she probably doesn't."

"It's all in how she's asked. Maybe I should ask her."

"Just like you asked me, huh? You really are sick, Benson, and not just your body temperature."

He let out a short laugh and said, "Someday. Maybe she won't even care if someone else did the killing for her."

Daria shook her head at him and said, "Anyway, I told her I'd be back tonight. See you later."

"Sure. Bring your gun."

She laughed and said, "Always," then pulled the door shut on her way out.

*   *   *

Tayo snapped his head up at feeling something crawling around on his back. More than one thing. He froze and fought to control his breathing, with the creeping sensations moving in every direction.

No, it doesn't hurt, whatever is going on this time. But is it normal? Would a normal back ever feel such things?

When at last everything had settled, Tayo sighed and stood, then he reached for his phone. He stopped and left it to remain on the kitchen table.

Then, he reached for it again and switched on its camera as he walked back toward the big mirror above his dresser. There, he fumbled around until he'd found a way to hold the mirror and camera correctly, and he snapped several photos of what he was relieved to not feel moving under his skin anymore.

Back at the table, with a tablet and marker, he looked at the photos and tried to find anything that he could reproduce on paper. After some study, he began to suspect that what had lodged on his back wasn't one single, tangled mess. There were regions where there appeared to be separate entities—symbols that were distinct. One was even repeated in another location. The rest *was* a tangled mess, and he stopped trying to identify others individually.

Using his clearest photo as a guide, he reproduced three symbols as well as he could, each on its own sheet. Then, he took photos of what he'd drawn.

*   *   *

"Oh, Daria, you are back," Anna said while rubbing her eyes. She stayed on the couch and pulled the blanket tighter up under her chin. Ozzy only studied Daria while peeking from beneath the cover.

"Yep, said I'd be back. You save any of that vodka for me?"

"Only a little," Anna said with a laugh. "Of course, there is more in the cabinet, though."

"Good, I could use a drink."

"You seem quite pleased with something. I will not pry, but I do wonder how your evening has been."

"Mom, I don't mind telling you. That text before? That was from Benson."

Anna sat up, clutching the blanket close, and stared at her daughter.

"He is dead. You shot him. Remember?"

"Yeah, I know. We left him in that alley. Somehow, he wasn't dead, though. Isn't that something?"

"He sure looked dead. I know you are a good shot with that gun of yours too."

"That was a crazy scene, and we got out of there quick. No one checked him. I probably should have squeezed a couple more into him to be sure."

"Daria, I am glad you did not do that. Are you saying that you met with him? Is that where you have been?"

"Yeah, mom. I have to say, he seemed kind of strange, even more than before."

"Stranger than before you shot him?"

"Yeah," she said with laugh. "I think he might be sick too. Who knows? Your name came up, though."

"In what way?"

"Nothing important. I think he'd want to see you again. You did work with him for quite a while."

"I wish to see no one from that past. The only past I am tempted by is back in Russia. The Shield and everyone associated with it can leave me to being alone."

"Sure, Mom. I get that. I might see Benson again, though."

"Even though he seemed odd to you?"

"Maybe because of that. It was weird, but he seemed so persuasive. There's something different about him."

"I would say to stay away from him. That damn Lancaster Wolfe was a persuasive sort as well. He was—"

"Swearing again? Just from thinking about that guy?"

"Oh, you are right, Daria. That was a dark time in my life. I do not value the company of Wolfe again or even Benson."

"Well, we're pretty sure Wolfe is really dead, aren't we? I mean, back at that cabin, with all the weird stuff that happened."

"Yes, he is gone, and that is good."

She finished her drink and set the glass down.

"We are going to bed. Are you staying up?"

"At least long enough to have a drink. Or two. Then, that's it. I'm exhausted."

* * *

But what are these symbols? I may need to determine that prior to devising a way to destroy this thing. Or even if I am to survive.

Tayo retrieved his laptop from his bedroom and set it up in the kitchen, where he sat with a cup of coffee to begin his search. Before even switching it on, he stretched and yawned as he stood up, twisting from side to side, feeling his back carrying a dead outer layer.

No, this isn't wise. Besides normal fatigue, I've begun perhaps the strangest challenge any living human has experienced. I must rest. In the morning, I can—

A soft squeak from somewhere in the living room caused him to turn sharply and stare at the entryway to his kitchen. He held his breath and listened.

Several seconds of quiet passed, and he let out the breath he'd held back.

A gentle stab hit his back, somewhere near where he'd been struck by a blade, near his left shoulder. He winced and reached for it, then it was gone. He stood, still staring at the door.

With no squeaks and no stabs, he walked over and peeked around the corner. The room remained quiet, the TV dark and silent, and the streetlights mostly barred from entering by the thick curtains.

He allowed himself a deep sigh, which he stifled at the sound of a low squeak, seeming to come from the far corner.

Expecting another pain in his back, in the same place, he waited and stared around the corner and into the room. For a minute, he paused, and nothing stabbed him again.

Will I lose another finger? Is that a mouse coming for another one? If it will let me sleep, I would owe it my gratitude. If it has any honor, it will allow me to—

A single loud squeak threatened to peel the paint off of the walls, back in the far corner of the living room. Tayo snorted out his breath and scurried into the living room area only enough to rush into his bedroom, where he quickly shut the door behind him.

Any observer might think I'm terrified of a mouse. Yes, I am terrified. But that is certainly not a mouse.

He allowed his breathing to calm before he undressed, looking all around at the small room's walls and trying to be prepared for more stabbing. He was left alone long enough to get into bed and when he reached for the lamp on his nightstand, he pulled back and left it on.

I have enough to fear already. Why add darkness? I cannot be blamed for attempting to minimize my torment.

He accepted the darkness only of his closed eyes and though his back didn't attack him again, he did hear what he thought was low, distant squeaking through his door.

I could be imagining that. Surely it could just as easily inhabit one of these walls. But it does not. Perhaps it does have some honor and wishes that I sleep and prepare for more horrible things tomorrow.

A pillow over his head managed to block out the squeaking, but he found, as his fatigue pulled him into a dark night, that his imagination of the sound chose to act without compassion.

Chapter 4 – A Research Project

Imaginary or real, a deafening squeak in Tayo's left ear caused him to toss aside the pillow still covering his head and sit up. He held his breath as he looked around the brightening room and listened. Only silence. He glanced at the clock and saw that he'd slept until 8:00.

He remembered his back, causing a spike to his heart rate, and it began to settle at not feeling anything there beyond the unusual weight of its unidentifiable burden. The throbbing from where he'd severed his finger, though, resumed and pounded with every pulse.

The entity has allowed me a fair amount of sleep. It's insane to think of thanking it any way, yet I am grateful. Likely, that won't last beyond the next calamity, whatever that might be.

While shaving, not wearing a shirt, he glanced many times into his own eyes, not knowing what he hoped to see there. He knew only that looking anywhere but at his back would be best.

He slipped on a t-shirt and khakis and took a seat at his kitchen table after setting a pot of coffee to brew. While getting water at the sink, he'd resisted the proper action of dealing with the tablecloth. That can wait, he'd told himself.

There might very well soon be other bloody articles deserving attention.

Before the pot had finished, he'd poured himself a cup and sat at the table, his black eyes scanning one website after another, image after image of symbols.

He stopped to rub his eyes, and he finished the entire cup, got up, and poured another. As the morning sped by, he searched every source he could find, studying every single symbol, and every family of symbols, looking for even a remote match.

Perhaps what I see packed under my skin is random? Could it be similar to gibberish spoken by a fool, none of it making sense?

Staring at the screen, scouring his memory for any possible Internet destination to continue his hunt, he gasped and arched his back from the uniform pain that had just erupted everywhere on his back.

They are moving again? Of course, it let me sleep, and now its workday has begun. I don't wish to know what it's doing, but I'm certain I will learn of it regardless of my wishes.

He pushed the laptop aside and lay across the table, taking deep breaths, fighting to not cry out from either pain or the insanity of it, and felt his invaders busy beneath his skin.

∗　∗　∗

"I slept good, Mom. How about you?"

"The longer I am rid of Lin and the rest of them, the better I feel. The coffee is done, Daria. Would you like a cup?"

"Yeah, thanks. A couple of those waffles when they pop up too."

They both sat at the table, eating and drinking, and when Anna had finished her cup, she said, "Oh, I just remembered that my phone rang last night while I was bathing."

She handed a bite to the dog on her lap.

"Right. While you were drinking, you mean."

"Yes, well, that too. I deserve to treat myself after all those years of chasing after the Words of God."

She picked up her phone, tapped it a few times, and held it to her ear. She set it back down and shook her head while letting out a deep breath.

"I do not wish to hear even from Tayo again."

"Why's that? He was a pretty good guy, wasn't he?"

"He is a remarkable man, Daria. I have never met a man more focused and sincere than him."

"And still? You don't even want to call him back?"

35

"I will return his call. Can a person be too good, Daria? If so, that is Tayo."

Daria sipped her coffee and studied her mother over the brim of her mug.

"You kind of miss that creepy Wolfe guy? Is that it?"

"Yes, he had a creepy nature to some degree. Mostly, he was just very intense. That is not always a bad thing."

"You know, that's how I'd describe Benson now too. And more confident than any man deserves to be."

"He never was that way before. Not before you killed him."

Anna grinned at her daughter and finished her cup. Daria didn't offer a smile in return.

"I really thought I did, Mom. I was sure he was dead."

* * *

Tayo hadn't blinked in a while, and his black eyes darted from left to right as the screen scrolled down, displaying endless rows of symbols, none of which came close to matching the three sketches he'd laid out on the table.

His heart jumped at the sudden chiming and rattling of his phone, and he laughed in relief at the realization that it hadn't come from someplace inside his walls.

"Oh, Jenny!" he said with a wide grin. "How are you? Did you sleep well?"

"You're silly, Tayo. Yes, I did, but I've been awake for many hours. How are you this fine day?"

Tayo glanced at the screen for a moment, shaking his head.

"I'm doing very well. I'm not thrilled with the cold of Baltimore, and I'll be happy to be back home soon."

"When?"

"I must complete my missions first, which I don't expect will take long. Then, we can—"

"Tayo, you and that mission. You are waiting around for something senseless that Lin Finity must have exaggerated. There's no real reason for you to stay there. Whatever she described will likely never show up. She was talking nonsense."

"Oh, I have to tell you about that, Jenny. Don't be alarmed because everything is fine, but the entity of which Lin spoke is indeed in this world."

"What? Where? What is it?"

"It's a, um, kind of like a vision. Sometimes, when I'm not focused on the world as I should always be, I can see some kinds of shapes. They're like symbols. I believe that might be what Lin foretold."

"You see symbols, Tayo? Perhaps you are only having some sort of degenerative eye issue?"

"Jenny, my eyes are fine. They must be because I've been pursuing extensive research to identify the symbols. My eyes are working very well."

"And have you learned anything about them?"

"No. Nothing. I don't even know where else to look—I've exhausted every resource I know."

"Well, if you were home, you could just ask Samuel. He's the most scholarly I have ever known."

"I've been so distracted that I haven't even considered asking for his help. Yes, and he maintains the church records, but he also has a library of what he calls ancient texts."

"I've heard that story too. I know no one who has seen any such books, though."

"I've never known him to be dishonest, Jenny. He might be someone that I could ask."

"So, you're coming home?"

Tayo frowned at the brown-stained gauze taped where a finger should be, then he took a quick glance at the dried tablecloth folded into the sink.

"Not just yet. There are still things that I would have to complete before leaving here."

"I say, you should just walk away from your furnishings and clothing and everything else. Your life there is over, Tayo. It's time to come home for good, not just an occasional visit."

Tayo felt his back beginning to crawl, slowly working around in every direction.

Oh, you are reminding me, aren't you? As if the finger is not enough? Yes, I could only imagine the revulsion and fear Jenny would feel at the sight of me. No, I am not leaving. I have honor as well.

"Soon. Are you able to meet with Samuel and extend my questions to him? I know he doesn't involve himself with cellphones and such things."

"Yes, of course. What questions?"

"I can send you renditions of a few of the symbols which I've drawn out. You can either print them or show them to him on your phone."

"Okay, I can do that. I'll print them, though. I won't want to hang around with him while he's rummaging through imaginary books in his imaginary library."

"You are wise, and you are funny, too, Jenny. Okay, let's end this call for now, and I'll send you three photos. Oh, and Jenny? Please just tell him that I'm involved in a research project, and we're looking for the historical context of these symbols."

"Ooh, top secret business, huh, Tayo?"

She laughed, which brought a smile to his face.

"Yes."

"As you wish. Send the photos and then, maybe give your eyes a rest, Tayo?"

My eyes? Please, Jenny, do not give this thing any idea related to my eyes!

"Thank you. Yes, I'll try to rest. Stay well."

*　*　*

"Are you planning to see Benson again, Daria? Despite him being odd now, try not to get too attached. We will be going back to Russia soon. Ozzy too."

"Mom, there's no way, whether I ever see Dead Benson again or not. I don't remember anyone in Russia anyway."

"You are calling him Dead Benson? That is a very strange thing to do."

"No, that was just for the fun of it. Even though I really think I shot him right through his heart."

"I have seen you at the range, and I do not believe you miss often. That was an unusual day. Perhaps that accounts for it."

"Maybe. Yeah, I mean, it's not like he can really be dead, is it?"

Anna stared at her daughter before answering. She started to speak but stopped herself.

After a few moments, she said, "We have seen much, but have we seen dead brought to life? I do not think so. Many things are possible but not that."

"Mom, we can't really even be discussing this, can we? Of course, he's not dead. He's just a weird guy now—probably from all we've been through."

"We have been through many things. That is true."

She looked at her phone but didn't reach for it.

"You've got no good reason not to give him a call back, do you?"

"I do not suppose so."

After glancing at her daughter, Anna again focused on her phone.

"Well?"

"Perhaps a drink of vodka first would be—"

"Mom! You just had waffles, and you're thinking about swilling down some booze now?"

"Yes, well, I do not know anything about swilling it. Maybe just—"

"How about just giving that guy a call? Oh, you know what? I bet he just wants some of that cash you cleared out of headquarters. We all went our separate ways, and I doubt he ever got a cut. He deserves some."

"Yes, he likely does. He was a very dedicated member of The Shield."

She stared at her phone again.

"God, Mom. Oops. I mean, Hell, Mom."
Anna looked up to see Daria grinning back at her.
"Fine. I will call Tayo."

*   *   *

Tayo had just ended his call with Jenny, followed by emailing the three photos of the symbols he'd drawn, when he heard squeaking behind his stove.

Oh, no. Not the mouse again. Where is your axe, little mouse?

The axe found his back.

"Ah!"

He gasped and reached for it, allowing his phone to clatter onto the tabletop. He writhed in silence as the sharp edge twisted around, digging in deeper.

It was a joke, mouse! Can you read my mind too?

While panting and reaching with both hands for the handle of the sharp tool behind him that he knew didn't exist, his phone rattled and rang on the table. He leaned over enough to see that it was Anna Kelgina.

Chapter 5 – Got Me Going

"Mom, you can't just ring the guy, then hang up."

"Well, yes, I can, Daria. I just did. I will call him soon. I am surprised he has not left for Nigeria."

"Probably because of that curse Lin put on him. Why on Earth would he volunteer for something like that?"

"First, it is not a curse. And second, he—"

"Not a curse, huh? Tell me, then: what exactly did Lin set him up for?"

"You know as much as I. After Lin left in that rainstorm, we—"

"Oh yeah, that rain. I've never seen it rain that hard."

"Yes, it was a gigantic storm. After Lin left, I know only what Tayo told us. It was something about him having to fight something from another world. It did not make sense to me."

"It still doesn't. Really, though, he did kind of volunteer."

"Do you remember how he acted at Lin's cabin, after he fired a rocket at her? He was like a hypnotized man."

"Yeah, and he was still like that in St. Simons. I think maybe he's nuts. And I bet he's not as good as he lets on. He's probably got a nasty side to him, just like—"

"Dead Benson?"

Daria grinned and said, "Yeah, he's kind of nasty."

"And apparently, that has impressed you. I will tell you who was nasty: Wolfe."

"Yeah, Mom, but you seemed to be okay with that."

"Well, Daria, he was a memorable sort of person, that is all. Anyway, that is all behind us now. Soon, you and Ozzy and I can—"

Daria's phone rang and buzzed on the end table next to where she sat on the couch. She picked it up and smiled after tapping it a couple of times.

"Do not tell me. Benson again?"

"Yep. Tell you what: save some vodka for me, and I'll see you later."

"Daria, it is early in the day."

Daria only shook her head and grinned at her mother.

"Well, I mean that it is too early that I would leave none for you. Later, perhaps."

"Hey, live a little, Mom. Think of all we've been through."

She grabbed the car keys, got up and wrapped her coat around her, then put on her furry hat. She stopped at the door, and Anna said, "You forgot your gun."

Daria laughed once and said, "That's what you think."

*　*　*

Anna remained on the couch, scratching around Ozzy's ears and listening to Daria drive away.

"Maybe I will have a small amount. Do not tell your sister, okay?"

Ozzy only tilted his head and stared back at her.

"Thank you."

She smiled and stood, stretched her arms out, and before she could take a step, heard three steady pounds on the door.

"Ozzy, that cannot be Daria. Who knows that we live here? No one."

She left the dog comfortable on the couch and walked toward the door, saying, "Perhaps it a postal employee."

Through the peephole, Anna saw the back of a warm hat, but she noticed that there were no clouds of vapor being exhaled toward the street. She hesitated until the stranger turned and focused his serious eyes on whoever might be watching him through the door.

She unlocked the door, pulled it in, and said, "Benson, you really are alive."

"Who would've thought?"

He blew on his hands, even though he wore gloves, and said, "Um, inside would be good. Why don't you invite me in?"

"Oh, I am sorry. Of course, please come in, Benson."

He soon stood inside, and Anna closed the door. She waited for him to hand her his coat, but he didn't even unzip it. He did look around the living room of the apartment that she shared with her daughter, though.

"Hell, it's cold in here. Trouble paying the heat bills, Anna?"

"It is actually a good temperature in this room. You are cold only from standing on that porch. You will warm up."

He laughed and said, "Right."

"It is a surprise to see you."

"Because I was dead?"

"We did believe so. We believed Daria had shot you. She does not miss."

"Nope, she's a good shot. I'd like to sit."

"I apologize again. Yes, of course. Have a seat."

"I like the sound of that."

He walked over and sat next to Ozzy, who promptly jumped to the floor and stared at him from a few steps away.

"Perhaps he does not remember you, Benson. He mostly saw you down in that damn tunnel, not in a home."

"That damn tunnel. And that damn elevator room up top. And that goddamn alley where—"

"Where Daria shot you. Yes, I know. We did not wish for you to be shot. Daria has not said much about that."

"What's to say? She probably thought I was a cop or something. Winged me. I thought it best to just lie there awhile."

"Like a dead man."

"Yeah. It was easy."

"You looked dead."

"Yet, here I am."

"Not to appear rude, but why *are* you here, Benson? The Shield is disbanded, never to return. Even Wolfe is long gone."

"Ran out of cash."

"Oh, you must think that—"

"I don't 'think,' Anna. I know. You wouldn't leave all that cash down in the office. How about spreading some of that around?"

"You have used a curious choice of words, Benson."

"Depends on what I'm thinking about."

She stared at him, and he stared back. Ozzy let out one short growl, causing her to look at him.

"Ozzy, be polite. He is an old associate that you might not remember."

She looked back at Benson.

"You are correct—I do have some cash. Not enough to 'spread around,' though."

She caught him glancing at her breasts in her tight, low-cut sweater before he said, "I'm guessing you have lots to share. If Wolfe were here, I bet you'd offer him something."

She shook her head while holding his gaze, then she grinned and said, "Yes, well, Wolfe has departed. At Lin's cabin, we watched some unbelievable thing destroy him. I do not believe he will be back."

"He's full of surprises. I'd say, be ready for anything. Wolfe mentioned how capable you were. He said you were always prepared for whatever came up."

She looked down at her hands in her lap and frowned before speaking.

"As Assistant Director of The Shield, much was required of me."

"Yeah. He said that."

"Must we speak of a dead man like this?"

"Got something against dead men?"

"No, it is just that—"

"Where's the thermostat? I'd prefer to heat things up."

"You are still not warm? Okay."

She rose and walked to the entryway to the kitchen, where she set it to a higher temperature. She turned quickly, and his eyes, which had been focused at a lower level, turned up to hold her gaze.

"There. Perhaps you are not well?"

"I feel great."

"You really did appear dead."

"Just now? On your couch?"

She laughed and said, "No, Benson. In that alley."

"After you and the rest of them left, Wolfe came back. He got me going again."

"I did not know that he had medical training."

"Nope. Never did."

"Well, we do not need to dwell on details from that past. I can give you some money, but I have a family, and we need to—"

"Mother, daughter, and dog."

"Yes, and we will likely leave the country soon. There is no reason for us to remain."

He let out a deep breath, and Anna felt cool air against her cheek.

"Alright. Whatever you can bare. I mean, 'spare.'"

She saw him again glancing at her chest. She waited until he looked back up at her eyes.

"As a precaution, that money is not kept here. If you and Daria wish to have coffee again, she can—"

"I don't drink coffee. She didn't either."

He continued to stare into her eyes.

"Yes, well, I can ask her to deliver an amount to you. Now, if you do not mind, I need to make a phone call and run some errands."

"Without a car?"

"You wish to call attention to how you sent Daria scurrying somewhere with a false text message, only so that you can ambush me here?"

"I wouldn't call it an ambush."

"But the rest is true. Okay, I meant that I will walk to take care of some things."

He sighed and stood up, still packaged up in his coat and hat.

"Thanks. Dealing with life isn't easy without money."

He walked to the door and stopped.

"I like that it's coming from you and from your daughter. You're both pitching in."

He held her gaze for a moment, then opened the door and stepped out onto the porch.

"Maybe go lie down for a while, Benson. You should not be that cold."

"I do need to find some way to warm up. See you, Anna."

She quickly closed and bolted the door and leaned her back into it. Ozzy growled once and jumped back up onto the couch.

* * *

Tayo had bagged up his tablecloth to prevent any unwanted attention, and he'd finished a quiet lunch. His priorities remained split between his back, which felt only heavy and thicker than it should be, and the walls, where nothing resembling a mouse announced its presence.

The plate and utensils had been rinsed and were waiting in the sink, and he'd just opened his laptop for more research, though he felt that he'd exhausted every resource he could find.

His phone rang and rattled next to the laptop, and he paused to express his wishes to anyone or anything that could help.

Let that be Lin. Let her say it was all a misunderstanding and that this thing needed to be returned to whatever pit it inhabited. I hope she saved the receipt.

He laughed at his thoughts and tipped the phone up, saw that it was Jenny, and smiled despite the caller being unable to rescue him from his unusual fate.

"Hello, Jenny. Have you had a good day?"

"Yes, Tayo. I did some shopping, mostly new shoes, and the weather here today is very good. More importantly, I was able to get prints of the photos you sent over to Samuel."

"I thank you sincerely. It's likely a dead end, but there is always hope. Did he seem surprised at the sight of them?"

"Oh, I don't know. I had to leave them for him. His staff said he was out visiting the sick at the hospital."

"Soon, perhaps, he'll tell you something that can help explain what they are."

"No, I think he'll call you. I put your name and phone number on the top sheet. I'm not sure that the woman who accepted them even knows who I am."

"That's all fine, Jenny. I will await his call, then."

"You really don't know what those are? They're just something you imagined?"

Oh, Jenny. How I wish they were only from my imagination. I would immediately imagine them gone!

"Yes, but they're persistent company. I feel that they must have some meaning."

"You know, you could just come home, then you and Samuel could research them together."

"I can't, Jenny. Not yet."

"Because of Lin Finity."

"No, that's not accurate. It's because of the task for which I have offered myself. Lin is gone, remember?"

"Yeah, Tayo. Yeah, I remember. Gone but not forgotten, it seems."

"Jenny, you know it's not like that. Yes, she's quite astounding and memorable, but those are not words bearing any affection or thoughts of romance."

"What of Anna, then? I'll never forget how she swept you away from the university in Makurdi. Tayo, you had only one year left, and you ran off with Anna to—"

"Jenny, please. Anna enlisted me to help decipher the Words of God. Do you remember? I must always apply myself to help humanity in whatever ways that I can. She, too, isn't a focus of my affection. You are, Jenny. Only you."

"I believe you, Tayo. I feel the same about you. Your short visits aren't enough. In between, all I see is your face on a screen, and I hear your voice, but you are so far away. How many more years—"

"Jenny, it will not be years! This task may not even present itself, and then I'll return to you. Soon. I promise."

"I do like the sound of that. Okay, Tayo. We're sitting down to dinner here, so I must go. I hope Samuel can help you. And I hope you can come home."

"Yes to both of those hopes. Goodbye, Jenny."

"Goodbye, Tayo."

* * *

Lee Ternity sat in silence on a patio chair on her deck behind her house in Jacksonville, Florida. She let out a deep breath, stretched her arms out to the front, then let them drop. She opened her eyes and turned to see the eyes she knew had been watching her.

"Don't ask again, Alessa. I already explained this to you many times."

"I just like it, Mom. You know that. None of my friends have a mom that can do that."

"Well, that's certainly true. Maybe nobody else anywhere. Anyway, are you about ready to stay with Grandma for a while? It took her a while to get ready for you but now, I need to get going."

"I like staying with Grandma. Why are you leaving?"

Lee paused to look at her daughter's angelic face. She smiled and reached for another donut from the box on the table next to her.

"Alright. It's for a very good reason, Lessa. Do you remember that friend of mine named Lin?"

Alessa nodded and said, "Lin Finity. I like that name."

"She picked it. That wasn't always her name."

"How come she changed it?"

"Well, she said it was because she realized that she's infinite. Her spirit. She sensed that she has no limits."

48

"Isn't everybody, Mom?"

Lee stared at her daughter for a second, then took another bite.

"Well, Honey, it's just the way her life was going. It just fit. Hey, I never told you that Lin kind of gave me a new name, too, but I'm not officially changing mine."

"What's your new name, Mom?"

"Lee Ternity. You're still Alessa Turner, and I'm still Lee Turner. It's just a fun thing. Like an inside joke."

She waited for her daughter to smile or comment, but she only looked out at the trees ringing their backyard.

Without looking back at her mother, Alessa said, "I don't think it's a joke."

Lee stopped chewing.

"How do you know that?"

"She's like you? Can she do what you just did?"

"Um, yeah, something like that. Anyway, to answer your question, I'm going to help another friend of Lin's. His name is Tayo. He called and asked if I could help him with some things for a short while."

"Why does he need help?"

"Well, Honey, Lin kind of asked him to take care of something, and I think he's having a rough time. I won't be gone long."

Alessa turned from the trees and held her mother's gaze.

"I have to go too."

"No, Honey, there's school pretty soon, and—"

"Mom."

Lee looked at her daughter's eyes, big and unblinking, and she sat so still that she could have been a photograph.

"Sure, Lessa. Alright. Let's pack and get going."

"After you eat a donut?"

Lee smiled and said, "Yep. There's time."

Chapter 6 – To Never Dream Again

How long ago did I forget the research and begin to sit here, paralyzed, listening to the walls and anticipating the axe?

After closing the laptop, he stood and stretched, allocating some attention to the thought of lunch.

I will certainly not cut up a hot dog for lunch . . .

Still pondering his menu options, he heard his phone rattle first, then ring on the table that no longer had a tablecloth.

"Anna, thank you for returning my call. How are you?"

"I am doing well, Tayo. I apologize for not calling back right away, but you did not state that it was an emergency."

"You're right—I did not state that."

"And besides, I had an unusual visitor. Benson, who we thought was dead, paid me a visit."

"Didn't Daria shoot him in that alley, Anna?"

"She believed so. I believed it as well. Apparently, he does not die so easily. He claimed to have suffered only a superficial wound."

"It was enough to incapacitate him, though? You said he wasn't moving and didn't look to be alive."

"That is an unusual story, to be sure. He said that Wolfe returned to headquarters and administered some sort of care."

"I have never known Wolfe to possess any medical skills. He didn't seem to have a modicum of compassion needed to tend to anyone's health either."

"That is all true. He did seem to be more of a taker than anything else."

Anna smiled at the memories.

"Well, it's good that he has survived. Has he been well?"

"Tayo, he is more odd now than ever before. He came here for money."

"I'm surprised he doesn't have a stash of that himself. Did you offer him a portion?"

"No. Well, not today. I told him that it was not kept at my home, so I would have to relay some to him another way."

"That all sounds reasonable. We three, and Daria, appear to be the only surviving members of The Shield."

"Yes. And you, Tayo? You have money?"

"I do. It's more than enough to live comfortably in Nigeria. Soon, I will return."

"When you are done with your promise to Lin Finity?"

Tayo paused to let out a breath, and he shook his head while studying the walls of his kitchen.

"Or when it is done with me."

"I do not—"

"What Lin described and that for which she enlisted my aid has indeed appeared. It's why I called you."

"What is it, Tayo? Are you okay?"

"For the moment, yes, I'm okay. It's quite a puzzling, stressful ordeal, though."

He held up his left hand, wiggled the remaining fingers, and saw that his dressing was red and moist, needing a change.

"Do you need help?"

"I've called for Lee, but it will take her some time to travel here. I was hoping you could indulge me with your presence. I have no expectations from you other than to be near if I might need anything."

"You wish for me to cook for you, Tayo?"

Anna laughed and so did Tayo.

"I will likely remain able to feed myself."

"Vodka, then?"

Tayo paused and reflected on how he avoided alcohol and anything else that might cloud his clarity. Then, he paid attention to the throbbing where another finger should still be attached.

"I didn't hear a laugh along with that question, so I will take you seriously. Yes, Anna. Please bring a bottle. I just might decide to share that with you."

"I have never known you to drink, Tayo."

"There are many things in my life which are startlingly new to me."

Anna hesitated, listening for more. Tayo remained silent.

"I will come over, then. Plan to have a shot with me."

A quick look showed that Anna had ended the call, so he laid his phone on the table. With more pain invading his back, he crossed his arms and slumped forward, trying to think only about his breaths, afraid to blink and waiting for whatever might be next.

* * *

He didn't remember closing his eyes, but he dared not open them. A pain in his back, near his left shoulder again, almost convinced him to sit up, but he didn't. Instead, he listened to the noises in the wall to his left.

Then, the squeaking came from the right. It yelled once, then went silent. Still lying motionless, he felt his heart beating hard against his right hand, wedged between his chest and the table. He resisted the urge to look when low squeaks, sounding more like singing, started with a low volume in all four walls and crescendoed.

A knife was at his back—he was sure of it. A stab would be more merciful, he thought, as he felt the blade slowly twisting its way through his skin, seemingly attempting to match the depth of the cut with the angry squeaks which had become shrieks, coming from every direction.

Resolving to not flinch, no matter what he witnessed, Tayo sat straight up and opened his eyes.

All four walls were so close that they almost touched him. Each seemed to be rocking, independent of its neighbors, as they shuffled their way closer, surrounding him, containing inside them things he could not guess, about to begin a deadly crush.

A single, vicious squeak exploded in his right ear, so near that he knew that if he were to turn his head, he'd be looking directly into the angry, murderous eyes of a mouse so large that—

Tayo opened his eyes at the sound of his phone ringing next to his head as he rested on his kitchen table.

Oh, I'm thankful it's only my phone. This must surely be Lin calling. It was a joke, she will say. No such entity could possibly exist, and it certainly couldn't plague us here in this world. Yes, it's a relief that Lin is calling!

He looked at the phone and saw a number that he didn't recognize. Still, he tapped to answer and said, "Hello?"

Only silence.

"Lin, is that you?"

More silence.

"Even if calling from some other realm, Lin, please, find a way to speak."

Nothing. He held it away to study it and saw that the call had ended. A quick search on his laptop revealed that it was a local number, somewhere relatively close in Baltimore.

It still might be Lin. Call again, Lin, even if you can't speak. It's still a comfort. Please be nearby.

He glanced at each wall in turn, reached back to rub behind his left shoulder, eliciting no sensation at all, then he laid himself back down across his crossed arms.

* * *

A steady pounding caused Tayo to sit straight up and without thinking, he looked at every wall and found that they were the expected distance away from him.

I must seek a way to never dream again.

He stood, slipped his phone into the front pocket of his khakis, and left for the front door. On the way, with every step, he watched the far corner, but anything that might be lurking in there resisted calling out to him.

The knocking had stopped before he'd left his kitchen and after being sure the corner of the living room wouldn't attack, he turned his eyes back toward the front door. In between the two locations, he caught sight of something unexpected through the large window.

A dark figure stood there, facing his apartment. He wore a heavy overcoat and a wide-brimmed hat and though he was turned toward the window, his head tipped forward so that the brim covered his face.

Tayo's heart lurched, and he ran the remaining steps to the door, yanked it open, and peered outside, ready to scream while knowing he had no acceptable excuse for such behavior.

The sidewalk was empty.

Perhaps I am truly losing my mind? I can no longer count how many mice have invaded my walls, and now I see shadowy strangers looking at me even when they can't look at me because their hats cover their faces?

He let out a deep breath, then took in a deep draw of the cold Baltimore air as his heart settled. Before closing his door completely, he looked at the sidewalk, and his heart resumed its pounding.

Two large footprints, fresh in the falling snow. But only those. None arriving or leaving.

Birds can land and leave impressions such as those.

He slammed the door, locked it, and rested his back against it.

I'll research birds common in this region, and I'm sure I'll quickly find the type which have bodies shaped like boots. Oh, and they travel in pairs. That's actually a good thing—they mate for life, birds such as those. Yes. Birds.

* * *

Walking back to his kitchen, before he'd reached the doorway, he felt a quick stab behind his left shoulder. He frowned and twisted, knowing it was foolish to believe that he could lessen the pain by squirming away from it.

He stopped and looked at the walls, but they only looked back in silence. The knife dug in farther.

I might be truly losing my mind because I'm relieved to fight only a knife and not a giant mouse too. This thing which I battle might indeed have some honor. I can—

"Ah! No!"

A giant, powerful hand had grabbed the back of his neck. He tried to spin out of its grip, grasping both jambs of the doorway to the kitchen, but he couldn't escape it. His head had become fused to his neck and his neck to his back. All would move in unison like a plank or not at all.

Turning slightly, he saw nothing behind him. He tried to turn the other way but never made it that far.

"Ah!"

The grip tightened and drove him to the floor, his body in the living room and his shoulders and head in the kitchen. His glasses had flown off to the side. The mighty hand wouldn't allow him to rotate his head, and his nose and forehead were ground into the cool linoleum.

Oh, what is this? A mouse with one giant, powerful hand? And what . . . three tiny paws? That's almost funny.

The clamp on his neck grew, and it felt like the hand had found extra fingers, all of them squeezing his neck and crushing his face into the floor.

Lin? Lin, I need you! This is not what—

The hand spread out to hold him from his shoulders to past his hairline. Tayo lay still and felt his throat becoming blocked, and his breaths required more effort.

At least the knife has withdrawn. And there are still no mice. I am grateful that . . . that they are not . . .

Tayo's raspy, struggling breaths were the only sound in his quiet kitchen as his tortured consciousness was wrung out of him like cloudy water from a rag.

* * *

While feeling like he was breathing through a straw, Tayo awoke, still facedown on the floor. He found that he could move his arms, and he pushed himself up. Something heavy clung to his neck, but it no longer pinned him down.

He reached up with his right hand, touching gently behind him, and found something large and unyielding under the skin. He thought it might be a large bean bag that somehow had gotten stuffed in there.

Is this how tumors begin? I had believed that their growth was not so immediate and painful. Still, if it's only a tumor of some type, then I can—

It moved, shifting itself mostly to near his left shoulder. Tayo held his breath, feeling the pressure of it but no pain.

Then, it lumped together near his right shoulder.

Oh, dear God. That is not a tumor!

It waited there and besides a swollen feeling, there was no other sensation.

I will not complain. While it resides at one side, breathing is more easily managed.

Like a rubber band, it snapped toward the left, but it all bunched together in the middle, crunching against the back of his throat.

May I complain now? Yes, I surely will because I can barely breathe! Lin, what is this?

When his phone rang in his pocket, he didn't even suspect that it might be Lin. He took it out and saw that it was Anna.

"Anna."

His voice was a rasp dragged over the edge of a board.

"Tayo? What is wrong? You do not sound well."

"Anna," he struggled to say, "no, I am not well. Please, tell me that you are en route."

"I am. Daria wanted food, so we are at a drive-through. Would you like us to bring you something?"

Yes, Anna. A hot poker to stab this thing.

"No, I can't think of food right now."

"Oh, and I forgot the vodka."

"That's fine. I . . ."

"Tayo, what is wrong?"

"The thing I told Lin I would engage in battle."

After a moment of silence, Anna said, "Yes?"

"It is winning. It's lodged in my neck. My speaking ability is compromised."

"Tayo, what is in your neck? I do not understand."

It is not something good, I can assure you of that!

"I don't know what it is, Anna. Please, come. I don't feel welcome or safe in my own home."

"There is a long line. I need food. Daria too. And Ozzy. We must stop and get him something. Then, we will be there."

Yes, take all the time you want. When my neck explodes, it's best if no one is here to witness that. And I will not help you clean up the mess.

"Thank you."

.

Chapter 7 – A Bloody Corpse Cooling

Tayo had laid himself out on the couch and even though the room was warm, he'd covered every part of himself, leaving only his eyes to peek out. And he kept his eyes focused on the window and the sidewalk just beyond it.

When those mating birds land in the snow again, I'll see them.

Someone walked past, too quickly to be studied properly. Tayo thought he'd seen a hat. He held the blanket close with both hands.

The figure walked into view again, from the door side of the window, and abruptly stopped, giving Tayo a profile: a short, bushy beard and a nose but no more, beneath the tilted brim of a hat.

Then, the stranger turned toward the window and froze. So did Tayo.

Can he see me? Is there really even anyone there?

Tayo watched the brim of the hat rise and fall several times, never angling up high enough to reveal whether there were eyes hidden in that shadow.

No, that can't be! He reads my thoughts? What madness is this now?

His heart began a steady thumping, pumping blood to his swollen neck with every pulse, when the invader turned and walked back toward the left.

A minute passed. Only faint sounds of traffic came through the glass.

Then, a loud, steady, determined pounding on the door.

That is not a bird! It sure isn't two birds! If I find the courage to open the door, and no person is attached to the knocking, would I not give up what's left of my mind?

He sat up, still clutching the blanket.

But if there truly is someone there, what then? Shall I tell him that I thought he was a bird? Would he only laugh and go on his way?

He stood and let the blanket fall to the couch and floor.

Oh, it's probably Benson. Anna said he was looking for money, so he probably traveled here with the hope of garnering some of mine. Yes, I'll tell Benson to move along. Before I command a giant mouse to attack him!

He'd made it as far as the door and though he strained to take each breath, he forced himself to be still enough to peer through the peephole.

Of course! A brim of a hat! Why would I expect more than that?

He sighed as well as he could and reached for the knob.

*   *   *

Tayo unlocked and pulled in his door only enough to peek through at whoever had come to visit. But the door swung away from his hand from a rough shove and when he stepped back, the stranger stepped in, closing the door behind him.

"Who are you? What do you want?"

He glanced down to see a black semi-automatic pistol held low in the man's right hand, the gaping hole of the barrel sizing him up.

"Easy. Tayo, right?"

"Yes, but what does—"

"Shh. Have a seat."

He didn't gesture with the gun—that aim never left its target. He pointed to the couch with his left hand.

Tayo backed toward the couch and sat. The man rarely took his eyes off of him, and he walked first to the window and drew the drapes. He stood with his back to the corner from which Tayo's mouse had screeched at him.

"You have my attention," Tayo said, sounding like a rock dragging over broken concrete. "What do you want?"

"What's wrong with your neck?"

"I am ill. If you leave, you might be lucky and not contract it."

"I'll take that chance."

"How do you know my name?"

"Samuel."

"You know Samuel?"

"No."

"He told you my name?"

"No. I read it on your drawing."

"Why would you have any interest in that?"

"When people ask questions like Samuel was asking, it gets noticed. More than that. It gets people dead."

Tayo wished he could find comfort in the blanket on which he sat, but he only stared, almost groaning with each breath.

"No more questions, huh? Good. I'll do the asking. Where did you learn of those symbols?"

This is about those symbols? Why? How could anyone else know of them?

"I made them up. I strive to be an artist. I wished that Samuel would offer his—"

"Just stop. Those symbols have been around a long time. You didn't invent them. Besides Samuel, who else knows of them?"

"No one. I sent those to my good friend Samuel so that he—"

The stranger quickly closed the distance between them, and Tayo felt a cold metal ring against the perspiring skin of his forehead, nudging his glasses down along his nose.

"My only required task is to kill you. I could just do that now. If you'd like to live another minute, you should try being honest. Really, there's no time for anything else."

Tayo knew that he looked comical, despite the dire circumstances, as both eyes tried to focus on the trigger finger. He looked back into the man's eyes.

"Samuel's secretary. Samuel does not have electronic devices. She likely delivered them to him."

"Then, it's just her and Samuel?"

"Yes."

"Good. They're both dead. So far, so good."

Tayo gasped, and the man backed the gun away but still pointed it at his face.

"So, it's probably just you now. Where are the rest of them?"

Tayo felt his back thick with symbols, and his head spun at the idea that others knew of them.

How could any of this be? This makes no sense at all!

"My imagination could only come up with—"

A sharp but controlled strike from the base of the gun's grip against Tayo's temple caused him to wince, and a few stars circled lazily before vanishing.

"No time for that, remember?"

Tayo flinched but not from the hit to his head.

Ah! That strike has awakened more stabbing of my back? No, this is not the time!

"Very well. I, um, saw them on a website and since Samuel is a good researcher, I asked him, only out of curiosity."

"Where? Show me."

"In the kitchen."

He stepped back, never lowering the gun, and tipped his head for Tayo to lead the way.

Can he see the axe that has once again found my back? Can he see that?

Standing beside the table, Tayo opened his laptop but before pointing it at a website that didn't exist, he said, "Before you kill me, can you at least tell me what these symbols represent?"

The man sighed and said, "Sure, why not? You'll be dead in a minute anyway."

"You may take your time with the explanation."

"You're being funny, even now?"

"I assure you, I am far from any laughter."

"Yeah, I bet. Alright, I can tell you what I know. They're ancient, and they're deadly. No living person is allowed to even know about them. That's where I come in."

"But you have seen them too? You are allowed?"

"No, I haven't. I didn't look."

"But you know about them."

"I know next to nothing, just that they're ancient and deadly. That's why I have to kill you. It's nothing personal."

"It feels somewhat personal to me."

"Yeah, I bet. After you're dead, I'm heading back to Lagos, and anyone that even knew Samuel is finished too."

Jenny! No, he can't be allowed to kill Jenny!

The axe twisted and began sawing its way deeper into his back. With his right hand, Tayo began tapping keys, using just one finger. He smudged around on the mouse pad, looking for links that didn't exist. And he fought to not gasp when he lost control of his left arm.

I have fought with honor. Why must you abandon all ethics by trying to destroy me now, even while I face imminent death?

His pleas went unanswered, and he noticed his lost arm moving on its own. He struggled to focus on the laptop, trying to mimic a convincing search. His breaths dragged in and out.

A quick glance showed that his left hand was reaching for the counter, where several items rested, including a butter knife.

Oh no, what madness is this now? It will kill me with a dull tool before this stranger can do it cleanly with a sharp bullet?

Still working the keyboard, he looked quickly to see that his hand had grasped the knife's blade, and the thick, shiny handle extended out.

Oh, please, be merciful! At least use the sharper of the two ends!

"I don't see anything. And I don't believe they're anywhere on the Internet. They would have come up in the searches we always—"

A deafening squeak erupted from the wall to the stranger's right, and he turned to look.

Tayo's left arm moved more quickly than humanly possible, and the flat end of the knife's handle penetrated the man's left temple. He stopped talking, but he didn't fall.

Tayo watched his hand pull the embedded knife, causing the man's head to face forward again. His eyes were still open.

It's protecting me? Why? And shouldn't a dead man fall to the floor?

He gave up on the laptop and looked directly at the man's head, which spouted a stream of blood that flowed as his body stood still and twitched quietly. Tayo's hand still held the knife, and he saw that the small serrated section had ripped open some fresh new wounds on his fingers.

What do I do? Why does he not die?

Quickly, his hand jerked the knife blade toward the back of the man's head, prying the handle forward and pushing his left eye out of its socket. The very end of the knife's handle protruded there, carrying a thick, slimy coating.

Is there no limit to the gore that has become customary in this kitchen?

All twitching stopped, and the body slumped to the floor. Tayo's hand had let go of the knife, and he again had control of it. The stabbing of his back had stopped too. The wall was silent.

Lin, I have changed my mind. Do not come here. This apartment has become some gruesome subdivision of Hell.

* * *

He coaxed his eyes away from the bleeding corpse on his kitchen floor and held up his left hand. The bandage had ripped loose from the stub of his missing little finger, and the next two showed ragged slices on the inside. He held it palm down over the table, forming a fresh pool.

How many times must I bleed on this table? Should I add a decorative bowl?

He heard only a steady drip in an otherwise quiet apartment. The man's head had turned to the right, and Tayo couldn't see his face, which, if it were alive, would be searching for something lost beneath his stove.

I did lose a quarter under there some time ago. Perhaps, while you're down there, you could—oh, I am losing my mind!

He looked at the sink, remembering how he'd allowed his tablecloth to dry out there before sending it away with the trash. He bent to twist the knife out of the dead man's head and clattered it into the sink too.

Think, Tayo. You are logical. What is the rational solution?

He studied the length of the counter adjacent to the sink.

It's long enough. If I were to convince him to recline on that surface, with only his head in the sink, then all leakage would—

"Ah! Let go!"

A hand had taken a loose hold on his ankle and when he pulled it free, the man's arm dragged across the floor at a regular pace, matching, it seemed to Tayo, his pounding heart.

"You are alive?"

The body said nothing.

It is likely some artifact of his nervous system's signals being thrown into disarray from the violent gouging of its major component, his brain, causing him to—

"Ah! Oh, it's only you, phone."

He picked it up, careful to stay out of the range of the sweeping hand, and saw that it was Anna.

"Anna?"

"Hello, Tayo. I am sorry we are not there yet. Ozzy is very particular about what he—"

"No! I mean, no, Anna, that's fine. I would like a few moments to perform some necessary cleaning before you arrive anyway."

How to clean blood? Should I not know the best way by now?

"Well, we have found him some treats that he has deemed acceptable, and we—"

"Mom, you spoil that dog too much."

"Yes, Daria, that is true. Tayo, we have all found food to our liking and will be at your apartment in a few minutes. I am sure your home is spotless, so please, consider leaving it as it is."

Oh, that's funny, Anna. Yes, of course. Every neat and tidy home has a bloody corpse cooling on the kitchen floor.

"You are probably right. I tend to be a perfectionist, that's all."

"Yes, and that is why you were so valuable to The Shield. Just do not try too hard with every little detail—that can drive a person mad."

I can assure you, Anna, that it would be a very short drive for me!

"Yes, you're right. I'll relax, then, and await your arrival."

*   *   *

Tayo looked around the kitchen and confirmed what he already knew: the room had no storage space for a dead body. He thought of his bedroom closet but remembered that it contained stacks of books, which would take too long to relocate. Only the small closet near the front door could be modified in time.

Before attempting to move the body, he opened the closet door and saw the shelves that he'd built in there to more efficiently store and display shoes, gloves, and hats. He'd brought a plastic trash bag with him, and he stuffed all of those items in, tied the top in a knot, and tossed it toward the doorway to his bedroom.

I face a dilemma like I'd never imagined possible: do I section the body to fit on the shelves? No, of course not. I must remove the shelves. Now, I wish I had not employed such durable carpentry techniques.

He pulled at a shelf and found that it refused to move. So, he raised his right foot up and stomped it, splintering the wood and prying loose some of the nails. Determined pulling and yanking of the pieces freed it, and he tossed it all next to the door. He kicked and pounded the other shelves into pieces, and the pile of cracked boards, bent nails jutting out of many, rested against the wall.

Back in the kitchen, he paused to look down at the body, which had stopped adding to the pool beneath its head.

Could I distract Anna and Daria long enough that they never notice a trail of blood from here to the closet? Perhaps. But that dog. The dog will surely resist my attempts at thwarting its natural senses. Could I call Anna and demand that she leave the dog in the car? No, that would only raise suspicions.

65

He found another plastic bag, put it over the man's head and before letting him back down, flipped him over onto his back and next to the puddle.

Even a tiny leak will alert that dog. I must seal the bag. At least his annoying arm gestures have stopped.

He looked around the room and realized that he'd never find a twist tie long enough to cinch it tight around the neck. An idea flashed, and he removed his belt and used that.

This is a time when a soul having substantial, measurable weight would be a benefit since this man's has left him. If he ever had one.

The body mostly stood in the narrow closet, with its back to one side wall, its knees against the other, and its torso leaning forward and the bagged head resting against the other as well. It kept trying to tip toward the door, so Tayo pushed the head back inside, looped a metal hanger around it, and connected that to a hanger on the rack.

Good, I'm still keeping things organized. Oh, I'm truly losing my mind . . .

He stood in the doorway and studied the pool of blood on the floor. His eyes darted at the puddle, then all around the room, then again at the mess on the linoleum.

He drew in a quick breath at the pounding on the door. With a quick shake of his head, he moved the laptop to the counter and flipped the round table over to cover the blood.

If my intellect had been a sliver to the left on any reasonable scale, I never would have—

He looked down at his shirt and saw that it carried wet red streaks.

Oh, my intellect is farther to the left than I'd like!

He quickly pulled his shirt up and off, looked around the room, then tipped the table up to push it far enough under that it couldn't be seen. He grabbed one table leg and rocked it.

Not a perfect solution. No one could expect a madman to devise a perfect coverup. Especially with guests at the door!

He moved to the kitchen's doorway and stood facing the front door, only then recalling that his back was a mass of chaotic symbols.

I must take the time to find another shirt before I—

Anna opened the door and walked in, carrying Ozzy, and Daria waved and closed the door behind her.

Chapter 8 – It's Not A Ghost

"We purchased dinner for you, Tayo. I hope you do not mind."

Anna held out a fast food bag and began walking toward him.

"Stop!"

Anna froze, and she and Daria and Ozzy stared at him. Ozzy quickly lost interest in him and began sniffing and looking around the room.

"I mean, um, what I need more is my coat from that chair. Can you toss that to me?"

"I believe going without a shirt in this warm place is the smartest idea, Tayo. A shirt would be one thing. But a coat?"

"Yes, that coat. Would you throw that here?"

Anna turned and looked at Daria, who only shrugged and said, "Maybe he's got what Benson's got."

"Very well."

Anna swung the long wool coat several times, then let it fly. Tayo quickly put his arms through the sleeves, never turning his back to his guests.

"Well, we are all warm, so we will probably like to remove our coats. Not Ozzy, though."

"Funny, Mom."

Daria began slipping hers back over her shoulders and reached for the knob to the closet near the front door.

"Stop!"

They froze again, all staring at Tayo.

"You will likely need your coats again too. Yes, it's warm in here now, but that changes often. Soon, it will be cold."

Anna stared. Tayo stared back.

"Fine. I will keep it near in case the climate shows such disruptions."

"What's with the scrap lumber?" said Daria, looking at the demolished shelves next to the closet.

"Oh, that. I'm attempting some remodeling in that closet."

"Yeah? What, with dynamite?" she said with a smirk.

"It resisted my efforts and required substantial force. I didn't have time to place it out with the trash."

"Let me see how things are going," said Daria, and she again reached for the knob.

"No! I would rather you wait until it's complete."

"Alright, well, I think I'll hang up my coat," she said, her hand turning the knob. "I can always get it if—"

"Please, no!"

Everyone stared across the quiet room.

"It's already completely full with things hanging. There's no room."

Am I having fun with this situation? Could that be considered the first irrefutable evidence of madness?

"Very well, Tayo. May we have a seat? You said you needed company because what Lin sent to you has arrived?"

"Yeah, that curse," said Daria.

"I do not believe it is a curse, Daria."

"Sure, Mom. Whatever."

Anna set Ozzy on the middle couch cushion, and he immediately tried to jump to the floor. While holding him down, she and Daria each took an end. Tayo sat across the small room in an upholstered chair but only after he'd looked out the window in each direction.

Did the nameless murderer have a partner? I hope not—that closet isn't big enough.

"So, Tayo, you said the thing has arrived. I did not believe there could be a thing like you described in Allentown."

"Still don't know why you'd agree to something like that," Daria said with an eye roll.

He focused on her and said, "You know that Lin has had a profound effect on me. It started with her eyes, but it's more than that."

"She is mostly a frightening thing, Tayo. And she has been gone for a long time. You should no longer be bound to whatever errand she has assigned to you."

"It's not an errand, Anna. It's something that can be of great benefit. To everyone. If I'm successful."

Daria pointed at his left hand and said, "Right. How's that working out so far?"

Tayo looked down and said, "Not so well."

He looked up at Anna.

"The entity, from what I've ascertained so far, is capable of—"

"I don't mean to be rude," said Daria, "but you don't sound so good. Too many cigarettes, maybe?"

She grinned and waited.

"No. No, Daria, it is not from smoke of any variety. As I was saying, the entity, which Lin has called a Hunter, can launch individual attacks, targeting, apparently, whatever it wishes."

"Let me guess," said Daria, again looking at the hand that he hadn't had time to redress, and which was wrapped in a washcloth, held in place by a tight fist. "It messed up your hand?"

"Yes, that's certainly one way to describe it. It found a unique way to destroy the little finger of that hand."

"Tayo, something sent here by Lin Finity, something as horrific as she has described it, came all that way to attack a little finger?"

He closed his eyes halfway and looked from one to the other.

"Mom's got a point."

He blinked a few times and cleared his throat.

"I believe it's only . . . warming up."

"As are you," Anna said while pointing at him. "You are beginning to sweat and still, you insist on wearing a coat?"

"The heating system is notoriously unpredictable and refuses all attempts to repair it. It will be cold soon."

"Alright, but how bad is your finger?"

Tayo hesitated, looking from Anna to Daria.

Daria did not question about the finger in the box, did she? No, they believe it is still in its correct placement.

"It, um . . . I don't wish to alarm you."

"Go on, Tayo," said Anna.

"Very well. The skin of the little finger began to peel down in four segments, beginning near the very end. One segment retained the nail, but the other three were—"

"You can't be serious," said Daria. "Under that washcloth, you have a finger with all the skin peeled back? That's pretty gross, Tayo."

"No, Daria, it is gone."

"It disappeared?" said Anna.

"No. I removed it. I didn't know if the peeling would continue or not. I didn't wish to find out."

"We sure wouldn't be sitting here talking to you if you didn't have any skin."

"Daria, that is not helpful. Tayo, you cut off your own finger? How?"

"With a steak knife. It was easier than you might imagine, Anna, since that hand, prior to the self-skinning, had gone numb."

"Mom, maybe we should get the hell out of here. Tayo, I like you, I really do, but this is—"

"Daria, wait. Tayo, you really are being attacked? Where is your lost finger now?"

"Oh, it's in a box in the kitchen."

"Why did you not rush to an emergency place?"

"It was, um, crawling around on its own, and I thought—"

"Give me the keys, Mom."

"Daria, no. Tayo, that finger by itself was still alive?"

Ozzy squirmed and tried to get up, but Anna held him to the cushion with both hands.

"Must it be alive to move?" said Tayo. "I've never had to come to a conclusion about such a thing."

"No, I do not believe anyone ever has."

"Alright, so what about your voice? You sound all scratchy, and you can barely breathe."

"Yes, Daria, that's complements of the Hunter as well. There's some swelling of my neck, and it conflicts with respiratory functions. My hope is that it won't continue to grow because—"

"It is growing? Tayo, tumors do not grow as we watch them!"

"I don't believe it's a tumor, Anna. It . . . sometimes moves around on its own."

"Sure, why the hell not?" said Daria. "Just like the damn finger. Mom, we should just—"

"Daria, stop. He needs our help. We must do whatever—"

A single loud squeak came from somewhere near the closet by the front door.

Oh, you are really too much! Why not just stab my brain and end it?

Anna looked over at the closet and lost her grip. Ozzy jumped down and ran over, where be rose up on his hind legs and began clawing at the door.

"He thinks he's a cat, Mom."

"Daria, I believe a dog would be curious about a mouse too. What do you think, Tayo?"

I think too much has been asked of me. Lin, if you are somehow listening, you should—

"Aw, he just wants to help," Daria said as she stood. "He just can't open the door. Ozzy, hang on. I'll get it."

"No! There's no mouse in the closet!"

"I heard it. Daria heard it. Ozzy too."

"No, it's in the wall somewhere. I've been trying to locate him for some time. He is not in the closet!"

"Well, okay, Tayo. I am sure a missing finger and a tumor are enough. We do not need to agitate ourselves over a mouse."

With his head tipped forward, he said, "It's not a tumor . . ."

Daria walked over to the closet, and Tayo felt his heart pounding. She picked up the dog and walked back to the couch, gazing into the kitchen on the way back. Tayo wiped at the sweat beading on his forehead.

After setting Ozzy down, and holding him there long enough for her mother to pin him down, she started walking back toward the kitchen.

"What the hell's going on in the kitchen, Tayo?"

"Stop!"

She kept walking, and he jumped up and rushed over to stand behind her while she studied the scene.

"I decided to begin refinishing that table too. That's the first step: turn it upside down."

Daria turned to look at him with her eyebrows raised.

"You're awful ambitious lately."

"Yes, I have the time, and—"

Daria took a step closer and grabbed one of the upturned legs.

"It's best if you don't alter its position in any way."

"Yeah? Why's that?"

She rocked it a few times and said, "Hey, there's something under there. Oh, you know what? It might be a mouse!"

She began to lean over and reach for the tabletop near the floor, and Tayo took hold of her other hand, dragging her a step back.

"Geez, Tayo. I was just curious."

"It's not likely to be a mouse. Come back to the couch, please."

"Sure. Let's go sit in the sauna awhile."

Everyone sat in their places, including Ozzy.

"So, Tayo, how can we help? I do not even see this Hunter thing that you believe is here."

"Is it like a ghost?" said Daria.

"Oh, if only," said Tayo. "No, it's not a ghost. It seems that it can cause much trouble, though."

"Like peeling your finger?" said Anna.

"I should have looked at that when I was in there. Tayo, go get it."

"Daria, that is an invasion of his medical privacy. You cannot demand such a thing."

"It's just a finger, Mom. Only the little one too."

"Yes, well, maybe we can view that later. Tayo, what of your back?"

Yes, what of my back? When will the axe strike again?

"It has not grown for some time. There's a possibility it will revert to normal."

Do I believe that? No, I do not.

Ozzy struggled to get away, and Anna said, "Ozzy, be good, and maybe we will buy you your own mouse at the pet store."

"Mom, that's just ridiculous."

"It was mostly a joke, Daria. When Tayo catches his, he will give us one."

"That's even more ridiculous."

"Yes, well, Ozzy is just a curious sort. Tayo, I do not know how we can help."

"I thought it would be a comfort to have company,—"

Until I killed a man and hung him in the closet.

"—but on further consideration, perhaps what I need most is a good night's sleep. I'm grateful for the dinner that you brought for me."

"We thought of getting you a chili dog," Daria said with a smirk. "Guess a hamburger was a better choice, huh?"

Tayo only stared at her and shook his head slowly.

"Daria, you are tormenting a suffering man."

Daria scoffed and said, "Oh, alright. Sorry, Tayo. I hope your back stops growing and your finger feels better. Oh, wait."

"Daria, just stop. Tayo, maybe we will leave you to get a good night's sleep, okay? I can call you in the morning. We are not far away. We can even bring you breakfast."

"Since you wrecked your kitchen too."

"Daria. Tayo, we will go. It is always possible that the worst has come and gone. You will be fine."

"I can only hope that you're right, Anna."

They all stood, Tayo still wearing a coat and the others putting theirs on. At the door, they all stopped to look at the closet when a series of high-pitched squeaks blew up.

"Tayo," said Anna, shaking her head, "you will likely need to kill whatever is in there."

Again?

Tayo sighed and said, "Yes, that is certainly a requirement."

Daria pulled in the door and stepped out onto the porch. Anna followed, carrying Ozzy.

"Until tomorrow, then," said Anna.

"Good luck with the mouse, and the closet, and the tumor, and the finger, and—"

"Yes, Daria is right. We wish you well, Tayo."

"Thanks, Anna. Thanks, Daria."

The door closed, and Tayo leaned his back into it. He felt an unfamiliar sensation of hot tears drawing thin lines down his cheeks as he rammed his numb back into the door over and over.

* * *

Tayo ate his meal in silence, seated on the couch and without the burden of a coat in the hot apartment. His blacks eyes stayed focused on the closet door the entire time.

I am forced to acquire many new skills. The cleanup of blood. Disposal of a body. Even clumsy carpentry. What could possibly be next?

No mouse interrupted his dinner, and he thanked the dead man for remaining dead and not swinging his arm around, especially while he had company.

Oh, I am learning rudimentary surgical techniques as well.

He looked down at the washcloth, still held tight over his wound. He relaxed his fist and pulled the cover aside, observing that no healing had commenced.

He brought the empty bag and wrappers into the kitchen, dropped them in the trash, then spent some time giving his wound a proper wrapping. Then, he leaned over, tipped up the table, and looked at the shirt smashed into the dead man's blood.

I'd like to retire to bed and dream that this was only a dream. But it would be here when I awaken and since the refuse is collected tomorrow, my proper course of action is already determined.

He righted the table, bagged up the shirt, then wiped everything clean. All rags and paper towels got stuffed into the bag too.

Why do I not have a supply of body bags in the pantry? Wouldn't that be reasonable? Only for a madman.

He opened the closet door and peeked in through only a narrow gap. Two eyes, one in and one out, along with a smeared butter knife handle, caught the light streaming in and stared back. Tayo slammed the door shut.

No, you will not inspire feelings of guilt. Let's try to remember who threatened to kill whom, shall we? Yes, we shall.

He reopened the door and breathed a sigh of relief at noting that his imagination had made a fool of him: the bag still covered the man's head. He grabbed the collar of his coat, lifted, and unwound the hanger. The body began to tip out of the tight space and when Tayo tripped and fell, the body landed across his legs.

Of course. Let's be thorough. Now, I need to dispose of the pants too.

After changing clothes, he dragged the body to his back door, the one that led to the alley behind the building, and looked down at the ice that had built up on the metal steps.

No little thing is ever easy, is it?

He looked up, catching stinging sleet with his cheeks, then back at the course he needed to navigate. Carefully and quietly placing his steps, he brought his burden to a half-empty container, open at the top, where he rolled the body in.

You wished to kill me? That did not work out so well for you, did it?

Walking away, wiping his hands, he stopped in his tracks.

No, I must go back and remove the bag and belt. No corpse ever accidentally fell into a refuse bin like that! Especially after having fallen so violently onto a butter knife!

He threw a leg up on the snowy edge and rolled himself into the trash, coming face to bagged face with his victim. He began unhooking the belt just as he heard someone approaching, their shoes splatting in the cold puddles.

He lay still, watching his breath condense on the cold plastic, as the sounds drew nearer.

This is certainly an interesting life. It will likely end soon, though, which might be good because—

His phone rang and vibrated in his pocket, and with his heart racing, he rolled onto the corpse, snuffing out the high-pitched tones. The footsteps passed by, and Tayo waited for complete silence. Then, he peeked over the edge.

This has not been a fun day.

He lay back down, slipped out his phone, and saw who had called.

Oh, Jenny! You will have to wait for a call back!

* * *

Cleaned up and seated on the couch, Tayo started to call Jenny, but he stopped himself.

That dead man most likely didn't work alone. He had my number, and he had the skills to find me with only that one thing. They might be listening in on my calls. Jenny and I cannot speak of the symbols. To do so would imperil her.

He completed the call and waited.

"Tayo, hi. I called earlier to see how you—"

"Jenny, wait. This will be an unusual request but please, play along with me. Every time we speak, I will first give a list of topics that are open for conversation. We can't speak of anything else. *Nothing* else, Jenny. Can we do that?"

"Tayo, I don't understand."

"It's a, um, sociological experiment I've devised for analyzing relationships conducted over substantial distances. It's only for a short time. Can we do that, please?"

"I suppose so. Should I understand this?"

"No, there's no way that you could. We must not make any mistakes, though. There can be no random comments about any other topic. Can we do that, starting this very moment?"

Tayo listened to the silence from his phone. Finally, she spoke.

"Okay, Tayo. Sure. What would you like to talk about?"

"I will tell you about the weather here today. Jenny, it was cold and snowy, and there is ice in many places."

More silence. Tayo continued.

"I believe there's a moon up there somewhere, but there are too many clouds for it to be observed."

A long pause ensued, then Jenny spoke again.

"Is this all code for something?"

Tayo hung his head and rested it in his other hand.

"No. It certainly is not."

Chapter 9 – If She Still Lives

We're driving all the way to Baltimore, Mom?"

"Yeah, Lessa. The flights are booked. This is probably the quickest way."

They'd packed a few things, and Lee started the car. She'd called her mother and explained that there was a change of plans—Alessa would be traveling with her. And she mapped her route so as to make an important stop on the way.

"You'll need a coat, Honey. Maryland is cold this time of year."

"Okay, Mom. Can I get some boots too?"

"Sure, Baby. Whatever you want. Did you pack anything to keep you busy? It's kind of a long drive."

"No, I'll be fine. I always have a lot of things to think about."

Lee looked over at her daughter, who sat looking straight out at the approaching roadway.

"Yeah, I know the feeling. Life is kind of funny sometimes. There's a lot to try to figure out."

"Like what you do. You know, like after you eat a dozen donuts."

Lee laughed and said, "I only ate eleven. You had one of them, remember?"

"I'll have to be quicker next time."

Lee turned and grinned at her and said, "Baby, nobody's that quick."

* * *

Before opening his eyes, Tayo listened, a new habit that he thought he'd probably never shake. He heard only light traffic at the front of his building and the approaching trash pickup crew in the alley.

At least the walls are silent. Will that dead man remain quiet as well?

He listened to the truck's brakes squeal it to a stop, and the hydraulics mechanism grabbed the container and began to lift it up high to dump it in back. He'd watched the operation enough times to know that no human contact was needed. Still, he thought it best to suspend breathing until they'd resumed their route.

A loud metallic clunk indicated to him that the container had been set back onto the pavement. No more sounds came from the alley.

The truck should move. I should hear the engine working, taking all of that far, far away.

The alley stayed quiet.

There is no screaming, which is good. But would they scream at the sight of a body in the trash? Probably not—perhaps that occurs often. Most likely, one of the workers has begun a call to emergency services. He's calling the police or an ambulance. Or both. Yes, probably both. Soon, I will hear the sirens that—

With a squeal and a revving engine, the truck continued down the alley.

Oh, my goodness. My heart has had no preparation for activities such as this. But at least my—

"Ah! Not again!"

Tayo reached back with his good hand to feel the squirming and shifting under his skin, and he found that the swelling behind his neck was no longer dormant. He thought that maybe it had gained the resolve to make up for lost time.

A squeak in the wall to his left caused him to snap his head around, and he groaned at the pain that that brought him.

A squeak from the other side of the room only caused him to close his eyes and take a deep breath.

A growing lump in my neck and mice in the walls. It is already a miserable Tuesday!

He fell to one side on the couch and lay facedown until the symbols had settled, but the swollen neck seemed to have a plan, and that was to grow. Still, he knew he'd better get started on his day.

What choice do I have? I cannot just lie here and die, can I?

He sat up but didn't stand.

That does deserve a fair amount of consideration. I will retain that as an option for after breakfast.

* * *

"No, Lessa, I don't think a jean jacket is going to cut it. Really, Baltimore is cold."

"Okay, Mom. But you only have that jacket. Is that warm enough?"

"Honey, I stay warm no matter what. I only wear that for style."

Alessa sighed and let the thin coat swing back into the rack. She followed her mom toward the winter coats.

"How about this one?"

Lee held out a thick plaid coat with big buttons. Alessa shook her head.

"Uh-uh."

"Really, you don't like it?"

She shook her head again.

"Alright, how about this, then?"

She grabbed the hanger and held next to Alessa's shoulder a long gray coat. Its hood, lined with fake fur, hung down the back.

"I like it, Mom. It's really long!"

"Well, we won't be running and jumping. Should be fine."

Alessa smiled and nodded.

"Try it on, alright?"

She did, and it fit well.

"Boots. You'll need boots too."

"Are we going to the North Pole?"

"You want to?"

Alessa smiled again.

"No. Tayo isn't at the North Pole."

"Nope, he sure isn't. Hey, how about these?"

She pointed at a pair of tall black boots that laced up the front.

"I like them. I like those, Mom."

"Good. Alright, let's pay and get going. We have some driving to do."

"Mom, do they sell cards here?"

"Yeah, Baby. Why?"

"Can we get one for Tayo?"

Lee stopped to look at her daughter's serious face.

"Sure, Lessa. That's a good idea. Come on."

* * *

While preparing a breakfast of toast and eggs that he'd boiled two days earlier, before he'd been attacked, Tayo kept an intermittent focus on the small box on the counter, the one with a soup can holding it down. The one with something scratching its way around inside.

Did you sleep well, my finger? Oh, I am seriously losing my mind. This is certainly not what's meant by someone talking to themselves.

Seated at the table, which he knew he'd never refinish, he poked at his eggs with a fork, a piece of burnt bread in his bandaged left hand. The walls had no comment.

Well, I am quite the attractive bachelor. Be sure that the photograph includes not just my butchered hand. Try to capture also the bizarre symbols and the restless tumor, though I know that it's not a tumor.

He took a bite and chewed, looking from wall to wall. He took another bite, grateful that he heard nothing and could see nothing of his back.

With the plate dumped in the sink, he paused to look at the box.

No, I do not need to see it.

In the bedroom, he put on his favorite black and white striped shirt, buttoned it up the front and at the cuffs, and sighed while looking into his eyes in the mirror.

"What a sad excuse for a man I have become."

At least I can still speak, though it's strained and difficult. I should try to feel grateful for that.

"And since no one is here, it would not be insane for me to keep talking as I—"

A sharp ballooning of the mass on his neck gagged him, and he held himself up with both hands on the dresser as he fought for every breath. When he saw the terror in his eyes, he quickly looked away.

Oh, you have taken this up a notch, haven't you? You have located a region of great importance to my survival. Go ahead and squeeze it. Someone else will have to drag me into the alley, though. Or should I climb in while I'm still able? Should I not end my life with one final considerate act?

He staggered back to the kitchen and picked up his phone.

"Tayo, good morning. We are out again for food, Daria and I. Ozzy too. Would you—"

"Anna."

"Tayo, is that you? What is wrong?"

"My destruction has begun."

"Are you being choked?"

"Yes. It is the thing that—"

"It is that mouse?"

Oh, which of us is more insane?

"No. It is the tumor."

"Told you it was a tumor, Mom."

"Not now, Daria. Tayo, can you call for help?"

"I am doing that now."

"No, not Daria or me. Or Ozzy. Someone who can really help?"

"I can't," he said in a voice like a dull saw ripping drywall. "This is too . . . unusual."

"He's sure right about that, Mom. What the hell would he tell them about that finger, huh?"

"Daria, stop. Tayo, we will forget our breakfast and come to assist you."

"Thanks. Please . . . be quick."

He ended the call and leaned over the sink, fighting to draw in each breath and forcing each one back out like a slow leak in a truck tire.

*   *   *

Minutes later, he heard them at the door, so he walked over and let them in. Past their staring eyes, he noticed dark clouds gathering and before too much cold Baltimore air could rush inside, he closed and bolted the door.

"Still haven't cleaned up, huh?" Daria said while looking down at the splintered closet shelves with a grin.

"No. Time."

Before he could stop her, she yanked the closet door open.

"Hey, I thought you said it was full of stuff?"

Oh, I can't believe what I'm about to say. My mind is barely connected to my head anymore.

"Garbage day."

"But you kept the scrap?" she said with her eyebrows raised.

"Daria," Anna said, with Ozzy in her arms, "do not pester Tayo. He has enough issues already."

"Fine."

"Tayo, you are not breathing well. Will you survive?"

While walking to the chair in the living room, Tayo said, "I hope."

"Sticking with the short sentences, huh? That's smart."

"Daria, please. Now is not the time. Tayo, what can we do?"

They'd sat on the couch, with Ozzy on Anna's lap, and they gazed at Tayo, waiting for his answer.

"Lin."

"Yes, she caused all of this. That is true. But what—"

"Go there. Now."

"To Lin's house? Why? Is she not gone?"

"Then, Gabriel."

"Or Jack, or her daughter, or even that mutt of hers. Sure, Tayo. That makes sense."

"Daria. Tayo, should we not call first, at least?"

"No. Might leave."

"Yes, we must leave if we are to go there. I do not under—"

"Lin. Might leave."

"You think that if she still lives, she would run from the disaster she has caused for you?"

"I would."

"Daria, that is not helpful. Okay, Tayo, we can drive there. Do we need to bring anything?"

He held up the small mirror still in his hand.

"Your mirror? You wish to bring that?"

He nodded, set it down, and pointed at the wall.

"That one too?"

"I think maybe his brain is swelling, too, Mom."

Anna gave Daria a look, and she only smirked back at her.

"Okay. Anything else?"

"How about that finger in a box? That's a fun thing," Daria said with a grin.

Anna looked at her, then at Tayo, and said, "Yes or no?"

He shook his head.

"Food."

"Okay. We will pack food too."

Tayo sank back into his chair, breaths wheezing in and out, while Daria rummaged around the kitchen and Anna removed the mirror from the wall.

*   *   *

"Very well, Tayo, the things you require are in my car. We can go anytime you feel ready."

Before he could answer, Daria said, "I took a look at what's left of your finger. It stopped and kind of pointed at me. Really creepy."

Tayo managed a grin.

"I would call that progress," Anna said with a smile. "You must be feeling—"

Tayo lost the smile and shook his head.

"Yes, well, we should go to Lin Finity's house. If she is alive, she must at least remove the tumor from your neck."

Tayo nodded.

"It looks like a pillow. Is it soft, Tayo?"

He shook his head and pulled his shirt away from his neck. Anna stood, and Daria said, "Ew, Mom, I wouldn't go near that thing."

"I am curious, Daria. I will be quick."

She walked over and touched it, then tilted her head while staring at it. She poked it, then tapped it many times.

"It is quite solid. Tayo, that is not good."

He sighed as well as he could while straightening out his shirt. He winced as a tiny corner of the axe touched his back.

I have no time for the axe. I have not yet become angry at anything: not the symbols, not the finger butchery, not the tumor . . . not even killing a man and throwing him out with the trash. So, why do I suddenly not like Anna's dog?

"I can find your coat for you, Tayo. Where is it?"

The axe broke his skin and began to dig in. Tayo only stared at Ozzy, who had climbed down and sat next to the couch. He stood and walked toward the dog, who only stared up at him.

"Never saw a dog before? That's Ozzy," Daria said with a smirk. "Come on. You must remember him."

I remember him, but I don't remember hating him. I do now. Ah, this axe! I hate that dog. Maybe he caused this growth on my neck. Maybe it's all from him. Could that be? Could ending this nightmare be that simple? Could I banish the axe if—

"Daria, of course he—"

Tayo lunged the remaining two steps and took Ozzy's neck in both hands. He stooped down with his arms straight out, the dog's front legs kicking and swinging wildly and his back legs scraping the wood floor.

Daria grabbed one of Tayo's arms and said, "Hey, what the hell? Let him go!"

"Tayo, are you insane? Put Ozzy down!" Anna said as she pounded on his shoulder with both fists.

"Oh, you're really asking for it," Daria said, and she reached inside her purse to pull out her gun.

Before she raised it high enough to shoot him, he felt the axe withdraw and released Ozzy, who scurried around behind Daria's legs, where he continued to whimper. She still had the pistol trained on Tayo's chest.

"Daria, there is no longer any need to kill anyone."

"I still might. Just to make a point."

Tayo stared at her but didn't move.

Yes, a bullet would be quicker and easier. I no longer hate your dog, but shooting me is still worthwhile. I'll even climb into the trash box before you fire.

Daria stowed her pistol and reached down to pet Ozzy.

Anna said, "I decided that we should try to call Lin's house first. That will give you, Tayo, some time to calm yourself."

Tayo let out a raspy breath and went back to his seat, in a rough voice, saying, "I hope she is alive. And I am sorry about Ozzy."

"You should be. Try it again. I dare you."

"Daria, please. The man is afflicted. Look at how his neck behaves."

"Yeah, for sure. That damn finger too."

Anna took out her phone, tapped a few numbers, and listened.

"There is no one at her home."

"Try again, Mom. We either fix this guy,—" she tipped her head toward Tayo—"or I finish him, and he's out the next trash day."

You do not see the comedy in your words, do you?

"Okay, Daria."

Anna tried the call again while saying, "Like you killed Benson?"

Daria sneered but didn't reply.

Chapter 10 – A Plan To Murder

Anna heard someone answer, and she switched the phone to speaker.

"You'd better have a good reason for calling," Lin said.

When Tayo grinned and gave a thumbs-up sign, Anna smiled back at him, but she quickly lost it.

"I believed I would never have reason to call you again. I am sadly wrong."

"Anna, you're done with The Shield. Lancaster Wolfe is gone. Just get on with your life."

"It is something we wish to do, but we cannot. I call today about Tayo. He has sent for Lee, but he does not believe her strength can do more than keep him alive. Maybe not even that."

"Just slow down, okay? What's wrong with Tayo?"

She glanced at him, sitting with his eyes closed. She turned to see Ozzy still hiding behind Daria, whose hand was kept close to the pistol in her purse.

"His destruction has begun. Those were the words he spoke to me before the back of his neck swelled up. He struggles to speak now."

"His neck swelled up, huh? Maybe he's coming down with something. Hold on, okay?"

Anna stared at the silent phone until Daria spoke.

"That's nervy, Mom. She put you on hold. You know, if it wasn't for her nutty powers, I'd—"

"Daria, that is not wise. I would not want Lin to hear such talk."

"Fine, Mom. I'm just saying."

A different voice spoke through the phone.

"Your name is Anna? I am Gloriana. Tell me what you see of the man Tayo."

"He is sitting down and not moving. He called me and said he needed—"

"But what do you see?"

"His neck behind him is large like a pillow. I am afraid something is growing in there. I touched it once, and his eyes said he would like to scream, but he made no sound. It felt hard. Not soft."

"Is there anything else unusual in his home?"

Anna looked around the room, then at Daria, who only shrugged.

"I do not know—we have never been here before. We are still in his apartment in Baltimore. I wish he could travel himself, but he cannot. We are packing to come to Lin's house, Daria and I. Ozzy too. I do not wish to be around things that—"

Lin said, "Wait. You were coming to my house? Who said you could do that?"

Daria sneered and tipped her head from side to side.

"Tayo insisted. He required that we bring his hand mirror."

"What are you—"

"And the mirror from his wall. We packed that too."

"You're not making any sense at all. I don't—"

"He said one of his fingers began to peel open on its own. And then—"

"What? What did you say happened to his finger?"

"Perhaps I heard him wrong, but whatever it was, it is gone now."

"What do you mean, it's 'gone?'"

"He used a knife. He placed it in a box. We can hear it scratching around in there. Then, his neck—"

"Oh, you can't be serious. This is some kind of joke, right?"

"No, Lin. When we arrived, he said he felt his neck beginning to grow, and he knew he could not cut that away from his body and confine it in a box. And Lee was still not with him. We have not yet put Tayo in the car because he tried to strangle Ozzy. After that, he—"

"What the hell is going on?"

"I cannot even guess. I should have gone back to Russia. I should take Daria and Ozzy and—"

"Stop already! Look, Lee should get there soon. Tell me where you are, and if I feel like traveling soon, maybe I'll come and help."

"Lin," said Gabriel, and no one in Tayo's apartment heard the rest of what was said.

After several seconds, they heard Lin say, "Tell me his address, just in case."

Anna repeated Tayo's address as he spoke it to her slowly, and they heard more voices besides Lin's until she ended the call.

*   *   *

"She is alive," Tayo said, with his eyes still closed.

"Lucky for you," said Daria. "Tell her to get her hocus pocus going and help you out."

"She must have only left the area for a while, then. But she does not wish for you to visit her, Tayo."

Who would? I have become a disaster.

"Anna, the pressure is becoming less. I can speak more easily."

"Good. Tell Mom and me why you tried to murder Ozzy."

"I began to hate him and thought he might be responsible for the strife I'm experiencing."

"Why the hell would you think that? He's just a dog!"

"I know that now, Daria. I believe my thoughts were attacked just as was my finger."

"Oh, right. The curse started peeling your brain. Nice try, Tayo."

"Daria, that is not helpful. We do not understand what is going on here."

She turned to Tayo and said, "What is this thing that is attacking you? We do not see anything in this room. Is it invincible?"

"She means 'invisible,'" Daria said, rolling her eyes.

"I believe it is both," said Tayo.

If I show you the symbols, and if the man in the trash has a partner, would that not lead to your murder as well? Perhaps it's already too late. Yes, both of you would be in line for slaughter now too.

"I can show you. It is an . . . unusual sight."

"More than a skinless finger in a box? Please."

"Daria, please. Yes, Tayo. Show us."

Oh, I cannot. I belong in a sweaty tent at the far end of a circus encampment.

Tayo took out his phone, set it to display one of the symbols, and turned it for Anna to see.

"Well, what is this? Some scribbling on a piece of paper?"

"That is only a rendition of the actual—"

Daria's phone began ringing and buzzing, and when she reached into her purse, Tayo recoiled. She looked up at him with a grin.

"It's only the phone this time."

She took it out and pointed it at Tayo, saying, "Leave our dog alone."

She looked at who'd sent a text message and grinned again.

"I have seen that grin before. It is Benson, is it not?"

"Yep. This is weird, though. He says he's outside, and he has a surprise."

While Daria grinned and typed her response, Anna said, "Well, it is strange enough that he is here at Tayo's home. Tayo, has he been here before?"

"No, he never has."

"Mom, I'm going out. He wants you out there too."

"What? Did he say why?"

"Nope. He only said to hurry because he's cold, even with the heater on."

"Yes, he did say that he would get cold easily."

"He said it? I thought I told you that."

"Oh. Um, we have been so busy that I forgot to say. Benson visited after you left yesterday."

Daria stared at her mother while putting away her phone.

"We haven't been *that* busy. Did you have a nice little visit with him, Mom? He did say he wanted to see you."

"He has become an odd man. That much is true. He told me that he was cold, too, just like he—"

"Did he get around to asking you anything?"

She tipped her head and grinned at her mother.

"He joked—at least, I hope he was joking—about asking you something."

"No, he did not. But what is going on out there?"

Daria shrugged and said, "Guess we'll find out. Come on."

* * *

Standing on Tayo's porch, their breath sending vapor clouds all around, Anna and Daria looked both ways.

"There," Daria said, pointing. "That car over there that's idling. That's probably him."

"There is another person in the car, too, Daria. What can this be about?"

"No idea. Let's go see."

* * *

Daria rapped on the tinted window and when it was powered down, Benson, with a coat and a scarf and a thick hat, grinned out at her.

"Hey. Get in."

He turned farther to see Anna and said, "You too."

Neither of them moved, but Daria leaned over to see the passenger.

"Who's your buddy?"

Before Benson could answer, she noticed that the man's hands were behind his back, and he'd been gagged.

"Benson, what the hell?"

"I'll explain. Try the backseat."

They stared.

"No, seriously. I bet this is important."

Anna held open the back door, and Daria sat and shuffled her way across the seat. Anna followed, and she froze at what Daria said.

"Benson, there's a knife stuck in you! What the hell?"

He turned only his head to the right to try to see the handle of a folding knife protruding from his back near his neck. It was in as far as it could go.

"Oh. Yeah, that could be kind of upsetting."

He chuckled as he pulled out the long, clean, shiny blade, waved it at his companion, causing him to lean back into the glass, and tossed it out the window.

Daria turned toward her mother, and they stared at each other for several seconds, their mouths hanging open.

"You got stabbed, and you just left it there?"

"Life goes on," he said and laughed. "Even when it shouldn't."

"Benson, first," said Anna, "what are you doing here? Let us start with that."

"Looking to get some cash from Tayo."

He turned his head again to the right, but he couldn't look directly at Anna behind him.

"I still plan on you delivering, Anna."

She turned to Daria and said, "Money. He means money, Daria."

"Yeah. We'll see."

Anna frowned at her daughter, then looked back toward Benson.

"Question two will have to be about this person confined in the vehicle with you."

"That's a fair question. Sure. I'll tell you. He was about to surprise your little party in there and kill all of you."

"Oh God, Mom, we left Ozzy in there with psycho Tayo. Why did we do that?"

"That is not the biggest idea right now, Daria. Did you not hear? This man had a plan to murder us?"

"Benson," Daria said with a smirk, "if this is some kind of joke, you can forget about ever again—"

"It's no joke, and I'm sure not forgetting."

He turned the rearview mirror and grinned at her reflection.

"Why would we be killed? That does not make sense!"

"Oh, maybe it does, Anna," said Benson. "I asked him some important questions, and he seemed to understand that only honest answers would help."

"You tortured him," Daria said with a grin. "You did, didn't you?"

He winked in the mirror.

"Yep."

"Like how?" she said with a grin. "What did you do?"

"Daria, that should not be our focus right now."

"Just wondering."

"I do not understand any of this," said Anna. "What is going on, Benson?"

"He said he had two partners, one of which has since disappeared. He said the three of them are like a secret agent society or some bullshit like that. It's about something that Tayo knows that he can't be allowed to know."

"And what could that possibly be?"

"We didn't get that far, Anna. We're sure going to, though."

"But why kill Daria and me too?"

"Probably Ozzy, too, Mom."

"Yep, he'd probably kill the dog too. Alright, you know what? Let's ask him."

Benson fumbled around in his coat pockets, outside and inside, and said, "What happened to that damn knife of mine?"

"You threw it out the window," Daria said with a smirk. "Litterbug."

"Daria, not now."

"Nah, that was his. Ah, here it is."

From inside his coat, he brought out a long blade. Anna and Daria stared at it. He reached over and removed the gag, but the man didn't speak—he only looked from Benson's eyes to the gleaming metal.

"I do not believe we need to be a part of all this," said Anna, and she reached for her door handle, pulling it enough to turn on the dome light.

"Hold up. I need you to confirm his answer. After that, you can both go back inside."

Anna pulled the door shut. Benson flipped the mirror so that he could see her.

"I never did tell you something. The skirts and heels are sweet. About time. Show off those legs. Shorter would be better too."

"She's copying off of Lin."

"Daria, that is not completely true. I was thinking of changing what—"

"No, you weren't, Mom."

Benson tapped the knife on the mirror, drawing Anna's attention.

"Whatever. It's hot."

"And you're cold," Daria said with a grin. "Perfect match."

Benson only chuckled and snapped the point of the knife to the man's chest, right over his heart.

"Quiz time. Are you listening?"

The man nodded.

"What is it that Tayo knows but shouldn't know?"

He shivered, wearing only a black t-shirt, and Anna could see that the very point of the knife was through the thin cloth.

"Someone will come for you too. All of you."

"Here's the deal," said Benson. "You give us a straight answer, and I'll let you go. We'll take our chances. How does that sound?"

The man let out a deep breath and despite the cold, sweat trickled down from his scalp.

"Numbers. No one can know about the numbers."

"What, like a secret code? A combination to a safe?"

"The capitals."

Benson shook his head and said, "Like in D.C., you mean?"

"No. He has seen the capital numbers."

"What the hell is he talking about, Benson?"

"I don't know, Daria, but is he making sense? Did Tayo—"

"Wait," said Anna. "Daria . . . what Tayo started to show us. Benson, it maybe is true."

"Alright, so he's legit, then," said Benson. "I've heard enough. I think we're through here."

"What does that mean?"

"What do you think, Anna? Oh, you both can go if you want. Or you can both stay. I kind of hope you stay."

Anna quickly got out of the car, and Daria scooted over toward the open door. But she hesitated.

"Mom, you go on ahead."

"Daria? No, you cannot possibly want—"

Daria pulled the door shut and locked it. When Anna stared, she waved at her, then tipped her head toward Tayo's apartment. Anna took slow steps back from the car.

"I'm going to ask her someday soon, just like I asked you."

"Don't you dare, Benson."

"Take a second and imagine it. It'd be hot, right?"

Daria sighed, and a few seconds later, she said, "Oh, I don't know. I guess."

He still held the pointy blade against the man's heart.

"Maybe right after we're done here. Sounds fun to me."

"You're a sick man, Benson," she said with a grin.

"You said you'd let me go."

Benson turned enough to wink at Daria, then tightened his grip on the handle and looked at his prisoner.

"Yep. I sure did."

Chapter 11 – Stab It Again

Anna scurried back into Tayo's apartment and slammed the door shut. She looked over at him, still in his chair and holding his neck with one hand. His big black eyes stared back at her. Ozzy sat on the couch, watching them both.

"Is everything okay, Anna?"

"I cannot even determine a guess anymore. I have been carried headlong into an asylum."

Actually, you just walked in.

"Would you like to trade places?"

She glanced down at the swelling under the skin of his neck and said, "No. I would not."

"Daria is gone?"

"Oh, Tayo, there are problems outside. Benson captured a man who said he wanted to murder all of us."

Tayo sat up, and his eyes grew wide as he stared at Anna.

"What man? Here to kill us?"

"He said you knew some things that you should not know. Does that make sense? All I could imagine was what you showed on your phone."

Tayo sank back into his chair, and he grimaced while fighting to turn his head from side to side.

"It's growing again. I won't survive."

"You do not know that. It might not grow any larger. Does what that man said resemble truth to you?"

He sighed and looked down.

"Anna, he's not the first. Another was here."

She looked around the apartment and said, "Here in your home? Where did he go?"

"I . . . got rid of him. I'm not surprised that he had a partner, though."

"And that picture on your phone is what causes these problems?"

"Oh, not just on the phone. The risk to you and Daria—"

"And Ozzy."

Tayo paused to squint at Anna.

"—cannot be avoided any longer, so I'll show you."

Anna stood and looked down on him as he untucked and began rolling up his shirt while he turned to his left. She gasped as more and more of the welts and markings were revealed.

"But what is this? What have you done to yourself? Have you joined some occult society?"

"I didn't do this. That thing that Lin sent after me? That's it. Right there."

"It has become part of you?"

"Yeah, and these symbols are—"

"Numbers. The stranger said they were numbers of some sort."

"Sure, why not? I can't identify them, though. I don't believe there's any record of them anywhere."

Anna moved the curtains aside to see the idling car with fogged up windows.

"And for those, we should all be dead?"

*   *   *

"Now would be a good time. Come on."

He looked in the rearview at Daria's eyes, open wide and staring at the passenger's chest. Only the handle could be seen.

"I don't believe you just did that."

"Had to."

"Yeah, but, um, you didn't stab him. You just . . . you just slipped it right in there. All the way."

98

He grinned into the mirror until she met his gaze.

"Good choice of words. Reminds me that you need a lap to sit on."

"You get sicker all the time."

"I might be running out of time. Who knows?"

She stared again at the dead man slumped against the door and window.

"Besides, you like it bizarre, don't you?"

"I, uh . . ."

"This would be a first for you. Don't pass that up."

She started to speak but stopped at the sight of his eyes in the mirror.

"Remember me being dead? How good that was? Now, here's another one that can watch us."

He reached over and stretched the man's eyelids up. They stayed up.

"Sort of. He's trying."

She shook her head slowly, gazing into the mirror as her frown gave way to a grin.

"God, how did you—"

"Hell."

"Right, Hell. How the hell did you get so damn persuasive?"

"Turns out, it took a lifetime."

*   *   *

Anna left the window and again studied Tayo's back.

"Your lump seems bigger than before. Can you still breathe?"

"It's becoming more difficult. Soon, I might not expend the effort necessary to converse with you."

"You will certainly not compose sentences so long."

Tayo nodded. Ozzy scratched an itch.

"I am sorry that Lin did not wish to help you, Tayo."

"I'm surprised, but I have to accept that. I did volunteer, so I need to find the strength to face this thing on my own."

"What kind of thing is it? I do not understand any of this."

"Lin said it was a Hunter. It hunts in a place where there's no life, and she and that woman you spoke with, Gloriana, somehow brought it here."

"Do you understand even a portion of that?"

"I do not. I believe I got caught up in the notion that I could—"

"You were caught up in your adoration of Lin. That is what I believe."

Tayo sighed and offered a barely noticeable grin.

"Yes, that's certainly a component of it. She has quite a style. As do you recently."

"It is a good look, even though it is hardly suitable to cold and ice."

"Still, it's good. I'm truly miserable, Anna, and scared too. You might find this foolish, but your new style alleviates a small amount of that."

She smiled and said, "Why, thank you, Tayo. I am happy that I could help. Can I bring you ice? Or a heating pad?"

Tayo laughed softly, sounding mostly like wheezing, and said, "Perhaps a priest would be a more logical choice."

"An exorcism? Is that what you mean?"

"I don't know what I mean. I only know that—"

He winced and tried to press down on his misshapen neck with both hands as it grew rapidly. With one hand, he pulled down on his lower jaw and fought to bring in air.

"Tayo, what can I do?"

He held his jaw, gurgled, and stared at her through his glasses with big, unblinking black eyes.

*　*　*

"See? That didn't take long."

Daria climbed back over the seat and worked at smoothing her camouflage dress back down.

"You're even colder than last time."

"Yeah. That kind of sucks. Keeping the camo on was nice."

"You think? The audience didn't applaud."

"Good one. Yeah, he's pretty quiet now. Won't be trying to kill you and your mom either."

"Or Ozzy."

"He really would have killed the dog too."

"They're as sick as you."

"Speaking of sick, what do you suppose is next for us?"

"Oh, this was a bad idea. I don't think we're ever again going to—"

"Sure. Now that you had your fun. Hey, I know. Let's get your mother, and we could all—"

"Stop. Just stop, Benson. Leave my mom alone."

She cracked open the door.

"Sure. Alone with her would be good too. Yep, that'll work."

"You're sick."

"Yep."

"You shouldn't bother my mom. Probably."

"Probably, huh?"

She groaned, slammed the door, and began the short walk to Tayo's apartment.

* * *

The wheezing from Tayo dwindled, and he stood and raced past Anna and into his kitchen. Before she could get farther than the doorway, she saw him open a drawer and take out a steak knife.

There you are, my old friend. Still bloody from that finger?

"Tayo, what are you doing?"

Is she suggesting that I should use the butter knife instead?

He turned to look at her, barely making a sound, staring with big eyes. He reached up with his right hand to hold the point of the knife above the mass under his skin.

You wish me to speak when I cannot even breathe?

"Tayo, you wish to stab yourself? Is that a wise solution?"

101

They both looked at the front door as Daria pushed it in, stepped inside, and slammed it shut. She saw them in the kitchen and rushed over.

"What insanity is going on in here?"

"Tayo is being attacked! He cannot breathe!"

"And stabbing that thing is going to help?"

"What else can he do?"

Yes, what else can I do? You have two seconds to submit your suggestions.

They both watched him as one tear leaked out onto his cheek.

Time has expired.

He raised the knife, still holding Anna's gaze, and plunged it toward his back.

The point found his skin, but the stabbing missed the mark as the growth bunched up near his left shoulder.

You know that I'm about to stab you? How can that be?

"What the hell? Tell me I didn't just see that."

"Daria, it is true! It moved!"

"Stab it again!" said Daria.

The thought had occurred to me. You obviously relish the idea more than I, though.

Tayo changed hands with the knife and struck and again, the mass dodged his attack, wedging itself near his right shoulder and stretching his skin.

"Quick! You have to be quick!"

I imagine it's easy to offer advice to the madman who must do the stabbing.

Tayo held the knife in front of him, passing it from hand to hand. The tumor huddled over his spine, twitching.

Who is the more clever of us, huh? Me? Or the tumor?

"Do it, Tayo. You need to breathe!"

I did notice that, Anna.

"Good advice, Mom. Tayo, maybe I should stab it for you."

"Daria, you would do that?"

No, surely she could not do that.

"Sure. It's the easiest thing. Just slide it right in."

Maybe next time, Daria. Yes, next time.

Anna never looked at her daughter. They both watched Tayo fake with his left, and when it moved to the right, he quickly changed hands and stabbed it. It tried to get away, but he held it in place, where he began twisting the blade and causing streams of blood to squirt and drip onto the kitchen linoleum.

How is that, tumor? Can you tell I'm displeased with you?

"Oh, this is a madhouse!"

"Mom, keep it together. If he lives, we'll—"

"I will live," Tayo said in a strained voice before raising the knife and plunging it in again.

"That's gotta hurt," Daria said while shaking her head.

With the knife sticking in him and while Anna and Daria watched, the mass deflated like a popped balloon until only the smooth skin of Tayo's back remained, with saggy stretched areas and knife holes and blood.

* * *

"You had better just stay lying down on that couch," said Anna, and Daria tossed a folded blanket onto him.

Anna unfolded it and covered him, and he let out a deep breath.

"Anna, it's the things on my back doing this to me. The man outside spoke of symbols. He—"

"Won't be saying any more about that."

"Daria, what do you mean?"

"Mom, I'm just saying that Benson's handling things. That guy won't bother us."

"It took that long for you to have a discussion in his car?"

"Yep."

Anna stared at her for a second, then turned to Tayo.

"What were you saying, Tayo?"

"I don't understand this, but these things on my back, they have some kind of power. Four have already left their places, and each one has caused something horrible."

"Your finger?"

"Yes, Daria. That was the first."

"Your neck was the next one?"

"Yeah, Anna. Then, I went after Ozzy. Please, believe me, I would never harm your dog."

"I believe you, Tayo. What of the fourth?"

"Oh, um, I'm not sure. I think it kind of departed quietly, not causing any damage. Maybe it missed?"

Anna stared at him, and he held her gaze for only a moment before looking down at the blanket covering him.

"Yes, well, that is a frightening tale that you tell. I do not wish to see your back again, but you must have some idea—"

"Hey, I want to see it. You showed my mom?"

"Can I perhaps recover to some degree, Daria?"

"Let him rest," said Anna. "Tayo, what do we do next?"

"You call Lin. I can't accept no for an answer anymore. Ice won't help."

"Neither will a heating pad," said Daria. "I can just about guarantee that."

"And I do not know how to contact an exorcism professional," said Anna.

"That's all true," said Tayo. "Lin will just have to help in some way. Even her advice could be the difference between life and—"

"More parts of you rattling around in boxes?"

"Daria, you are sometimes not helpful."

Chapter 12 – A What? A Bird?

"Just make the call, Mom. She's too far away to do anything to you anyway."

"Many weeks ago, Tayo determined that her distance was expanding all the time. We cannot know that we are safe, even here."

"Well, just don't piss her off, then."

"Fine. I will call."

"Thank you, Anna," said Tayo.

She picked up her phone and listened to Lin's ringing. Tayo and Daria sat and watched her.

"Put it on speaker, Mom."

"Fine."

She tapped it and set it down.

"What, Anna?"

"Lin, it is Tayo. He—"

"Yeah, yeah, I know. He's got some kind of neck thing. You need to—"

"No, he is done with that for now. He stabbed it, and it—"

"What do you mean, 'he stabbed it?'"

Daria gestured like she was doing the stabbing. Anna frowned at the smirk on her face.

"With a steak knife. Lin, it did not want to be stabbed. It dodged several times. But Tayo was quick, and the knife found it. He now has stretched skin and several holes with blood. Whatever was in there is now—"

"You know that sounds crazy, don't you?"

"Yes, of course, it does. I did not understand the world any longer after seeing all that you have done. I understand it less now."

"Don't try to understand it—that's the problem. Just accept it. Is Tayo okay?"

"He can speak again. But not much. Here he is."

Tayo leaned forward in his chair to be closer to the phone laying on the coffee table.

"Lin? Are you there?"

"Yes, I'm here, Tayo. What's going on with you?"

"The entity to be hunted, for which you enlisted my help, has officially arrived. I had hoped you were either joking or greatly exaggerating in your description of it. If anything, you painted too pleasant of a picture."

"What is it, Tayo? Where is it?"

"It is with me. It is a part of me now."

"Where? How?"

"It's on my back. Under the skin. I can sense that it is weak. Confused somehow. But it's getting stronger. Every time one of the symbols comes alive and vanishes from my back, the effects are worse."

"You have symbols on your back? What kinds of symbols?"

"They are like nothing I have seen. Before they began their attempts at destroying me, I was able to initiate some research. I can find nothing in any published literature that matches them."

"How many are there?" said Gabriel's voice.

"Doesn't that Gabriel have anywhere else to be?" Daria whispered. "Always with Lin?"

"Daria, shh."

"There were forty," said Tayo. "Thirty-six remain. Three have manifested themselves: one damaged my finger; another affected my neck in a deleterious way; and the third brought some level of clinical madness to me—I remember not desiring to attack Anna's dog, but I could not stop myself."

"What happened to the fourth one?"

Tayo paused to look at the inquisitive eyes all around him.

I could tell all of you a very intriguing narrative. Shall I do that? Would I change, in your view, from a humble victim to a homicidal maniac?

"I do not know, Gabriel. Fighting to maintain my physical being has been trying. I did not view my back until after my attempts to murder Anna's pet. The fourth symbol could have left in unison with any one of the three, or it might have departed quietly on its own."

"Are you sure that four are missing?"

"Yes, I am fairly certain."

"Okay, and there were forty to begin with?"

Anna saw Daria grinning and counting on her fingers, and she snapped her fingers softly and frowned.

"Yes, Gabriel. I cannot anticipate what might happen next. Can we meet? The three of us?"

"I don't think I can help you," said Lin. "I barely feel like Lin right now. I'd try to explain it to you, but I know it sounds crazy."

"I understand, Lin. My hope is that you can witness this adversary of mine, even if you can't help right away. But at least you will know, and perhaps you can devise some way to help or at least provide some advice on how I might prevail against this thing."

"Well, it doesn't sound like it's just one thing. Okay, I'll meet you halfway. Can you drive, or will Anna be able to drive you?"

"The way I feel at the moment, I can surely operate an automobile. But I don't know if or when my face might swell up and make vision impossible."

Daria filled her cheeks with air, then let it out to show a big smile.

Anna pointed at her.

"Or perhaps my leg will expand like an aluminum foil pouch as the corn kernels inside are heated, pinning the accelerator pedal to the floor."

Anna and Daria paused to look at each other for several quiet seconds, Anna not blinking and Daria whispering, "Didn't think of that one!"

"So, Anna can drive you, then?"

"She has agreed to chauffeur me as needed. She cannot mask her displeasure at the spectacle I have become, though."

"She'll just have to get over it."

"Your voice is carried by the phone's speaker ability. She can hear you. Daria too."

"It is true, Lin," said Anna. "I will drive Tayo as he needs. I can force myself to be around him, but I do not wish to be near you. I have seen too many frightening things you can do."

"Oh, I've learned some new ones too."

Daria lost her smile, and Anna froze before speaking again.

"Like what? What are you—"

"Look, just drive him to French Creek State Park. Get on Route 345, and you'll see my Temt8tion at one of the parking areas. Let's plan for three hours from now."

"Thanks, Lin," said Tayo. "I can't guarantee that I will even be able to speak by then. But it will help my morale to have you involved in some fashion. I'm certain I have little dominion remaining over my physical form and if my confidence were to crumble any further, I would have no chance. I will see you in three hours."

"See you soon, Tayo."

Anna leaned forward, saw that Lin had ended the call, and picked up her phone.

"Well, perhaps that is encouraging, Tayo. Do you believe Lin can assist you in some way?"

"Before you fill up with popcorn?"

"Daria, let the man respond."

"Yes, Anna. It is as I told her: I sense that my confidence is key in this sordid agenda which has trapped me. Having her seeking a solution will help my morale to a great extent."

"Well, I hope that it is enough."

"Hey," Daria said as she stood up from the couch, "maybe we could get Benson to tag along. Like a convoy or something."

"Oh, Daria, I do not think—"

"Nope," she said, looking through the curtains. "They're gone."

"They?"
"Yeah, him and the . . . the guy."

* * *

"No, I don't think we'll need the mirrors, Anna."
"Why did you insist on packing those earlier?"
"Why do you think, Mom? What if you had that sick crap all over your back, and you—"
"Daria, Tayo is right here, and you should—"
"Anna, she's right. My nemesis deserves a much harsher description than that."
"Okay, well, we will unpack them later, then."
Daria sat up front, with Anna driving and Tayo slouched in the backseat.
"We drove much like this to St. Simons only several weeks ago," Anna said before she started the engine. "Do you remember, Daria? It was a warmer place than this."
"Hell yeah, it was warmer. Can we stop at home first? I need a better coat."
"Yes, we surely will. I would like to change too."
She started the engine.
"Tayo, are you hungry? We can stop and eat while we travel."
"My appetite is suffering from these circumstances but yes, I will eat. I don't know how much strength I might need for the next attack."
"Just don't strangle me," said Daria. "I'll shoot you before you can get a hand—"
"Daria, Tayo will resist his urge to strangle you, okay?"
"Anna, you make it sound like I already want to. I do not."
"There. You see, Daria? Let us drive in peace."

* * *

With the car parked and idling in front of her apartment building, Anna ran in to change, with instructions from Daria on which coat to bring out.

"Tayo, this must really suck for you."

"It's not pleasurable, Daria. I've never known such a nightmare."

"I'd be pissed at Lin if I were you."

"I can't be. It's true that she was instrumental in delivering this thing to the world, but her intentions were good."

"How can you be sure about that?"

"Because I know her heart. It's a good heart. And her eyes. I'll never forget how they were so bright when—"

"Oh, please. Again with her eyes? That's just some spooky bullshit that—hey, what the hell?"

They watched Anna step out of the building with two coats in her arms. She'd changed into a shorter skirt and higher heels, and her sweater was thin, tight, and low-cut. She opened the back door and threw the coats at Tayo, then climbed in the behind the wheel.

"What the hell, Mom? We're going to a fashion show?"

"Daria, I felt like having a change. I enjoy this style. Is that so bad?"

"No, not at all. It looks good. Aren't you cold, though?"

"Well, Daria, we are not walking to the Pennsylvania park, are we?"

"You're kind of a smartass, too, Mom. That's what Benson called me. Can you believe that?"

"You did say he has become more unusual than he already was. So, yes, I do believe what you say. I do not wish to be considered a smartass, though."

"Bet he'd call you that too."

"I have no wish to see him ever again. I really am considering returning to Russia with you. And Ozzy."

"I'm not going to Russia. I don't think even Ozzy wants to go."

"Yes, well, for now, we are all going to see Lin Finity in Pennsylvania."

* * *

"This spot is good, Mom. Anywhere around here."

Anna turned her car into a gravel parking lot located in a large, open area. Far away in each direction, a thick pine forest had them hemmed in.

"She is late. I believe we are on time."

"Why this park, Mom? Seems kind of remote, don't you think? Is she planning to murder us, cut us up, and bury us in—"

"Daria, what is going on with you? Your thoughts seem to be drifting into darker regions lately."

"Oh, I don't know why, Mom. Maybe a wiggling finger in a box? Oh, how about seeing Tayo stab himself while whatever he's stabbing is running away? Under his skin? Or maybe it's because—"

"Daria, we can finish that analysis later. Tayo, I know that temperatures are low, but your back scares me."

"You're kicking him out, Mom?"

"He did try to strangle Ozzy. Do you remember? Maybe he will—"

"I don't sense an impending eruption from my back," Tayo said with a deep sigh. "But I understand. I'll wait at that table,—" he reached between Anna and Daria to point toward their right—"and minimize the risk to you both."

"Mostly Ozzy."

"Yes, Anna. I really do regret that."

He got out, swung the car door shut, and began walking toward the picnic table that was mostly covered in snow, holding closed his long wool coat.

"That's kind of mean, but I feel better with him the hell out of here."

"You are becoming obsessed with Hell. But you are right. I feel more safety now too."

"Uh-oh," said Daria. "I bet that's Lin's car."

She pointed past her mother and through the window at a sleek black car approaching slowly.

"I think you are right. I hope that we are ready for whatever might happen."

"You sure are dressed for it. Are you hoping that she can check you out? You like antagonizing her like that?"

Anna turned toward Daria with her eyebrows raised, then she looked again at Lin's car.

"I do not seek to—"

"Oh, you want her approval, don't you? You're a Lin Finity groupie, aren't you?"

"I am not sure that 'groupie' is an accurate term, but I—"

"Uh-huh. Sure, Mom. Well, she'll never say that she approves, but I bet she will."

"Oh, Daria, do you think?"

"Hell yeah, Mom."

They watched as Lin, Gabriel, and Taylor got out of the car.

"Geez, doesn't she go anywhere alone?"

"She certainly has in the past. Tayo determined that she was likely alone when she killed a man in Georgia. Daria, you must remember all of the reports that we studied?"

"Yeah, I'm just saying. That's Gabriel and that girl, right?"

"That is her daughter. I believe her name is Taylor. Oh, look. Only Lin and Gabriel are coming to see Tayo."

"And you. She'll probably stop to see you too."

Anna glanced down at her skirt, high on her thighs, then she again watched Lin and Gabriel getting closer. She could hear the snow crunching from their steps, even through the closed window.

* * *

"Great, Mom. They really are coming after us first."

"Daria, they are not coming after us. She probably wishes only to extend a greeting."

When Lin looked in at her through the window, Anna hit the button to lower it.

"Hello, Lin. We meet again."

Lin only stared back. Anna watched as she fidgeted with her hands on her legs and frowned.

"Yeah, wonderful. I can see you don't want to talk to me. That's fine."

"I do not even want you this close to me."

"Oh, Mom," Daria said from her side and out of Lin's view, "give her a break. She's never hurt you in any way."

Lin leaned enough to view in and saw Daria's smile and thick black hair. She'd put on a puffy parka, and she sat looking at Lin with a slight smirk.

"No, but I came close to hurting you."

Daria stared in the silent car as Lin gazed calmly at her.

"Still having fun playing with cameras?"

"No. No, I'm done. I swear."

When Lin's eyes flashed a blazing green for only an instant and she grinned through the open window, Daria pushed herself as far from her as she could.

Anna didn't look at Lin's burning eyes.

"She will not have fun, Lin. There is no need to destroy either of us."

"I might destroy you just for copying my style."

Anna barely hid a smile as she peeked down at her short skirt, then she looked out at Lin.

"It is a good look, but I do not wish to die for it."

"Don't worry. I won't kill you. Not this time anyway."

"Thank you. Tayo is on that picnic table."

She pointed across the field to the table Tayo had swept clear enough of snow to sit.

"Whatever is ailing him belongs far from me and Daria."

"Fine, I'll leave you two alone, then."

"Ozzy too. He has already been strangled."

"Mom," Daria whispered. "Just let her go, alright?"

Anna swung a hand up to shush Daria. She watched as Lin looked first at her, then Daria, then Ozzy in the backseat.

"Just stay out of my way. All three of you."

She stood, and Anna quickly closed the window.

"Hell, that's one scary woman, Mom. Really, you shouldn't push her."

"It was you with that smirk on your face that caused her eyes to flare up. I do not wish to be destroyed by her, Daria."

"Right. Wait for Tayo's back to explode and kill all of us. That's a hell of a lot better. We'll all end up in little boxes in his kitchen."

* * *

Tayo sat with his back against the table, his arms crossed, shivering and watching Lin and Gabriel draw near across the snow. Every step they took crunched the frozen top layer and when he closed his eyes, he could judge their distance by the loudness of their steps.

They stopped, both looking down on him, and Tayo noted that Lin wore jeans and a warm coat, her blond hair fluffing out from beneath a thick hat, and Gabriel's long, wavy brown hair rested in the calm air.

"Tayo, what's wrong with you?" Lin said.

He looked at her through his thick black glasses, and he tipped his head back to view her more directly, causing his short dreadlocks to fall to each side. He knew that his eyes were attempting to plead for help even before he spoke.

"Lin."

Oh, my voice is not good. I hope I can communicate effectively. This is quite important to my continuing existence.

"I'm here, Tayo. What happened to you?"

"The thing you told me about. It's here."

"In this world? We really did bring it here?"

"Yes. But *here*," he said, wondering if the act of speaking might be damaging his already compromised vocal cords.

"I'm sorry, but the damage to my neck has rendered speaking a difficult activity."

"I can still understand you. But it's here? With you, you said?"

Yes, with me. Not beside me. Not near me. With me.

"Yes. Lin, it is destroying me."

"What exactly do you mean? You said it was in your back?"

"Yes, it resides under the skin of my back."

"But you're leaning on it now, aren't you?"

Oh, why not, Lin? It seeks to annihilate me, and I must still cater to it and keep it comfortable?

"It would be a blessing if that could injure it in any way."

"That doesn't hurt you, though?"

That's humorous. You're funny without even trying, Lin. Excuse me, but I won't laugh.

"I have no sensation that might confirm that I still have a back."

Before closing his eyes, he saw Lin and Gabriel fall silent and look at each other for a moment. Then, he heard Lin continue.

"I'd like to know what it looks like."

He opened his eyes and said, "I can show you. It's cold—St. Simons would be preferable—but the enormity of what I've been tasked with accomplishing warrants the discomfort. Still, I'd like to make it brief, so please, ready your phone's photography capabilities."

He watched her pull off her mittens one at a time, and she handed them to Gabriel.

What is cold compared to all else that has tormented me? It's nothing. I'll shiver if I must, but Lin must know. She must see my adversary.

He took off his coat, folded it on his lap, and turned to face away. He unbuttoned his shirt and after taking a deep breath, he pulled it down over his shoulders, all the way to his waist.

He heard Lin gasp softly, but Gabriel made no sound that he could hear.

Yes. You see, Lin? You see what you have brought me? I don't believe even you can explain this with any accuracy.

The seconds dragged on, Tayo counting them out to himself as a distraction, and when he suspected that Lin had forgotten their objective, he reminded her.

"Lin, it's exceedingly cold today, especially without benefit of a shirt. Please, take your photo soon."

"Oh, yeah. Sorry, Tayo."

He heard the sound effects of her phone's camera snapping a few shots and when they'd stopped, he quickly got dressed and turned to face them.

"I don't know what that is, Tayo. Gabby, do you?"

I suspected that you would not know, Lin. Gabriel, you might be my only hope.

"Yes, I have some idea. But we should go and discuss this at your house. Tayo needs to get back to Baltimore soon too."

You have some idea? I would like to hear it!

"Lee will get to your apartment soon, Tayo," said Lin. "Those look like some kind of welts. She might be able to help with them."

"Yes, you are correct. I—"

Oh, not now!

He felt the familiar, merciless axe strike behind his right shoulder, and he knew that it was at the location of the last symbol in the top row.

Why must it be an axe? Can you not just tap me on the shoulder and state your intentions to begin destroying me again? I promise that I won't argue.

"If you're cold, Tayo, maybe—"

"It is not due to the unfavorable temperature here. It's . . . I think—"

Forgive me, but I'm too compromised to even finish my sentence.

He fell forward onto his hands and knees in the snow, with a quick thought that maybe he could be suffocated by lying there long enough. Taking deep breaths, he heard Lin.

"Gabby, do you see that too?"

"Yes, Lin. Something is happening with his back. It might be another symbol reaching out to cause destruction of some sort."

"Tayo, are you okay?"

I never knew how truly comical all of my friends and associates could be!

"No, Lin. The state of being 'okay' is quickly becoming an unrecognizable abstraction."

"Is it trying something else on you?"

He felt the axe as if it were just breaking the skin, just starting to cut into muscles and tendons, but it had stopped and dug in no farther. It was unlike the other instances of symbols rising up to attack.

"No, I suspect we should all study our surroundings. This feels different. I don't believe it will risk killing me. I am its host, and my estimation is that it wishes only to eradicate my will. It has a different plan."

Tayo closed his eyes, and he didn't move, but he was able to continue with his controlled breathing. He heard the alarm in Lin's voice.

"Gabby, I don't like the sound of that."

He remained on his hands and knees, his eyes closed, in a snow-covered field that had fallen completely silent.

He heard Lin say, "Gabby, there."

A long moment went by without a word. Then, Lin spoke again. "And there."

Do I wish to see what is happening here? Do I dare?

Tayo turned his head to one side and opened his eyes. He saw many small things just inside the treeline, and they all seemed to be moving toward them. He looked in the other direction and fought to retain control of his breaths.

What have we done this time? How can a symbol on a man's back produce such a situation?

He closed his eyes and turned his face back to the snow. The cold soaking through at his knees was a welcome distraction.

* * *

"Mom, what the hell?" Daria said as she pointed straight out through the windshield.

Anna looked, and Ozzy climbed forward between them to look as well.

"What are those things by the trees? They are moving, Daria?"

"Yeah, Mom. Oh, and look,—" she turned to look out her side window, and Anna looked past her—"over there too."

Anna quickly looked in every direction and said, "They have us surrounded. They are everywhere."

"Well, who the hell are 'they?'"

They waited in silence and watched whatever was approaching them.

*　*　*

Lin said, "Cats, Gabby?"

"I believe these are larger than regular household cats."

"Yeah, they're bobcats."

I have brought a herd of cats here to attack us? What nonsensical insanity is this?

"There must be a hundred of them."

Why not a thousand? Why not a million?

"We'd be safe in your car, Lin, but you'd have to use his magic for us to move him in time."

"Or you could carry him. But that still wouldn't save my paint."

"What?"

Yes, what are you saying, Lin? Is our safety not paramount?

He heard Lin say, in a calm voice, "My Temt8tion has perfect Oblivion Black paint. I'm not about to let that get all scratched up by a pack of possessed bobcats."

This could be considered supremely entertaining if it weren't lunacy too!

"Lin, it's just paint, and—"

"Besides, moving Tayo like that would tire me out."

Moving me 'like that?' Moving me in what way?

"I'm still not strong enough to be doing that."

"No, not yet, but you will be soon if—"

118

"I want to try out what I showed you before—that new mayhem of mine."

Oh, here we go. She's eager to try out some new destructive power. Yes, of course, I'm completely safe in the snow, on my hands and knees. Perhaps crying will help.

"You do like calling that mayhem, don't you?'

"Yes, I do. It's spinning mayhem, remember?"

"Lin, there must be a better way than killing all those cats."

You can kill them all, Lin? How on Earth can that be done?

A few seconds of silence passed.

"Tell me something, Gabby. If they're possessed like that, do they still hear God's voice at every moment?"

"I don't think so."

Why would anyone care? If you can kill them, then please, kill them!

"And do they wish to do that thing's bidding, that Hunter thing?"

"No, they can't. They'd never behave this way."

What is wrong with these two? Is there really time for a philosophical debate, trying to determine what God thinks of this? I fear He has fled the park like anyone rational would!

"Anyway, we're out of time," she said.

Tayo looked again to his right, at a line of hunting bobcats that were all so close that he could see their eyes focused on him.

How will it feel to be shredded alive? It will take much less effort than sawing off a finger, or stabbing a back, or whatever else might befall me.

* * *

"Those are some type of cats, Daria."

"Yeah, I see that now. Mom, what the hell is going on? There's at least a hundred of them!"

"It probably has something to do with Tayo and that goddamn back of his."

"Swearing now is a-okay with me, Mom. Yeah, exactly. His goddamn back. Maybe it's because of that goddamn Lin?"

"Perhaps, Daria. Yes. Or maybe that goddamn—no, I cannot say it that way. I mean, perhaps it is because of Gabriel."

Daria frowned at her and shook her head.

* * *

Tayo focused on the bright eyes of the closest of the cats.

I will face my death. I don't believe I will even resist. Yes, Lin is powerful, but there are too many. You must be the leader. I see that you have stopped, and you are crouching there, contemplating which part of my anatomy you will remove first, aren't you? The throat would the quickest death. Yes, I will even expose that for you to—

Tayo felt like his heart would stop as the top half of the cat, with staring eyes and mouth open to expose its fangs, slid to the left and crunched into the snow. Its bottom half, with every leg twitching, teetered and fell over to the right.

No! No, what madness is this now? What just happened?

He looked at the sectioned cat's neighbors and saw nothing but bloody pieces.

They were not struck. There is no weapon here. Not a drop of blood flew in any direction. How do living things become sliced after being assembled and living?

Some heads contained eyes that still pointed at him, and others had fallen to permit them to study the cold sky. Furry, wet, red body parts littered the field.

I am thankful to be alive, but I never knew that there was so much to fear in this world. Lin, you did that? Lin, what did you do?

He closed his eyes, remembered to take another breath, and held his head low, near the snow. Many quiet seconds passed before Gabriel spoke.

"They are in pieces, Lin. You have succeeded. That is quite stunning, but I'm sorry you felt a need to do it this way."

"It's what a crow would do, Gabby. We kill threats if we can. Without regret."

I should not question anything any longer. But what is this talk of crows?

"Broken hearts or broken bones, Gabby."

Yes, and slaughtered animals too. Why break bones or hearts when one can do whatever insanity just happened?

"Yes, Lin. You have sent them back to God. You have saved us."

Yes, that's the important thing—the attacking animals are with God now.

"Saved my paint too."

I do not understand this. Lin, I remember you being more compassionate.

"Are you okay, Lin?"

"I'm fine, but I think I'm still kind of a bird."

A what? A bird?

"It will pass. And you have prepared quite a feast for the scavengers on this cold winter day. There is always some good in everything."

"What do you think of my spinning mayhem?"

"I'm very impressed, Lin. I hope if you ever have occasion to use it again, it will be for no more than chopping down more trees."

"Or candleholders."

"Yes, but never chocolate in any form."

These people are more insane than I am becoming with each animating symbol.

"Or any other living things, Gabby. I remember not wanting to kill."

"I know you do, Lin."

I do not know that you do, Lin. Should I fear you as well?

Tayo opened his eyes and raised himself up onto his knees. He looked up at Lin, who was gazing down at him.

"It did not harm me, Lin. I feel as I did before. It's prohibitively cold to check again, but I believe my back contains one less symbol now."

"Each instance is getting stronger, isn't it?" Gabriel said.

"Yes, I believe that's true. How will I survive even the next one, let alone all thirty-five that remain?"

"I don't know," said Lin, "but you need to get back to Baltimore. Lee can help."

That is wishful thinking. She'd have an easier time reassembling your dissected cats.

Gabriel gave Tayo a hand up, and they walked in silence to Anna's car. Tayo opened the back door, sat next to Ozzy, then closed it. Lin and Gabriel continued around to the driver's side.

* * *

"Tayo," Anna whispered, watching Lin and Gabriel walk around the front of her car, "what just happened?"

Daria turned to look at him and so did Anna, causing her skirt to slide farther up on her thighs.

"I don't understand anything anymore, Anna."

Anna and Daria looked at each other, then Daria looked down at her mother's legs.

"Good, Mom. Smart. Piss off Lin after whatever the hell just happened."

Anna glanced down and then back at Daria.

"She will not destroy us. I do not know how that happened to those cats, but it probably could have eliminated us too."

"Right. Well, maybe she just wants to look into our eyes while she slices and dices us."

Anna turned to look out at the cat parts strewn everywhere and didn't answer her daughter. Her breaths stayed shallow and her eyes rarely blinked as she stared at all the cat pieces and puddles.

Tayo watched from the backseat with Ozzy as Lin stood by Anna's window and looked in. After several seconds, she thumped it with her thick mitten. Anna hesitated, then turned toward her and powered down her window.

"Lin, how . . . what just—"

"It's like everything else: just forget what you saw. You need to get Tayo back to his apartment before Lee gets there."

Daria stared and shook her head twice, quickly, when Lin leaned over and stared into her eyes.

"Did you like that? It was so quick you didn't even see it. Still feel like taking a photo of me?"

Daria only shook her head as she stared back. She didn't smirk. She didn't even smile.

"Good."

Tayo shook quietly as he sat behind Anna and when Lin looked around her and met his gaze, he couldn't think of what to ask her first. She spoke, and he didn't get a chance.

"Lee might be able to help you, Tayo. Let her try. Gabby and I will try to figure out what this is all about, okay?"

I must return to my hellish apartment with no resolution in sight?

"I'm not inclined to plead for assistance, but I would indeed treasure your help, Lin. If you had not been here—"

"Maybe none of that would have happened. Maybe that thing was coming after me this time, not you."

That is possible. It did cause the dog to be strangled. And that stranger met an unkind but well-deserved fate.

"Instead, perhaps my leg would have exploded."

He knew that the strength and surety in his eyes had diminished, but he couldn't be sure whether the terror he felt was on display there. He thought it probably was.

"Do the best you can, Tayo. I need to find my own life right now."

"I don't understand. Where is your life?"

"Let's just say I only flew back into town yesterday."

It's possible that nothing I will ever hear will ever again make sense.

He watched Lin turn her gaze down toward Anna's lap, and a quick glance showed that Daria had managed a modest grin.

"Anna, he'll be in good hands with Lee. I will never see you or your daughter or your dog again, do you understand?"

"You despise Ozzy as well?"

"All of you. Never again. Got it?"

"Yes, Lin, of course. I want only to be a large amount of miles from you. I did not want to see you this time. But Tayo—"

"Just go. Take him home."

Lin took a step back, and Anna zipped her window shut.

"Hell, Mom, why are you asking her about Ozzy? Of course, she hates all three of us. You're going to get us killed."

"You are more likely with your photography antics."

"Yeah, maybe. Sometimes, I wonder just how far she can be pushed."

"Do you see how close those cats came to giving her a push? That is how far. It is not far."

She started the engine and cruised slowly toward where the road disappeared into the dark forest. Tayo and Daria and Ozzy watched the skies as large, hungry birds circled the slaughter scene.

Chapter 13 – A Thing For Boots

"Tayo, you slept like a dead man on the journey back here, but you still appear exhausted."

"Who wouldn't be, Mom? Geez, the guy's a disaster."

"Daria, that does not help anyone."

"Just saying."

"You're right, Anna, and she is too. I think I'll lie down in the bedroom for a while."

"Watch out for mice."

"Daria."

She only grinned back at her mother.

"Tayo, when we heard a mouse in that closet before, that was—"

"Something else. I know only that it's related to what's on my back."

"It makes no sense to me. Does it to you?"

"No. I sure will lie down, though."

He got up and walked the few steps to his bedroom, then closed the door behind him.

Anna set down everything that she'd packed to take to Lin's earlier, then waited for Daria to look her way.

"Do you see the wisdom in returning to Russia?"

"What . . . just because Tayo's got an insane back, Lin learned how to butcher a bunch of animals all at once, Benson is out there killing—"

Anna stared.

"Oh. I mean, he probably would be if we asked him to. Come on, Mom. He was like that even with The Shield, remember?"

"Yes, he always did seem off to some degree."

"Well, he's added a few degrees of offness. Still, I think I'll text him and see what he's up to."

She took out her phone, and Anna stood and stretched.

"We should have picked up food. I will look in the kitchen."

"Just not in the little box on the counter, the one that's pinned down by a giant can of soup."

Anna shook her head and sighed before leaving for the kitchen.

Daria called after her, "Maybe don't move that soup either."

*   *   *

Daria typed, "So, what did you do?"

"Dumped him," was Benson's reply.

"Where?"

"Don't ask."

"Right. Now, where are you going?"

"Someplace warm."

"Like Florida?"

She waited and listened to her mother rattling the cabinets and looking in the refrigerator. A phone rang in there, a different tone than her mother's.

"No. Something in camo."

Daria grinned and glanced up at the kitchen doorway. No one was watching her.

She typed, "And lace."

She stared at the phone, willing a reply before she could make herself look away. It arrived.

"Yep. Best parts."

"Daria, there are things to eat that are not fingers."

She put away her phone, looked up, and saw her mother looking around the corner into the living room.

"You were on the phone?"

"No, Mom. Just checking. Was that your phone that rang? Did you change your ring tone?"

Anna glanced at Tayo's bedroom door, then crept in and sat next to Daria on the couch. She spoke in almost a whisper.

"No, that was Tayo's phone. It is charging on the counter."

"Who called?"

"Daria, that is private information. It is none of our business."

"Still, who was it?"

Anna smiled and said, "Someone named Jenny."

"Oh, that's nice. A neighbor, maybe?"

"No, I am sure not. I did not study the number completely, but it started with 234. Daria, that was a call from Nigeria."

"Oh, right. He's from there. Cool that he has a girlfriend back home."

"Well, we do not know that. It could be a grandmother."

"Hey, did he ever come on to you?"

"Oh no, Daria, he was always way too professional for that."

Daria grinned and said, "So, did you ever come on to him?"

"Daria! You are being silly."

Daria still grinned.

"There was only one time that I had a fleeting fantasy of an encounter with him."

"I bet that's long gone now that he's all mutated and stuff."

Anna smiled and said, "He is not really a mutant. He is a suffering man. Can you show some compassion?"

Daria shook her head and said, "Probably not."

Her phone rang, and she took it out and smiled.

"Got to go."

"Benson again? Daria, is that wise?"

"What the hell else are we doing, Mom? Babysitting some psycho that's all—"

"He is not completely a psycho."

"Some defense. Look, you go eat something. I won't be gone long. He's just kind of hard to tell no."

Anna sighed and said, "Yes, Mr. Wolfe was at times like that as well."

"Oh, so you flirted with him, didn't you?"

"No, Daria, I have never flirted with him. He was just a very determined type."

"Fine, Mom. I'll fill in the blanks myself."

"As will I about you and Benson."

Daria only nodded and grinned.

"If I must remain in this haunted home, a bottle of vodka would help. I meant to bring one earlier."

"Now, you're talking. Good, I'll bring you one."

"Maybe some for you too."

Daria shook her head and smiled at her mother.

"There is a lot of haunting here," Anna said with a shrug.

"Yeah, for sure. See you later."

She wrapped herself up with a coat, hat, and gloves and left through the front door.

A second later, a mouse called to Anna from the wall behind her as she sat on the couch with big, unblinking eyes.

* * *

Tayo hadn't yet fallen asleep, but he did lie still, under a blanket, and at the sound of a squeak, his eyes popped open.

Usually when that arrives, there is also—

"Ah!"

He grabbed at his back and writhed from side to side, feeling skin and muscle and bone cleaved and pried apart by a sharp, heavy blade. Curled up on his side, he held his breath and waited.

As quickly as he'd been cut, the pain vanished.

Perhaps it's timing its strikes? It could be waiting for a specific number of heartbeats before striking again. If so, I should slow my heart, no matter the fear, because then—oh, I'm losing my mind!

He sat up and cast the blanket aside as he stared at the bedroom door.

Are Anna and Daria still out there? Alone with the mouse? Oh, Tayo, it's not a mouse. You must continue to think clearly. Your rationality could be the first defensive weapon you will lose. Don't yield it so easily.

He opened the door and looked out. Anna sat very still on the couch and turned only her eyes to meet his gaze.

"So, you heard it too?"

"Yes, Anna. Whatever it was, I—"

"Maybe it really is just a mouse," she said.

"It's not a mouse."

They both fell silent and waited, only their eyes studying every wall, occasionally each other's, then the walls some more.

Anna let out a deep breath and said, "Would you consider continuing your rest out here?"

"I surely would."

He took a seat at the other end of the couch and looked around until he felt sure that they were alone. He'd waited for another symbol to activate, but they remained as they were. He felt nothing there.

Then, he sighed and looked at Anna.

"Daria has left?"

"Yes. She went to see Benson about something. Oh, and I heard a phone in the kitchen earlier."

"That's mine. I can check that later."

I hope that it was Jenny, and also, I hope that it wasn't. What actions might I take, or not take, that will result in her death too?

"She said she'd bring back vodka too."

"I still believe I would join you in sampling that, Anna."

"You are sure you wish to drink alcohol now, Tayo?"

"I could easily be dead soon, and I wouldn't—"

"No, you would not enjoy it then."

∗ ∗ ∗

Daria arrived first at the apartment that she shared with Anna. She let herself in and hurried to change into a much shorter dress, which wasn't camouflage, and much shorter boots, like she and her mother both thought Lin would recommend.

She took a look in a full-length mirror and smiled at the sight of so much of her legs being exposed. A brush rested nearby on the dresser, so she gave her long black hair a few strokes, leaving it teased up and wild.

Standing in the hallway, she looked around, trying to decide which room. Her bedroom was kind of sloppy, but the living room was neat. Maybe the couch would do.

Oh, the heater! she remembered and set the thermostat all the way up.

She reached up into the cabinet, took out a bottle of vodka, and stopped at the sound of slow, steady pounding at the door.

"Yep," she said out loud, "that's how a dead man would knock."

Smiling at her own joke, she stretched her arms straight up enough to raise the hem of her dress and crossed the living room to let him in.

Through the open doorway, she saw his grim smile, and he said, "Kind of cold out here."

"Wouldn't that keep you fresh longer?"

He grinned and said, "Right. Because I'm dead."

"Still, come on in. I'm not sure we should be meeting here, but Mom's over at Tayo's with Ozzy, and I needed to pick up some—"

He'd grabbed her hair in one strong fist and pulled her backwards toward him, where he wrapped an arm around her waist and whispered in her ear.

"Didn't I say camo?"

With her head tipped back and held in place, she said, "Well, there's lace underneath."

"And under that?"

He relaxed his hold on her hair, but he kept her faced away with a cold hand on her belly.

"Hmm . . . I do need somewhere to sit."

He spanked her once, still holding her waist, and lifted her dress high enough to see for himself.

"That's nice. Is that yours or your mom's?"

She laughed and said, "Mine, of course. You get sicker all the time."

"Comes with being dead."

He spun her around, held her lace with both hands, and squeezed her in tight. Their lips met and when she tried to back away, he reached up with one hand to hold her in place until she quit struggling.

"There. Cold is good, right?"

With her eyes still closed, just before she'd leaned in close enough to kiss him again, she said, "Yeah, cold is good."

Still kissing, he bolted the door behind them.

"Show me your room."

"Happy to. It's a little messed up right now."

"I kind of am too."

"Yeah, I guess you are. Death will do that to a guy."

She took his hand and led him toward her bedroom, but he yanked her arm, stopping her, and they both looked into her mother's room.

"In here."

"Benson, that's my mom's room. Why don't we—"

He pulled her in for another kiss and with his other hand, he reached up under her dress and patted the thin lacy material.

"Oh, fine. That seems kind of kinky. Might be good."

"Yep."

He led her inside and stood her next to the bed. He held up a finger, at once telling her to stand still and not speak. He lay on his back, his head on Anna's favorite throw pillow.

"Undress for me."

She grinned while lifting the dress up and off and when she reached down for her short boots, she saw him shaking his head.

"You got a thing for boots, don't you?"

"Indulge a dead man."

She laughed and stretched her last garment down over her thighs, down to her ankles, and then kicked it aside.

"I can guess what you're going to say next, Benson."

Without a trace of a smile, he said, "Have a seat."

He quickly undressed, and she did.

"Oh, my. That's cold. You sure you're not sick?"

"I think you mean 'ill.' You like sick. You're getting to be a sick girl yourself."

She began a steady beat, her hands on the cool skin of his chest, feeling the warm air circulating through the room from the furnace on high.

She closed her eyes and said, "Yeah, I kind of am."

The furnace fan was the only sound as Daria continued, stopping once to brush her hair back, then again placing both palms on his chest.

"You know what I'm going to say next, don't you?"

She grinned, eyes still closed, and said, "Mm-hmm. To tell you when there's no turning back."

"Yep."

"Oh, I'm there already. Why so fast, I have no idea."

"Because I'm dead. You know that."

She opened her eyes and laughed once, but the smile faded and she only moaned softly.

"Whatever. I'm there. I mean, I'm almost *right* there."

"Good. You're sure?"

"Oh, hell yeah, I'm sure."

She bounced a few more times before he said, "Tell me you're Anna."

She froze, her hands still on his chest, and stared down at him, her eyes showing shock even as she grinned.

"Benson, what the hell?"

"Do it. You'll like it."

With his hands guiding her hips, she let out a low moan and began her steady up and down again, then said, "I'm Anna."

"That's just lazy. Say it right."

"I am Anna."

"Again. And say what you're doing."

He rubbed his cold hands along her flexing thighs.

"Benson, you're—"

"Do it, Anna."

She closed her eyes, never slowed, and said, "I am Anna, and I am having sex with Benson."

"Yes, you certainly are, Anna."

She shook her head but never opened her eyes and never slowed.

"Keep going. Get into the part."

After a quick grin, she said, "I am Anna, and I am loving to have sex with Benson."

"Yep."

"I am Anna, in my own bed and having sex with a dead man."

She smiled when he said, "Good ad-lib."

"This dead man named Benson is cold and giving me a big climax soon."

"Yep. That's right, Anna."

She breathed deeply and slowed her motions. Her mouth opened and her head tipped, but her eyes remained closed.

"Every time we do this, who will you be?"

She couldn't smile, and she couldn't stop.

"I will always be Anna. You are having sex with Anna, who is naked for you, and she cannot even think of stopping."

"Good, Anna. Good. More."

She panted a few times and said, "I am Anna, and I have always wanted sex with a dead man."

"Yep. One that you killed."

"Yes, that is true. I want to kill them then have glorious sex with them."

"You're such a pervert, Anna."

"I have always been so."

He reached up with both hands to hold her breasts.

"You like that, Anna?"

"I like that. I like cold, dead hands touching me."

"You like doing as you're told for me, Anna?"

"Yes. That is a truthful statement. All you say seems true when sex is happening."

She started to shake gently, but she kept a slow, steady rising and falling.

"Let yourself go, then, Anna. I sure am."

"You are sick."

"Yep. You too."

She let herself go and so did he.

* * *

"Lessa, baby, it's getting late. We're not going to make it all the way in one drive. Let's stop."

"Can we stop someplace with a pool?"

"Sure. I'd like that too. Are you hungry?"

Alessa smiled but kept looking through the windshield.

"Not as hungry as you!"

"Nope."

"Besides Tayo, Mom, who else is there?"

"I don't know for sure. I only talked to Tayo, and he didn't say anything about anyone else."

"Maybe your friends will be there?"

"Oh, you mean Lin, right? Yeah, I hope so."

"Lin Finity. Does she have a boyfriend?"

"Yeah, Jack. She has a daughter, too, named Taylor. She's always with someone named Gabriel too."

"I like that name."

"Gabriel?"

"Yes. Does she have a dog too?"

"Yeah, a really big one. His name's Nomad."

"I like big dogs. I hope he's there."

"Yeah, he might. Hey, how about this place?"

She pointed off to the right, and Alessa turned to look.

"I like it. They have a restaurant too! That's good for you, Mom."

"That seems like a joke but really, you're just telling the truth, aren't you?"

"I try to."

* * *

"Tayo, explain your requirement that we pack those mirrors."
He glanced over the arm of the couch to where both mirrors rested, the big one leaning against the wall.
"It's an odd mix of curiosity and revulsion that I feel for what has happened to my back. I didn't wish to try to view them in a mirror attached to your vehicle."
He got up and stooped down next to them, then picked up the smaller one.
"You do not wish that Daria or I perform an inventory if needed?"
"Anna, I know that my malady isn't something for which I should feel embarrassment as if it's due to poor hygiene practices. Still, it's not a source of pride either."
He turned the hand mirror to see his own face and sighed. He spun it around until it mostly faced the larger reflecting surface.
Oh, are you there? Do I see you now?
"We would never ridicule you, Tayo."
"I believe you, it's just that—"
You hide far back in these cascading reflections? How could that be?
"Yes?"
"I, um . . ."
I see nothing, not with my eyes. But you're there, aren't you? And if I can't see you, why am I sure that you are drawing nearer?
"What is it, Tayo?"
"In the mirror. Anna, it—"
You climb from one image of the mirror to the next one closer as if through a line of windows? You are coming for me?
"What is in the mirror?"
"It's, um, I think—"
You are almost upon me! No, I refuse to allow that! I cannot stop your sadistic axe, but I can surely shatter these windows of yours!

A sharp strike of the smaller into the larger cracked it, and most of the shards slipped to the floor. He then hammered the hand mirror against the floor, destroying that as well.

"Tayo! Are you possessed?"

Wouldn't that be easier for all concerned?

"No. At least, I don't think so."

"What are you doing? Why have you wrecked those if they are so important to you?"

He rejoined her on the couch, but he didn't answer right away. He stared straight forward and breathed deliberately.

"Mirrors and windows, Anna."

"I do not understand."

"They are both made of glass. Sometimes, windows act as mirrors. Other times, mirrors become windows."

He still stared forward. Anna waited, shaking her head slowly.

"Nightmares can navigate through windows but maybe only when they are infinite."

"Tayo, have you lost your mind?"

Have I?

"Perhaps."

Chapter 14 – Three Of Me Now

Daria awoke in her mother's bed, naked except for her boots and toasty under the bedspread. She looked both ways and saw Benson, fully dressed, sitting in the room's one chair.

"Tell me that didn't just happen."

He grinned and shrugged.

"What the hell. Why do I listen to you?"

"Because it feels good. Nothing wrong with that."

"Well, it's still sick for me to pretend I'm my mom."

"Yep. My kind of sick."

She peeked out over the edge of the blanket.

"Maybe your kind too?" he said.

She pulled the blanket up to cover her grin and talked through it.

"You're just going to sit there and watch me get dressed?"

"Hell, yeah."

She lowered the covers, revealing her smile, and said, "Fine."

She threw the blanket aside, rose, and dressed herself quickly while Benson watched her every movement.

"Alright, we need to get out of here. I need to grab some vodka and get back."

"Don't need me for that."

She stopped herself, walking out of the bedroom, and turned to see that he hadn't even stood up.

"Oh no, you're not staying here. Get up, Benson."

He laughed once and stood and after they'd put on coats, with a hat and gloves and scarf for him, Daria grabbed two bottles of vodka, and they stepped out into the cold Baltimore air.

*   *   *

Anna heard the rapid pounding on Tayo's door, and she said, "Oh, that must be Daria. I will get it."

She walked over, opened the door, and saw Daria grinning, with Benson shivering behind her.

"Oh, Benson, I have not seen you in some time."

"Seems like only minutes ago," he said, and Daria turned and frowned at him.

"Mom, let us in. It's too goddamn cold out here."

"Yes, it sure is. Very well. Come in. I do not think Tayo will mind."

Inside, with the door closed, Daria quickly slipped off her coat, but Benson kept on all of his winter apparel.

"Tayo."

"Benson. It has been some time."

"Yep. Thought I was dead, didn't you?"

"I did hear that. You seem well."

"He isn't," Daria said with a smirk. "I think he's sick."

He looked at Tayo and shrugged.

"Women, huh?"

Tayo didn't get up, but he said, "Please, come in. Have a seat."

Benson paused to look at Daria, but she held her jaw tight and looked away. Tayo moved to the chair, and Benson took the center of the couch, a Kelgina on each side.

"This is comfortable. Nice couch."

"Thank you, Benson. It's old, but sometimes older is better anyway."

Daria took in a deep breath and exhaled loudly.

Benson said, "Maybe it's just pretending to be older."

Anna leaned forward to look first at Benson, then at her daughter, but she sat back without commenting.

"Yes, your apartment is comfortable, Tayo," she said.

Ozzy jumped onto her lap, and he sat there with his head tilted, gazing at Benson. He stared back. Seconds dragged by.

"I remember the dog."

"Well, I am not sure that he remembers you," said Anna. "You are out of context. If we were far underground, perhaps then."

"I kind of belong underground."

He looked up from Ozzy's constant stare, ignoring Daria's grin and shaking head, and focused on Tayo, who said, "We are certainly done with The Shield. I'm surprised this many of us survived. Many did not."

"Yep. More dead than you suspect, I bet."

More quiet seconds crawled past.

"I brought some vodka, Mom. I set it next to the closet over there."

"Oh, I see it now. Thank you, Daria. With all the oddness happening, I often wish to be in my own bed, with a comforting drink."

Benson said, "Sounds like a damn good place to be."

Ozzy watched Benson. No one spoke. Daria stared across the room and held her breath, then looked at the mirrors that Tayo had destroyed.

"What the hell happened?"

Anna only looked at Tayo, who hesitated then said, "I didn't enjoy their reflections."

Daria squinted at him with her head leaning, then said, "Sure. Whatever."

Benson said, "It's cold in here."

"You think everywhere is cold," said Daria.

Tayo said, "We can make it warmer than this," and he started to get up, but Ozzy began a low growl.

Benson slowly turned from Tayo to look at the dog. The growling continued.

"He is out of his sorts, Benson," said Anna. "Ozzy, try to be a gentleman, okay?"

He made no attempt. His growling continued.

"I left the motor running anyway. I'll go."

You're very odd, Benson, but I surpass your best efforts. I have mysterious features that can stab me at will. Can you boast about that? No, of course, not.

"You left it running?" said Tayo.

"Always. Keeps it warm."

Daria sighed, Ozzy growled, and Anna and Tayo stared at Benson.

"Yep. I like warm."

He stood and since his gloved hand was so near, Ozzy bit it and shook his head from side to side before letting it go. Benson never resisted. He only looked down at the dog, who was looking up and growling.

"Ozzy, that is not polite!" said Anna. "Benson, I apologize for him. He is not behaving like himself."

"I like that. Pretending to be someone else is good too."

Daria sunk back into the cushions, crossed her arms, and took a deep breath.

"Yes, well, at least he only bit at your glove."

Benson held up his gloved hand to look and said, "Not true."

The room remained silent.

"Alright, I'm going."

He started to walk toward the door, and Ozzy barked once.

"Benson, I am truly sorry for his behavior. He must not be feeling well."

"Yep. Biting is a *dead* giveaway."

He looked at Daria and winked.

Daria slumped down and looked from face to face.

At the door, Benson turned to hold Daria's gaze and said, "Bye, Anna."

He quickly looked at Anna, and she said, "Goodbye, Benson. If you are sick, you should lie down somewhere."

"Yep, I will. Not here. Careful with that dog."

He stepped out and pulled the door shut. A long, silent moment ensued.

"He is surely more odd than ever, Daria."

"Told you, Mom."

"Well, Tayo, we will give him some time to be on his way, then Daria and I should go. Ozzy too. You will be okay?"

"Yes, Anna, and thanks for the visit. I'd like to make a phone call anyway."

"Jenny, I bet," Daria said with a grin.

"Daria, that is not any of—"

"She's right, Anna. I do wish to call Jenny."

Anna took a look out the window and said, "Well, he is gone. Daria? Let us leave Tayo in peace."

* * *

After Anna and Daria had left, Tayo sank back into his chair and let out a deep breath.

I don't wish to call attention to my eyes by thinking about them, but they do need rest. Only for a moment.

It seemed like only minutes had passed before Tayo awoke, and he opted to leave his eyes closed and listen rather than look. He heard nothing from his chair in the living room and since he was curious what time it was, and if a glass of vodka was still close, he opened his eyes.

The room was dark.

The mouse let me sleep? Am I in its debt now?

After his eyes began to adjust, he was able to see the clock on the wall. It was near 9:00.

How did I sleep so long? I intended only a few moments.

He looked at the empty glass on the small table next to him.

I'll blame it on the spirits.

He looked around at the quiet walls.

The liquid variety, that is.

With both hands on the chair's arms, he sat up only a small amount, then collapsed back into the worn cushions.

I cannot do this another day. Yes, I'm dedicated. Yes, I'm focused and resolute. But how do I survive this? Can anyone help? Does anyone even know what this is?

Still holding the chair, he dragged his back from side to side, confirming that there were no feelings there. Only when the axe drops, he reminded himself.

He got up and took a slow walk into the kitchen, paused to look at the walls, and heard nothing inside them.

It would be kind of you to allow a man to have a snack in peace before you again try to destroy him. At least, there is no squeaking that—

He turned his head to listen to a faint scratching sound. Scanning the room and listening, with his head at different angles, he let out a deep sigh when he'd focused on the small box on the counter.

Do you ever rest? Oh, that's me in that box. Part of me anyway. The voice in my head, which is a party to a conversation with myself, is also imagining a discussion with my severed finger. So, are there three of me now?

He rubbed his face, tried to ignore the box beneath the can of soup, and opened the refrigerator. He saw nothing of interest.

Yes, I could easily walk to the grocer's for supplies. Why not? They're open twenty-four hours. Oh, I know why not: because disaster trails along with me but not leaving its own set of prints in the snow. Still, could I not buy a mouse trap?

He laughed out loud then jumped when his phone rang where it was charging on the counter.

I should change the tone to a squeak. That would bring some welcome amusement to my life

"Jenny, hello. You're up at a very early hour. Is everything okay?"

"Hi, Tayo. Yes, I'm fine, but I wasn't sleeping well, so I thought I'd see if you were still up."

"Yes, I am. I napped and was considering finding something to eat. I'm glad you called."

"I almost didn't. I don't know what's on the safe list for talking."

He heard her chuckle from so many miles away, and he smiled even while studying the small box containing his finger.

"That's very unusual, I know, but I'll explain now. Jenny, there was some danger that I feared might come to you because of those images that I sent you."

"Tayo, that's strange that you should mention that. I don't think it was related to those, but Samuel has been killed."

Should I act surprised as if I didn't know? How deceitful am I willing to become?

"You said that he has been killed? Do you know how?"

"Not for sure, but people are talking. They think he was beaten to death. Tayo, why would anyone harm him?"

"It's hard to imagine a reason for that. Samuel was a good, kind man."

"So, there is no sociological experiment, then?"

"Not anymore."

"Why would those images that you can see cause danger for me? How could that be?"

"It's because I didn't imagine those images or the rest of them. They are—"

"There are more, then?"

"Yes. Jenny, they're part of the task assigned to me by Lin. They're what I'm fighting."

"Oh, Tayo, you should never be involved with Lin Finity. Who is she to assign anything to you? And what is this thing that you are fighting?"

"She only asked, Jenny, and I said I would do it. It's another good thing that I'm doing. I don't know what this thing is, but it's related to those symbols in some way."

"Lin sent you photos? Tayo, this makes no sense."

"No, it just appears as symbols. I don't understand it myself. The main theme today is that I no longer believe you're in danger. I'll have to find a way to finish—"

His phone gave him notice of another call coming in.

"Jenny, can you hold a moment? There's a call, and I should see to that. Please, don't hang up."

"Okay. I'll wait."

"Thank you."

He tapped a couple of times and said, "Hello?"

No one answered. He waited several seconds.

"Hello, who is this?"

After more silence, he looked at the phone and saw that the call had ended.

Oh, this can't be. This happened before, and I placed a butter knife in the caller's head. And then, I had to—oh, Jenny's still in danger! There's no time to review those actions!

"Jenny, I'm back. It was only a wrong number."

"Well, I'm relieved that we were able to speak about whatever we wanted. I'm sorry about Samuel, but we—"

"I have to make another unusual request. Please, just do what I ask and don't question it."

"Tayo, this is becoming not funny at all."

"I know. It will all be resolved soon, though, I assure you. Don't tell me where, but can you please, just for the next several days, go stay with someone?"

"Sure, I could go to—"

"Stop! You must not tell me. Just go, and don't use your phone, alright? Don't even turn it on until Friday, and I'll call you."

"Tayo, you're a wonderful man like no one else I've ever met. But you sure are strange too."

He grinned and let out a deep breath.

"I welcome your assessment of me, and I will say nothing in my defense. You are wonderful, too, Jenny. We'll talk Friday?"

"Sure, Tayo. Good luck with whatever you're doing."

I will soon be fighting for my life, with an axe in my back and a mouse in the wall. Yes, I will need good luck.

"Thank you, Jenny."

Chapter 15 – Murderer On My Phone

Anna unlocked the door to their apartment and set Ozzy down inside. He yipped and ran down the hallway.

"What is going on with him now?"

"I'd say he's the least of our worries, Mom. You staying up? I think I'm going to hang out and have a drink before bed."

"I will have a quick drink but then, I need to sleep."

She laid her coat over the back of a chair near the door and said, "Ozzy has never acted in such a way before. I must see what he is doing."

She started walking, her heels tapping the wood floor, and Daria said, "Yeah, I'm kind of curious too," and followed her.

They both stood in the doorway and looked in on the dog, pawing at Anna's bed, tugging at the quilt, and the pillows were all in disarray.

"Why would he be so interested in my bed?" said Anna.

"Beats me. He's probably losing his mind, too, just like the rest of us."

"Ozzy, leave my bed alone!"

He stopped and stared back at her, then he jumped down and left the room. Anna quickly smoothed out the blanket and arranged the pillows. When she'd finished, she turned and saw that Daria had left, so she joined her in the living room.

"Oh, good, you are already pouring. I will take a glass."

Daria filled one and handed it to her as she sat on one end of the couch.

"Drink up, Mom. I know I will. I really do think I'm losing my mind from all this."

"I have seen far too many things that belong nowhere in this world. It started with Lin and all—"

Daria's phone rang, she looked down to see who had texted her and got a big smile.

"Do not tell me. It is Benson again, is it not?"

"Yeah, it's him."

Anna gulped down the last of her drink and stood up.

"You have a pleasant conversation with the man you attempted to shoot. I am going to bed. I believe I will call and check on Tayo first, though."

Daria never looked up.

"Good idea. Who knows how many things have attacked him just since we left. Goodnight, Mom. Enjoy that comfy bed."

Anna stopped and stared.

"We have the same type of bed, you and I."

"Um, yeah. That's why I figured. Anyway, goodnight."

Anna left, with Ozzy padding along beside her.

*   *   *

Tayo set his phone on the kitchen table, sat, and rested his head in his hands. His missing finger throbbed. Blood from the stab wounds in his back still oozed. He suspected that the axe would strike again, with renewed wrath, and that the mouse would again pay him a dreadful visit. He couldn't even be sure that he wouldn't launch another attack on Anna's harmless dog.

And now, as if I have insufficient activities on which to focus, another assassin will be coming for me? Do not kid yourself, Tayo. That's who just called you.

The finger in the box continued its muffled scratching, but the walls were silent. No axe found his back.

I'm not proud that I want alcohol, even this time of day. I'm being destroyed, and my personal destroyer cares not a whit for any clock. But my body is severely damaged, and my will feels that it might be leaking out of those stab holes in my back. Or maybe where my finger should be. I'll just sit instead.

146

He allowed his eyes to close, and he found that concentrating only on his breathing provided a relatively safe haven. Or, at least, it made ignoring everything else easier. But the ringing phone wouldn't allow it.

"Hello, Anna. I trust you made it home safely?"

"Hello, Tayo. Anyone else might think you are overly dramatic. Not I. That is a real question these days. Has anything else bad happened since we left?"

"No."

How about a speechless call from a murderer, Anna? Have you ever heard the silence of a man, through a phone, that will soon come to kill you? No, of course, you haven't.

"I hope you do not mind, but I looked in your refrigerator earlier. Tayo, you have nothing to eat. Would you like me to bring you something tomorrow?"

A gun, Anna. A really big gun.

"I'm not usually inclined to elicit charity from anyone, but in this—"

"Tayo, it is not charity. Daria and I wish to help you if we can. Ozzy too."

Oh, you could help, Anna, if you have a way of contacting Benson. You said he dealt with the second man? Yes, and I can imagine how. I wish him to intercede with this third man, the silent murderer on my phone.

"Thank you, Anna, I would most assuredly welcome any breakfast you can bring here. I don't wish to be a complainer, but all that I'm experiencing is weakening me. Food intake must be a minimum requirement for me to continue."

"Good. I am sure to be hungry too. As will Daria. Ozzy, too, I bet. We will bring you hot breakfast sandwiches, then. Is there anything else you need?"

Tayo hesitated.

Yes, a killer to kill a killer. But why would he assist with such work again? Oh, Tayo, he wanted money, didn't he? Shield money?

"Yes, there is something else that would be of immense assistance."

Tayo, you are now someone who puts a contract on another's life?

He rubbed his chin while staring at the twitching finger box, felt his burns and stabs and amputation, and offered a deep sigh.

Yes. I'll try to consider myself blameless but yes, I wish to pay for a murder.

"Anna, do you have a way of contacting Benson?"

"I do not, but Daria does. You wish to speak with him?"

"Yes. It's a life and death matter."

"Daria did say that he was dead," Anna said with a laugh. "He is perfect. When we arrive, Daria might arrange for you to speak with him."

"Thanks, Anna."

*   *   *

"Hey, dead guy."

"That's me. What's your name again, though?"

Daria got a big grin and squirmed on the couch.

"I am Anna. I like sex."

"Not just any kind. You can tell me what kind when you see me."

"Oh, yeah? When?"

"Tomorrow night."

"I'll wear lace."

"Your own, Anna."

"Oh, Benson, you're sick!"

"Yep. Your own skirt and heels too. No bra, though. Just a tight sweater."

"You have things all planned out, don't you?"

"Eh, some of it I make up as I go."

"Yeah, and it's all sick."

"Cold too."

"Yeah, you're sick and cold."

"And dead. That's what you want, isn't it?"

Daria hesitated.
"Yeah. I never knew."
"You do now."
"Fine. Okay."
"I'll text you."
"Okay."
Daria chugged her glass, almost spilling it from smiling the whole time.

Chapter 16 – I Tire Easily

"Daria, are you ready? We will do the driving through to pick up breakfast food."

"Yeah, coming."

Anna opened the front door, letting in a blast of cold Baltimore air.

"Mom, go on and start the car. I want to change first. I'll be quick."

"And I will sit in the cold?"

"No one tells you to wear short skirts all the time, Mom. That's on you."

"I believe you made a joke, did you not?"

"Ha! Yeah, I did. Go on. I'll be right out."

Anna sighed and pulled the door shut. Daria ran to her room, put on jeans and a sweater, grabbed a small travel bag, and hurried to her mother's closet.

"Oh, this is nice," she said, fingering the thin material of a short black skirt.

She slipped it off of the hanger and stuffed it in the bag. She had room to cram in a pair of high heels and a thin sweater and turned to join Anna in the car parked in the street.

"Oh," she said out loud. "Almost forgot."

She pulled open a drawer in a dresser and saw Anna's underwear collection. She pushed a few aside and found what she wanted.

"Wow, Mom, that's really tiny—shame on you. Bet that doesn't cover much. Pink is nice, though. The things I do for that dead guy!"

* * *

Tayo peeked through the slim opening of his front door and said, "Oh, it's you."

"Did you expect others, Tayo?"

"No, Anna, I don't want to see anyone else. Please, come in."

They'd brought bags of food from the drive-through and after dumping their coats and hats near the closet, Daria had placed all of it on the coffee table.

"Oh, perhaps we should have gotten coffee too," said Anna.

"There's already a pot made in the kitchen."

"Easy enough," said Daria.

She left for the kitchen, and Anna turned to Tayo.

"That is good. We will have fresh coffee too."

"Thanks for bringing food."

"You are welcome. Has everything been treating you okay?"

Anna took a bite of her sandwich, then tore off a piece to feed to Ozzy, who was seated next to her on the couch.

Oh, you heard that question, didn't you? That wasn't an invitation to bring out the axe.

"I, um, mostly feel okay."

He winced and snapped his head to look behind him before again looking at Anna.

"Well, we can only hope, Tayo."

Daria walked in with coffee for all of them and took a seat on the other end of the couch. Anna gave Ozzy another bite. He swallowed it quickly and growled once.

"Oh, see, Daria? This is perhaps one of his favorite breakfast foods."

"You spoil him."

He growled again after turning to look at Tayo.

"And why is he growling?"

"I believe maybe he just feels energized from his meal."

He began a low, continuous snarl.

"Maybe he just wants dog food, Mom. Ever think of that?"

Perhaps the dog only has behavioral issues, and the cleaver in my back is unrelated. Yes, Tayo, of course. That's a comforting story.

"Has Ozzy ever acted that way before, Anna?"

"No, Tayo, I do not believe so. He mostly has a gentle soul."

"But he's still growling, Mom. What's wrong with him?"

"I did not want to speak and ruin our meal," said Tayo, reaching over his shoulder with one hand. "But something is occurring again."

"You feel those things back there?"

"Yes, Anna, when they decide to initiate some sort of action. I feel as if I'm being cut up by something very sharp."

Ozzy barked at Tayo, but he stayed on the couch.

"You feel a knife in your back?" said Daria. "I bet that doesn't feel good."

You can be quite amusing, Daria.

"No, it does not. But it's more like an axe."

"Ooh. Hope it's not contagious."

Tayo paused to study her a moment.

"It likely isn't."

He turned away from Daria and looked at Ozzy, who was staring at him with a low growl.

"Anna," he said before frowning and reaching for his back, "something about his eyes is changing."

"I don't see anything," said Daria. "Oh, wait. Now I do. Mom, his eyes are turning white. That can't be good."

The growling got louder.

"They are completely white. Anna, perhaps refrain from moving."

Ozzy barked once and kept growling at Tayo.

Daria said, "I'm thinking of running for—"

"Ah!" Tayo said and tried to grab at his back with both hands.

"—for the door," said Daria. "This is—"

"His teeth!" said Tayo. "A symbol is taking your dog, Anna!"

Ozzy's fangs grew too long to remain in his mouth, and he lowered his head as he stared and growled. A thick white foam developed and bubbled out of each side of his snout, where it clung to his black fur.

"A mouse would be a hell of a lot better!"

"Daria, that helps no one!"

"Yeah, but he's—"

Ozzy jumped onto the coffee table, found the edge of the slippery surface with his front paws, and launched himself at Tayo. But Tayo was quick enough to kick him with both legs, sending him flying back toward the couch.

He landed facing Daria and just as he lunged at her throat, Anna grabbed his collar from behind, holding his snapping jaws close to Daria's face.

"Mom, get that damn dog off of me!"

"I cannot hold him forever! Tayo!"

Over the sound of Ozzy growling, the wall behind the couch emitted a high-pitched squeaking.

"Not the mouse too!" said Daria.

"It is *not* a mouse!" said Tayo, and he rushed over and grabbed Ozzy's back legs, one in each hand.

Anna stood, still holding his collar with both hands, and lifted him up off of Daria, who sat staring at him with both hands covering her throat. Tayo held his legs, which were kicking as Ozzy turned his head from side to side, snarling and sending frothy white streams all around.

"We must contain him!" said Tayo. "Quickly—in the kitchen!"

With the dog kicking and squirming and his front legs swiping at the air, they carried him out of the living room. Daria rushed in after them, and Tayo tipped his head toward a bottom cabinet and said, "There! That one!"

She jerked it open, and Anna tried to shove him through the opening. From his thrashing around, his head clunked on each side repeatedly before Tayo could help push him in.

He slammed the door and sat on the floor with his back against it. The force of Ozzy's attacks shook him, and the mad howling and growling were barely muffled.

"What do we do?" said Anna.

"He's kind of in a box. We need a big can of soup."

"Daria, I am serious."

Tayo looked around and said, "She's right. That table will have to do. Can you move it over here? Put one of the legs up against his prison."

"Daria, help me."

"Nope. It's being refinished."

"Daria!"

They maneuvered the table over as Tayo had suggested, and he sat on it, adding enough weight to keep it in place.

"Never thought I'd see that, Mom."

"No, neither did I. He is insane."

Between rapid breaths, Tayo said, "No, Anna, he is not. A symbol has taken him and forced him to attack us."

"Do we need to kill him?" Daria said as she pulled open a drawer and rummaged through the utensils.

"Daria, you would stab Ozzy?"

"No, Mom. Let's dress him up and take him to a party."

Anna shook her head at her daughter, then looked at Tayo.

"The mouse has left us. You hear, Tayo?"

"Yes. It has gone silent."

"Maybe your back can start to behave like a normal back again?"

"Back to being a back," Daria said with a smirk.

"The pain is less," said Tayo. "Yes, perhaps."

They all listened to the constant snarling and snapping inside the cabinet.

"Not less enough, I'd say. Tayo, you have a hammer and nails?"

"Daria, we cannot entomb him. We will still need to feed him. And if I want to pet him, we will—"

"Mom, this is a horror show. You're not making sense."

"Oh, I am sorry, Daria. You are right. But my mind is *not* right. I *left* it somewhere. Hey, that turned out funny. I said—"

"Mom, just take a few breaths, alright?"

"Yes, Daria."

After a minute of them listening to Ozzy growling and scratching at the door and Anna taking measured breaths, Tayo said, "He's losing some strength," and hopped off of the table but kept his hands close to it.

"He is still insane, Tayo."

"It might take a while, but I believe he'll recover, Anna. My back feels mostly better. I would wager that I've lost one more symbol."

"This is a nut house," said Daria.

"Yes, well, you understand now why we should have gone to Russia."

"Yep. I'm starting to get that."

*　*　*

They'd waited long enough to be sure that the table would prevent Ozzy's escape, then they all took seats in the living room, Tayo in the chair and Anna and Daria on the couch.

Daria got right back up and left for the front door.

"Daria, are you leaving?"

She leaned over, picked up a bottle, and said, "Nope. I sure am having a drink, though."

"As will I," said Tayo, and Anna stared at him.

"For breakfast?"

"These are unusual times, Anna."

"Very well. Me too. Tayo, do you have glasses that—"

"Oh, Anna, I'd recommend that we not agitate Ozzy by going in there. I'm okay with drinking from the bottle."

"Ew, no thanks," Daria said and quickly returned with three glasses.

"Tayo, you have the makings of a great vodka drinker. Daria, perhaps reconsider. Maybe the bottle is better?"

"I'm doing all kinds of crazy new stuff these days, but I'm still using a glass. So is everyone else. Who knows, maybe that back garbage of his is contagious?"

* * *

"What if Ozzy never gets back to normal, Mom? What then?"

Anna reached for the bottle in her daughter's hand, poured more in her glass, and rested each on its own leg. Ozzy howled.

"I think he should find his way to normalness soon."

Daria scoffed and said, "We might have to kill him. Just telling you, Mom."

Tayo got up, stepped close enough to reach over the coffee table, and sat back down with the bottle.

"You seem to speak of murder more often than other times."

"Well, hell yeah, Mom. I mean, with those fangs of his, he—"

"You are always seeming to be familiar with Hell too."

"Look around, Mom. Tell me what you see."

She shook her head and grinned, watching her mother only look at her hands in her lap.

Tayo set the bottle on the table and said, "He will return to you, Anna. Just as the mouse cannot stay, Ozzy will find his way."

"Ha! Nice poem, Tayo," Daria said with a big smile. "You should drink more often."

"You must know that I could not have prepared that in advance either."

"Well, that much is obvious," said Anna.

She finished her glass, got a grin, and pointed at him.

"Unless you,"—she waited for Ozzy to take a breath—"have contrived all of this for your own amusement. Did you, Tayo? Have you been waiting years for the correct circumstances to present that poem?"

Daria and Tayo stared at her for a few seconds, then at each other.

"Here, Mom," Daria said as she poured more for her mother. "Doctor's orders."

Anna sighed and took a sip.

"Well, I know only that vodka is a help. I am glad you went home to get that, Daria."

"Good place to get it, as it turns out," she said with a grin.

"You mean, as compared to the store for liquors?"

"Um, yep. Sure."

While I'm waiting patiently for the next disaster from the toxic scribbling under my skin, must I listen to the drunken drivel of these two? A mouse mixes more meaning into its utterances than these past coworkers from The Shield.

"There is much more in Russia."

"Well, hell yeah, Mom."

I don't wish to invite the malicious mouse to return, but it has a knack for ending such conversations, doesn't it?

"Again with Hell?"

"Yep."

Tayo emptied his glass, then looked across the small room at his guests. All of them heard Ozzy reach a high level of snarling before he fell silent.

I am just insane enough at this point to send a formal invitation to—

"Ah!"

He dropped the empty glass onto the raggedy carpet and reached for his back.

"Geez, we're not even really done with the last catastrophe," Daria said with a sneer. "What now?"

"Tayo," said Anna, "is it your back?"

He stopped and squinted at her, one hand still grabbing at the blade in his back.

Who is more insane, huh? Anna has been a good friend for a long time, so she probably doesn't deserve sarcasm. Still, I'm being cut in two, so . . .

"What makes you think that, Anna?"

"Oh, good one, Tayo," said Daria. "Mom, really?"

"It is my mind, Daria. Forgive me, Tayo. It is failing me. It is also soggy with vodka."

Tayo shook his head and frowned, grasping with both hands over his shoulders.

"Where's the mouse?" said Daria. "Shouldn't there be a—"

The lamp on the table next to Tayo's chair flickered. Everyone turned to see, then it shut off completely. With the curtains drawn, the room became darker.

"This is getting creepy," said Daria.

Only now? You know that there's a living, peeled finger in a box in the kitchen, don't you? I stabbed something growing on my neck, and your dog, your pesky, annoying, biting little dog is still caged by a cabinet. Oh, and you should have seen the once-living garbage I removed from the closet. After I'd put it in the closet. After I'd killed it.

"Yes, Daria," Tayo said in short, controlled bursts. "It is beginning to resemble a creepy story that—"

A squeak in the wall near the door called to them, followed by a loud cracking sound.

"Oops—this mouse is too big for your walls, Tayo."

"Daria, try to offer encouragement."

"I'm just saying that—"

Another, louder crack was followed by the sounds of drywall chips falling to the floor.

"Uh-oh," said Daria.

What waits in the wall? Oh, it's the vodka, isn't it? Go ahead, Tayo, you madman. Complete your asinine, absurd alliteration. Very well: why worry whether woe is waiting? When it wishes, its will will willfully—

"Ah! My back!"

A louder crack came from the wall, more pieces fell to the floor, and all eyes scanned the walls as the squeaking traveled around the room once and went silent.

Tayo and Daria stared at the cracked up wall. The glass shook on Anna's bare thigh until she lifted it to her lips.

"Really, Mom? Now?"

"Oh, Daria, if we are to die, then I wish—"

The wall split open a short distance above the floor, and the end of an electrical wire poked out.

"What the hell?" said Daria.

"You are correct with geography this time," said Anna.

Tayo leaned forward to study it and too quickly for him or anyone else to react, it ripped a path along the wall, drywall and wood splinters flying like from a sprinkler as a length more than equal to Tayo's height set itself free.

Hypnotized, they could only stare as a loop formed close to the free end and with sparks flying, it snapped itself around Tayo's neck and dragged him from his chair.

"Mom, we have to help him!"

"Tayo, what can we do?"

I doubt that I have time to explain circuit breakers to you, Anna. Instead, I suggest you call a coroner. Perhaps a psychiatrist. Maybe both. In any order.

He managed to say, "Stay. Back. Save. Yourselves."

It pulled him up to his feet and slammed his back tight against the wall. With one hand, he tried to free his throat, and the other attempted to reach around behind him for the wire.

"Mom, how can we help him?"

"I do not know, Daria. We will have to clean up this mess somehow, though. Does he have a broom? I should have—"

"Mom! No, forget that. We need to—"

A loud snap sent sparks out in a bright cloud as the wire touched Tayo's chest.

"Ah!"

"Mom! It's killing him!"

"Ah!"

Fireworks sprayed across the room along with the odor of cooked flesh.

Anna reached for the vodka bottle and said, "When it is done, we will have to—"

"Forget cleaning up! Maybe forget the booze for a minute, too, huh?"

A thick stream like from a roman candle erupted from the wire, it tapped onto Tayo's forehead, and he went limp. A second later, the wire died, and he slumped to the floor.

Anna and Daria stared at him.

"Ew. I can smell him burning."

"He is not ablaze, Daria. He is only asinged. Is that a word?"

"No, it sure as hell isn't. I think it's done with him, though."

She got up and approached him cautiously, one slow step at a time. The wire remained motionless. So did Tayo.

Just as she reached for the man who appeared dead, his eyes popped wide open, and Daria jumped back with a gasp.

"I believe I am alive," he said.

"Most dead guys don't talk," she said with a smirk.

"Most?"

She shrugged.

"We're just glad you didn't get murdered. Can you get that noose off your neck?"

"Yes, Daria, I believe I can now."

He freed himself but remained seated.

"My back is better."

"But your home, Tayo," said Anna, who had never left the couch or let go of the bottle and glass. "It has become quite a mess."

Daria shook her head and glared at her.

"Does that really matter right now? How many dead guys do we want in our lives?"

Anna tipped her head and stared at her. So did Tayo.

Oh, does she know? How could she know? Maybe she worked part-time for the garbage collection service, and she saw the body, and she knew that I'd killed him, but she didn't say anything because she might want to blackmail me? Is that what's happening here?

Daria looked at the questioning faces for a few seconds, then said, "You know, like all those Shield people we knew. That's all."

She doesn't know. I'm a lucky man.

Anna let out a deep breath, and Tayo staggered back to his chair. Daria took her place on the couch. After he'd picked up his glass, brushed it off and picked some pieces of wall out of it, then held it out,

Daria stood and poured more for him. He took a long drink before looking at both of them.

Daria stared back at him, then grinned and said, "You got another one, don't you?"

My insanity is so plain to see now?

Tayo offered a pained smile, then said, "A mouse that squeaks, a rotting finger that reeks. A back that's a wreck, a noose around my neck. This thing kicks my ass, but still, refill my glass."

"Aw, keep drinking there, Tayo. How about that, Mom?"

Anna stared at the floor and said, "Tayo, do you have a broom?"

Daria looked at him, and he shook his head and looked down.

"Yeah, I think it's all a bit much for Mom."

Anna said, "Maybe it's okay to let Ozzy—"

"No," came from both Tayo and Daria.

"But he is—"

"Mom, he really needs a time out."

Anna tipped her head to study her drink.

Tayo crumpled back into his chair and said, "I'm exhausted."

"Why, just because you had an axe in your spine, got strangled, and then electrocuted?"

"Yes, I tire easily. So, you are both stuck here until it's safe to let out your dog."

"Telling you, Mom. We might have to—"

"Daria, let us not murder him, okay?"

She turned toward Tayo after seeing her daughter smirk.

"I prefer the comfort of my own bed, but I would like to lie down for a few moments," Anna said.

Tayo only pointed toward his guest room.

"She does have a nice bed."

Tayo and Anna stared at her.

Anna finished her drink and said, "I believe I will sleep like the dead."

"*With* the dead," Daria said softly with a hand over her mouth.

"What is that, Daria?"

"Nothing. Hey, do dead folks even bother with sleep?"

* * *

Tayo and Daria sipped their drinks for only a few minutes, then Tayo said, "Oh, that wasn't beneficial to me."

"Getting zapped, you mean?"

"Yes, Daria. Do you suppose I could . . ."

"Oh. Yeah, of course."

She stood up from the couch, and Tayo mostly crawled toward it, and he lay there on his back while she took his chair.

Fifteen minutes later, Anna walked into the living room, stretching her arms and yawning, and stopped to listen for sounds in the kitchen. Daria had fallen asleep, and she opened her eyes.

"I think he is okay," Anna said. "We can free him and—"

"Do you remember those fangs, Mom? I do. Let's let him cool down, alright? Just to be sure?"

"You are perhaps right, Daria," said Anna. "We must be careful. We can never be sure what might be next."

"Like another mouse?" said Daria. "Why a mouse, Tayo? What the hell is that all about?"

I have never even asked myself that question! Yes, why does my tormentor manifest as a mouse?

"Oh, Daria, I think I might know. As a child in Nigeria, I was once left unattended in a small room where we stored grain. I heard my family leave through the front door, talking and laughing, and I became alarmed that they'd forgotten me. I rushed toward the door but in my clumsy dash, I toppled a heavy bag of grain, blocking the door from swinging in.

"Behind the bag had been a family of mice, and they ran in every direction, squeaking and scurrying, blinded by their fear. One ran up my leg and then under my shirt. They have sharp little claws, and it raced all around, scratching and squeaking and—"

A loud scratch sounded from behind the wall near his sink.

162

"Hey, like that?" said Daria.

A squeak followed her question, then two more loud scratches.

"Yes, but now it resides in my walls, Daria. Oh, this isn't good. It has taken my childhood nightmare, which was real, and is making it a real nightmare for me again as an adult."

"Well, it is good that we have eaten," said Anna, standing and brushing down her skirt. "Perhaps Daria and I should go. Ozzy too. You could—"

"Ah!"

"Let me guess," said Daria with a grin. "The damn axe, right?"

"Ah! Yes, that's it."

"Daria, you are lacking in compassion. You—"

She stopped when Daria snapped her head around to face her, with her eyes completely black.

"Oh, Tayo, your mouse has taken Daria!"

"It is not a mouse! Run, Anna!"

Anna ducked into the kitchen and peeked around the wall, but Tayo remained on his back on the couch. Daria jumped up from her chair, snarled and growled, then leapt high in the air, scraping the ceiling, and landed on his lap.

"Daria! Leave Tayo be!"

Daria howled at the ceiling, then reached for him, but he'd grabbed both of her wrists.

"Anna, she's not exclusively Daria anymore!"

Daria stared with black eyes down at Tayo, snapping her jaw.

"Tayo, do you see? What is that?"

A thick, black, gooey mess ran out of the side of Daria's mouth, dripping onto Tayo's chest.

"It's hot! Wow, it's hot!"

Daria's hands were raking, reaching closer to Tayo's face with every attempt. Anna screamed in the corner.

"Anna," said Tayo, "do not scream! We must handle this! The neighbors cannot know!"

"But, Tayo! Daria!"

Her nails had just begun to reach his face, and the next swipe left three long cuts in a cheek.

"Daria, you are murdering him!"

She grunted and snapped, her hands a blur as she found more flesh to rend.

"Anna, find that wire! Quickly!"

Anna picked it up and watched the scene on the couch.

"Not just to watch, Anna! Wrap her up! Put the noose over her and around her arms! Hurry!"

Tayo's face was more wound than skin, and blood ran down everywhere. Anna looped it over her daughter and pulled it tight, drawing her arms back and her hands away from Tayo's face. He managed to shove her to the floor, and she lay there writhing, biting and snarling, her eyes big and black and slimy sludge oozing from her mouth.

"That is not my daughter!"

"No, Anna. Not at the moment."

They both stood and watched from across the room as Daria's eyes gradually closed, and her spasms dwindled. She slept there, wrapped in electrical cable, her face still covered in slop, with blood and shreds of skin all over her hands.

"My back feels better. The axe is gone."

"Well, your face is your newest suffering. You should wash that. I will watch her."

"The mouse that isn't a mouse is gone too."

"Tayo, we have earned another drink, even at this early hour."

"I can't argue with the logic of that. I'll clean up my face, then I'll help clean up Daria. Then, we will have that drink. And then, Anna, you must call Lin."

"That is not wise, is it? She frightens me, and she said she is pondering your predicament, and she—"

"Anna, the next attack might kill us all. You must tell her everything that has happened."

"Yes. Your axe, your mouse, your—"

"No, please not that. Nothing about the mouse or axe. Just the unfortunate events."

"Why not tell her?"

"It's too humiliating."

"How would that be so?"

"Lin will come to know soon that I'm a broken man. Would not a devastating monster handing out such destruction be more flattering than a squeaking mouse hiding in a wall?"

"That is a valid point. No mouse. Or axe."

*　*　*

Daria still slept on the worn area rug in Tayo's living room, and he'd cleaned up his face, revealing that the cuts weren't very deep. He sat with Anna on the couch, they clinked their glasses, and each finished their drink.

Anna blew out a deep breath, took out her phone, and tapped a few numbers. After hearing the first ring, she set it to speaker and laid it on the couch cushion between them.

Chapter 17 – Plucking Something Out

"Didn't I make myself clear? Do you wish to die without ever seeing Russia again?"

"No, I do not wish to die! I want only for Daria and I to go to Russia! Ozzy too!" She shifted the dog on her lap so that she could hug him closer. "We do not want any of this! We cannot—"

"Stop! Hang on, Anna. I want everyone to hear this."

Anna took a deep breath, let it out, and fidgeted with the hem of her short skirt.

"Okay, go ahead."

"Lin, I am sorry to call with you again. Tayo insists. And while he can still speak, he wishes—"

"You should be sorry. Next time I see you, maybe I'll kill you,—"

Anna held her breath and waited. Tayo's eyes didn't blink. Neither did Ozzy's.

"—and maybe I'll kill your daughter, and then maybe I'll kill that dog of yours too. It won't be pleasant, either, because—"

"Lin," said Gabriel in the background, "perhaps we can postpone all that killing for a while. I'm curious how Tayo is."

"Fine," Lin said. "Okay, Anna, tell us: what is going on now?"

"Ozzy is a gentle soul, and he would never attack us the way he—"

"Your dog attacked you?"

"Not just me, Lin. He attacked all of us. His eyes turned completely white, and he grew long fangs. He was phoning at his snout, and—"

"'Foaming.'"

Anna glanced at Tayo and saw that he grinned and nodded once. She scowled and focused again on the phone.

"Yes, that is more accurate—I am forgetting English as my mind leaves me. Ozzy was foaming from the snout, and he leapt at Tayo. Tayo managed to kick him, which only caused him to focus on Daria. His fangs were at her throat, and—"

"Good," said Lin. "She's a brat anyway."

Anna noticed that Daria was rubbing her eyes with one hand.

"Yes, well, I grabbed his collar and held him long enough for Tayo to wrestle him into one of his kitchen cabinets. He leaned against the door until Daria and I could arrange his table to block it. He is still in there. The growling has stopped, but we are in no hurry to look inside."

"Hang on."

Anna looked up at Tayo, who only shrugged and said, "These are unusual circumstances, Anna. Being placed on hold is not by any means a slight."

Lin spoke again.

"So, you have things under control again, and you can—"

"No, Lin, there are no situations under control. The growling from Ozzy became loud howling, and then it stopped. Lights flickered in Tayo's apartment, then part of his wall began to crack near the entrance. Pieces of wall broke loose and fell, the lamp near the door died, and the end of a wire left the wall. It ripped itself free, making an extensive mess of dust and chips on the floor, and I do not know how we will clean up all the—"

"Anna. Don't worry about cleaning up. What happened next?"

"I am sorry, Lin. I am not thinking in a straight line anymore. You are right. That is not the important idea. The wire continued to free itself until a long length was curling and whipping around, and sparks were exploding from the end of it. I heard more growling, and I still think it came from that wire. It made a lasso—is that a correct term?—around Tayo's neck and started to drag him to—"

"Anna, this is insane. A wire came to life and attacked Tayo?"

"Yes. Yes, that is true. It got him by his throat and pulled him to the wall. It did not strangle him, but it continued to shock him until he lost his consciousness."

"Is he dead? What happened to him?"

"No, he lives still. Daria and I managed to free him. We put him on the couch. I wanted to get a broom because the wall was broken and all over the floor, but Daria—"

"Listen to me: forget about cleaning up the mess. Is Tayo okay?"

"Tayo is a distance from okay. I believe he has mentioned that to you. After we separated him from the wire, the wire became just a wire again. Daria and I managed to wake Tayo, but he is not well."

"Okay, so at least things have settled down. Can you put Tayo—"

"Things did not gain any settling. I am grateful Tayo was awake because Daria was taken next. Her eyes turned black. Lin, they were entirely black. Some oily, slimy sludge oozed from her mouth, and she began to shriek."

"Good God," said Jack from some distance from Lin's phone.

"There is no God here," said Anna. "I believe He, too, is afraid."

"Hang on, Anna."

When Anna looked at Tayo, she saw that he only looked down, shaking his head slowly.

"Okay," said Lin, "so your daughter got possessed. Then what?"

"She sat on Tayo as he lay on the couch to recover from electricity, and she began clawing at his face. He held her wrists while I watched from a safe distance and screamed. I thought it wise to keep at least myself safe because someone had to survive to—"

"Anna. What happened to Tayo?"

"He was not as successful as he probably wished, and his face is ripped up like ribbons. He did manage to instruct me to retrieve the wire that had attacked him. I did and somehow, we managed to wrap Daria up with it. Tayo pushed her to the floor, and she lay there hissing and snapping at us until she fell asleep."

Anna stared at the phone, Daria stirred, and Tayo continued to look down. Several long, quiet seconds passed. Anna picked up her phone, walked into the kitchen, and returned with a normal Ozzy trotting alongside. She set the phone back down.

Anna and Tayo waited, then Gloriana said, "Is the girl still asleep?"

"Yes," said Anna.

"And the dog you call Ozzy. Is he still imprisoned?"

"No, I checked and saw that he was himself again, so I let him out."

"Tayo has survived? He will live?"

"That is a real question. He would say that he will not. I do not know. It can be a tossed coin."

"His back," said Gabriel. "Has he shown you his back?"

"No. I will ask him to reveal it."

Tayo shifted around and pulled his shirt all the way up, showing all the symbols but not the punctures where he'd stabbed himself. Anna pointed at each one and counted.

"He has shown it. More of the markings have become absent."

"There are still many more, though?" said Gabriel.

"Yes. There are now thirty-one."

"Wait," said Lin. "By my count, he had thirty-six, then the cats went crazy, so that should leave thirty-five. Now, you just told me about Ozzy, the wire, and your possessed brat daughter."

Daria sneered and mouthed something silently.

"That should leave thirty-two," said Lin.

"I counted thirty-one, Lin," said Anna. "I will ask him again to—"

"No, don't bother. Leave him be."

"Very well."

"What will you do?" said Lin. "Has Lee arrived yet?"

"No, Lee is not here. What would I like to do? Take my daughter and my dog and flee to Russia. There were no murderous symbols on anyone's back in Russia."

"Can Tayo speak?" said Lin.

"He can only barely focus his eyes. He wishes for your assistance, Lin."

"Hang on."

Tayo sighed, and Daria, who lay on the floor, completely awake and wrapped tight with the wire, waited quietly with them. The seconds crawled past.

"Anna," Lin said, "I have to go—we'll see you soon."
Anna picked up the phone and saw that Lin had ended the call.
"Well, that is good, is it not, Tayo? Lin Finity is on her way."
"Better clean up, huh, Mom?"
"Oh, you are right, Daria. I need to find a—"
"I was kidding, Mom."

*　*　*

"I should be more involved, Lessa. I know I should. But did you ever learn much about maps in school?"

Alessa sat with a big, unfolded map on her lap as Lee navigated her car on the outskirts of Baltimore.

"No, Mom. I can read all these little words, though."

"Good. It helps to have a copilot. Are we getting close?"

Alessa moved a finger along one of the squiggly lines, then looked up at signs along the highway.

"I think we're on the right road."

She looked back down, then held the map closer to her squinting eyes.

"I hope we're close."

"I think we are. And, Honey, don't be surprised by anything you might see, alright?"

"Like what?"

"Oh, I don't know. Maybe Tayo isn't feeling well. He's having some problems in his life."

"This is serious, Mom?"

"Yeah, Baby, I think it is."

"Okay, Mom. I can be serious."

Lee looked over quickly and saw her daughter gazing out through the windshield. She looked back at the road.

"For how long, Baby?"

"I don't know yet."

Lee risked a glance and saw her daughter staring calmly at the highway.

* * *

Daria rolled from side to side and sat up. She looked down at the wire holding her arms to her sides and said, "Hey, a little help?"

Tayo stared and didn't make a move. Daria looked back at him, studied his face, and said, "What the hell happened to you?"

"You don't remember?"

"Nope. Cut yourself shaving, then you both felt like tying me up?"

She grinned at her mother, who said, "Things are just becoming a place for insane people here, Daria. We will explain someday."

She reached down and helped get her free of the wire.

"My clothes are wet too? What the hell kind of party did I miss?"

"It is not important right now."

"Hey, I'm just relieved you all left my clothes on."

Anna frowned and cleared her throat.

"Or did you just put them back on?"

She raised her eyebrows and stared at her mother.

"Daria, you heard that Lin is coming to visit, so we should—"

"Run like hell?"

"Again with Hell?"

"And, once again . . . look around, Mom."

"She's making sense, Anna. You two don't have to remain here. I understand your apprehension at being around Lin."

"You mean, 'fear,' right, Tayo?" said Daria. "Isn't that what you're saying?"

"Even that would be understandable. She commands powers which—"

"Which don't scare me. Maybe Mom but not me."

"You would be only wise to fear her, Daria. But it is up to you. I wish only to rest. It has already been a difficult day."

Daria looked at Anna, who said, "I choose to stay. And you, Daria?"

"Fine, Mom. I'll stay. I'm glad I changed. This place is a mess."

Anna looked at the drywall and splinters scattered around the room, plus the broken mirrors, and said, "That is true. Tayo, if you have a—"

"Mom, just let it go. Really, we'll get it some other time."

Anna exhaled a long breath and leaned back into the couch cushions. Tayo closed his eyes and laid an arm over them. Daria took the upholstered chair and got out her phone.

"Let me guess: I'll be keeping on my heels," she typed.

"Yes. 'Your' heels, Anna."

"Whatever the dead guy wants."

She grinned and stowed the phone.

*   *   *

Anna jerked and sat straight up, dumping her dog to the floor. He stood and stared at her with his head tilted.

"Oh, I am sorry, Ozzy. I just do not like being haunted."

Tayo let his arm flop off to the side and opened his eyes.

"It let us sleep. That's a good sign."

Daria stretched and yawned and said, "No axe, huh? That's always good."

"Yes, Daria. My standards for proclaiming it to be a good day have taken a drastic slide."

"Yep."

"Do your attackers tend to let you sleep, Tayo?"

"So far, yes. Perhaps it has some honor?"

"Maybe it just wants some damn sleep too," Daria said with a smirk, which turned into another yawn.

Tayo met Anna's gaze and said, "I would be grateful for even that."

"So, for the moment, things are good. I do not know if Ozzy slept, but I bet he would like some fresh air."

172

"And a fire hydrant," Daria said with a grin.

"Well, Daria, he has limited options."

She stood, with Ozzy looking up at her, just as a squeak blew out through the trench that the wire had torn open, followed by loud scratching inside the wall behind the couch, followed by Tayo saying, "Ah!" and reaching for his back.

"Just what the hell is this shit?" Daria said with a sneer.

In between gasps, Tayo said, "I believe you have identified its origin."

He winced, stretched his legs out on the couch, and rolled to face the back.

Anna had forgotten Ozzy and watched Tayo, her mouth open as if preparing for a scream.

"What about Ozzy, Mom? Hell, it's safer out there anyway."

"Oh, yes, that is a right idea."

Another loud squeak froze everyone as they looked all around the room. Tayo again buried his face in the couch back, both hands reaching for the axe.

Anna rushed for the front door, opened it and while watching Ozzy run out, said, "The leash! How did I forget that?"

"Because you're going insane, maybe?"

"Thank you, Daria. That is helpful."

"Hey, at least you look good in your skirt and heels. I like the black stockings too."

Anna stared at her daughter for a moment, started to speak, then rushed outside, pulling the door shut after her.

* * *

Tayo writhed quietly on the couch, trying to reach his back.

"Um, Tayo, are you going to be alright?"

"My response . . . at the moment . . . would be . . . no."

"Um, anything I could—"

"Ah!"

Daria jumped up from the chair and backed herself into the corner farthest from him. She stared at him until the wall above him erupted in squeaking and scratching.

"Oh, shit. I should have gone with the damn dog."

"You have . . . a dog. And I . . . have a . . . mouse!"

"Yeah, a damn angry one."

*   *   *

"Ozzy! It is too cold out here. Be quick!"

He never turned to look as she called to him and carefully placed each heel on the ice of the steps, holding the rail tightly. By the time she'd reached the bottom, he'd taken care of his business and was sniffing around wherever he could, leisurely meandering down Tayo's street.

Anna glanced down at the frozen sidewalk, her breaths puffs of white vapor, and began taking choppy steps to catch up with him.

When she'd wrapped her hands around him, she said, "I do not blame you for escaping that madhouse. But, Ozzy, you cannot wander around this city on your own."

She turned and took short, cautious steps back toward Tayo's apartment. Still holding Ozzy, she pushed in the door, set the dog down as she walked in, and slammed the door behind her.

*   *   *

"Mom, it's about damn time."

"Hello to you, too, Daria. Tayo, what is going on with you?"

How do I explain it? It makes perfect sense, though I know it's a thought more appropriately confined to the squirming brain of a madman locked in an institution.

He got up, took turns gazing at Anna and Daria, then down at Ozzy, and shuffled into the kitchen.

Must I do everything myself?

"Mom, this isn't good. Did you see that nut? Maybe we should just—"

Tayo appeared in the doorway from the kitchen, a long steak knife in his hand, staring at all of them. Then, he held both hands over his ears as loud squeaking caused Anna and Ozzy to run over and huddle with Daria.

The mouse settled down, and Tayo walked calmly to the couch and lay down.

It'll be easy. It's similar to a Bible verse, the one about plucking something out. Well, something offends me, and I'll do much better than a simple pluck. I'm actually not an amateur at this anymore.

"Mom, what the hell?"

"We are officially there, Daria," she said as she picked up Ozzy and backed them all farther into the corner.

"Let's make a run for it."

"No, it might see us."

"It?"

"The mouse!"

"It is not a mouse!" said Tayo, and he sat up with the knife in his right hand. "And do not tell Lin."

"You should reconsider your goals, Tayo."

"Mom, this isn't going to be fun."

Right or left? It doesn't matter—first one, then the other.

Tayo yanked up his right pant leg and started long, steady strokes with the serrated blade. Blood came out in a trickle, then a stream, then a gush, soaking the couch cushions.

Larger than a finger, so it's more work. But easier to aim, unlike stabbing my back.

Daria hid her face in her mom's hair, Anna squinted but still watched, and Ozzy gazed at the scene with no change of expression.

It's only fair that I feel nothing. I can focus on my knifework.

With a loud grunt to accompany every cut, especially those for the bone, Tayo had sawn his way through, and he tossed his foot to the floor, where it rocked once then settled.

I'm making good progress!

He paused only for a second to watch the blood pumping out of the bottom of a leg without a foot.

That's not a surprise.

Then, he started on the other.

Without any knocking, the front door swung in.

"Mom, that's that Lee woman," said Daria. "Remember her?"

I'm too quick, Lee! More than halfway there!

"Yes, Daria. Do not make a sound, though."

"Because of the mouse?"

It is not a mouse!

Anna didn't answer.

Lee wore her black leather jacket, tight jeans, and black snakeskin boots. Alessa wore her new light gray coat with the hood up, a ring of fake fur around her face, which was turned toward Tayo and, like Ozzy, showing no emotion.

Lee snapped the door open and shoved her daughter out onto the porch. After slamming the door shut, she hurried toward Tayo while tucking her sunglasses into a front pocket of her jacket.

Chapter 18 – That's His Foot?

Lee looked over at the three cramped into the corner but only for a second. She quickly walked over to Tayo, and she placed one hand on his, the one doing the cutting near his remaining foot.

God, what am I doing? She's really here, not some imaginary cast member in my grisly drama?

He stopped and looked up at her, his eyes wide and lips trembling, squinting and tilting his head to one side.

Lee, you are here. And now, I feel what I have done. Oh, I really feel it . . .

She coaxed him back onto the pillows, crossed his knife arm over his eyes, and climbed up to sit on his lap.

Your hair is beautiful, Lee. I will die while knowing the touch of it. If I could just twist it around my fingers . . .

He reached for her with his other hand, and after she'd grabbed that wrist, she held it close to his side.

But I have no strength. It has all flowed out of me. Only a trickle is left . . .

"What the hell," Daria said softly.

Anna only shook her head and watched.

* * *

Alessa stood on Tayo's porch, facing the closed door, with her hood up to help with the cold of Baltimore in January. Lin Finity, Jack Madison, and Lin's daughter, Taylor, arrived at the bottom of the three stairs leading from the sidewalk.

Jack looked at Lin, who only shrugged back at him.

"You must be Lee's daughter, right?" he said.

Alessa turned only her head to look behind her.

"Yes. I'm Alessa. You're my mom's friends?"

Lin said, "Yes, we are. It's nice to meet you."

Alessa turned back toward the door.

"Nice to meet you too. You are Lin?"

"Yeah, and this is Jack."

Alessa still looked at the door.

"Um, and this is my daughter, Taylor."

Silence.

"Is everything okay in there?"

"Things are often how they're meant to be, Lin, though they might not appear to be okay."

Lin turned to look first at Jack, then at Taylor. Taylor scoffed and looked down the street, in the direction of the fast food that she'd wanted, and Jack shook his head with a grin.

"Well, why did your mom put you on the porch?"

"She came to help the man in there. She said his name is Tayo. My mother didn't want me to see the blood, I suppose."

"Uh . . . what blood?" said Jack.

"The blood from Tayo's ankle as the knife in his hand cuts him."

"Mom, let's just get out of here. Like you said, Lee can—"

"Taylor, wait," said Lin. "Alessa, he's in there cutting himself? And your mom didn't want you to see it?"

"She thinks it will upset me. She's often kind and protective."

Jack climbed the stairs, stood next to Alessa, and grabbed the doorknob. Alessa stepped to one side. Lin joined them on the porch, but Taylor stayed on the walkway, looking at the sky.

"Alessa, you can wait out here, but Jack and I need to go in. Taylor, Hon, are you coming in?"

"I, um, I . . . changed my mind. You go ahead, Mom."

"Honey, are you—"

"Really, this is good. The porch is good."

A loud peal of thunder rang out, and a light, cold rain began.

"Honey, is that from you?"

Taylor looked at Alessa and said, "Nah, what are you talking about? It's just a freaky storm that came out of nowhere. Go on. I'll just hang with Alessa."

"They'll be fine, Lin," said Jack. "What's a little thunder and rain? Come on."

He turned the knob and pushed in the door, entering the quiet room first, and Lin followed close behind, leaving Alessa and Taylor alone outside.

*　*　*

"Uh-oh," Daria said as Lin and Jack opened the front door and walked in.

"Daria, do not make trouble."

"Wonderful, Jack," Lin said. "Look over there."

"I see them."

Anna squeezed Ozzy more tightly as she watched Lin looking her up and down. She glanced down at her skirt, then back up to hold Lin's gaze. She noticed Lin scoff at her loudly enough to be heard.

Lin's eyes next scanned Daria, and both Anna and Daria held their breath and waited. Both of them studied Lin's eyes closely.

When Lin turned back toward Tayo, Anna and Daria looked too. They saw Lee sitting on him and holding both of his wrists, the bandage over Tayo's missing finger soaked with fresh blood. The blade was coated and couldn't reflect any light.

They all watched what looked like a struggle, with Tayo trying to free himself but Lee too strong to be overcome. She leaned over, and her long, straight black hair hung down on both sides of her face, keeping her mostly hidden.

"That's his foot?" said Jack.

"It sure is," said Lin. "He almost got the other one too."

Tayo's couch cushions, which had been a cream-colored fabric, had become soggy sponges, more brown than any other color.

179

Anna caught her breath sharply when she saw Lin grab Jack's arm and begin the short walk toward them. She fought to not run as Lin planted herself directly in front of her, blocking the view of the couch.

Lin's eyes glowed with their own soft, green light.

"Don't worry," said Lin. "This just happens. I'm not planning to destroy you."

"Thank you, Lin."

Lin moved only her eyes to peer at Daria and said, "You? I haven't decided yet. We'll see, won't we?"

Anna felt Daria shrug once, but she didn't hear any reply.

"Shouldn't we be helping?" said Jack.

He started to turn, and Lin grabbed his arm and kept him looking away, all of them huddled together so that none of them could see.

"No, Jack, we can't help with that. Let's just give Lee a second and some privacy."

* * *

Lee went to her home—that place that she'd found so many years earlier, before the birth of Alessa, after struggling with her own health defects that she'd brought with her into life. Even as a child, she'd come to realize that no one would be able to help her. She'd accepted that if any healing were to happen, she'd have to do it herself.

It had seemed, even to her, that the place she'd found—a lush green field of grass in a peaceful valley—was only a make-believe land created by a desperate, dying girl. Still, she traveled there often, seeking a cure or at least just a respite from her approaching demise.

For a long time, she didn't find what, if anything, could be done there that might help. Brushing down the grass in different directions didn't help and even after finding forty stones and trying a variety of arrangements, nothing had changed. She'd always returned feeling refreshed, but her health hadn't improved.

A time came when she had to face that she was near the end. Her afflictions were getting worse, and she'd traveled to her home for what might be the last time.

With no ability to think clearly remaining, from her hands and knees, she'd arranged the stones into one last pattern, knowing that she'd likely never return after failing again.

She'd placed the stones in a figure eight.

And everything changed.

As if the sky had opened up above a dark, desolate landscape, she'd felt every tiniest piece of her shift into their proper locations and when she let out a deeper sigh than she ever had before, every bit of her snapped into a perfect alignment like a limitless expanse of puzzle pieces.

She knew it immediately: her health concerns had been driven out. Her struggles in that imaginary world, which she'd begun to call home, had succeeded. The figure eight was key.

Standing once again in her home, before addressing her mission of healing Tayo, Lee paused to remember Gabriel's words after she'd spoken of her home: Gabriel had said that the shape that she makes with her forty stones is the symbol for infinity, not a figure eight.

Lee looked up at her sun, burning brightly in the clear blue sky and never moving from directly above her, and smiled at the understanding of Gabriel's wisdom. It *was* infinity. That sun above her shone down infinity with every ray of its healing light.

Infinity. Healing everything. Never aging. That's why Lin had given her the name Lee Ternity, a more accurate name than Lee Turner.

She shook her head to end her reminiscing and wondered how Tayo would appear in her home this time. When she'd healed his broken leg in Allentown, a much easier operation, he'd appeared as a wood bench that needed a thorough cleaning. They'd both enjoyed how she'd rubbed away at the dirt and when she'd returned, they'd found that Tayo had been healed.

She looked at where she'd seen him before as a bench in her home, but there was only the edge of a meadow, with lightly waving plants. A few insects darted above them, flitting in random directions.

She felt the hairs on the back of her neck stand all at once, and a harsh memory of when she'd tried to help Lin's daughter invaded her thoughts. She'd tried to face something impossible— the Hunter—and nothing she'd done had had any effect except to weaken her and make the situation worse. The cloud in the sky had continued to grow, blocking more of the sun, and her stones had scattered on their own. She remembered only laying herself across them, fighting to hold them in place, and weeping. She'd had no choice but to return to her life.

Now, that same feeling began with her neck, and it spread throughout her: the dread of facing an unbeatable foe that had nearly killed her before. And she knew without a doubt that it was behind her.

She held her jaw tight and turned just enough to take a quick glance. She froze, staring at the meadow in that direction, but she couldn't define why. Something was there . . . hiding in the weeds. Watching her. Waiting to pounce.

Leaving would be the wise decision, she knew, but then she remembered why she was there. Tayo was damaged in so many ways, not just bleeding to death from sawing at his ankles. There was no time for fear.

Help Tayo. That's all. Don't fight that thing, that Hunter. Maybe it'll stay where it is. If not, and if it were to attack, she accepted that she'd never return.

Staring in the opposite direction of the Hunter, at the tall weeds at the edge of the grass, Lee felt that she was using some unknown part of her, from somewhere deep inside, to will him to appear there.

Can I do that? she wondered. Have I arranged every encounter here without knowing it?

As the hair on her neck stiffened more, and her heart continued to pick up its pace, and she wondered when she'd feel it grab her in a deathly embrace, she saw something odd, a short distance inside the tall plants. An empty place. All around, tall weeds waved about from the light breezes, but a region, about as far across as her height, showed no plants at all.

Relieved to finally have a destination, she began a steady, cautious walk in that direction. While walking, she recalled how she'd felt in previous healing efforts: sometimes getting weaker as she walked, sometimes even lighter. Instead, she felt a steady temperature increase, and she wondered if it could be from her sun.

She stretched the collar of her t-shirt around as she neared the weeds, and she parted enough of them to look down at a pool of water that had never been there before. By its darkness, she guessed that it was quite deep. And long stalks lay across it in all directions, creating a barrier much like a sloppily constructed fence.

She knelt beside the odd pool and reached in a hand, and she felt that it was warm like bathwater. She tried pushing aside the weeds and found that they resisted any attempt to move them. They flexed, but she couldn't convince them to allow a larger opening.

Feeling a spike of fear, she stood and turned to look behind her, and whatever waited for her there, across her grassy field, seemed to have stood up as well. She snapped her head to look again at the warm water.

Tayo's in there? she asked herself.

Then, it occurred to her that she'd never tried to hold her breath in her home. So, she gave it a try, and she found that she might never need to take another breath.

Well, she realized, it's not like this is a real world anyway.

She looked back down while she was kicking off her snakeskin boots. She lost her jeans next, then her t-shirt. She reached back down to the pocket of her pants and found what she needed to tie her long black hair into a ponytail.

With a deep sigh, she knelt again and with both hands, she tried stretching out an opening wide enough to dip her head under the surface. She took a deep breath, even though it might not be needed, and felt the warmth of it as she plunged her head in, still holding the fence weeds with both hands.

Lee prepared herself for whatever her eyes might show her when she'd open them but before she could look around, she felt two warm hands, one on each side and squeezing her ribs. She fought to climb back out, but the weeds she held only bent farther when she pushed on them, and the tight grip began forcing her into the pool.

She battled the urge to scream as her panic spiked, and she felt her shoulders pressed into the weeds as her hands flopped back around by her sides, trying to grab whatever had captured her. But her attacker's strength was too much, and she felt the weeds scraping her as she was jammed deeper into the water. The plant stalks peeled first at her bra, ripping it off of her, then when she'd been pushed in so far that only her legs kicked above the surface, her underwear got stripped down along her legs as she submerged completely. The weeds closed above her, with her lost clothing clinging to the branches.

Held only by warm water on her naked body, Lee sank even as she tried to swim back to the top. She flapped her arms and kicked her legs, and she looked all around as she hoped that she'd soon reach the bottom.

Her hands touched it first, and only then did she open her eyes. At first, she thought she'd nearly landed on some sort of large plant, its many fronds extending out in every direction. It lay there motionless except for its limbs, which undulated only slightly from her disturbing the calm water.

It surprised her that the words that came to her at the bottom of that dark well, in a magical realm that she'd found when she was but a child, were, "Tayo, is that you?"

Before she could laugh at the silly thought, she again felt the iron hands at her sides, pressing her into the strange plant. She fought and kicked, but her legs were soon held still by thick bands wrapping around her ankles and pulling them down. More found her wrists and though she shifted and squirmed, trying to break free, they stretched her arms out to each side.

Two more vines found her thighs and circled around them several times while another pair, one from each side, found her waist and twisted around, rubbing warm against her skin.

She could only tip her head back, trying to keep from being smothered in that lonely pit, as the last lash took her neck. All of them, working in unison, pulled her flat and drew her down to the bottom.

Knowing that no scream would help her, she still felt an urgent need, or perhaps an urging, to take a deep breath of her watery grave. Crazed by the need to take that breath, she barely noticed two more thin, skillful vines gently begin to pry open her mouth.

She resisted but felt her consciousness, if that's what sustained her even in that mysterious corner of her home, beginning to fade. She barely noticed other fronds, warm and smooth, as they found other, more private parts of her. All of them felt soft and rubbery as they slid across her skin, pausing to squeeze before sliding again.

With a feeling of sinking into a lost ocean that didn't exist, Lee succumbed to what had turned into forceful but gentle coercion, seeming to desire her to become a permanent guest in that unknown well.

She took a deep breath, inhaling the warm fluid, and felt it flow through her. Despite the tragic death being handed to her, an unusual, unexpected pleasure took hold as she felt that she'd warmed the water held inside her. Its temperature was increasing with every moment and though she didn't understand why, there came a time when she knew it was warm enough, and she exhaled—a heated stream of that water flowed through an already warm pool. It flowed over and around the curious plant beneath her, and Lee, still held tight and caressed all over and in every way, naked at the bottom of a pool that could never be found, felt every sense bleed out of her and mingle with the water of her tomb.

* * *

She felt hot sunshine first, drying and warming the bare skin of her back and legs. The grass beneath her felt soft and cool, and an unidentifiable pleasure seemed to roll away to the horizon like weak thunder.

Lee opened her eyes, picked her head up, and looked around. She found that she lay beside her stones, which had suffered a scattering that demanded her immediate attention.

Up on her hands and knees, the last of the pool's warm water dripped off of her in many places while her back had mostly dried. Satisfied with the arrangement—a perfect infinity symbol—Lee Ternity stood and looked around her home.

A long gaze toward the pool showed a continuous, living surface, with an unbroken landscape of gently twitching and swaying plants. She dared a glance in the opposite direction and though she stared and saw nothing, she again felt the hairs on her neck telling her to flee.

She looked all around to confirm that she was completely naked and that her clothes were nowhere in sight. She gave one more look in the direction of the pool that had itself fled, and she shook her head, thinking that her boots, at least, better still exist back in her real life.

At a feeling of being watched from the other direction, she told herself that it was definitely time to leave.

So, she did. Lee returned to her life.

*　*　*

Still sitting atop Tayo, Lee opened her eyes, first looking down at the man she'd healed, then toward the corner, where Lin and Jack faced away, blocking Anna and Daria's view.

She took a deep breath, let it out, and said, "Lin, I'm glad you're here."

Lin is here too? Has she brought some sort of salvation with her?

When Lin let go of Jack and turned away, Anna and Daria saw that Lee was awake and sitting straight up on Tayo's lap. She brushed her hair back with both hands, yawned, and rested her hands on his chest.

"Look what she did," said Jack.

I feel nothing from the knife's activities. I still don't. She has corrected me again?

Anna followed his pointing finger and saw that both of Tayo's feet were again attached, and only blood stains indicated that they'd ever been cut. She gasped and held Daria tightly.

"It's what she does, Jack. Nice work, Lee. And I'm not staying."

She must have. Otherwise Lin would not be offering praise.

"You have saved me again," Tayo said.

He hadn't yet opened his eyes. His right arm fell off of the couch, but the other one, the one with the knife, still lay across his forehead until Lee removed it from his hand.

That knife and I are developing an odd, abusive relationship.

Lee stood up and before she could take a step, she closed her eyes and rocked side to side gently.

"Check the finger too. I think I patched you up pretty well."

Anna and Daria stared at Tayo's reattached feet.

"I might never comprehend the skills you possess," Tayo said as he wiggled all of his fingers. "I am in a horrible predicament, and I'm certain more damage will come to me."

"Well, that's why I'm here," said Lee. "Oh, I think I need to sit awhile."

She turned away from the couch, dropped down onto his lap, and slouched back into the cushions. Her head slowly tipped back, and her eyes closed.

"You people are frightening," said Anna. "Normal people cannot do such things. I saw a foot that was alone by itself, and now it is back on its own leg."

"Mom, don't make any trouble, alright? Let's just get out of here."

"Yes, Daria. We are no longer needed. Goodbye, Lin and the rest of you too."

Anna, no, don't go. This affair isn't over.

Anna tried to get through between Jack and Lin just when thunder exploded above the apartment building.

She and Daria turned toward Tayo's front window when they heard rain begin to hit it. She looked at Lin, who only shrugged with a grin, her eyes big and still glowing.

Anna clung more closely to Daria when they all heard a muffled roaring of wind coming from somewhere down the road. It grew louder, and Anna couldn't look away from Lin's bright eyes.

When the wind hurled trash of all kinds into the window, Lin still only held Anna's gaze. But her grin became a smile. And she nodded.

The wind died down, and the rain stopped.

If my wishes are answered so quickly and easily, I should wish away what's on my back.

"Anna, I believe God is indicating that you should remain," said Tayo.

"I do not believe God wishes—"

More thunder rattled the building.

"That would be a coincidence. Lin, please excuse us, we are—"

A continuous, deep rumble above them rolled on for ten seconds, freezing Anna in place as she looked up at the ceiling.

"Okay," Anna said, her voice breaking. "We will remain."

"Not for long, though," said Daria. "I'm not causing any trouble, Lin, and I sure as hell ain't going to go for another photo. But you people scare us. Even you, Lee. What the hell was that? Some kind of voodoo bullshit, except you didn't chant anything, and you're not waving dead chickens around, and you—"

Daria tensed up as soon as Lin's eyes flared with blazing green light. She shook lightly when Lin stepped over and stood almost nose-to-nose with her.

"Oh . . . right," said Daria. "Never mind."

I'm too weak to laugh, but I can acknowledge the humor of that even without seeing it.

Anna allowed herself to be pushed farther from the corner so that Daria could wedge herself behind her.

"Please, Lin, she means no genuine harm."

Lin leaned her head to one side, her eyes continued to glow, and she said, "I sometimes do."

Anna looked at the floor, but Ozzy continued to stare at Lin and never blinked.

Without looking away, Lin said, "Tayo, can we see your back?"

They heard his weak voice as he still lay on the couch, Lee asleep on top of him.

"Yes, of course, Lin. I no longer feel anything there, but evidence suggests that there is one less symbol."

Jack remained in the corner beside Anna, but Lin approached the couch. Tayo twisted toward the couch back, shifting Lee around but not waking her. Jack, Anna, Daria, and Ozzy stared.

"I'll need help. I'm too weak now."

"Try to get some rest," Lin said, and she rolled up his t-shirt.

Even from the corner, Anna and Daria could see the complex mass of welts and shapes, all bunched together and overall, forming a rectangle. Near his left shoulder, much of his skin had healed.

Lin said, "Do you know why you were cutting off your own feet?"

"I suspect it wants me weak and immobile but still alive. Its attempts still seem random and rather unfocused, though. I dread the likelihood of it applying more intelligence and strategy to its efforts. I will not survive, Lin."

"You'll survive. Lee will keep you going until we can figure this out. Do you mind if I take a photo?"

Anna and Daria both flinched when Lin turned to look at them. Daria raised her hands and shook her head a few times. Lin offered her own smirk and turned back to Tayo.

"No, not at all," said Tayo. "Do you know what these markings represent? Do they have meaning?"

"I know some. They were common long ago, but they were used with a particular type of power to cause great damage. The entity that you are fighting is using those symbols. Let's hope we can defeat it before it learns how to control them more."

Lin took out her phone, snapped a few photos of Tayo's back, then put it away. She pulled down Tayo's shirt, but he didn't help and remained facing the back of the couch.

"Tayo," Lin said, turning her head quickly to look at the broken mirrors on the floor, "what was the deal with the mirrors? Anna said you wanted to pack those and take them?"

"I might never voluntarily view any reflection again."

"You broke them?"

"Yes."

"Why?"

"I did not relish the sight they offered."

"I don't get it."

He rolled toward Lin but only enough that he could turn his head to look at her.

"One mirror gives one reflection. A second mirror provides a different view. But Lin, I found that if both mirrors are aligned in a specific way, the images multiply to infinity."

"Yeah, I've seen that before, too, but what—"

"It is weak in the near reflections, but it gains strength if one were to focus further into the depth of that infinity."

"What's weak? What did you see?"

"I do not know."

In the quiet room, they all heard Tayo let out a deep breath.

"Perhaps it was a feeling that I saw with my eyes. Is that possible, Lin? I only knew that what the mirrors revealed was not beneficial to my mental state."

Lin glanced at the mirrors, touched Tayo's arm, and stood up.

"We have enough to figure out right now. I'd say you shouldn't play with mirrors for a while, okay?"

"I won't."

Sadly, I can't give such a guarantee about knives.

He turned his face back into the couch and didn't move. Jack only shrugged when Lin looked at him, and Daria still hid behind her mother in the corner, both watching Lin.

"I'd help more, Tayo, but I'm not quite myself. Not yet. Lee will keep you going until we know what to do, okay?"

I will surely keep going, Lin. Dedication. Perseverance. For the good of all mankind.

"Yes, Lin. I will do my best, and I take comfort in knowing that I am fighting in service of humanity."

Daria shook her head and said softly, "Oh, gimme a break."

Daria, that is not wise.

Anna caught her breath when she saw Lin spin around to face Daria, her eyes erupting wrathful green fire.

"Fine."

Daria shook her head and said, "No! No, no, no—"

As quickly as Lin's eyes had blazed, they settled but remained unnaturally bright.

The hair on Daria's left side, from the level of her chin downward, fell to the floor.

Daria stretched her eyes wide open when she felt her severed hair tickle across her hand on the way down. Anna and Daria both looked at it on the floor, then back up at Lin's green eyes, bright and focused on Daria like a bird of prey.

"Think of how close that cut came to your throat."

What cut? Lin almost cut Daria's throat? Oh, like she was a cat in a field?

Daria reached up with her right hand to hold her neck. She nodded and looked back at the floor. Anna looked again at her daughter's cut hair, then back at Lin.

"Thank you once more, Lin. Thank you for not killing anyone."

I can assure all of you that I will be the next to be killed.

"Hey, I'm just here for the photos. Jack, you ready to go?"

* * *

Tayo and Lee both snored lightly on the couch. Anna let out the breath she'd been holding, but she didn't let go of Daria, and she still

191

held Ozzy. Lin and Jack took the few steps needed to get them to the front door, where Lin turned to glance at the couch.

Before opening the door, Jack said, "Hey, I have an idea, but I'm not sure you'll think it's a good one."

"What's that, Jack?"

"Those photos will help, right? They'll help you and Gabriel and maybe Gloriana, too, figure out what's going on?"

"Well, we hope so. That's just one small part of fighting this thing, though. But yeah, the photos might help. What's your idea?"

"Why not have Daria take photos every time something happens, and she can just send them to you?"

"Oh, you know, Jack? That's a pretty good idea. Hey, you. Daria."

Daria still hid behind her mother and watched Lin from the corner. "Yeah, Lin?"

"I need you to keep taking photos of Tayo's back. Every time his back changes, you can—"

"Lin," said Anna, "I do not know much of these things, but I do know that if his back decides to be different, then bad things happen. We truly do wish to be far from all of these happenings."

"Well, now you can't. I need you to stay with Tayo. All I need is photos of his back."

"So," said Daria, "you won't need—"

"No, I won't need videos of him sawing his feet off."

"Ew. No, I mean that you won't need me to write up reports and stuff, right?"

"No. Just the photos. It's your chance to help Tayo serve humanity."

Daria didn't smile and didn't make a sound, and Anna slowly blew out a breath after seeing that her daughter wasn't smirking.

"Good, you're learning. It's the truth. And it's only the photos that I want. Don't be bugging me about how you're having a bad hair day, okay?"

Daria still stared. So did Anna.

"Okay, that was kind of a joke. Look, we have to go. Tell Tayo and Lee we'll figure this out."

Anna and Daria and Ozzy all still gazed at Lin and rarely blinked. Lin smiled, let out a big sigh, and shook her head.

"You know, I could just as easily have trimmed a couple of inches off of that skirt for you, Anna."

Anna looked down then back at Lin and said, "As horribly frightening as that would be, I will try to see it as fashion advice. Thank you, Lin."

She managed a small smile back at Lin.

"Still wouldn't be as short as mine."

Anna lost her smile.

"No. Never, Lin."

Lin laughed and said, "Okay, Jack, now we can go."

They left and closed the door behind them.

Anna sighed and let go of Daria, and she put Ozzy down on Tayo's chair.

"I truly do not understand the world, Daria. Look at Tayo, asleep on a bloody couch. He has his feet again."

"Yeah, and his finger too. Mom, I thought for sure Lin was going to kill me this time."

"Instead, she only trimmed your hair. That is frightening, too, in its own way."

"You should have let her shorten that skirt."

"Since when do you care about any type of skirt, Daria?"

"First time for everything."

Chapter 19 – You're Already Dead

Jack had just pulled Tayo's apartment door shut, and he crowded up against Lin on the porch with Taylor and Alessa. A weak rumble of thunder rolled away beyond the buildings, and Lin shook her head at Taylor.

"Honey, how are we getting storms like that? You weren't, I mean, you didn't—"

"What are you talking about? Storms just happen, Mom. You know that."

She shook her head and looked into Alessa's big brown eyes. The girl only stared back at her calmly.

"Alessa, I don't know what Taylor told you, but you really shouldn't think that she caused that weird thunder in January."

She paused, studying Lin, then she said, "I've learned to believe all sorts of things. I live with my mother."

"I know your mom too. She's a very talented and strong woman, and she—"

"Uses the magic."

Lin's face went blank. Alessa blinked once and continued a steady gaze.

"See, Mom? It's alright. She knows all about this stuff."

"Just how much do you know?" said Lin.

She studied each of Lin's eyes for a moment.

"I know that there is good, and there is evil. Healing is good. Storms are not evil, but they can still cause harm."

"Well, lots of things can cause harm. Your mom is here to help Tayo, who's trying to fight something that causes more harm than anyone can know."

"I know."

Again, Lin froze and stared at the child.

"What do you know?"

"How much harm it can cause."

"How? What do you mean?"

Alessa looked into Lin's eyes for a few seconds, then turned slightly and faced the closed door.

"I just mean that I know Tayo is a good man. I'm glad my mother is helping to heal his body."

Lin squinted, watched the girl, then said, "Yes, well, she does have that ability. So, you understand what she does?"

The young face turned, with cheeks red from the cold air, and Alessa held Lin's gaze.

"No. I can't. Can you?"

Lin started to speak but stopped and only stared for a few seconds.

"Well, maybe I don't actually understand it, but I do know that she—"

"Uses the magic. Is she done in there? I'm getting cold standing out here on the porch."

She held still, cheeks rosy and not offering a smile. She looked up at Lin and waited for an answer. Lin nodded and continued.

"Yeah, she's done. She fixed him right up. It was nice meeting you, Alessa. There's no reason you can't go join her now."

"Goodbye, Taylor. Goodbye, Lin."

She reached for the doorknob, and Taylor said, "Wait a second. I'm going with you."

* * *

Daria's phone buzzed and after she'd taken it out and saw the sender's name, she said, "Speak of the devil."

"You have your own devil that gives you calls, Daria?"

"It's just a joke, Mom. How about you?"

Anna looked down as she smoothed her skirt, then she looked back up.

"I believe Wolfe had a devil portion to him. He even had higher temperatures than a normal man should."

"And just how do you know that? Oh, I think I was right: you two did—"

"It was noticeable from some distance, Daria. Did you not notice when he strangled you in that Shield meeting?"

"Yeah, his hands were hot. So, you think he had some creepy devil bullshit going on?"

"I do not believe I used those words. I only said—"

"I know. I'm just trying to call them like I see them. That guy gave me the creeps. So, maybe that's why that Gabriel character did that weird stuff outside that cabin? That's what it took to kill him?"

"I do not know. That all still seems like a bad dream."

Daria tipped her head toward the couch and said, "Yeah, well, the bad dream isn't over, is it? What the hell just happened here?"

"These people are not normal at all, Daria. I miss normal people like there are many of in Russia. Do you? Even your new companion, Benson, seems very odd. Much more than before."

Daria chuckled and said, "Yeah, but at least he isn't a devil. He's not hot at all. In fact, he's cold. I mean, he's actually cold."

"Well, could that be because you killed him?"

Anna looked at her daughter with a grin, but Daria kept studying Tayo and Lee, still asleep on the blood-soaked couch. She watched as Daria nodded but didn't reply.

"You do think that you killed him? Daria, how could that be?"

"Oh, no, I was just lost in thought, that's all. There's just something wrong with his temperature. I'm sure that's it."

She looked again at what he'd texted: "Anna, dress up for me. Then, undress for me."

*   *   *

"Taylor, what are you talking about?"

"I told you I was bored, Mom. I'm just going to hang here for a while and see what happens."

"For how long, Honey?"

"I don't know. I'll just fly home when I'm ready."

"I know you're joking. You are joking, aren't you?"

Taylor stared and shook her head.

"I miss it, Mom. I don't even care about learning anything to do with those nonsense numbers. Crows don't need that. I already have all kinds of tricks."

"Oh, that's for sure. Okay, Hon, I guess you know what's best. I'm actually kind of glad you'll be around to help Tayo and Lee."

"I'll try not to kill those Kelgina women and their dog."

"That would be best, Honey. They might be some kind of help anyway. Hey, remember how much Lee always eats? They could be the ones that run out for groceries."

"Right. At least they're good for something."

Lin gave her daughter a hug and kissed her cheek.

"Bye, Honey."

"Bye, Mom. Come on, Alessa. Let's go see what's going on."

*   *   *

Daria grinned, shook her head, and said, under her breath, "Pervert."

"What did he say to you?"

"Oh, I think I'll just keep that a secret, alright?"

She typed, "Yes, I shall. My own skirt and heels from my own closet."

She grinned and hit "send" just as the door opened, and they both turned to watch Taylor and Alessa step back inside, close it, and look around the room.

* * *

"Mom," Daria whispered, "what's that girl doing here?"

"Daria, let us just wait and see," her mother whispered back.

Taylor looked first at them in the corner, with Ozzy sitting on the chair and returning her gaze. She saw Anna glance toward the couch, so she followed her look and when she saw the couch, she froze with her mouth open.

Tayo lay there like a dead man, his left arm still covering most of his face. His right arm hung limply toward the floor, seeming to point at the discarded bandages that had covered his missing finger.

Lee slouched against the back cushions, seated on Tayo's lap. She twitched lightly and snored, each breath stretching her tight t-shirt beneath her black leather jacket. In her right hand, a slimy knife rested where it had dragged across her thigh, adding wet streaks.

Taylor covered her mouth with one hand at the sight of Tayo's bare ankles and feet, still wet from his amputation efforts. The seat cushions were shiny and brown, and at the very edge of the fabric, extending out over the floor, a single drop of blood hung, twinkling in the light.

Then, it dripped into the puddle beneath it, adding a soft "plink" to the quiet room.

Taylor gasped and grabbed the doorknob, jerked the door open, and disappeared back onto the porch. She pulled the door shut behind her with a decisive boom.

* * *

Taylor still held the knob, and her breaths were shallow and quick. Her wild eyes looked only at Lin's.

"Honey, did you change your mind?"

"I can't stay here. Just looking at Tayo reminded me of what that thing tried to do to me before. I hate it."

"Well, I'm glad you'll be coming home with us. We can all—"

"Mom, I can't go home either."

"What do you—"

"I don't belong in there. I don't belong at home. I belong—"

"No, Hon. You're wrong. You do belong home. It'll just take more time for you to see that."

"I don't want to see that. I know what I want."

* * *

"You are Anna, and you like sex with a dead man."

Daria laughed once and typed, "Sex with the dead is so good for Anna."

She laughed again, sent it, and put her phone away.

"And who are you?" said Anna, looking in Alessa's direction.

Alessa turned her head slowly and said, "I'm Alessa. That's my mom."

She pointed at Lee.

"It is good that you waited in the outside. These are things that make me wish for the outside as well."

"My mom was successful with him."

"Yes, and I am glad it is over."

Alessa turned back to Anna and said, "No."

"You are not glad?"

Alessa stared a moment, then said, "It isn't over."

She walked toward the couch and sat on the coffee table, facing her mother.

Daria's phone buzzed, and she read, "Anna should try killing during sex."

Daria gasped and held the screen to her chest.

"What, Daria? Is he sending inappropriate photos?"

"Mom! No, he'd never do that. He's just funny, that's all."

She typed in, "That's crazy. Besides, you're already dead."

With a smug grin, she pocketed her phone again. She and Anna both looked up when they heard thunder.

* * *

"Hon, is that you?" said Lin. "Are you doing that?"
"I know where I belong, Mom."
"You don't even know how to do that, do you?"
"It's all intent," said Taylor. "Isn't that what you always say?"
The rain picked up, carried by an increasing wind, and louder thunder echoed off of the old brick buildings lining Tayo's street.

* * *

"We should leave whether Lin allows us or not, right?"
Daria didn't answer. She looked at the new message that had just arrived: "Makes it easy to practice."
"Daria, did you hear? Should we not just leave?"
Daria held her phone at her side and looked at her mother.
"Hey, maybe we're going about this all wrong. I should just take a shot at Lin and put an end to it."
Anna stared while Daria grinned back at her with a shrug.
"You cannot go around killing people!"
Alessa turned quickly, still seated on the table, and looked from Anna to Daria, her face a photograph with moving eyes.
"Oh, um, we're not really going to kill anyone. It's a joke. We do some weird joking around, that's all."
Alessa's expression never changed but after a few seconds, she turned back around to face Lee.
Anna and Daria looked at each other, with Anna shaking her head and Daria smirking, and she said softly, "Creepy as hell."

* * *

"Can you just give it more time, Honey?" said Lin. "Let's go home and stay under those blankets awhile, okay?"

Taylor looked up at the sky, her eyes glowing.

"Honey, please don't. Just give it more time, okay?"

"Mom, I wasn't healthy almost my entire life. Lee healed me and almost right after that, I became a Glyphin. Remember that? Remember how I couldn't control it, and you had to take me away?"

"Yeah, Hon, of course, I remember that."

The wind began to whip the rain into Taylor's face, but her bright eyes remained fixed on the sky.

"I felt afraid again."

"When?"

"Now. In there. I don't like feeling afraid."

"No one does, Hon. You don't have to stay here and help."

"I didn't feel fear when we were with the family. I just lived every day. Mom, I had no doubts about anything. No fear either."

"I know, Honey. I felt that too. Still, can you stay, please?"

She looked again at the sky.

"I miss it too much."

*　*　*

"Oh, Daria, do you see? How does it rain like that?"

They held the curtains open and watched the beginning of a downpour in cold January.

Daria didn't respond, so Anna said, "You had to shoot Benson because he was shooting you. You could not shoot at someone like Lin for no reason."

Daria didn't respond.

"Daria?"

"Yeah, I suppose. Maybe I just need the right kind of practice."

They both flinched when a giant black bird flew past the window.

"What the hell was that?" said Daria.

"It was only a bird. There is no reason to—"

More black birds flew past in each direction, some near the window and others farther out.

"It's just one damn weird thing after another, isn't it?"

"Oh, Daria, must swearing be thrown at birds as well?"

"Mom, it's just too freaky that—"

They froze and looked up as every last bird, in unison, flew straight up and out of sight.

"Look," said Anna as she pointed toward the porch. "Lin and Jack are finally leaving here. But where is the daughter?"

Daria looked at her mother with a smirk, one finger pointing straight up.

"No, that cannot be. Can it?"

Daria only shrugged and shook her head.

Chapter 20 – Shh . . . And Don't Stop

I don't have the ability to even describe what just happened. Comprehending it? I lack the necessary intellect.

Tayo rubbed across his eyes with his left wrist, and the lack of throbbing at the site of his amputation made him take a deep breath and wiggle his fingers around.

I feel no pain in my ankles, but I didn't even as I cut them. Perhaps I'm bleeding out while I lay here wiggling my fingers? That would be a surprising level of foolishness.

He moved his arm aside and saw what caused the pressure to his thighs and abdomen. Lee still lay slumped back, snoring and holding the knife.

Tayo looked to the right and saw Alessa watching him in silence. He held her gaze before looking past her. Anna and Daria were both turned to the window, holding the curtains aside and talking softly.

A glance at his chair caused Ozzy's tail to wag, and Tayo wished he could smile at the dog as it tipped its head and stared at him.

I'll laugh again someday. I make that promise to myself. Unless I'm dead. Oh, but maybe I can impose that last action—forcing my almost-dead face to smile—before my eyes close for the final time.

He turned away from the Kelginas and their dog and shook Lee's leg lightly. She drew in a sharp breath and opened her eyes. She turned to look at him with her eyes again drooping shut.

"Tayo. You feel okay?"

"I believe all parts of my body are restored. And though I'm profoundly grateful to you, still, I can't say that anything is okay."

"I understand. I—oh, I think I need a minute. I didn't have time in my home."

Tayo squinted at her, and she said, "I'll try to explain some time."

She looked straight out and saw Alessa watching her calmly.

"Lessa, you didn't . . . I mean, you weren't—"

"I didn't watch, Mom. You need to do your thing, don't you?"

"Yeah, Baby. Just give me a second."

Lee sat up straight and brushed her hair back on both sides. She closed her eyes and took a deep breath, giving Tayo a chance to glance at Alessa, who only shrugged at him.

As Lee let out her deep breath, she stretched both arms straight out in front, dropped them to her lap, and opened her eyes.

"All better, Mom?"

Lee fell back again, one hand on her forehead, and said, "Oh, not quite. Fixing this stuff is . . . it's . . ."

Her eyes closed, and Alessa took the knife from her hand and laid it beside her on the table. She turned to Tayo.

He said, "My damage was severe. Perhaps a second round of that will be necessary."

"I saw it before I had to wait on the porch."

"I did not want to do that to myself."

She nodded but didn't blink.

"I know."

*　*　*

"Mom," Daria whispered, "how could she know? Who does she think she is?"

"We are surrounded by unusual characters, Daria. I wish that we—"

Daria's phone buzzed, and she grinned at her mother before taking it out to see that Benson had texted, "You can use my knife."

She shook her head and grinned, and Anna said, "I am waiting to hear you state again that he is a pervert."

"Funny, Mom. I guess I don't even have to say it anymore."

They both looked toward the doorway as Tayo's phone rang on the table in the kitchen.

"Hey, stay off those feet for a while," Daria said and walked out of the room.

"Your humor is most welcome, Daria," Tayo said, without a trace of a smile.

As she approached Tayo with it, his eyes were wide and he shook his head slowly.

Is that my next assassin? How many of you are there? No, Tayo, that's not the most accurate question. That would be, "How many of you must I kill?"

"Geez, relax. Just Jenny. She's probably not that scary."

I have an incapacitated healer asleep on my lap. My restored limbs rest on wet cushions. An odd child is studying me and seems to understand my situation more than I. And two Kelginas and their dog are standing there, watching me, because Lin has threatened to destroy them if they leave. Yes, Jenny, everything is fine. How are you?

Tayo sighed deeply and accepted the phone. He looked at it as it continued to ring, then, when it had stopped, he slipped it into his pocket.

"I wouldn't feel like talking either," Daria said with a smirk, and she walked back to the corner to stand with Anna.

Alessa spun around enough to face Anna and Daria and said, "I think my mom needs food."

Then, she turned back to Tayo and said, "I don't believe you have donuts and cookies, do you?"

Tayo laughed, and it sounded more like wheezing, then he said, "I surely do not."

"Fudge?"

"Certainly not."

"I'll go," said Daria. "Really, I need to get out of this nightmare apartment of yours."

"Daria," Anna said with a frown, "that is not polite."

"He just sawed his feet off, Mom. I think that qualifies. Anyway, sorry, Tayo. But I really do need some air."

"Tayo, we can pick up some sweet food for Lee. We won't be gone—"

"What do you mean 'we?'" said Daria. "I was thinking of stopping to see Benson for a minute."

"You still can. We will purchase food, and I will wait in the car with Ozzy while you run in."

Daria frowned at her mother while shaking her head, and Anna only grinned back at her.

"Oh, you want to get out of here, too, don't you?"

"We can discuss such topics while in a car in the outside world, Daria."

"Buy a lot," Alessa said without turning around. "I know she doesn't look like it, but she eats garbage food all the time."

"No, she does not have that appearance," said Anna. "Yes, we will return with a large assortment of things."

* * *

After Anna and Daria had dressed for the cold, picked up Ozzy, and closed the door behind them, Alessa took the seat that Ozzy had just vacated.

She didn't move, and neither did Lee, when Tayo's phone rang in his pocket. He took it out, checked it, and looked at the ceiling before answering the call.

"Hello?"

Seconds passed with his black eyes looking all around the room.

"Hello?"

He let out a deep breath, tapped it, and put it back in his pocket.

"That wasn't Jenny."

"No, Alessa. It was not."

* * *

"So, Lee does that voodoo bullshit to keep herself in good shape too? That's what's going on?"

"I would recommend you lose the habit of calling it 'voodoo bullshit,' Daria. If Lin were to hear—"

"Alright, fine. I'm just saying. She can eat all this crap, and it doesn't mess her up?"

"I believe that is true. Yes. We know so many unusual types of people."

"Yep. Speaking of unusual, pull over right here. Good."

She reached over the seat for the bag that she'd packed and lifted it over and onto her lap.

"What is this? Are you traveling away somewhere with the odd Benson?"

"No, nothing like that. It's just, um, some things he wanted me to pick up for him. Not a big deal."

She grabbed the door handle and said, "Just hang out with Ozzy. I'll be back quick."

When she'd cracked open the door, she saw her mother only staring at her with her eyebrows raised.

"Oh, and don't eat all those donuts. You don't know any of that voo—I mean, that magic stuff. See you in a sec."

* * *

She gave the knob a twist and found it unlocked, so she swung it in, stepped inside, and closed it behind her. She reached for the lock, but a sweet spike of panic mixed in with the pending excitement, and she wondered if she might have to run for her life.

"Oh, God," she said when the heat hit her.

She quickly peeled off her coat and tossed it onto the nearest chair. Benson appeared in the shadows of the passage to the hallway, where he leaned and shook his head at the sight. He wore jeans but nothing else.

"I'm glad you're here. What's that you're wearing, though?"

"Oh, um, I packed a bag. Somewhere I can change?"

She detected a slight grin in the dim room, and he said, "You're already there."

"You like that, don't you? Watching?"

"Yep. Dead watching the living. Hell of a pastime."

"Fine."

She pulled her sweatshirt up and off and tossed it aside. She unlaced her boots, kicked them toward the wall, and dropped her socks onto them, then stopped to grin at him.

"Bra or jeans, dead man? What's next?"

"Bra, of course."

"Of course," she said, unhooked it, and let it fall behind her.

She held her breasts with both hands and said, "I do kind of like showing these off."

"Yep. You should."

She shook her head and peeled off her tight jeans, leaving only her very small underwear. She hooked her thumbs in the elastic and waited.

"Keep going."

"I kind of figured you'd say that."

She soon stood naked in the sweltering heat of his apartment, her heart pounding, as the man mostly in shadows studied her up and down.

"You really want me wearing her stuff, huh?"

"Yep. The skirt and heels."

"Happy to, dead guy."

She wiggled into her mother's short, tight skirt and stepped into Anna's high heels. She crossed her arms, covering her breasts, and walked up to stand right in front of him.

"We don't have much time. She's waiting outside. We had to pick up donuts and stuff."

"Oh, that's interesting. Alright, let's get going."

He held her hips and looked into her eyes.

"Tell me your name."

She smiled and said, "I am Anna. I am Anna Andreyevna Kelgina. I am a sex-crazed Russian woman."

"Yep. Always have been. Tell me what you like best."

He grabbed her behind with both hands and pulled her close, squeezing her breasts into his bare chest, and she put her arms up on his shoulders.

Daria grinned and shook her head before saying, "My best sex ever is with a dead man."

"Cold?"

"Oh yes, I like them cold. Cold like Russia."

She gasped when he lifted her and began walking to the bedroom, and he didn't close the door, but he set her down to stand on her mother's pointy heels near the bed.

After slipping off his jeans and lying on the bed, he said, "Take off the skirt for me, Anna."

She grinned and shimmied around until it dropped to the floor. She stepped out of it, looked down at him, and said, "Pretty impressive for . . ."

"A dead guy?"

"Yes. You are a very dead person. May I select a seat?"

"Be my guest."

She straddled him in the hot room, and while he caressed her thighs, she lowered herself down, paused to grin at him, then dropped all the way.

"Ah, there . . . I have found a useful seat."

"Am I cold, Anna?"

"You have a very cold thing, Benson," she said with a sigh, then began steady motions while he continued to rub her thighs up and down.

"You like that being cold?"

"Mm-hmm . . ." she said with her eyes closed, biting her lower lip.

He let her keep up a good, steady pace and when she turned her head up to look at the ceiling, he said, "You're there?"

"Almost. Not quite."

"Here."

She looked down at the knife that lay flat on his upturned palm. It was the same one that he'd used in the car.

Daria tried to rise up and off, but he held her arm with his other hand.

"Just hold it, Anna. Indulge a dead man."

She sighed and said, "Very well. I can easily hold that tool for murder."

She took it by its handle and supported herself with her left hand on his chest. She picked up the pace, tiny beads of sweat appearing all over her smooth skin from the intense heat of the room.

"Oh, I'm getting close now," she said softly.

"Too close to turn back?"

"Mm-hmm."

He guided her right hand so that the point of the knife was just touching his chest at his heart.

She looked down and shook her head, but she didn't resist.

"Just look at that point."

She stared at the sharp metal that had just killed a man and felt the handle hot in her hand.

"You don't have to stab."

She bounced, licked at her lower lip, and stared at the knife in her hand.

"Not this time."

She laughed once without a smile, and it evolved into a low moan.

"Just imagine: to stab right when you're sliding into ecstasy."

She kept staring, and she didn't grin or make a sound.

"Whoa, slow yourself down."

She groaned but did as she was instructed, delaying her satisfaction, still staring at his chest so close to being pierced. She shook her head slowly, but she also tipped it to get a better view.

When he reached under his pillow, she looked away from the blade to see that he'd taken out his phone.

He paused and said, "Nope, don't stop, Anna. You are Anna, aren't you?"

"Mm-hmm . . . I am Anna, having sweet sex with a cold dead man."

"That's right."

He hit a number on speed dial, set it to speaker, and laid it on his chest, close to where he could soon be stabbed.

"Shh . . ." he said with a grin. "And don't stop."

* * *

"Ozzy, does your sister really think that I would eat all of those donuts?"

The dog only stared at her from the passenger seat.

"Well, I would like to eat several of them, I will admit. I think we all deserve to—"

Her phone chimed, and she took it out, tapped it to answer, and said, "Hello, Benson. How are you?"

Chapter 21 – When My Head Explodes

"No one spoke?" said Alessa.

I must converse with this odd child and hope she isn't discerning enough to know that that was another assassin?

"It was likely an incorrectly placed call. My voice was probably not what they'd expected."

She stared at him for a few seconds, then looked again at her mother.

"Do you eat donuts and cookies, too, Alessa?"

"Sometimes. I have to be quick, though."

"Ah. I bet I know why. Your mother is quite amazing. I can't comprehend what she does."

"No one can. No one in this world ever will."

Tayo flopped his head to the side to look at her, and she moved only her eyes to hold his gaze.

I'm attempting conversation with a photograph?

* * *

Daria still held the knife to Benson's chest, but her other hand covered her mouth. She stared at him with big eyes, shaking her head slowly and still seated on him but motionless.

"Hi, Anna. I'm doing great. Except for that daughter of yours murdering me."

"Well, I am sure she did not mean that. It is good that her aim was off that day."

Daria had moved her hand back to his chest, and she grinned and stayed quiet. She blinked and started some very slow motions.

"It wasn't."

The phone was silent for a long moment.

"Yes, well, whatever the issue was, it is good that you are not dead in that alley."

He winked at Daria.

"Well, I'm sure not in that alley. That's true."

Daria covered her mouth again, stifling her laughter.

"Is everything okay? I am waiting for Daria outside. She said she needed only a brief visit."

"Oh yeah, everything's fine. I just wanted to say hi."

"Hi, Benson. I do not intend to be rude, but will she be outside soon?"

"Yeah, she's coming."

Daria didn't smile, but she nodded as she stared at the knife's point, a few trickles of sweat tickling down her chest between her breasts.

"I could use a donut, too, you know."

Daria never slowed, but she closed her eyes and shook her head.

"I can bring one up to your apartment for you, Benson."

She shook her head more and grinned, but she didn't stop.

"Hang on."

He muted the phone.

"I like how you kept going."

"Well, I'm almost there."

"You have to choose: either I play this game with her alone, sometime real soon, or she joins us right now."

Daria froze on his lap, tilted her head to look and confirm that the phone was muted, and said, "You're sick! You're not getting either of those, you pervert!"

He unmuted his phone.

"It sounds like you have some really tasty things down there."

She tried to move the knife away, and he grabbed her wrist, holding it in place. The very end of the point pushed into his skin.

"Well, there are donuts and cookies . . . things like that."

"Hang on," he said and muted the phone again.

To Daria, he said, "Tasty. You know I wasn't talking about the donuts."

"You are such a perv."

"You've already imagined both of those options. Admit it."

She hesitated a few seconds, then nodded.

"You choose, or I choose."

"Fine. Have my tasty mom all to yourself."

He grinned and nodded, then unmuted the phone.

"I think I'll pass on the treats this time. Just hang tight,"—he paused to grin at Daria, who shook her head and smiled—"and Daria will be out in a second or two. She's coming."

He tapped his phone and pushed it off of his chest.

"You're really close now, aren't you?"

She bit her lip and said, "Mm-hmm . . ."

"Even better than before, I bet, because you know that *both* of those choices are gonna happen."

She began to tremble.

"Both of them. You're imagining both."

She nodded, and looked at the ceiling, bouncing slowly in the sweltering room.

"Who's the real pervert here?"

She never answered, and she never stabbed him, but she finished everything else.

* * *

Lee needs sleep. I can't deny that. I suppose she needs a donut too. But must I try to entertain this child as well?

He'd felt his eyes sagging closed, but they popped open at a loud squeak from the wall behind his couch. He turned only his eyes to look at it. Then, he looked at Alessa.

"That's nothing to—"

214

"You don't have to explain anything. Do you still feel okay?"

He stared at her with his head tipped to one side as another squeak sounded from across the room.

"Usually,"—he paused to study her before continuing—"when I hear such sounds, I'm soon confronted with some type of difficulty."

"That's why you called my mom."

"Yes. She's generous enough to help with my injuries, but I don't believe she can solve my problem."

Lee rubbed her eyes, slid off of Tayo's lap to sit on the floor, her back against the couch, and resumed her snoring.

"No. She can't."

Tayo stared at the girl.

*　*　*

At the door, Benson said, "You should leave your skirt and heels here, Anna."

"Oh yeah, you're right. I told my mom I was dropping some things off for you."

"She didn't know that you meant her skirt? Down to the floor?"

Daria chuckled and said, "No, she sure as hell didn't."

She pulled the clothing out of the bag and left it on a chair in his living room. She looked down at it, then turned to Benson.

"Hey. I think I know why you want me to leave that here."

"Smart girl."

"You're disgusting."

"Just part of being dead."

She nodded and grinned.

"You like dead, Anna."

"God, yeah. Who knew?"

"You mean, 'Hell, yeah.'"

"Right. Hell, yeah. Are you going to make my mom say that she's me?"

"Huh. I never even thought of that. Maybe."

"Pervert.

"Yep."

She stepped out and pulled the door shut after her.

* * *

Tayo gave each wall in his living room a long look, then he let a deep sigh leak out and turned his head toward Alessa, seated in the chair near the window.

"The mouse is taking a nap."

"It's not a mouse," she said, still gazing at him calmly.

"No, it certainly is not. Still, I'm grateful that—"

A loud crack was followed by Tayo grabbing at his left leg and saying, "Ah!"

He held it with both hands and between quick, shallow breaths said, "No mouse would be this vicious."

She held his gaze for only a moment, then she studied the walls in each direction.

"Are you not frightened by this? I can tell you that I surely am."

"You have every reason to be frightened. I believe my mom can help with that, though."

There must be some limit as to how much Lee can do. Should I risk her death over a mere broken bone?

"Yes, I'm sure that she could. But she's exhausted already. It's only one bone, so let's let her sleep."

"She said you were a good man."

I know that I'm being selfish, but I prefer to ensure she's alive at the time, which I'm sure is near, when my head explodes like a balloon on a pin.

"I'm trying to be one."

"You are."

Yes, she's odd, but she's making me wish I were alone and could cry. Funny that a bone that broke inside me, without any valid reason, did not elicit that feeling.

"Thank you, Alessa. I've seen enough to conclude that you, too, are—"

He looked down from her eyes and saw the "get well" card that she'd stood up on the table next to her. He looked back into her eyes and when she offered a kind smile, he couldn't prevent one big tear from rolling down his cheek.

Still holding her gaze, he wiped it away just as the front door swung in, and Anna and Daria stepped inside.

*   *   *

"We brought tasty treats," Daria said with a smirk while taking off her coat.

She took Anna's from her and hung them up in the closet while Anna delivered the first box of donuts to the coffee table near Lee. Alessa vacated the upholstered chair and sat on the floor, leaning her back against the wall.

"Is Lee okay?" Anna said.

"Yes, I believe so," said Tayo. "I believe she needs to rest, though."

Alessa crawled over toward her mother and said, "She probably needs a donut even more."

She shook her mom's shoulder lightly.

Lee's eyes opened, and she said, "Oh, okay."

She looked over and said, "Hi, Lessa. How long was I out?"

"Not long, Mom. You probably need to rest more, but maybe a dozen donuts will help too."

Lee's eyes found the box, and she flipped the lid up to see an array of powdery confections, all crammed together like eggs in a nest.

"Ooh, I think you're right," she said with a tired smile.

She looked around and said, "Who else wants one?"

"No one," said Anna, sitting in the chair with Ozzy on her lap. "I do not generally eat such things anyway."

"Hell, Mom," Daria said with a grin. "Most people like a big serving of a tasty treat."

She held her mother's curious gaze before Anna turned back to Lee and said, "Well, there is more in the kitchen anyway. So, you and your daughter can—"

Lee had already set the box on her lap and held one in each hand, alternating taking bites of them. Alessa had returned to her seat by the wall.

"Yes, well, I can make coffee too. Tayo, is the pot on the counter in there?"

"Yep. Right next to that little box, Mom. Remember that?"

Anna looked at Daria, who was grinning and shaking her head.

"Yes, Daria, there is an empty box in there now. Which is good."

"I'd get up," said Tayo, "but I, um, think I better just lie here awhile."

He glanced at Alessa and though she again mimicked a photo, Tayo could detect a slight smile. He thought she might have nodded once too.

"Come on, Mom," Daria said, tipping her head toward the kitchen. "Let's boil some coffee."

"You do not spend much time in kitchens, Daria. Still, we can make a pot."

She followed Daria out of the room. Ozzy remained on the chair and though Alessa studied him for a while, she stayed where she was.

Tayo had watched her make that choice and despite the pain, he smiled in her direction.

Maybe odd is sometimes a misinterpretation of kind and caring.

"Oh, that's better," Lee said, licking bits of icing and powdered sugar off of her fingertips. "It's only a dozen, but still."

She smiled at her daughter, who managed a small grin in return.

She turned her head toward Tayo and said, "You going to be alright for a while? I need to get outside and get some air."

"You must know by now that I can offer no such assurance."

"He's right," said Alessa.

Lee looked at her, shook her head then stood, still holding the empty box.

"Lessa, come on. Get your coat. Let's take a walk."

Are you also proficient in finding traces of blood, splattered in and around a trash container? Please, take your hike in the other direction.

"Sure, Mom. Before it gets too dark."

"See you soon, Tayo."

Alessa bundled up in her long coat and boots, and Lee slipped on her black leather jacket and grabbed her sunglasses. They closed the door behind them just as Anna and Daria walked in with a full pot of coffee and mugs.

Chapter 22 – Not Much Of A Boss

Anna scooped up Ozzy and sat with him on her lap, and Daria took Alessa's spot on the floor. They each held a cup of hot coffee, and Tayo's rested within reach on the table.

He looked at it and said, "I must disclose that never before has coffee rested on that coffee table."

"So, what did you call it before now?" Daria said with a sneer.

"Daria, it can still be called that. It does not depend on what items have been there."

"Geez, it was a joke. Hey, Tayo, what's the plan for that couch?"

It's hard to ignore the soaked cushions beneath me, especially when reminded of that discomfort. Daria is correct, though—something should be done.

"I don't know. I believe placing it outside for pickup would attract unwelcome attention."

"Probably rats too," she said with a smirk.

"Well," said Anna, after a quick glance at her daughter, "is it possible to throw it away only a small portion at a time?"

"Like those closet shelves that you smashed to hell."

"Daria. She is right, though, Tayo. But until then, what can be done?"

"If I had a tablecloth, that could be used to—"

"Why don't you have one? I know you have plenty of money."

"Yes, Daria, it's not poverty to blame. It was, um, damaged, and I haven't been able yet to replace it."

"Mom, why don't you run out and get one?"

Before she could answer, Daria said, "Tayo, anything else you need around here? Maybe a bigger box in your kitchen, just in case, you know, like if something—"

"I'm hopeful that I won't need another box. But thank you, Daria, for devising plans to assist with my imminent destruction."

She took a sip and smiled before saying, "Anytime."

A squeak came from the wall right behind Daria, and she crawled halfway across the room before she turned and said, "Mousetraps too. Get some of those, Mom."

"It's not a mouse," Tayo said and closed his eyes.

Anna and Daria watched in silence as he lay on the couch, taking deep, measured breaths until there was a loud snap.

"Ah!"

"Oh, Tayo, was that you?"

"No, Anna. Not me. *Inside* me."

"No way," said Daria. "That was a bone breaking?"

"Yes."

"You're right, then. It wasn't a mouse. That's a serious problem you got there, Tayo."

"Thank you, Daria. Yes, but it's not my only problem. I wish to enlist more assistance from Benson."

Daria grinned at her mom, then said to Tayo, "I know exactly what you mean. He's good at handling problems."

Tayo still lay motionless, with his left arm covering his eyes.

"Do you have the ability to contact him?"

"Yeah," said Daria, "we can call him anytime. Hey, Mom, since you're going out for tablecloths and mousetraps and stuff, why don't you—"

"It is *not* a mouse," Tayo said softly, still not moving.

"Right. Mom, drop by. He won't mind. Offer him something sweet. He wanted some."

"He really did want a donut?"

"Uh . . . yep. Yeah, that's right."

"Do you not wish to come with me?"

Daria coughed, and it turned into a giggle.

"Wow. No, I'll just, um, hang out with the guy with a broken bone."

"It's more than one," Tayo said and let out a deep breath.

"Geez."

"Very well. I will make the needed purchases and talk to Benson about helping you, Tayo."

"Bring him sweets too. He really did want a taste."

"Okay. I will be back soon."

"More like 'on your back soon,'" Daria said softly with a hand over her mouth.

"What is that, Daria?"

"Oh, nothing."

Dressed for the cold, Anna slammed the door shut behind her.

Daria shrugged at Tayo and said, "Not exactly sure why, but I kind of hope she gets it."

Tayo lifted his arm and when he saw Daria grinning at him, he set it back down.

*   *   *

Anna held a small bag containing two donuts in one hand and knocked with the other.

Almost like a reminder of Lancaster Wolfe's intense body heat, she felt the warmth rolling out of Benson's apartment when he opened the door.

"Anna."

He looked at the bag in her hand.

"Good. I really do need cash."

"It is not money. I have not had time to travel to where it is kept."

"So, what's in there?"

"A donut. Daria insisted. She said you truly did want something sweet."

"And here you are. Come in."

She stepped inside and immediately began ridding herself of her coat.

"Oh, Benson, this is so hot! What illness do you have?"

"No illness. But I've been told I'm sick."

She squinted at him, finished with her coat and handed it to him, then tried to pull down her short skirt.

He watched her hands tugging on the hem and said, "Don't bother. Really good legs."

"Oh, well, thank you, Benson."

"Lin Finity style. I like it."

"It really is a good look."

"A good look that looks good on you."

She looked into his eyes as he stood close, still holding her coat. Without looking, he heaved it toward a nearby chair.

"Yes, well, I did not think it appropriate at Shield meetings to have on such clothing."

He reached out with one hand to brush her hair aside, and he touched her cheek on the way, causing her to take a quick breath.

"It's not appropriate now either."

"You prefer jeans, Benson?" she said, followed by a deeper breath.

"Nope. That's not what I mean."

"Oh, you mean—"

"Yep."

She turned her head slightly but continued to hold his gaze.

"How long has it been, Anna?"

"Oh, I—"

He pulled her toward him and stifled her with a kiss. She squirmed and made a muffled whimpering sound, but he didn't release her. She closed her eyes and relaxed as he continued to kiss her with only the furnace rattling and circulating hot air all around.

He pulled away just far enough to say, "It's been too long for you," and kissed her again.

"And you?"

"Dead guys don't get much action."

"Your lips are cold."

"Yep. I'm cold all over. How about that, huh?"

She smiled and said, "Because you are dead?"

"Yep. Killed by that daughter of yours."

She raised her eyebrows as she studied him.

"You just kissed a guy your daughter shot. How about that?"

"Well, I am not sure that—"

He reached behind her and swung open the closet door, revealing a full-length mirror, attached on the inside. With his hands on her hips, he spun her around to face it.

"Stay still. Just watch."

She stared as he slid his fingertips inside the top band of her skirt, and she drew in a sharp breath at feeling a bunch of wiggling icicles on her skin.

"Oh, Benson, I do not know if—"

"I need something sweet."

He kissed her neck and worked his hands deeper, fingertips rubbing her skin and stretching the elastic.

"I'll have that donut later. After."

She took a deep breath and looked first at her own eyes, then his, looking over her shoulder, then at his cold hands. She watched as he worked at her skirt until it was halfway down her thighs, and he held it there.

They both took a long look at her lacy underwear, exposed in the dim light of his sweltering apartment.

"Hmm. Something sweet. Wrapped up nice and pretty too."

"Your hands are so cold."

"Everything is. Alright, let's see those legs."

He pushed her skirt down until it fell along her thighs. Without looking, Anna raised each of her heels up and out of it.

"Good girl."

After lifting her arms straight above her, he got a hold of the bottom of her thin sweater and peeled it up and off. He waited until she'd brushed her hair back on both sides, then he moved her arms straight down at her sides. She held them there, and he reached around, unclasped her bra between her breasts, and worked it over her shoulders and let it drop.

She gazed at the reflection of her bared breasts as he grabbed her upper arms and forced them back, causing a gasp. She took deep breaths, and she watched her breasts rising and falling, his hands cold vises on her.

"And just like that, Anna Kelgina is here in my apartment, wearing only her heels and panties."

She pursed her lips while observing her nakedness from bottom to top, then gazed into his eyes in the mirror, but she didn't speak.

"Not the boss this time."

She still watched her own breasts as a thin sheen of sweat appeared.

"Are you?"

She didn't smile, but she shook her head and said softly, "No."

He grinned and said, "About damn time."

* * *

"How much farther, Mom?"

"I think it's just another block, Lessa. I need more than donuts."

"And cookies."

"Yeah, I ate the cookies too. Some hamburgers would be good."

Hand in hand, Lee and Alessa walked the cold streets of Baltimore near Tayo's apartment, aiming for the fast food restaurant they'd passed on the way in.

"French fries too."

"Yeah, Baby. All of it."

* * *

Benson let go of Anna's arms to pull his t-shirt up and off, showing the lean muscles everyone believed he'd gotten from years in some military somewhere. He took hold of her wrists and placed her palms on her hips.

"Stay," he said, and she only nodded.

He stepped away and returned quickly with a chair from his kitchen, which he placed in front of her, turned her way, with its back against the mirror.

He reclaimed her wrists, leaned in close above her right shoulder, and said, "Left or right knee. Last choice you get."

She sighed and looked down at her right knee as she lifted it up and placed it on the chair's soft cushion. In the mirror, she mostly watched herself, wondering how she'd lost her clothes so quickly, and Benson seemed more like a shadow behind her.

"Hands on the back. Both of them."

Anna grabbed the top rail of the chair's back, and she didn't make a sound when he reached around with two neckties and hastily fastened her in place.

"Oh, and look at that. Anna Kelgina's not going anywhere now."

She felt her heart pounding while noticing her breasts hanging forward, shifting with each breath as she leaned into the chair. She heard him removing his khakis and tugged weakly against her restraints, knowing that he'd tied her down too tightly.

When she felt a cold hand grab at her underwear, she let out a soft squeal.

"You can protest if you want."

She shook her head, then it got tipped up when he gathered her hair in a tight grip.

"Yep. Thought so."

She felt him tugging at the last remaining piece of clothing she still wore. Then, she let out a long breath when she found that he'd been completely truthful: every part of him was cold.

"And . . . there you go."

She held onto the chair.

"Not much of a boss at all."

Her knee slid forward and back along the soft fabric.

"You're just obedient. Like a pet."

The chair rocked up onto its far legs and back down with a clunk each time.

"Aren't you?"

She hesitated and felt her hair pulled more forcefully.

"Aren't you, Anna?"

Lost in his coldness in the steamy room, Anna gasped as she was compelled to look up at the ceiling, the chair legs thumping a steady rhythm on the wood floor as he rocked her, and she rocked it.

And she knew that he was right.

"Yes."

"Yes, what?"

The chair pounded, her knee kept sliding, and the grip on her hair tightened.

"Yes, I am an obedient pet."

"Even for a dead man?"

With an uncontrollable wave about to crash, she could barely focus on her response.

"Especially for such a cold . . . dead . . . man."

*   *   *

Daria glanced at the clock on the wall.

"Gee, wonder what's taking her so long. Bet she forgets the tablecloth."

"That's not her most urgent task."

"Nope. Giving Benson a treat."

The door snapped open, and Anna rushed in, holding in one hand a plastic bag and a smaller paper bag.

"Speak of the devil," said Daria.

"Well, I am not exactly a devil, Daria. But you did speak of me?"

"Yep."

She pointed at the bags in Anna's hand while she took off her coat.

"Lookie there. Donuts. And here, I thought you were going to give old Benson something sweet."

Anna dropped her coat near the closet and looked at the bags in her hand. Then, she saw that Daria was grinning at her.

"Well, Daria, I, um . . ."

"Yeah, Mom?"

Anna smiled and said, "He is dead, remember? I do not recall dead individuals wanting sugary treats."

Tayo looked from one to the other, squinting.

"That's funny, Mom. 'Sugary treats.'"

"Yes, well,"—she tossed the plastic bag toward her daughter—"perhaps all the blood can be covered."

"Thank you, Anna," said Tayo. "I can delay disposal of this furniture until it's more convenient."

Daria grabbed both of Tayo's ankles and started to lift.

"Ah! Please, no!"

She set them back down.

"Oh, yeah. Broken bones. That's gotta hurt. We'll get to that later. Mom, you want some coffee?"

"I have worked up a thirst. Yes. Thank you."

"You did, huh?"

"Well, um, he keeps his home on the tropical side. It is a dehydrating thing."

"Right."

"Anna," said Tayo, "did you petition for his assistance?"

"I did find time for that, yes."

"You found time? What does that mean?" Daria said with a big grin.

"Oh. I, um, what with shopping for home items. That is all."

"Right."

"Well, Anna? What was his response?"

"He agreed to help. He stayed close behind me when—"

"I bet he did," Daria said with a smirk.

"—when I returned. He is in his auto parked in the street."

"With the heat cranking."

"Yes, Daria, because—"

"He's dead."

"Yes," Anna said with a short laugh.

* * *

The front door jerked open, and Ozzy jumped up onto Tayo's legs. "Ah! Please, no, dog!"

Daria scooped him up and set him on the floor while Lee and Alessa walked inside.

"Hey, everybody. I feel a lot better. I had some hamburgers and—"

"Fries," said Alessa.

"—and a lot of other stuff. What's going on here? Tayo, you don't look so good."

He looked at every pair of eyes focused on him before speaking.

"I do not wish to complain, but—"

"He's full of broken bones," Daria said with a grin.

"Why does that cause a grin?" said Anna.

Daria ignored her. Tayo spoke.

"It is only two that have snapped."

"So far," said Daria.

"That really is not helpful, Daria."

"Just saying."

Lee said, "Well, let's get you fixed up. I can—"

"I fear that this episode has not reached its conclusion," said Tayo. "If I remain still, the pain is tolerable."

"You really want to lie there with snapped bones?" said Lee.

He let his head flop to the side and looked at Anna.

"Anna, if any vodka remains, I believe that would offer some level of comfort."

"Great," said Daria. "Let's all get drunk and bet when his next bone will snap. Hell of a drinking game."

Everyone stared at her, and she looked from face to face. Even Ozzy watched her closely.

"What? Too much?"

Chapter 23 – An Unusual Attack

Tayo's apartment contained precious little space, but there were two small bedrooms in addition to the kitchen and living room. A lot of liquor had been consumed, Lee and Anna had helped Tayo make a necessary trip to the restroom, then assisted him back to the couch.

While he was out of the room, Daria spread the tablecloth over the soaked cushions, under the quiet watch of Alessa and Ozzy. Then, Anna and Daria had retired to the sparse spare room, and Lee and Alessa took Tayo's room.

All had waited and listened for any signs of mice, but the walls offered no squeaks, allowing everyone some measure of sleep.

Daria's back was turned to her mother's, and she cradled her phone close, completely muted—even the vibration. At 2:00 am, she'd glanced at the clock on the nightstand, then at her phone. She grinned at the text: "Anna, come out to the car."

She texted back, "I can't. We're all sleeping. Maybe tomorrow."

"Are you in a bed?"

"Yep."

"With your mother?"

"Yep."

"Nice. Both naked, I bet. Make room for me. I'm coming in."

"NO! Alright, I'll sneak out. Need to get dressed."

"No. Just a coat."

"It's too cold."

"Hang on. I'll call your naked mom."

"No! Alright, just a coat. See ya."

She slipped out of the bed, careful to not bounce the mattress around, and crept out into the living room, where she'd left her coat.

Tayo lay on the couch as they'd left him, and she paused to hear his soft snoring.

"Damn drunk," she said under her breath with a smirk.

Wearing only the coat and her boots, she quietly exited the apartment and started to shiver. A car idled not far down the street, its soft rumbling sending out puffy clouds of exhaust into the still air, and Daria began crunching the crusty snow on the sidewalk.

The passenger door was unlocked, so she quickly climbed in.

"God, it's freezing out there."

"Hell. You mean, 'Hell.'"

"Hell yeah, it's cold. Almost as cold as you."

"You're a smartass, Anna."

"Yep, that's damn smart. Cold too."

"Back seat," he said and opened his door.

She got out, too, and joined him in the back.

"Car's warm, though," she said. "That helps."

"Off with the coat."

"No, it isn't that warm in here."

"Keep the boots if you want."

She started working her arms out of the thick coat, grinning at him, and said, "Why can't I say no to you? What's the deal?"

"That's easy. With a dead guy is when you feel the most alive."

She stopped, with the jacket pulled down off of her shoulders, her bare breasts lit by a nearby lamppost, and stared at him.

"God, that—"

He pointed at her.

"Hell. Hell, that makes perfect sense."

"Hold it," he said. "What happened to your hair?"

"That damn Lin. I pissed her off, and she decided to give me a trim."

"Huh. Good thing your head was the only possible target."

"Funny, Benson, but true. Hey, earlier, when you and my—"

"There's no time," he said and loosened his belt. "Let's not talk until you're where I like you best."

She grinned and nodded and said, "Yeah. Where I can't stop. That's a good place for me too."

He finished undoing things and said, "For you."

She looked down at how ready he was for her just as his left hand brought out the knife that she'd held to his chest the last time.

He laughed and said, "Hold it with both hands."

"Oh, I see. My choice, huh?"

"Nope."

She looked up at him.

"Not the knife, right?"

"That's right, Anna."

She reached across and did as he'd instructed.

"Check out how cold."

She leaned over to him, then backed away only enough to say, "Damn, yeah, that's cold."

He coaxed her back to where he wanted her and raked across her hair, brushing it all off to one side. And when she tried to speak more, he wouldn't let her.

Many minutes passed, and he said, "Alright, Anna. Time to have a seat."

She shook her hair back and accepted his offer, and she groaned as she settled in. He handed her the knife, and she held it with both hands, the point near his heart.

"Cold feels good this way, too, huh?"

"Mm-hmm. Yep," she said as the springs in the seat squeaked softly.

"Cold and dead. Think about that."

She grinned and shook her head, but she didn't argue.

The windows fogged, the engine barely made a sound, and only Daria's steady movements and occasional deep breath filled the quiet car. His hands touched her all over as she rose and fell.

"Are you there?"

"Yeah. I'm there."

"That was quick. Anna, you have to make a choice."

"Oh, hell, what this time?"

She bit her lower lip and let out a long breath.

"Stab me in the heart right at the best moment."

"I hope to God—Hell, I mean—that there's a second choice."

"You don't think you'd like that?"

She hesitated, imagining what it would be like, and a spike of morbid excitement surprised her.

"I, um . . ."

"Yeah, think about that."

She closed her eyes, and he watched a slight grin appear.

"Or, we get photos of us next time. You like photos."

"Well, that would be better than—wait, who do you think will take those pics?"

"You know who."

"All I know is that you're a pervert."

"You like perverted. How close are you now?"

She moaned and said, "Hell, I am *so* close . . ."

He watched her closely and said, "Your mother will take the photos."

She didn't make a single comment, and he nodded quietly at her. She only moaned again and sighed, then softly said, "You are such a damn pervert."

"You've made your choice."

She nodded.

"You like how cold feels. You'll agree to almost anything."

"Mm-hmm. I guess so."

"Imagine she's here with us now, right there on the seat. Can you see that?"

She closed her eyes, kept her rhythm, and breathed deeply.

"Yeah. I can."

"Perverted can be pretty sweet, huh?"

She nodded and dropped the knife, placing both hands on his shoulders.

"Are you just about to get there, Anna?"

While biting her lower lip, she said, "Oh, hell yeah . . ."

"One final thought."

"What's . . . that?"

"Your mom will be naked too. She'll even undress herself."

She picked up her pace, and a long moment passed before she said anything, with Benson grinning up at her obvious smile the entire time.

"Oh my . . . this is bigger than . . ."

"And I'll be calling you both Anna. You won't remember which is which, and you won't care. Just two naked Annas in a bed. Lucky me, huh?"

"Oh hell, what are you doing to me . . ."

"Something like that."

Daria shuddered and leaned down to kiss his cold lips in the hot car as a powerful climax twisted and churned all through her.

*　*　*

Tayo awoke early, in a room that was quiet and dark. His dry mouth couldn't distract from the pain of his broken bones, and he left his eyes closed and only listened.

This is an unusual attack, my strange personal tormentor. I don't believe you're done with my skeleton. Which part will be next? Please do not split my skull between my eyes so that I can see to each side. Like a fish. No, like a man with a split-open head.

"Good morning, Tayo," Anna said as she entered the room. "How was your sleep?"

The insanity of such a question as I lay here with two bones broken and likely more on the schedule!

"I slept very well. Vodka has redeeming qualities."

"Yes, I do agree."

235

"Hey," Daria said as she walked in, rubbing her eyes. "If nobody cares, I'm going to take a shower. That alright, Tayo?"

"Yes, of course. The door's lock isn't functional, though."

"That's alright," Daria said with a grin at her mother. "Not like my mom's going to barge in and take pictures of me."

Anna stared without blinking and said, "Daria, why would you even concoct such an idea?"

Daria shook her head, grinned, and pointed at Anna before leaving the room. Anna turned back to Tayo.

"Well, I do not always understand her. But, Tayo, the couch cover seems to be working for you."

"Yes, and thanks again for—"

A loud crack came from somewhere near Tayo's legs, and they both stared at a shiny white bone, its end ragged and shattered, sticking out through his skin near his ankle. Tayo contained his scream with one hand over his mouth.

"Oh, Tayo, let me wake Lee up. May I? You need to be repaired."

Yes, like an automobile or appliance that has gone too far past its expected lifetime. Please, Lee . . . patch me up before my skull splits between my eyes!

Daria hadn't yet started her shower and when she heard the commotion, she returned to see. Lee and Alessa joined them too.

Lee said, "Tayo, did this just happen?"

"That particular bone? Yes. But there are still those two others that were sent for my enjoyment yesterday."

"Have you had enough? Can we get you fixed up already?"

"I don't know if my Hell of snapping bones has ended yet, but I'm beginning to long for death. Please, Lee. If you would."

"Polite to the end," Daria said, shaking her head.

Anna turned and frowned at her.

"Could be the end. Who knows?"

She took out her phone, tapped it, and started to point it at Anna. But Anna pushed her arm back down and said, "Daria, you wish to take a photograph of me? Why?"

"That look on your face."

"It is just my everyday face."

"Fine," she said and put the phone away.

Lee rubbed her eyes a few times and stood beside the couch. She looked at Anna and Daria and Alessa and said, "This isn't easy. Remember how exhausted I was last time?"

"I'll save you a donut."

"Daria."

"All I'm saying," said Lee, "is that if I'm wiped out, carry me or drag me to bed, alright?"

"If I survive," said Tayo, "I will try to relocate you to where you can recover."

"Good. Thanks. Alright, here I go."

She swept her leg over and straddled Tayo, crinkling the plastic beneath him. He looked up at her with big black eyes, and she rested her palms on his chest. Her head tipped forward, and his breath wheezed out as his eyes rolled up high and closed.

Lee went home.

*　*　*

"Shouldn't she be done by now?" said Daria.

"Well, some time has passed by, but how could we know?"

"She's not looking so good either. I think it almost killed her the last time."

"I am not so sure she can be killed."

"Where's my gun?"

"You are sometimes less funny, Daria."

"Fine. Maybe you should call Lin?"

"To what end? She is far away, and I do not believe she can heal anyway."

"I don't know. She might have some kind of advice, though."

Lee started to tip, and Daria nudged her back to an upright position.

237

Anna sighed and said, "Perhaps you are right. She is a frightening thing, though."

"Hey, it's just a call."

"Well, okay."

"Put in on speaker too."

Anna sighed loudly and said, "Okay, Daria."

She tapped Lin's number, set it to speaker mode, and laid it on the coffee table.

"Hey, now it's a phone table."

"Daria. Stop."

* * *

With Lee and Tayo unconscious on the couch and Alessa sitting quietly against the wall, Anna and Daria listened to Lin's phone ringing.

"What now, Anna? Did Tayo fill with helium and float out through a window?"

Anna looked at Daria, who had a hand over her mouth to hide a giggle, and they heard Jack somewhere farther from Lin's phone.

"That's a good one."

Anna shook her head at her daughter before speaking.

"No, he is not a balloon, at least not yet. No, Tayo is—"

A loud crack came from the couch, causing them both to swivel their heads around.

"Oh," said Anna, "did you hear that? That is the fourth one. He—"

"Fourth what?" said Lin. "I didn't hear anything."

"Fourth bone breaking inside Tayo's body. That was a big one, and I thought you surely would have heard when it—"

"This can't be happening. His bones are breaking now?"

"Not all of them, Lin."

"Not yet!" Daria said with a big smile.

Anna pointed at her and frowned.

"Has his neck been broken yet?" they heard Gabriel say.

"No," said Anna. "It seems that his less consequential bones are considered, well, less consequential. They are snapping within him."

"Uh-oh, that's gotta hurt!" Daria said after another of Tayo's bones fractured loudly inside him.

Anna looked away and shook her head.

"Oh, Lin, this is not pleasant. A leg bone sticks out as if someone stabbed it into him. I thought that there would be more blood, but no, it is white. Just white. It is whiter than I would have—"

"Anna, slow down," said Lin. "Stop talking a second and just answer me. Is Lee still there?"

"She is sleeping with him."

"What?"

"Mom!" said Daria. "She means that Lee is doing whatever voodoo she does, and she—"

"It's not voodoo," said Lin. "You know, I think I can have some fun even from way over here at home. Want me to try?"

Daria made an exaggerated grimace for her mother to see.

"Sorry," she said. "No, don't try. I just mean that Lee is sitting on him, and they're both unconscious. That's what my mom meant. Oh, but *that's* not good."

"What now, Daria?" said Lin.

"I just heard another bone crack apart, and God, I can see it almost jabbing through his skin. But the bad part is that Lee is getting more pale every second. What if she can't help him? What then?"

"I will have to call emergency vehicles, Lin," said Anna. "They can reset his bones, and if they have smelly salts, they can—"

"Smelling. Smelling salts."

"Yes, well, they can wake up Lee, and then—"

"Then, you'll all go to jail or an asylum. Do NOT call anyone, do you understand?"

"Okay, but—"

Lee shook her hair back, opened her tired eyes, and looked around the room.

"Oh, Lee has opened her eyes. How is this possible? Daria, do you see?"

"I see it, but I don't—"

"See what?" said Lin.

"His bone has returned to his body, and it is moving around in there. That is good because—"

Lee's eyes closed, her face seemed to sag, and her head hung forward, her chin almost touching her chest. Another bone had popped out of one of Tayo's thighs, ripping through his khakis.

"Lee is becoming pale again! Tayo's bones are again outside of his skin!"

"Daria," said Lin, "take a photo."

"Yuck! No way do I want—"

"Can you see how green my eyes are? Do it!"

"Okay, okay!"

She got out her phone, took a photo while muttering, "Better things to take photos of," and sent it.

"There, it's on its way."

Lee stretched her arms to both sides and managed a strained smile. Tayo's bones had returned into his body. Daria clapped quietly and pumped her fist into the air.

"Lin," said Anna, "Lee is again waking herself up, and Tayo is healing. It is a miracle, and I maybe should have waited before calling."

"That's okay. Don't worry about it, Anna. Make sure that daughter of yours, the one with the weird haircut,"—Daria sneered while flicking around her chopped hair—"sends a photo of Tayo's back. Got it?"

"Yes. Yes, of course, Lin. I will say goodbye now."

"Bye."

Anna looked down on the phone, saw that Lin had ended the call, and tapped off her phone.

* * *

"Oh," Lee said with a big yawn, "that was kind of impossible. I heard you talking in between. What was going on?"

Anna said, "We called Lin. You seemed to be in depths higher than your head, and we did not know if you would survive. We thought maybe Lin would have some advice."

"What all did you tell her?"

"Well, we, um, we mentioned that—"

"You looked about to die yourself, Lee," said Daria, shaking her head. "So, that's about what we told her."

Lee reached into the pocket of her tight, faded blue jeans and took out her own phone. Still straddling Tayo, whose head tipped lazily from side to side, she called Lin.

"Hey, some courtesy," Daria said with a grin. "Speaker, alright?"

Lee squinted at her for a second, looked at Alessa, who only shrugged, and put it on speaker.

*   *   *

"Hi, Lee. Are you okay?"

"Hi, Lin. I'm exhausted, but yeah, I'm okay."

"How's Tayo?"

Daria dragged her fingers across her throat while grinning at her mother, who only frowned and shook her head.

"Good as new. Well, except for the trauma. That poor man is going through a lot. I can fix his bones and stuff, but if he's terrorized by all this, that's on him."

"You're doing enough by healing him. That really is amazing."

"It tires me out, but it's not as horrible as you might think. I do what I can to make it fun for both of us."

"What? How?"

"Remember when I first healed his leg at that restaurant in Allentown?"

Daria nodded and winked at her mother, who only shushed her.

"Oh, okay. I get it. Yeah, I remember. I'll never forget that smile on his face."

"Good, because you won't see any more. I make it as good as I can for us, but really, Lin, he's being destroyed. He's not smiling anymore."

"That Hunter thing isn't killing you like when you tried to heal Taylor?"

"Came close," Daria said very softly.

Anna pointed at her with a frown.

"Not anymore. I've learned to not think about the Hunter. I sense it there, like something lurking in the weeds around my clearing. Something really nasty. But all I do is focus on Tayo. Don't ask me to try to destroy that thing. Lin, I don't think anything can."

"You are probably correct," said Gabriel from a distance. "It is wise to not even try. We will try to figure something out here."

"Gabby's right, Lee. We'll keep working on it, and you keep helping Tayo. Can you get that brat Daria to send a photo of Tayo's back?"

Daria frowned and pointed at herself, mouthing the word, "Brat?"

"Yeah, sure. Did you do that to her hair?"

"Pretty neat, huh?"

Daria rolled her eyes and scoffed.

"I'm guessing it could have been worse."

"Oh, yeah. Hey, could you fix her hair if you wanted to?"

Daria froze with an ear turned toward the phone and so did Anna.

"I don't know. Maybe. Do you want me to try?"

"Nope. It's a good reminder for her."

Daria shook her head and her lips formed all kinds of words that no one could hear.

"Alright. Look, I'm really tired, Lin, but I wanted to let you know that I'm doing alright at keeping him alive. Figure something out soon, alright?"

"We'll try. Good luck, Lee."

Lee tapped off her phone and wedged it back into her pocket.

"Well, Daria, Lin is expecting a photograph. You should not mind—you seem to like taking photos."

"You know, I think I might like having some taken of me too. Special ones."

She grinned and waited, and Anna said, "You are making Lin angrier by every extra second."

She looked down at Tayo and said, "Tayo, can we see your back? Lin would like to know what has changed."

He didn't answer, but he rolled toward the couch back and worked his shirt up as high as he could. Anna pulled it farther and held it there.

"Oh, fine."

Daria took a shot of his back, and Anna said, "Where his bones did their snapping, too, Daria."

With an exaggerated sigh, Daria took photos of Tayo's damaged legs and sent them all to Lin. Anna smoothed Tayo's shirt back down, and he rolled onto his back. He looked from face to face, but he didn't smile.

Daria's phone chimed, and she read aloud the text Lin had sent: "Yes, I got the photos of Tayo's broken bones and his back. Thank you."

*   *   *

"I believe I should try to move around," Tayo said, still not budging and reclined on the couch.

"Probably need a bathroom break, at least," Daria said with a scoff.

"Daria, that is not—"

"Anna, she's right. That will be my first destination if I can navigate on these repaired legs."

"Let me guess: the booze is second?"

"Daria, you are rarely supportive. You have a dark side that grows darker."

"You've got a little wickedness going on there yourself, Mom. Like how you switched to those short skirts, showing off your—"

"You two?" said Tayo. "Lee, it would be easier for me if I didn't have to lift you as well."

"Oh, right. Of course."

She stood, walked over, and sat beside Alessa.

"Lessa, I hope you weren't too worried by any of that."

"I wasn't. I have faith in you."

"Why, thanks, Baby. I have faith in you too."

"That will help."

Lee stared at her, but the girl only watched as Tayo tried to right himself. He stood next to the couch, wobbled a little, then stood up straight.

"Lee, despite my tentative maneuvering, I actually feel good. Physically. Thank you. It's alarming how the memories of pain are reluctant to leave, though."

"Can't help you with that."

"You have done more than your share. Now, I really need to go."

He left the room, and the three women and one girl relaxed and waited in silence. The silence was cut short by a mad scream from Tayo.

His arm entered the room first. It was engulfed in flames. He waved it around, almost igniting the walls, then dropped to his knees.

Anna screamed, Lee began tearing the tablecloth off of his couch, Alessa watched calmly, and Daria fumbled around with her camera.

When the dog ran toward Tayo, Anna screamed, "Ozzy, no!"

He began pawing at the flaming arm, only to singe his paws, yip loudly, and run behind the chair in the living room.

"Tayo," said Lee, "try to hold still."

She wrapped the plastic around his arm, smothering the fire, and walked him back to the couch. Anna turned her head at the sound of Ozzy's whimpering and rushed to find him.

"Oh, you are now injured too?"

He struggled to keep from being picked up, but Anna and Daria managed to carry him into the kitchen, where they laid him in the sink and ran cool water over his burns.

While Anna continued trying to nurse Ozzy, Daria sent the photo of Tayo's arm on fire to Lin.

* * *

Anna left Ozzy sobbing in the sink, which was half-full of water, and peeked around the corner into the living room.

Tayo lay on the couch, taking deep breaths, and Lee was sitting on his lap like before, her eyes closed. Daria watched from across the room with her arms crossed. Alessa still sat on the floor, against the wall.

When her phone rang, she set it to speaker and laid it on the table. They heard Lin's voice.

"Anna, is the fire out?"

"Yes. The fire on Tayo is out. Lee is attempting to heal him."

"Good. So, everything is back to normal."

Anna looked up quickly when her daughter scoffed.

"No. Ozzy tried to help and was burned badly. Daria and I placed him in the kitchen sink and ran water to end his flames. He is still there. He is not happy. Neither am I. Or Daria."

"Can Lee help the dog too?"

"I hope so. He will never last for the journey back to Russia. We will go soon. When Ozzy is cured, if he can be."

Daria's head was shaking, and she was softly saying, "I'm not going to Russia."

"No, not yet, you won't," said Lin. "I need updates from your daughter. In fact, tell her she owes me a new one of Tayo's back. It must have changed after he played with fire."

"He did no playing. I will tell Daria to send something after Lee is done. Then, when Ozzy is himself, we will all—"

"Oh, Anna, I'm too tired from all of this to argue with you. If you leave, I'll destroy all of you."

Daria's eyes stretched wide open, and Anna caught her breath.

"We need your help until we can fix this."

Anna puffed up her cheeks and began to let out a long, slow breath. Partway through, she glanced at Daria and saw her pointing her camera at her. She shook her head and let all of the breath out.

"Fine, Lin. I believe you could locate us in Russia, so I will stay."

"Smart. Get going on that photo."

Anna tapped off her phone.

"Daria. You heard her. When Lee is done, you can play more with your camera."

"There are way better ways to play with a camera," she said with a grin.

Anna loudly forced out a breath and shook her head.

Daria nodded and winked.

Chapter 24 – Bottom Of A Lost Well

Lee opened her eyes when she felt the heat of her sun, the one that never moved from its place high in the clear blue sky of her home. Her first thought was of her stones, and she saw that they still formed the infinity symbol, although a few had migrated from their proper locations. She stooped down and arranged them, and instantly, she felt the effects of the donuts, hamburgers, and everything else depart, leaving her in perfect, eternal health.

She remembered Tayo. His arm had been burned badly by the entity, that Hunter thing, and at the thought of it, she felt the hairs on her neck standing up in formation.

She remembered that she'd felt that before, even though she'd faced a different direction that time.

It doesn't matter, she realized. A thing like that will always be behind me unless I turn and face it. And I'm not that foolish.

After a quick glance at her sun, shining down its healing green light, Lee focused on where she'd found that odd well the last time she'd healed Tayo. Again, the sea of gently waving plant stalks danced an outline around the compact area where none could grow.

As she walked toward it, recalling how it had played out the last time, she pulled her t-shirt up and off and left it on the ground. Since she was still walking, her bra was next, and she realized that her bare chest had never felt that intense heat from her sun.

She paused and leaned back, allowing the warmth from above to touch her all over and before she resumed her short journey, she kicked off her snakeskin boots, peeled down her tight jeans, and removed the last little item.

Not satisfied with standing under her sun, she lay down on her back in the soft, green grass and extended her arms out to the sides. After a few seconds and without thinking about it first, she eased her legs apart too.

I should go find Tayo or whatever he is down in that murky well, she thought, but this does feel awfully good. It's so much more than just heat.

She tipped her head up, blocking the sunlight with one hand over her eyes, and watched her bare breasts rising and falling as she breathed. The green, healing warmth seemed to hold her and caress her, and she laid her head back down, feeling fingers of sunlight touching her in so many places.

She exhaled a deep breath and felt a distant wave of pleasure begin to approach. She knew exactly what it was, but how her sun could do that, she didn't know.

Oh, she thought, could this be like when I'd healed Ben? That made sense when Ben was here, too, but now, just me, lying naked under the sun? That's enough?

The approaching tremor answered her question and before the first wave hit, she sat up, and that seemed to break the spell but not completely.

Oh, what is my home turning into? I'm here to help Tayo, she told herself. Not . . . whatever that was.

She stood and looked in the direction of the well, and she felt the hunger of what she'd just denied herself. She sensed that the wave was still poised to wash over her, but it waited patiently.

The sunlight seemed to be teasing her exposed shoulders and back, promising to finish what it had started if she'd only lie down again. Just lie down in the soft grass. Only for a minute or two.

She dropped to her knees and took a few deep breaths as the hunger simmered inside. She leaned forward to put her hands in the grass, and the sun rewarded her with its healing brightness all over her back.

After letting her head tip toward the ground, draping down her long, straight black hair, she dropped down to her elbows.

Just for a minute or two, she thought. I'm so close already. And the grass is so soft. And the sunlight is so warm, and the way it's touching me, knowing just where and how I like it, it wouldn't take long to—

She snapped her head up and quickly stood.

Oh, why would it ever stop? she asked herself. Why would I ever *want* it to stop? How much time would pass in my life while I'm here, naked in my sun's light, being touched and caressed and giving in to the ecstasy that it could—

Tayo! she yelled to herself. Go heal Tayo! Now!

The sweet hunger persisted as she walked through the tall weeds, feeling them all rubbing against her bare thighs, some softly dragging through between them, fueling the craving, and she soon stood looking down at the gloomy water. As she watched, the vines crisscrossing the surface parted, prying themselves away, leaving an opening not quite large enough for her to pass through.

That's odd, she thought. The last time, something forced me in there. Is that how it works? If I resist, something will drive me in there anyway?

Holding a deep breath in her lungs, and knowing it probably wasn't necessary, Lee extended her hands and did a slow-motion dive through the opening. The branches that had looked coarse and unyielding became soft ropes that restrained her, wrapped around her, seemed reluctant to let go of her, and held her tight enough that she had to wiggle to pass all the way beneath the surface.

She used short, fluttery kicks and sweeps of her arms to descend into the depths. The water had become almost as warm as her sunlight, and she couldn't prevent the smile that appeared. The water, unlike the light, touched her everywhere at once—not just what she'd exposed to the sun. Every feature that could be caressed received constant, willing attention that promised to never end.

She stopped swimming and rested, suspended at some unknown height above the bottom, motionless and immersed in the near darkness, with countless soft, warm hands touching, exploring, fondling . . .

Oh, I can't stay here! Somewhere, in another world, Tayo's arm is burnt to a crisp!

She reached down to resume her travel to the bottom, and her hands contacted the same slowly waving fronds of some plant-like thing at the bottom of the well.

Remembering the alarm she'd felt the last time, Lee mostly knew only the hunger that had been aroused by both sun and water. She felt her heart beating hard and knew that there'd be no resistance this time. Not even close.

She bent enough to find two soft plant arms and coaxed them to wind around her ankles. Knowing at least one of her wrists would have to be last, she wound two more around her waist. Another agreed to coil around her throat, and another held her right wrist.

Without a thought or the slightest hesitation, she swept all around with her free hand until she found a thick, writhing frond, and she slipped it up between her thighs. She fed it though bit by bit until it began to wiggle on its own, squeezing itself as high as it could go along her thighs, then bending over her to join the others in wrapping around her waist.

Oh my, she thought, that one really got itself in tight.

It kept creeping around her waist, a little at a time, all the while tightening, adding to the soft pressure that it applied.

The last frond was easy: she held her left wrist near it, and it looped all around several times.

She felt all of the plant's arms holding her tightly, rubbing against her wet skin everywhere, and the warm water painted pleasure to every part of her that it could touch.

The limbs holding her wrists and ankles began a gentle tug, and Lee didn't resist. They stretched her out as far as she could be stretched, then they pulled just a little bit more. She tested their strength and found them to be unyielding.

Lee wondered if she cared whether or not any of that helped Tayo. She thought that she might never escape the amorous clutches of the unknowable life at the bottom of a lost well in a world that didn't exist.

And when two small vines touched the corners of her mouth, she didn't wait—she opened her mouth and inhaled the deepest, warmest, most watery breath possible.

She held the water inside and felt it warming from being part of her. And when she finally exhaled it toward the plant, the pleasure from the vines holding her tight, stretching her out and suspending her in place, and from the relentless heat of the water kissing her everywhere at once, burned through her as she slipped into a bottomless night.

*   *   *

"Damn, look at that smile!" said Daria. "What the hell is Lee doing?"

"I am even more alarmed at Tayo's arm. How does a burnt arm of a man become unburnt?"

"I don't know, Mom, but look. She's waking up."

Lee tipped her head up and shook back her hair. Before opening her eyes, she let out a deep breath, then turned to the questioning eyes watching her from across the room.

Before speaking to them, she looked down at Tayo's arm and saw that it was healed. Whatever had happened in her home had worked, even though she thought it was the most selfish healing journey she'd ever taken. She smiled at the memory of it.

Then, she quickly looked behind her and sighed at seeing that she still had her black snakeskin boots. The rest of her clothing too.

She heard Daria first.

"Just what the hell is that, Lee?"

"That's . . . kind of hard to explain. It worked, though. Tayo's as good as new."

"I'm thinking maybe you are too," Daria said with a smirk. "That was some wicked smile you had."

"Daria, why must it be called wicked? Yes, it was a smile, but—"

"It's just satisfying to be able to help him," Lee said while brushing back her hair with both hands. "I'm happy that I can help."

"Looked like you were helping yourself," Daria said with a grin.

"Daria, please. Lee, that is astounding what you do. I do not wish to appear ungrateful, but may I ask that you also help Ozzy? He, too, was burned, and he—"

"Mom, he'll be fine. Just his paws got a little singed, that's all."

Anna looked at the chair behind which Ozzy still cowered. He'd stopped whining, but no one had seen him since he'd tried to help Tayo with his torched arm.

"Daria, I think he is badly injured. You would not like your paws burned in that way."

"My paws, huh? Good one, Mom."

Lee said, "Sure, let's give it a try," and smiled at her curiosity about whether she'd take another dive or not.

"Thank you," said Anna. "I will try to bring him."

She reached around the chair to pick him up and though he shrunk back, she was able to grab him and soon stood with him near the couch.

"Tayo's arm is restored, but is he dead? Why does he not move?"

Lee smirked and tapped Tayo's cheek several times.

"Oh, I, uh . . ."

He looked around the room before looking up at Lee. He shook his head slowly and said, "You cannot see, but there is a smile somewhere inside that I can't even ask my face to offer. Lee, that was an indescribable experience."

"Well, your arm is all fixed up. That's the main thing."

She shifted down from his lap to the other end of the couch, crunching and bunching up the plastic cover. Tayo bent his knees upward to give her more room.

"Can you set him on my lap?"

"Yes, Lee. He is a kind soul, and he will not consider a bite."

"I would if my paws were burned up," Daria said, rolling her eyes.

"Yes, well, *you* probably would. Ozzy, just sit for a moment on this lap, okay?"

He didn't answer, so Anna laid him on his side on Lee's thighs.

Lee touched only the top of his head, and he turned it to look up into her eyes. His eyes and Lee's eyes closed at the same time.

"This is some weird shit."

"Daria. Please."

Not even a second had passed before Lee opened her eyes, smiled, and said, "Well, that was easy enough."

Ozzy's eyes opened shortly after that, and he spun his head around to find Anna. When he did, he yipped twice, hopped down, and ran and jumped up into her arms.

"Ozzy, is it true? Your paws are just your paws again?"

He yipped three more times.

Daria inspected each of his paws and said, "Yep, all fixed up. Lee, that's some kind of powerful voodoo you got there."

Lee sighed and said, "It's not voodoo. I can't explain what it is, though, so don't ask me. I tried telling Gabriel about it, and—"

"Who exactly is that Gabriel?" said Anna.

"Oh, I don't really know. Just a good friend of Lin's."

"They're a really weird bunch," said Daria. "I mean, who chops off part of someone's hair like this?"

She held out her hair on each side, showing how much shorter it was on her left side.

"What kind of person can do that?"

"I can't explain her either," said Lee. "Don't even ask."

"I have something that I can ask," said Anna, still looking at Lee.

"Sure, what's that?"

"Would you consider a repair project for Daria's hair? It is only hair, not a burned arm or collection of burned paws, and even though it is not the most urgent—"

"No problem. Yeah, that should be easy enough."

Daria exchanged a long look with her mother and said, "I, um, I'm not so sure that—"

"Daria, it is your only best chance. It will require years to grow again."

"Fine. Alright, Lee, what do I need to do?"

"Nothing."

She patted the plastic next to her, causing Tayo to pull his knees up tighter.

"Just have a seat."

"I . . . um, maybe I should—"

"Daria, it will be okay. Go on. Sit. Ozzy has done it too."

Daria sat beside Lee, who took one of her hands.

"Oh, Hell, here we—"

Daria slumped over into Tayo's shins, her head resting against his knees, and Lee's head tipped forward, her black hair hanging down on each side of her face.

Lee went home. With Daria.

*　*　*

She felt the sunlight first. It warmed her through her clothes, and she waited, knowing that she stood in her grassy meadow, with a clear blue sky above that held a sun that never moved.

A quick memory of the well and all of its tantalizing sensations raced through her, followed quickly by an almost overpowering desire to tear at her clothing, to strip naked, and lie under the light that did so much more than heal.

But she felt a tiny hand in hers, and she looked down at a girl younger than her daughter. She could see mostly the top of her head, which carried a thick, almost buoyant growth of rich black hair that hung far down her back.

She wore a simple white dress, and Lee tipped her head enough to see that she was barefoot, her toes wiggling in the soft grass.

What drew the most attention from Lee was the softly, calmly flapping wings of a butterfly that boasted every shade of the rainbow. She couldn't be sure, but it seemed that the graceful insect had noticed her, and it, too, seemed content in the light from her sun.

Oh, this should be the easiest one yet, she thought. Even easier than that dog, who only needed to fetch a stick. Running through the tall grass had cooled his paws, and the odd smoke that had been spiraling in random directions from each of them had been quenched.

Lee knew that she needed only to nudge that beautiful bug along, convince it to exercise those magnificent wings, and take to the air. She wondered if she could resist following it if it were to fly in the direction of her well.

Before reaching any conclusion about that, she felt the hairs on her neck point straight out as if they dared not encroach on each other. Or perhaps they were pointing at the Hunter, telling Lee of its presence so that she could flee?

I'd better just take care of that butterfly and return, she thought, and she looked down at the young girl. She watched with the feeling of an approaching scream as the girl began turning her head to look behind them.

No, don't even look! Lee wanted to say.

She watched the girl yank her hand free and spin herself around to face the Hunter. She looked up at Lee and smiled—the cheerful, carefree smile of a child playing a fun, harmless game.

When Lee reached for her shoulder, intending to turn her away from the Hunter, to not even allow her to look in that direction, the girl's face became a ghastly, menacing mask with razor teeth that snapped viciously from a gaping mouth that left little room on her face for any other features. Lee jerked her hand to safety just in time, and the girl's pleasant smile returned—only youthful innocence eager to explore Lee's home.

That didn't just happen, did it? Lee said to herself.

She tried again, and the ferocious jaws, like a sprung steel trap, closed with a heavy metallic clunk, the eyes fiery and glaring up at her.

What is this? Lee thought. Why is she so determined to go to that thing? Can't she see how dangerous it is?

With her heart pounding and her neck hair still stiff, sounding the alarm, Lee waited until the sweet version of the child's face had returned. Then, she waited another moment longer—until the girl again focused her sight on what lurked in the tall weeds.

Knowing that it might be her last chance, Lee cautiously reached out one finger and prompted the graceful wings to take the butterfly up into the sky.

Well, good, thought Lee. Problem solved. I'd sure like to strip naked for that sun now, or dive into that well, dripping with hot sex, or—

The girl had started a determined walk toward the weeds and whatever waited within. Lee fought to turn her head, not wanting to and afraid to, but she couldn't spin around to watch the girl traipsing toward her own certain destruction.

I can't help her! she thought. My only hope is to return before this version of Daria is taken by that thing!

As her heart threatened to pound its way out of her chest, Lee returned to her life.

Chapter 25 – Gonna Leave A Stain

Lee opened her eyes and met Anna's hopeful stare. She let go of Daria's hand, seeing that she was still asleep, her hair again the desired length and leaning into Tayo, who only watched them all quietly. A glance across the room showed her that her own daughter gazed back calmly, not moving at all.

Lee shook her head and said to Anna, "It worked, but that was, um, I mean, she—"

Anna smiled at Daria and said to Lee, "You were very successful! I still do not say that hair is the important thing, but it is good that you fixed it. Thank you, Lee."

"Sure. Not a problem. But she, um, she seemed to want to . . ."

"Yes?"

"Nothing."

She shook Daria, who sat up quickly and looked all around the room, her eyes stretched open wide.

"What the hell was that? I mean, all I felt was like I had a dream, and now I can't remember it. I only remember feeling like I was starving."

She reached and felt her hair, causing her serious face to yield to a smile.

"Wow. You sure that's not voodoo? Because what else could—"

"Daria. She has already stated that it is not that. You might consider offering a thank you or two."

She turned to Lee and said, "Thanks. Really, that's pretty cool."

"You don't remember anything?" said Lee.

"Nope. Why?"

"Oh, um, it was just interesting, that's all. You said you felt hungry?"

"Yeah, but I don't remember what for. Glad my hair's fixed, though."

Daria rose from the couch and reclaimed the chair across the room.

"Hey," she said to Alessa, who sat close by, leaning against the wall, "like mother like daughter? Maybe you can do something like that too?"

"Something like that," said the girl, who froze with her eyes focused on Daria.

"Geez," Daria said, with her eyebrows held high, and looked away.

"We are all repaired, thanks to Lee," Tayo said after relaxing his legs more. "If I could scrape the remaining symbols from under my skin and—"

"Ew. Gross," said Daria.

"—and if no more mice appear, there would be only one major obstacle before me."

"That is why you need Benson's assistance?" said Anna.

Daria smirked and said, "He's dead, Mom. Remember?"

"Well, Daria, so I have been told. Still, if a dead man,"—she paused to grin at Daria before turning back to Tayo—"can help you as you have asked, then maybe I can finally go. Daria too. And Ozzy."

"Mom, you know that Lin will find us and kill us. Hell, she probably will anyway. But we have a better chance of surviving if we don't piss her off."

"You seem to like aggravating that woman, Daria. Someday, you will truly get us all slaughtered."

Daria sneered and shook her head. Tayo's phone rang. He looked at the caller and put the phone back in his pocket.

"Jenny?" said Anna.

"Yes. I will return her call soon. Right now, we should all—"

A hard kick to Tayo's front door caused it to swing in wildly, the knob banging into the nearby closet door. A man in a black overcoat, with a wide-brimmed black hat, stood with an equally black pistol in his hand. He began to raise it, with his passionless eyes fixed on Tayo.

* * *

Everyone in the room froze with their eyes locked on the gun as he lifted it up. His thin lips curled into a tight smile, but his eyes were cold and pointed intently on his first target.

Before he could squeeze off a shot, a sound like a pipe being jammed into wet earth was followed by the point of a blade jutting out of his chest, sending out a sloppy red spray. His smile never lessened as he stood in silence, looked down at what had pierced his beating heart, then fell forward, embedding the point in Tayo's wood floor with a solid clunk, his gun clattering to the side.

All eyes looked up from the body to see Benson, standing with his hands on his hips. He looked first at Anna, then his eyes rested on Daria.

"Get a photo of *that*," he said and nodded with a calm grin.

* * *

"It's the dead guy," Daria said as she arose from the chair. "Perfect timing, dead guy."

He looked at Tayo and said, "You wanted help? There you go."

Daria stood over the corpse and said, "That's gonna leave a stain."

She turned back to Tayo with a grin, but he only stared at the body on the floor.

"I can't fix that," said Lee.

"No one wants you to," said Tayo. "He was sent to kill me and since you were here, he would have killed you as well."

"Got himself killed instead. Nice how that worked out," said Daria.

"Daria, I am relieved that we were not shot to pieces, but killing is not to be celebrated."

"Oh, I don't know," said Benson. "Sometimes 'dead' is good."

Daria grinned and winked at her mother.

"Why was he coming to kill you?" said Lee.

He pointed over his shoulder and said, "Because of whatever that is under my skin. Please, don't request further explanation. My focus must now be on the removal of another body."

"Another?" said Lee. "What are you—"

"He's not the first."

"Tayo, you have already killed another man?"

"Yes. I'm not proud of that, Anna. I had no intention of revealing that fact to anyone."

"Revealing? You should be bragging," said Daria. "Way to go, Tayo."

"Daria. Please. It should not be a source of pride."

"Should have called me," said Daria. "I could photographed the whole thing for you. A scrapbook from Hell."

She turned to smile at Benson, and he pointed at her and nodded.

"Still, the body must be removed," said Tayo. "The next trash day isn't until—"

"Don't sweat it," said Benson. "I'll dump it."

"Then, I'm truly in your debt," said Tayo. "This is more calamity than we ever faced working for The Shield."

"Yep," said Benson. "But we were sometimes shooting at each other then."

"Oh, and good thing Daria missed," said Anna.

Benson scoffed while looking at Anna and said, "Right. Yep."

Lee took careful steps toward Alessa, keeping her eyes on the corpse bleeding onto the floor. She sat beside her and took her hand.

"Lessa, baby, try not to worry about this, alright? Things are just—"

"It's okay, Mom. People live. People die. Many live good lives. Some don't."

Lee stared at her. From across the room, near the man with a knife through his heart, Daria scoffed out loud and shook her head.

"Benson, I don't mean to seem ungrateful or unduly commanding, but if your offer to remove the intruder is still good, perhaps sooner is better than later?"

"Yep. The longer we wait, the more to mop up."

He reached down with both hands and grabbed the man's waist. He pulled and found that the knife wouldn't easily leave the floor. He jerked the body, unsticking the blade, spun it around, and lifted it up and over one shoulder. Then, he squatted down and retrieved the gun.

"Hey," said Daria, "isn't that knife—"

"Yep. Don't sweat it."

Daria grinned, took out her phone, and pointed the camera.

"Hey, hold that a second."

She snapped a couple of photos while Benson offered a smile.

"Mom, get in there too."

"Daria, no. This is not something to commemorate."

"The Hell it isn't. You'd rather Tayo was dead? And the rest of us too?"

Anna stared at her daughter, shaking her head and squinting, then she walked over to stand near Benson.

"Fine."

"Closer," said Daria.

"Daria . . ."

"Come on, we don't have all day. Snuggle up."

Anna moved in to stand just in front of Benson and with his free arm, he hugged her and pulled her in close.

While pointing her camera, Daria said, "Kiss the dead guy, Mom."

Anna grinned and said, "Which one?"

With the shutter sounding, Daria said, "Good one."

She rotated her phone and took a few more.

"Perfect," Daria said as she switched off her phone.

"Not quite," Benson said with a grin at Daria. "Good enough for now, though."

"Hell, yeah," said Daria.

* * *

Benson closed the door behind him after he'd stepped out onto the porch, the dead assassin still dripping and slung over his shoulder. Tayo let out a long, deep breath.

"I am living an interesting life."

"Do you believe that is the last of that type that will visit you, Tayo?"

"I hope so, Anna. As long as I don't get any more—"

His phone rang in his pocket, and before he took it out, he looked at all the staring faces in the room. Even Ozzy's.

"You gotta at least look," said Daria.

He got out his phone and displayed a big smile.

"Ah, it's only Jenny."

"You're not taking her call?" Daria said, shaking her head. "Don't you want something normal in your life?"

"Yes, but I don't wish for all of this abnormality to spill into my relationship with her. This is just too much for me to contain right now."

"I understand that, Tayo," said Anna. "I am not containing things too well myself."

"At least, you posed for some hot photos, Mom," Daria said, grinning at her.

"Hot? Anyway, I was coerced into that. That is not the type of photo shoot I wish to ever participate with."

"Yep, I know. We'll get you a better scene."

"Well," said Lee, "I'm hungry."

"You always are, Mom."

"Yeah, Lessa, I know but especially after healing someone."

"Oh, and you just healed three individuals," said Anna. "Tayo, Ozzy, and even Daria's hair."

"Yep. Kind of exhausting. Lessa, you coming? It's a short walk."

They got up and reached for their coats.

"Get some donuts too," said Daria. "Benson's always looking for sweet things."

She turned to grin at her mother, who quickly looked down at the floor, then at Tayo.

"Tayo," said Anna, "are you hungry as well?"

She turned to Lee.

"Perhaps we can ask for extra food to be brought back?"

Lee didn't wait for Tayo to answer.

"We'll get a lot. Bags full of stuff."

"And sweets."

"Daria, that cannot be the most necessary thing at this time."

"Oh, that Benson. We can't really tell him no, can we?"

"You might be right," said Anna.

"Because he saved our lives?"

"Yes, Daria. There is that."

Lee and Alessa left, a blast of cold Baltimore air washing in before Lee pulled the door shut.

* * *

"That kid's creepy," said Daria.

"Well, that is probably true, but her mother does astounding things. And she brought a card for Tayo. You see, Daria?"

Daria looked where her mother pointed and saw the card standing near the wall, where Alessa had been sitting.

"Alright, I guess she'd kind of sweet too. Hey, Tayo, your arm looks pretty good again."

How do I explain that the memory of burning flesh does not heal so easily?

"Yes," he said, looking at his arm as he held it up. "It was horribly burnt."

"Kind of tiring, I bet."

"Yes, Daria. Burning, healing, almost being murdered, seeing a murderer murdered, wanting mostly that his bloody corpse is taken away quickly, and—"

"Alright," said Daria with a roll of her eyes, "we get it. Why don't you rest, and Mom and I will get some coffee going."

"Thank you. Yes, that's probably more wise than the other option."

"Shit," Daria said while turning to her mother. "We should have added that to the shopping list."

"Well, Daria, we still have a full bottle."

"Good. Forget the coffee, then. Tayo, take a nap. Mom and I are having a drink."

She took Anna's hand and led her into the kitchen while Tayo laid an arm over his eyes, still lying on the couch.

* * *

Anna dropped onto a seat at the table, and Daria rattled through the cabinets for two clean glasses. She set them on the table while Anna unscrewed the cap, then poured for each.

After each had consumed half a glass, Daria said, "Mom, I gotta tell you something."

"As do I."

"Really? Alright, you first, then."

"Well, okay. It is about Benson."

"He's dead. I know," she said with a big grin.

Anna returned the smile and said, "For a dead person, he is surprisingly . . . vigorous."

"I know. The way he just killed that guy. That was—"

"No, Daria, that is not what I mean."

She held her daughter's gaze.

"Wait a minute. You and him? You two have already—"

"I could not say no, Daria. He seemed to take control of me. It was strangely similar to Wolfe. He was very convincing as well."

"You and Wolfe too? You really get around, don't you, Mom? Did The Shield hand out coupons for a good time with Anna?"

"Yes, well, I did not seek any of it. Benson seemed to have a plan, and my choice in the matter never arrived."

"He is kind of persuasive, isn't he?"

"Yes. And cold."

"He's really cold. Alright, how was it?"

"Daria! I cannot speak of such things!"

"Yeah, I didn't think you would."

"So, tell me: what did you wish to discuss?"

Daria took a long sip and kept the glass up to her lips, watching her mother over it. Anna waited patiently. Daria set down the empty glass.

She covered her mouth as she stifled a soft belch and said, "Me too."

"You too, what?"

Daria only grinned back at her.

"Oh, you cannot mean that, Daria! You and Benson too?"

She shook her head, kept grinning, and said, "Can't tell him no. Why is that? He's kind of scary, but he sure gets his way."

"Well, if it was only that one time, then that was not—"

"Nope. Not just one time, Mom. How about you?"

"It was only once."

She looked at the ceiling and said again, "Only that one time—"

"Oh, you want more, though, don't you?"

She looked down at her daughter, her serious expression changing to a smile, and said, "Well, I do give that some thought. Yes, he is odd and dangerous."

"Maybe that's why we like it, Mom?"

Anna snatched up the vodka and poured into both glasses.

"There is a certain attraction to that, yes. Our world is insane, Daria. We might as well be open about things."

She held up her glass. Daria looked at it, smiled at her, and clinked hers to it.

"Yep. I'll start. He's had this weird thing about playing with knives while we, um, you know."

"Really, a knife is involved?"

"Yep. The one he's been killing people with too."

"That is somewhat scary."

"Did he do that with you?"

"No, no knife was included. Did he talk about stabbing you, Daria?"

"No, he wanted me to stab him! Can you imagine that? He said it would be fine because he's already dead."

Anna laughed once and said, "Perhaps he is, Daria. You shot him, remember?"

"Yeah, and I don't miss."

"So, it might be because of the drinking I have just done, but I think I can summarize: we are both sleeping with a dead man?"

"How about that, Mom? We do live interesting lives."

Anna grinned, then lifted her glass and finished it. She raised a hand to her mouth as she hiccupped.

She held her daughter's gaze and blurted out, "He tied me up."

Daria grinned and shook her head.

"Alright, Mom, that's pretty good! How was it?"

"Well, there was talk about me not being such a boss anymore. Daria, I surely was not. I was secured to a chair."

"Mom, that's so kinky. I'm proud of you."

"Well, I am a bit older than you, and I deserve to be the kinkier of us two."

"Think again. He made me go by a different name."

Anna squinted, looking at her empty glass, then she looked up and said, "And what name was that?"

Daria got a big smile and said, "Anna. I was Anna."

Anna only stared, and Daria raised her eyebrows a couple of times.

"One time, I even wore your skirt and heels. Damn, that was fun."

Anna blew out a deep breath, reached for the bottle, and said, "What is happening to us, Daria? How does he have such control over us?"

"I don't know. Maybe because he's dead?"

Anna shook her head slowly and said, "It is good with a dead man, is it not?"

"Oh yeah, Mom. Yep. Maybe it *is* the vodka, but it's kind of strange for us to be sharing all this, isn't it?"

"Well, Daria, we are kind of like a team, are we not?"

Daria grinned, accepted her refilled glass, and said, "Yep."

She held her glass up and when Anna clinked hers into it, she said, "To teamwork."

And while sipping her drink, she watched closely as her mother nodded in agreement.

Chapter 26 – Next Time

Anna and Daria looked toward Tayo's living room when they heard the front door open. They got up and saw Lee and Alessa step inside, arms full of plastic and paper bags, and shut the door.

Alessa stomped snow off of her boots, and Daria rushed over to help with all that they'd brought back.

"Hey, thanks. We can't live on vodka as much as I'd like to try."

Lee smiled and said, "I know. I bought a few more bottles."

"Nice. Thanks. Tayo would thank you, too, but he's—"

"He's able to thank you himself," Tayo said, still lying on the couch. "I don't plan to ingest alcohol exclusively, though, so I hope some of those bags contain food."

"All kinds of stuff," said Lee.

"Donuts too," Alessa said as she unbuttoned her coat and kicked off her boots.

Anna helped with the bags, and she and Daria brought them all into the kitchen. Lee walked over to Tayo and said, "Still feel alright?"

"I'm definitely healed, but Lee . . . I'm still a damaged man. I can't even attempt to hide that fact."

"I don't know what to do about that."

"I know, Lee. You're doing enough. If you hadn't healed the physical damage, I would be confronted with that, still, and able only to push aside the trauma for a later time. Thank you again."

She took the chair, and Ozzy jumped up onto her lap.

"You're welcome. It's not over, is it?"

"It is certainly not. I should find encouragement in the mouse's absence, but that offers little—"

"Mouse?" said Alessa. "I like that you call it a mouse."

Tayo focused on the child and said, "You know that I don't refer to an actual mouse?"

Alessa nodded.

"It's good to call it that, though."

He scratched his head, then turned to Lee, who only shrugged.

"Lee, before the next onslaught, if you brought back any hamburgers and fries, then I would—"

"They're going fast!" Daria said from the kitchen, talking with her mouth full.

Lee grinned at Tayo, and he only sighed in return, his eyes weary, so she lost her smile.

"I'll get you some. Just rest."

* * *

In the kitchen, Lee found Anna and Daria seated at the table, which was covered in bags, some full and others being emptied, with a half-empty bottle nestled in the middle.

"Any burgers left?"

Daria snorted and said, "Only because we couldn't find them all!"

"Daria, we do not really eat that much."

"When I'm drinking, Mom? Think again."

"I'll just grab some for Tayo, then," said Lee, and she looked through the bags, found one that she liked, and took it out of the room.

They both watched Lee leave the kitchen, her faded jeans tight over every solid curve, and her snakeskin boots thumping confidently on the linoleum.

Daria whispered, "I wonder if Benson would like a shot at that?"

Anna whispered back, "Oh, I do not know. She is somehow more frightening than him."

Daria snickered and said, "She could beat the shit out of him and heal him, all while they're having sex."

"That would be an event to watch."

Daria stared and said, "You'd like to watch that?"

"No, I am just talking while full of vodka."

"Right. Nice to have that to blame for stuff. Anyway, it looked like Lee was having sex with Tayo when she was healing him. You remember that?"

"It did look that way. Hey, Lee healed you too. Do you remember whether . . . if you—"

"No, I don't remember anything. She might have had some kind of sex with me, though. Who would know?"

"Well, Daria, if I get some injury from all of this, which is then healed by Lee, then maybe I will—"

"Mom, you sound kind of eager. You want to see if Lee takes advantage of you, don't you?"

"I did not say that, Daria."

"I'd like to watch *that.*"

Anna stared.

"Take some pictures too."

Anna scoffed and said, "These are just odd times. You do not remember anything, so we could not compare notes anyway."

"Nope. Not for that. For Benson, though?"

She grinned and reached out her glass, and Anna met it with hers.

∗　∗　∗

"Here, Tayo," Lee said and set a bag on his lap. "Two burgers and some fries. That'll help."

"Thank you. Yes, it's a big help."

Until the mouse returns, sent forth by haunted symbols lodged under my skin. Yes, until that revisits me with a new, unexpected form of annihilation, I'll be happy with a burger. And fries.

He took out the food and got started, Lee again relaxing in the chair, with Ozzy on her lap and Alessa seated on the floor.

Tayo looked around while chewing and said, "None for you?"

"We ate on the way back."

270

"Mom eats quickly," said Alessa. "Donuts too. A lot of them."

Tayo nodded, his cheeks packed, and said, "Seems to work for her. It's getting late, and if you two wish to stay, you are most welcome."

"You already have a full house, Tayo. Alessa and I can just—"

From the doorway to the kitchen, Anna said, "We should probably return to our apartment, Daria and I. Ozzy too."

"I regret that I don't have more room," said Tayo.

"No, it's fine," said Daria, wiping at her lips with a napkin. "We can't go too far anyway because—"

"Like to Russia," Anna said, then covered a soft hiccup.

"Yeah, she's right. Because Lin will destroy us."

"Call if you need us, Tayo. As much as we wish to flee forever, we also would like you free of your monsters."

"Yep. Like Mom said."

Daria began putting on her coat, passing a full bottle from one hand to the other. Anna got ready, too, and they stopped at the door.

"Really, Tayo," said Anna, "just call if—"

Daria's phone jangled in her pocket, and she took it out and grinned. Anna looked over, shaking her head.

"Do not tell me."

"Yep."

Anna turned back to Tayo and said, "We will now say goodbye."

Lee and Tayo waved, and Alessa looked like a photo.

"Creepy, Mom," Daria whispered.

"Yes, well, we are going. Goodbye."

They left and shut the door behind them.

*　*　*

"I'm still kind of tired from healing you, Tayo. Alessa and I should probably just get some sleep. Will you be alright out here? Or are you going to bed?"

"I'll stay here for a while, then go to bed. Please, take the guest room. Will that be adequate for you both?"

271

"It'll be fine. If anything happens, just call me."

"Unless my face is on fire. Or if my head has been removed and placed on a table. Or—"

"Tayo," said Lee, "maybe it'll give you a break. Maybe it gets tired too?"

She looked at his solemn face, with no trace of a smile, as he said, "Yes, that's my goal: for it to expend its energy on wrecking me in creative ways."

Lee shook her head and said, "I know it's not pleasant. Lin and Gabriel will figure something out. I know they will. Just hang in there the best you can."

"I will. Thank you, Lee."

They left the room, and Tayo again laid his arm to cover his eyes. He listened to the quiet walls, waited for the axe to strike his back, and tried to focus only on his breathing.

* * *

On the short drive back to Anna's and Daria's apartment, in another section of Baltimore, Anna said, "Okay, so what did he say this time?"

Daria snorted once and said, "Well, for one thing, he called me Anna."

Anna blew out a long breath and said, "That is certainly a strange practice. What else?"

"Oh, nothing important."

They turned a corner and saw Benson's car idling near their apartment.

"Oh, just that," Daria said, pointing through the windshield. "He wants to stay at our place tonight."

"You cannot be serious, Daria. He has his own apartment, does he not?"

"Uh, yeah, but guess where he dumped that dead guy?"

Anna shook her head and said, "Well, I would not want to spend the night with a dead guy either."

"Oh, except for Benson, right? Because, you know, he's dead too."

"I do not know if it is such a good idea, Daria."

"Hey, cheer up, Mom. Maybe he brought your favorite chair with him."

Anna hit the brakes, put it in park, and turned to Daria with a frown. Daria continued to grin at her until she started smiling herself.

"Well, Daria,"—Daria raised her eyebrows up and listened—"we have chairs too."

Daria slapped her mom's leg and said, "Now, you're talking."

"I was making a joke."

"Sure, Mom. Uh-huh."

* * *

Tayo's head snapped to the left when he heard a soft scratch from inside the wall behind his couch. He held his breath and waited. His home was again silent, and he knew that Lee and Alessa had likely fallen asleep.

It felt like a pin. Just a tiny point at a vulnerable place on his back that he couldn't reach.

I can ignore the point of a needle. I've felt so much worse.

It became a blade, a length of it pressing into him, opening, he knew, a deep gash.

Speaking of only a sharp point wasn't an invitation for an increase in aggression!

The axe plunged in all at once, and Tayo lost any chance of entertaining himself with his own conversations. All he could do was lie in complete silence, a heavy blade cleaving through skin, muscle, then bone, until he felt sure that he'd soon see it erupt from his chest.

A soft squeak came from the wall, and the knife withdrew, leaving him soaked with sweat, taking choppy breaths and again able to speak internally.

I'm no longer joking. Lin. Or Gabriel. If you can hurry, you'd preserve what scant sanity remains.

* * *

Just as Anna was unlocking the door to their apartment, Benson came up from behind.

"Oh, look who's here," said Daria.

"Hello, Benson. Daria has told me that your apartment is, um, occupied?"

"Hey, girls. Yep. I even turned down the heat for him."

Daria grinned and said, "Mom will turn up the heat here, won't you, Mom?"

"Yes, of course, Daria. Because Benson is—"

"Dead. Yep, I'm dead. Look, get that door open already, alright?"

"Oh, I am sorry. I will blame my lack of focus on the vodka."

"We drank a lot," Daria said with a smile. "We had a nice chat too."

"Huh. All I did was transport a corpse."

Inside, Benson closed and locked the door. Anna walked right over to the thermostat and when she tapped on the display, the furnace started up.

"Good. Thanks."

"Take your coat?" said Daria.

"Not yet."

"Still cold?" said Anna.

He looked her in the eye and said, "All over."

She looked quickly at her daughter, who nodded her head and grinned.

"Yes, well, it is late, and I am kind of drunk. If you do not mind, I will take a shower."

Daria held up the bottle and said, "Another drink for me, then I'm done for the day."

Benson said, "I'll take the couch. Thanks again."

"Well, you are most welcome, Benson. Have a good night."

"I plan to," he said, and Anna glanced at her daughter, who was still grinning.

She turned and left for the bathroom and after closing the door, she leaned her back against it for a moment. Then, she turned on the hot spray and began to undress.

* * *

Daria uncapped the bottle, sat next to Benson on the couch, and took a drink. She passed it to him, and he chugged a few times.

"She's Anna. You're Anna. Pretty cool, huh?"

"Yes, I am sure that I am Anna."

"Now's a good time."

"For what?"

"Raid your mom's lingerie. Go find something lacy."

Daria stood up immediately, took a big sip, and set the bottle on an end table.

"I am Anna, and I like to wear pretty things."

He worked at his coat, looking up at her with a steady gaze.

"You might like stabbing a guy the most."

Daria didn't smile. She only looked down at him.

"Right at that moment."

She took a deep breath, then let it out.

"Even better when dressed sexy. What a contrast, huh?"

She shook her head slowly.

"You are what is known as a pervert, Mr. Benson. We can discuss that at a later time."

He tipped his head, still looking her in the eye.

"You can wait for me in my daughter's bedroom. I must go find some of my silky, lacy clothing designed solely for entertainment."

"You're more of an Anna than Anna. Go."

* * *

Anna finished her shower, which she'd turned up hotter than usual, and blotted herself dry in the steamy room. She tiptoed naked across the floor and put her ear against the door. She heard nothing.

It is not fair, she thought. It should be my turn. Oh, but maybe Daria has only fallen asleep, and Benson is waiting for me?

She leaned away and looked at the thin nightshirt that she always kept there. With a faint smile, she took it down and slipped it on, feeling it clinging to her hot, moist skin.

After a glance at her clothing off to the side, she didn't even give it any thought: she stepped into her heels, remembering Benson's comments after he'd stripped her in his apartment. He'd liked her in heels.

No, that is not correct, she thought. He expects me to wear heels for him.

A quick wipe with a towel cleared a patch of the mirror, and she brushed her hair, her open shirt inviting her to give them a glance.

She finished, fastened only a few of the buttons, all of them below her breasts, and imagined walking into the living room to see Benson waiting on the couch for her.

*　*　*

And what of Anna and Daria? Can they be affected by what has infected me? I don't even know where they live—is their home within this thing's range?

Still wet with sweat, Tayo jerked his head up to listen until he realized that it was likely Lee that was trying to be quiet, walking around in his kitchen. He heard a donut box rattle open, then silence, and he could imagine the sight of her stuffing in one after another.

And could this thing take Lee? That would be terrible—I would surely be obliterated already without her assistance.

He heard the box closed and the same soft footsteps leading back to the spare bedroom.

No, I don't think Lee can be affected. Probably not that daughter of hers either. That's a strange type of child. I suspect that no normal laws apply to either of them.

The bedroom door closed gently, and Tayo let out a deep breath. *Daria was already taken once. This thing knows her. It chose her. Why her? Did that cause some lingering effect on her?*

* * *

Daria opened her bedroom door, stepped inside, trying to not make too much noise with her heels, and closed the door behind her. She'd looked first at Anna's bathroom and saw that the door was still closed, but the shower had stopped.

She turned and saw that Benson had switched on a dim lamp and lay waiting on the bed.

"Anna. Tell me what you want."

Daria walked over to the bed, allowing the heels to strike the hardwood floor, and stood close, looking down on him. He'd taken off his shirt and shoes, and his arms were crossed behind his head on a stack of pillows.

Daria smirked and said, "Give Anna the knife first, and she will tell you exactly what she wants."

He grinned and reached behind the pillow, withdrawing a polished blade that glinted as he extended it out toward her, handle first.

She took it in her right hand and rubbed the flat of the blade across her left arm while staring into his eyes. She held it straight up, pressed between her breasts, which were barely covered by sheer fabric, and she slid it down over each one several times.

Seeing that Benson was mostly watching the knife touching her in places that he liked, she moved it to her left and dragged the flat side of it across her throat, feeling her heart pounding inside her chest.

"Anna likes playing with sharp things. So deadly. So dangerous."

"Have you always been like that?"

"No. Only recently has Anna become a sex-starved, perverted Russian woman that loves most to have sex with a dead man."

Benson smiled and said, "You have a way with words. Good, Anna. Did you bring your phone in the room?"

She tipped her head toward the nightstand and said, "It is there."

"You know why."

"Yes. We might need to call someone to join us."

"Good. I'm cold. Do you like when things are cold?"

Daria bit her lip and nodded, and he said, "Like I always say, have a seat."

She climbed onto the bed, swung a leg over him, and sat on his legs. She poked at his belt buckle with the knife point, eventually undoing it. He laughed and finished for her, pulling everything down. She rose up long enough for him to throw it all to the floor.

Still looking him in the eye, she kicked back one leg, then the other, and lay down over his legs and used both hands. One held the knife.

"That would make a good photo," he said.

She nodded and said, "You like when Anna poses? Anna likes to pose for pictures."

"Yep. Just need that photographer, don't we?"

Daria nodded, her eyes big and staring at him intently.

"Hot out of the shower would be nice."

Daria grinned.

*　*　*

Anna carefully opened her door and crept out to peek into the living room. She found it empty, so she leaned back to look down the hall and saw that her daughter's door was closed.

She began fumbling with the next button up and glanced into the living room again.

With the button lined up with its hole, she stopped and tipped her head back to look down the hall again.

Looking into the empty living room again, where a bottle and glass waited, she fidgeted slowly with the button.

After drawing in a deep breath, she looked down at what she was trying to fasten, saw that the thin cloth of her nightshirt kept no secrets, and gave up on the button as she let her breath out slowly.

She turned her back on the deserted room, facing whatever might be waiting in Daria's room, and gave up on the button. A faint smile appeared as she unfastened the next one down and spread the fabric apart, showing more of her breasts.

Oh, they are in there, are they not? Yes, but I should go to bed and leave them be.

Instead, she walked as quietly as she could toward the door but from the alcohol still circulating, she hadn't controlled her heels as well as she would have liked.

I do hear that something is going on in there already.

She heard faint voices and when she placed her ear to the thin door, she found that she could understand every word being said.

* * *

"Oh, hear that?" said Benson. "Guess who."

Daria grinned and said, "Our photographer."

They wish me to photograph them? Would I agree to that?

"She's right outside that door. Bet she's wearing something nice too."

"She likes wearing sexy things. She is hot from her shower."

"Yep, she sure is."

Anna held her breath, her heart pounding.

"She's going to join us any second now," said Benson. "Give her an interesting first view."

"Why would I do that?"

"Because you want to, Anna."

"I believe you are correct."

Daria grinned and reached back with her knife hand, pulling on her lacy garment until it was up around her waist, revealing only skin from there to her heels. Each of her knees rested beside his legs on the soft blanket. She squirmed them slowly, causing her hips to shift from side to side.

"There. That is a special sight for her eyes," said Daria. "I am so close to having actual sex with a dead man in my bed."

What kind of sight? What special sight for me to see?

"Yep. You can do better, though. Go on."

"Yes, Anna can."

She's calling herself my name? They are really doing that game?

She shifted forward, still looking into his eyes.

"Yep. Like that," he said.

He twirled her thick black hair around one finger.

"Ooh . . . it is so cold."

What is cold? And what is Daria doing?

"Cold is good for you. Go on. It'll be good for your mother to see."

"Yes, it will."

"Ah, that's it. Good, Anna."

I am certainly curious and wish to see. Yes, I might take photos if only I were in there too.

"Soon, I'll have two Annas in this bed," said Benson. "Not bad for a dead man."

Daria stopped what she was doing and said, "You can even tie her wrists one more time. She would like that. Especially when she is dressed like we know she is."

"I know she would. I could tell. And yeah, now's a perfect time."

Daria! You should not be telling him those things. I did like it, though. Is that what would happen to me in there? What more after that?

She turned and leaned her back against the door. Both hands found her thighs below the short hem. She sighed deeply as she touched her soft skin.

"I bet she's listening outside the door. Dressed all sexy and wanting sex."

"With a dead guy."

"That makes two of you."

"Teamwork. We do work as a team in many activities."

"Yep. That's the best. Teamwork for one more thing would be good."

Daria giggled softly.

Anna closed her eyes and let her imagination go. She knew that she was probably bumping the door softly, but she thought it couldn't possibly matter. Maybe it would be better if Benson took away her choice and dragged her into the room.

I will be just one more Anna for the dead man.

"Alright, Anna, time to have a seat. Come on."

She heard springs compressing and blankets rustling, then her daughter sighing deeply. Anna's hands stayed where they wanted to be.

"There you go," said Benson. "Nice and cold. Take that off."

She heard more rustling.

"How is that? They are bared for your enjoyment."

Now, my daughter is naked for him? Only on the other side of this door?

"That's a sight. Play with the knife some more."

Daria took turns bouncing her breasts up with the back side of the blade, then she took the handle in both hands and rested the point above Benson's heart.

What can they be doing with a knife? I wish to see!

"Best time for that photo—when you're at your peak and you plunge it in."

"Mm-hmm . . ."

"You know you'd like it."

Daria only sighed deeply and looked at the sharp point.

Then, Anna heard him say, in a louder voice, "Perfect time for a few photographs."

Anna held her breath. Even her hands stopped moving.

Daria giggled softly.

Still in a louder voice, he said, "Not just photos—every other perverted thing I can think of. Bet she'd like watching all of it."

"Watching? How about doing? Teamwork."

Anna let her hands continue.

Oh my, I believe I would!

With her heart racing, Anna grabbed the doorknob with only one hand, causing a soft rattle, and she stopped herself and listened.

Benson held a finger to his lips, then Daria turned enough to look at the door. They both waited.

No, I cannot do this, though I feel compelled.

"I bet she's curious," Benson said.

No, I am far past just curiosity. There is a hunger now.

She shook her head, smoothed down her shirt, and took the most quiet, careful steps that she could to her bedroom. Inside, she kicked off her heels, closed the door, and got into bed.

She couldn't hear them anymore, but her imagination didn't care. It spun every imaginable activity, and when she thought that some of those possibilities should shock her, things that she knew would be demanded of her in that room but that she should never even consider, she found that they didn't. They didn't bother her one bit.

Lying in a roasting room, wet with sweat, the words, "Next time," spoken in Benson's voice, teased and tormented her in an endless loop.

Chapter 27 – Offering Me Everything

"No, it's alright, Lessa," Lee said while rubbing her eyes. "He's awake. Come on in."

Alessa had peeked around the corner and saw her mother in the living room chair, her head tipped back and eyes closed again. Tayo still lay on the couch, with his left arm covering his eyes.

"I can bring you some donuts, Mom."

"Already had a pile of them, Lessa. Thanks, though."

"I was joking anyway. I saw that you left only one."

"For you, yeah. Did you eat it?"

"Of course, Mom."

She walked in, said hi to Tayo, and took her spot on the floor. He'd barely responded and when she looked at her mother, Lee only shrugged and raised her eyebrows. Alessa nodded but didn't say anything. Lee tipped her head back again.

*　*　*

Outside Anna's apartment, Daria said to Benson, "So, you coming back to Tayo's place? If you do, bring that knife."

Anna caught her breath and bit her lip.

"No, I have some things to take care of. Gotta make a phone call too."

"Oh, Benson, I did intend to get some dollars for you. Sorry, but so much has been happening that I forgot."

"Don't sweat it, Anna. Maybe next time."

Daria nodded, grinned, and said, "Yep, next time."

"Very well," said Anna, pausing to clear her throat. "We are going to visit with Tayo some more. We do not wish that, but we would not enjoy being destroyed either."

"Oh yeah, Lin Finity. Yep, she's a dangerous dame, that one. Call if you need me."

He looked at each of them in turn.

"For anything. Both of you."

He turned and began walking toward his car, with no sign of his breath in the chilly Maryland air.

"I'm kind of glad he's gone, Mom. I've been wanting to ask you: when you got out of your shower, what did you do?"

"Oh, um, nothing. I mean, of course, I dried off. But I was in bed shortly after that."

Daria nodded and watched her closely. Anna only looked back calmly for a second, then turned to watch Benson's car rolling away down their street.

"You didn't, um, get anywhere near my bedroom?"

"Oh, I, um, I did think of knocking, but then I realized it was late, so I did not."

Daria shook her head and said, "Alright. It's just that if you were to ever—"

"Daria," Anna said while looking her daughter up and down, "I did not know that you would ever wish to use a wardrobe like that. It is a good look."

"Aw, thanks, Mom. Yeah. I think Benson liked it too."

She grinned at her daughter and said, "I noticed that. Yes, he seemed pleased."

"As much as a dead man can be?"

"That is true, Daria. Okay, let us visit with Tayo. Can we even guess what might happen today?"

"Nope. No, we sure can't."

"If anything, it will not be good things. We should swing our car near the liquor store on the way."

Daria smiled and said, "Now, you're talking, Mom. Even Tayo would appreciate that."

"Perhaps Lee as well?"

"I doubt it. But maybe that creepy kid of hers. Might zap some of the creepiness out of her."

* * *

"There's no real breakfast left in the kitchen, Tayo," said Lee, without opening her eyes. "We can run out and grab something. What would you like?"

How about a normal human back? Where could one of those be purchased?

"I believe Anna and her daughter planned to return this morning. I don't believe they can help in any substantial way, but I'd still prefer their company while you're gone. For me, breakfast can wait."

"Suit yourself. Hey, do you remember anything from when I healed you that last time?"

He uncovered his eyes and looked first at Lee, then at her daughter, then back at Lee.

"I, um, remember little. This is not a criticism because no one can do what you do. But it felt that I was in an agonizing limbo, forgotten, and left to my own remedies, of which, of course, I had none."

"Oh, um, yeah. I remember getting distracted by a few things."

She smiled and leaned her head back into the upholstery.

A man's arm is burned to a crisp, like an overcooked French fry that has an elbow, and you were distracted? I don't ever wish to be ungrateful, but—

"It's a weird place that I go to—where I do the healing. It's just that the sun was hot. Stuff like that. It's a beautiful place."

"I can't understand, of course, but I do believe it. After that lengthy pause, what followed was a very comfortable experience. If it weren't for the extreme fear and trauma, perhaps it could even be described as pleasurable. But I don't remember any details at all."

Lee opened her eyes and stared at him, shaking her head, then she spoke.

"Tayo, what do you know about plants?"

"Plants?"

"Yeah, like maybe plants that live underwater. I just, um, think I saw some around there when I was working on fixing you up."

Tayo stayed silent and looked up at the ceiling. His black eyes moved from one side to the other, not taking time to focus on anything. After many moments, he again looked at her.

"It's startling to me that my memory could include a region that's pushed aside and obscured. Yes, Lee, I remember now.

"When I was but a child, I began a school science experiment that involved a plant. It had begun with little enthusiasm from me but after spending time in setting up a tank, preparing it for the plant, then receiving it from a local store and planting it, it became a fixation of mine.

"What kind of plant? Can you describe it?"

"Yes, but I can't remember its species, genus, or any other of its classifications. Perhaps I was too young."

"Well, yeah, that probably wasn't the important thing to you."

"No, keeping it alive was, though. Lee, it withered and, I believe, suffered in that tank. I tried everything that I could. Our local library had few books, and even the store from which it was purchased claimed to know nothing about it. Actually, it seemed that no one cared but me.

"I've never felt so weak and ineffective as I did then. Perhaps it's why I chose to discard the memory."

"What happened? Did you help it?"

"No. No, I did not. It had many fronds that pointed out from its center radially. In the beginning, they were lush and thick, and I could imagine that the plant had some volition and that it knew me. I believed that if I put a finger near, which I never did for fear of hastening its demise, that its limbs would coil around me. I knew that that would be the only way it could communicate with me."

"And what do you think it would have said?"

Tayo covered his eyes with his left hand and said, "'I want to live.' Only that, Lee: 'I want to live.'"

"Oh, Tayo, I'm sorry. I guess it didn't make it?"

"No. I watched its slow death for many weeks. As bad as that was, it might have been worse that I had to acknowledge all of the indifference around me. I alone cared and couldn't save it."

Lee heard Alessa's choppy breaths and looked down to see a single tear, thick and wet and creeping down her cheek. She still only watched Tayo.

"Lessa, baby, are you alright?"

She nodded, squeezed her eyes shut quickly, sending out a rush of tears, then opened them and continued to watch Tayo.

"Does that answer whatever it is you asked, Lee?"

Lee wiped at her own eyes with both hands before answering.

"Yeah, Tayo. Yep. I, um, think maybe the water needed to be warmer."

"You know about such plants, Lee?"

"Uh, no. I just . . . I think maybe—"

The door burst open, and Anna and Daria, holding Ozzy, lunged inside and out of the cold. Anna swung the door shut with a boom.

*   *   *

"We're back. We even brought breakfast," Anna said while removing her coat.

Daria dumped Ozzy onto the floor, took off her coat and gloves, and she and Anna both tossed their things into the closet. They turned to look at Tayo and Lee, who both sat in silence, staring.

Anna wore a short black skirt, black stockings, and high black heels. Her light gray sweater was perhaps a size too small and low-cut, showing a fair amount of cleavage. Her shoulder-length light brown hair had been teased up to give it a wild look. She stood with her hands on her hips.

Next to her, her daughter wore the exact same thing—only her hair was longer and black. Her hands were on her hips too.

Tayo and Lee looked at each other, then back at the two Kelginas.

"What? Breakfast is good, right?" said Daria, offering a slight squint in Tayo's direction.

"Breakfast is certainly good," Tayo said.

I shouldn't be thinking such things, but Daria has never looked better. Yes, Anna, too, but if I allow my eyes their choice, they will never leave the sight of her. I had better look away.

Ozzy approached the prone man on the couch, and Tayo looked down and reached out to scratch his head around his ears.

"I will just leave these things in the kitchen, then," said Anna, and her heels clacked on the hardwood floor as she left the room.

"I'll get some coffee going," said Daria, and her heels sounded just like her mother's.

Tayo again turned to Lee, who only shrugged.

She has left the room, and still, I see her. How could I have never noticed her legs before? Everything else, too, of course, but those legs of hers are like—

"Well, that solves the breakfast issue," said Lee. "Guess we don't have to run out now."

"No, you do not. I'm suddenly more hungry than before."

For breakfast, too, Lee. My hunger is also for breakfast. Even as I feel that needle finding a sensitive place among my tormenting symbols and poking at me. Will I soon hear the infamous mouse?

"Yeah, smelling it can sure do that."

Oh, you are right. I believe I did catch a scent. A scent of that stunning Daria, dressed in such a way that I can barely—

"Want me to get some for you? You don't have to get up."

Ah, that's good timing: the axe has come to play again. I'll dwell on that later. What Lee just said: getting some, not having to even get up, her long legs—

"Tayo?"

"I should probably move about anyway. I'll get it myself."

That sounds even better. I'll take what I want. Do I care if there are observers all around? No, of course, not! I'll take what I want!

Tayo stood and wobbled in his place near the couch, Lee and Alessa watching him closely. His head turned when Anna entered the room, followed by Daria, both sets of heels clicking and echoing through Tayo's brain even as the axe dug in deeper.

Even the damn mouse can watch. Hell, I've killed a man bare-handed. I can certainly do this. Bare is a delicious word. It will be so easy to pull up on young, tasty Daria's skirt, exposing what I know waits there for me.

"Tayo," Anna said as she drew near. "Daria has something for you."

He looked at the bag in Daria's hand, then down to her thighs in black stockings, mostly left uncovered by her skirt, then up at her breasts. He looked into her eyes, and she seemed happy to see him, and he knew that she'd still be happy, maybe even more happy, after he'd torn her clothes off of her and pinned her to the couch.

She's not really offering me only breakfast. She's offering me everything. I see the way she's looking at me. Well, young Daria, it's your lucky day!

Anna was near enough, and he delivered a solid backhand that sent her toppling. A loud squeak timed itself to the moment she'd hit the floor.

Ah, there's that mouse! I hear you, little mouse!

Daria was close behind her mother and despite the beginning of a scream, he knew that she wanted exactly what *he* wanted, so he grabbed her arms.

Before he could go any further, the axe really dug in, severing tendons and ligaments, and he looked up and screamed. He screamed loudly, but the mice were louder.

"Ah!"

Good, there are now mice in two walls at the same time!

Then, Ozzy's sharp little teeth dug into his left ankle. Tayo glanced down and sneered, then tried shaking him loose, but Ozzy held on tight.

Despite the jaws holding him and Daria fighting to free her arms, Tayo forced several deep breaths and refocused, reaching one hand up to Daria's sweater between her breasts. The walls erupted in squeaking.

Mice in every wall! I'm certain that they're cheering me on!

He planned to rip her sweater straight down, expose her breasts first, then move on to the skirt, then—

He heard the cracking more than he felt it and when his head hit the coffee table on the way down, he heard more than felt that solid clunk too.

Lee stood over him, ready to strike again. Daria had frozen in her tracks, mouth open, staring down at Tayo, then at every wall, each containing mice. Anna lay unconscious in the middle of the room. Alessa watched silently, only once turning enough to glance at the wall against which she leaned.

Daria dropped the bag on Tayo's chest and said, "Bastard."

She went to see about her mother and as she was waking but still dazed, Daria helped her to sit up.

Tayo tried to speak. "It . . . it was the —"

"You attacked me!" said Daria. "What kind of bastard would—"

"Wait," said Lee, and she held up a hand.

Daria stared and waited, her chest still heaving as she looked at every wall, with no sound coming from any of them.

"Tayo, what was that? Was it that Hunter thing?"

"Yes. I felt it tormenting my back, and that is usually accompanied by the squeaking."

"Yeah," said Lee, "we all heard that. What is it?"

"I'm not sure any of us should find out."

"So, you didn't want to attack her?"

"That is not completely accurate. It made me actually attack her. Even now, it's difficult to assign all of the blame to it."

"You still want to attack her?"

You mean, if I wasn't lying here with a broken neck? Lee, try to understand: I would probably appreciate her beauty with no Hunter lodged in my back. I would not ever assault her, though.

"No, I would never attack her."

"Last time I ever get you breakfast," Daria said with a scoff. "You do need some mousetraps, though. Big ones."

"I genuinely apologize. On my own, I would never behave in such a way."

"I believe him," said Lee, looking at Daria. "I think we all know Tayo better than that."

Daria shrugged and exhaled loudly, then she helped her mother up.

"Oh, there is still a ringing sound. I had better sit."

"Ringing? Yeah, I bet. He really clobbered you."

Daria helped her to the chair and after she sat, Ozzy jumped up and licked at her neck and cheeks, one of which bled from a break in the skin.

"Ozzy protected us, Mom. He bit that bastard's—"

"Daria," said Lee. "Really, he couldn't help it."

Daria rolled her eyes and said, "I bet that's what they all say."

Lee shook her head, and she couldn't help but smile.

"They don't all have monsters hiding on their backs, do they?"

Daria kicked at the floor and said, "I suppose not."

Lee turned back to Tayo and said, "I probably didn't need to hit you that hard."

"You acted in defense of Anna and Daria. I cannot find fault in that. But I do believe my neck is broken."

"You better just lie still, then."

"Yes. No cartwheels for a while."

With his eyes closed, he said, "I don't expect you to forgive me, Daria, but I am truly sorry. You as well, Anna. Without evil forces commanding me, I would die to protect any or all of you."

Lee turned to glance at Alessa and saw her wiping at her cheeks, a very faint smile apparent as she watched and listened to Tayo. She fiddled with the card in her lap. Lee turned back around.

"Well, how about some healing?"

"I cannot even nod. Yes. Please, Lee. Would you consider providing a remedy for the dog bites as well?"

"Good boy, Ozzy," said Daria.

"Daria, that is really not helpful."

"Just saying, Mom."

Chapter 28 – All Of Eternity

Lee glanced again at Daria, who stood near the chair where Anna sat with an indifferent Ozzy on her lap, picking a few dog hairs off of her stockings. She looked from one to the other several times and smiled.

"You two are like twins today. Looks good."

"It is a good look," Anna said as she rubbed her fingers to drop the hair on Tayo's floor. "Lin scares me immensely, but I cannot find fault with her fashion sense. I am also uncomfortable with the continuing mouse attack."

"And you?" Lee said, looking again at Daria.

"Well, um, it just seemed like a good idea to give it a try. With all the crazy shit going on, we're kind of like a team, you know?"

Lee nodded and said, "Yeah, I can see that. It's a good style."

Anna held back Ozzy's kisses and said, "Lee, perhaps you will be the next to try a style such as this."

Lee grinned, looked again at their heels, stockings, and skirts, and said, "Bet I could rock a little black dress."

"No doubt," Daria said with a smile. "You're in awesome shape."

"Your shape would model such a dress well," said Anna. "Maybe after these nightmares have gone far away."

The squeaking started again, causing them to pause and look around.

"Right. Well, this'll just take a second. Gotta patch up old Tayo here. Lessa, have another donut if you want. I won't be around to wrestle you for it. Not this time."

"You guys fight over donuts?" said Daria.

Lee looked right into her eyes and said, "Stay out of my way when I'm hunting donuts."

Daria puffed up her cheeks and raised her eyebrows.

"It's a joke."

Daria grinned and let out her breath.

Lee looked down and said, "Tayo, I don't dare sit on you. I'll just hold your hand this time. It should still work."

He mouthed something silently but didn't move.

She sat back on her heels next to him and took one of his hands.

Lee went home.

The squeaking erupted, joined by frantic scratching, and the power went out.

"Um, this isn't good, is it?"

"No, Daria. Little that happens here is."

*　*　*

Drawing in a deep breath and looking down at her stones, Lee saw that they were in perfect alignment—an exact symbol for infinity. All forty, including what she'd always called her anchor stone—the first one she'd found—rested in their exact locations on the green grass of her home.

Only after she'd looked up at her sun—which she always felt had been smiling down on her—did she notice that she felt its nourishing, pleasurable heat all over.

She felt it first, then confirmed it: every last bit of clothing had been left behind. She stood completely naked in her home, taking in all the heat the sun could give her.

Oh, she realized, that thing, that Hunter, is having a better view this time, isn't it? I wonder if it cares . . .

Remembering Tayo and his broken neck, she also remembered diving into that lost well, somewhere back in the tall weeds. Unlike the sunlight, which fell on her from a single place, the water, that murky, clingy water, soaked pleasure into her from every direction all at once.

293

It wasn't even a decision that had to be made. But she did promise herself that she'd only enjoy being immersed there long enough to settle down near Tayo. Down near his childhood plant that he'd nursed and prayed for and had to watch die. She knew that whatever ecstasy that plant and all of its delightful tendrils could give her should be enjoyed guilt-free.

She parted the tall plant stalks with both hands and aimed her steps toward the small clearing which contained only the well. Standing on its edge, satisfied that she hadn't bothered with clothing on this journey, she watched as the vines across its surface parted, leaving a narrow opening.

Feeling an almost careless abandon, she stepped around to the other side, away from where the vines had invited her in. A quick glance over the matted surface showed her a much tighter opening—less than half the size. And she knew without any consideration that that would be her entry because the vines would hold her even more tightly.

She pointed both hands together, touched her fingertips into the bath-temperature water, and took a breath, though she knew it wasn't needed.

Her head passed in easily, and she felt the anticipated squeezing from vines all around her after her shoulders had passed through. When her bare breasts were at the level of the vines, they cinched up tighter and if she could have, she would have gasped because of where they'd tightened up on her.

But it was only a playful squeeze, repeated several times, touching her in the right places, and then the vines relaxed, and she passed deeper into the well.

As her waistline approached the vines, they coiled around her but didn't prevent her from diving deeper. As she sank farther down, more vines wrapped around her thighs, mostly near their very tops, where they couldn't go higher if they'd tried. They snaked and twisted over her skin, holding her tight. The vines around her waist had remained in place, sinking into the warm water with her.

She tried paddling with her arms, attempting to draw herself down to the plant—to Tayo—but got only as far as her ankles at the surface, where the most aggressive of the vines wrapped tightly around. She could go no farther. Vines remained still and strong around her waist and ankles.

But those around her thighs continued to circle around, rubbing and sliding, in and out and back and forth, working to wedge themselves in as deeply as they could.

Lee stopped struggling. The hot water and soft touch of the vines, caressing her in the exact ways she would have requested if she'd been asked, held her with no chance of escape.

And she wanted no escape. It was a train that she wanted to ride to the destination that she knew was waiting for her, immersed in a forgotten well, touched and fondled as the ecstasy built, rising up like she'd never felt before.

Just as she was about at her peak, having long before forgotten about Tayo or his injuries, the vines around her ankles relaxed, and she slipped down below the surface. The strands around her waist unwound. The ones around her thighs remained and somehow, they continued touching her, slipping and shifting, as Lee descended to a height just above the plant.

She looked down on the plant, ready to prompt it to take her ankles and wrists, but the restraints around her thighs gently flipped her over to face straight up. Then, she felt the fronds from the Tayo plant wrap around her ankles and wrists, her neck and her waist, and they locked her in place, staring up at a distant circle of faint light.

Her arms were pulled to the sides gently until they'd reached the limit, then just a bit farther. Her ankle fronds pulled, too, and when she thought they could take her legs no farther, they did.

She waited for it. It didn't take long.

A single, last limb from the plant snaked up between her legs, wiggling a path through the surface vines that lingered around her thighs, all of them still squirming and sliding around.

That single frond rose a distance above her and then bent down toward her with a determined pressure. Lee gasped and what she'd thought was a held breath, which was really only water from the well, escaped. She sensed the heat of it dropping past her cheeks, its warmth seeking to heal the plant.

The wave of pleasure that had begun while she hung near the surface resumed and reached the same level, this time at the well's bottom, near the plant. Lee inhaled as much of the water as she could. She felt it flow to every tiniest part of her, but most of it sped toward a special place, where it bubbled and boiled and erupted into a cascade of ecstasy.

Almost unable to focus on anything but the rapture, the weak daylight circle above her began to retreat, becoming a pinpoint, then only darkness, and it took Lee with it, to a place where only pleasure could exist.

She had a thought that if an image of her, naked, held immobile and pleasured, deep in the private water could be taken or painted, someone would pay a fortune for it.

Her last thought was that she wished the best for Tayo, but she had no desire to ever return. All of eternity could pass her by, she thought, as the vines and fronds claimed ownership and caressed her at the bottom of a well that didn't exist . . . never to be found by anyone.

* * *

Lee opened her eyes but remained on the floor near Tayo. She let out a loud sigh, and when she sensed that she was still smiling from her visit to her home, she coughed once and looked down.

She still held his hand, which she shook lightly, causing his eyes to crack open. He turned them toward her without moving anything else.

"Lee," he said, his voice slow and strained, "thank you. I believe you have fixed my neck. Could you look at my ankle and confirm that it is restored as well?"

Lee took a quick look at it, saw that it was fine, and looked again at him.

"You can't tell?"

He drew in a breath and closed his eyes.

"I'm becoming unable to separate pain from memories of pain."

"Maybe if you get up and walk around, then you might—"

"No. No, this is good. I wish to stay here."

"For how long?"

Until I'm confident that movement will not cause the severing of my neck, sending my head rolling? I don't wish to cause enjoyment for Daria in that way.

"I don't know. I'd cover my eyes if I dared to move. Could you draw the drapes?"

"The power's already out."

"From the things in the walls. Yes, they are gathering in there."

"What does that mean?"

"I don't know. But I feel that dark would help me."

"Can we please tell Lin about your strange mice?" said Anna. "Perhaps that will help?"

Tayo sighed and said, "Very well. My dignity flows away as unrestricted as my blood anyway."

"Geez, kind of dramatic, huh?"

"Daria."

"Let me be the one to tell her, though, Anna."

"I cannot promise that, but I will try."

Anna looked over her shoulder at the window, and Daria said, "I'll get it. But this is a damn scary place."

I'm nearly dead, and I still treasure the sound she makes as she moves about. It unlocks a memory of the vision, and I find the feelings there still.

She yanked the curtains closed, darkening the room, then stood close by her mother, both watching and listening to the walls.

"I think maybe I have a construction, Daria."

Daria laughed once and said, "I think you mean 'concussion,' Mom."

"Yes, maybe one of those too. For a diseased man, Tayo, you—"

"I am not diseased," he said, just loud enough to compete with the squeaking and scratching. "Plagued, I think, is more accurate."

"Well, plagued or not, you have an alarming strength."

"How bad is it?" said Lee.

Daria leaned over to look into her mother's eyes, and she squinted to try to see in the darkness.

She said, "Her eyes don't look right. She might have hit her head on the floor too."

"I am glad I did not break open a wall. We still have not cleaned up—"

"I can't believe you sometimes! Forget about cleaning anything, alright?"

"Okay. We do not have a broom anyway."

Yes, we have a broom. But it's not worth speaking of it.

Daria scoffed and stood up. Lee spoke to Tayo.

"I'll be back. Just lie still, alright?"

Yes, of course. I'm practicing to be a corpse.

"Yes, I will."

Lee stood and looked at Anna.

"I can fix that."

"But can you fix the broken wall?" Anna said, followed by a weak laugh.

"Um," said Daria, "I think that means, 'yes, please do what you can to fix what is broken in my head.'"

Lee stared at her, shaking her head, before she spoke.

"Alright."

The squeaking started to move around the room, as did the scratching.

"We might be running out of time, though."

She walked over, nudged Anna's legs to one side, and sat on the edge of the chair. Anna's head flopped over, and Lee took one of her hands. Lee's eyes rolled up, but Anna's were already closed.

Lee went home again.

*　*　*

The heat from her sun warmed the spaces between the fine hairs on Lee's neck, which were all standing straight out. She knew why, and she also knew that she wouldn't turn to look at what hid in the weeds.

She did glance down at her stones, though, and saw that a few needed some attention. She stooped down, arranged them properly, then stood and looked to where she might find the well if she were to make a mad dash toward it.

A deep sigh leaked out unintentionally, and she remembered that she was there to help Anna. She found herself wishing that Anna somehow inhabited the deepest, warmest regions of that well, whether as a plant or anything else, but when a butterfly fluttered past, near her face, she turned to watch it land on the light brown hair of a teenage girl standing next to her.

Only then did she notice that she held the girl's hand. The girl looked only forward, and it seemed to Lee that it would be an easy time: just flick the thing off of her head, sending it on its way, then return to Tayo's apartment.

If I get the work done quickly, she thought, maybe I could take a little dip in the well?

While musing the possibility of sweet entrapment by vines and fronds and warmth and darkness, so far from any real world, Lee felt the girl yank her hand free. Before she could turn to look, she got shoved over and down onto the grass, bumping two of her stones out of place.

A deep loss of strength hit her immediately and when she glanced up, she saw the same vicious, snarling face that she'd seen on the younger girl when she'd healed Daria.

The teenager stared and seemed to snort as she turned and began moving, without using her legs at all, toward the Hunter in the field. Her back was arched, her head tipped back, and her toes dragged through the grass.

Do I have time to set my stones? she wondered. Or should I chase after her first?

While still watching the girl being pulled along as if by a cable attached to her waist, Lee reached around with one hand, fumbled with a stone, and tried to fit it in between its neighbors. Some health returned but not all of it.

She jumped to her feet and ran after the girl and when she got close enough, she reached around her waist with one arm and tried to hold her in place. But the cable's pull was too strong, and she was dragged along with her. The girl's head snapped to each side, sharp teeth aiming for flesh.

Lee leaned away from her and dug her snakeskin boots into the soft ground, managed to stop her advancing, and looked up to see the butterfly sitting calmly on the girl's head, its wings lazily moving up and down.

Feeling her strength dwindling, not understanding how the child could be drawn to something so evil, just like the younger girl, Lee made a desperate move, wrapping both arms around her waist, lifting her off of her feet, and tipping them both backwards.

They hit the soft grass hard, and the girl above her kicked and thrashed about. Right in front of Lee, in the girl's hair, sat the calm butterfly, holding tight and riding along, seemingly watching her, undisturbed by the two struggling on the ground.

As she felt her power leaving her, knowing that it had little chance of success, Lee figured she had no choice: she let go with one hand and quickly flicked the butterfly aside. It rose casually into the air and where it traveled after that, Lee would never know.

The girl had taken advantage of her opportunity and broke free of Lee's grasp. She stood and resumed the odd, effortless drifting like before, and Lee had to choose: die trying to save her or fix her stones and get the hell back to the world.

She chose the stones. Too weak to stand, she crawled back toward them and while lying in the grass, she reached out to properly place the last one.

It wasn't perfectly located, though, and she rolled over onto her back to feel the hot light from the sun that never moved. She thought of lifting her head up to see what would become of the teenage girl determined to go to the Hunter.

But she couldn't.

On the verge of tears, all Lee could do was leave her home, abandoning the girl to her fate.

* * *

Lee opened her eyes, still seated beside Anna, and a second later, Anna opened hers, then smiled and stretched her arms out.

"My head feels like a better thing, Lee. Thank you."

"Sure. Hey, um, did you feel anything strange?"

Anna grinned and said, "In addition to strange feelings I am already having, you mean?"

Lee shook her head, looked down, and said, "Never mind. Maybe it's nothing."

She stood and quickly held the back of Anna's chair.

"Oh, but that wasn't easy. I, um, I'm going back to sit with Tayo."

While she rejoined Tayo on the floor, Daria said, "What's she talking about, Mom? And what are you talking about?"

She called her daughter closer, got her to lean over, and whispered, "I was just thinking of Benson, that is all. Those are truly some strange things with him, are they not?"

"Yep. Strange in a good way, though," Daria whispered back before standing up. "I'm kind of drawn to it. Can't help myself."

"Yes. I am too."

* * *

"Lee," Tayo said with a shaky voice, "I don't ever wish to trouble Lin, but . . ."

He paused to take two slow, deep breaths.

"Maybe—"

"No, I get it. I agree."

After looking around at the scratching and squeaking in every wall, she said to Anna, "What do you think about giving Lin a call?"

"I think she is mostly a monster, and I do not ever—"

"Mom, really," Daria said with a smirk, "she's never actually hurt you. Hell, Tayo's the one that hurt you."

"You do mention a valid point, Daria. Fine."

She took out her phone and tapped a few numbers.

"Speaker, Mom—we need the entertainment. This place is cuckoo."

Chapter 29 – Thanks, Mouse

Lee remained on the floor, near Tayo, and Daria stood close to the chair where her mother sat with Ozzy on her lap. Alessa still sat on the floor, leaning against the wall and rarely moving. All eyes except for Tayo's watched the phone on the coffee table.

"This better be good, Anna."

"It is anything but good, Lin. I do not wish to see you or even speak at you again."

"Okay, what's going on this time? Tayo's ear fell off?"

Daria stifled a laugh, and Lee and Anna both looked at her with frowns. Daria only shrugged.

"I wish it were only that simple. Tayo is no longer injured. Lee has healed him. I do not even want to know how she can do such things. What kind of person could—"

"Anna, get to the point."

"Yes, well, as I was saying, everyone is fine now, thanks to Lee. She was even so generous as to repair Daria's hair. Do you remember her hair?"

Daria grabbed her hair on each side and grinned, looking around the room, but no one paid her any attention.

"How could someone make another person's hair fall off in just one—"

"Last chance, Anna, and then I swear, there will be no way for you to ever see me again because you won't be around. Neither will your brat daughter or your brat dog."

Anna held her daughter's stare and offered her a slight grin.

"Of the two, Ozzy is less of—"

"Anna!"

Daria covered her laugh with one hand while she pointed at Anna. "Oh, I am sorry, Lin. My mind is being lost."

She looked again at Tayo and Lee on the floor.

"I am calling because Tayo wishes you to visit again."

"Why? If everyone is okay, what's the point? Do you think we like driving for three hours each way just so I can disappoint myself by not finishing you off? Your wardrobe is really irritating. You must know that."

Daria shook her hair back and straightened her skirt. Anna held a leg out and smiled at the high heel that she wore.

"It really is a good look, Lin, and if your offer is still good about shortening—"

"Forget your stupid skirt. Why does Tayo want me there?"

She saw his head lifted up, shaking side to side, and she shrugged.

"He said there is something growing inside the walls."

He let his head rest on the floor again.

"I have never seen him so scared. I have heard it too. Ozzy has noticed."

"What do you mean? What's in the walls?"

"Tayo is awake now. He can tell you."

Anna rose from her seat, picked up the phone, and handed it to Lee. Lee held it close enough to Tayo that he wouldn't have to make too much of an effort.

Tayo didn't move, but he turned his eyes from side to side, studying the walls, which had become silent.

Daria whispered toward him, "Whatever's in there is nice enough to let you talk."

"Daria, do not antagonize the tortured man."

Daria smirked. Tayo held Lee's gaze for a moment, then he spoke.

"Lin? Are you there?"

"Yes, Tayo, I'm here. What's the problem this time?"

"I did not wish to render Anna unconscious."

"He sure did knock you on your ass," Daria whispered to her.

"I had no time to think before I struck her, and she fell to the floor. I also did not have the desire to try to assault Daria. At that moment, it became overpowering."

"Bastard," she whispered.

"Daria, not now," whispered Anna.

"You beat up Daria too?"

"No, Lin. I will use the word 'assault' and allow your own mind to supply details."

"Well, a good slap would have been enough—"

Daria made a move toward the phone, and Anna grabbed her arm, which she quickly pulled free. But she stayed by the chair.

"—because she's a brat, and—"

"I know you are trying to be amusing, Lin, but I cannot laugh. I can barely find the will to continue."

"So, I'm guessing you didn't get too far with her?"

"No, I did not. The dog distracted me with its surprisingly strong little jaw gouging into an ankle."

"Good boy, Ozzy."

"Daria, shh."

"The one where Lee just stuck your foot back on?" said Lin.

"No, the other one."

Daria scoffed, and Anna pointed at her.

"Okay, what else?"

"Lee awoke from her fatigue and convinced me to stop."

"Convinced you?"

"She is surprisingly strong, Lin. With one casual slap, she broke my neck."

"Good God," said Jack. "It's a nightmare over there."

"What about the kid?" said Lin.

"Daria is fine. She—"

"No, the other one—Alessa."

"Her. That one is unusual," Tayo said, causing Lee to turn for a quick look at her daughter. "She watched me calmly, even as my neck was snapped. As I lay there dying, I saw her studying the walls of this room. Lin, something gathers in there."

"What are you talking about? What do you think is in there?"

"I prefer to not learn that. It is coming from the numbers, I believe. Extra symbols are missing for which I cannot account. They don't seem to be correlated with the attacks. The entity appears to be busy assembling something."

"Hang on."

"She put us on hold?" said Daria. "What the hell?"

"Daria, I think maybe that is not so important right now."

She stood and walked to where Tayo could turn his eyes to see her, and when he did, she said, "Tayo, that phone is on speaker."

She tipped her head in Alessa's direction, and Lee saw her.

"It takes more than that to bother her, Anna," said Lee. "She'll be fine."

Anna glanced at Alessa, who calmly gazed back at her without moving.

"Well, we are all grateful for that."

She returned to her seat, and Daria leaned down, close to her ear, and whispered, "Creepy as Hell."

"Daria, please."

"Hang on, Tayo," Lin said through the phone. "We'll see you soon."

He let out a deep breath, then took in just enough breath to answer softly.

"Thank you, Lin."

Lee turned the phone to confirm that Lin had ended the call, and she set it back on the table.

"She is truly coming here again?" said Anna. "She is more frightening even than a giant mouse living in every wall."

"It's not a mouse," Tayo said weakly.

"Mom, really, has she ever hurt you? Not at all, right?"

"Well, Daria, there is always a time to be first."

Daria grinned and shook her head at her mother. Then, she looked down at her skirt.

"Today might be the day, dressed the way you are. That's gonna piss her off."

"Well, Daria, it is a good fashion style. And you are also—"

A scratching came from the wall behind the couch.

"Oh, boy," said Daria. "Glad it's over there."

A loud squeak came from directly behind her. She took a few quick steps to the middle of the room.

Thank you, Mr. Mouse. Though I'm mostly dead now, even those sounds she made deliver a sweet memory.

"You cannot stand there for the time it takes for Lin to arrive here, Daria. Come and sit. There is room."

She scooted to one side of the wide chair, with Ozzy on her lap, and patted the empty space. Daria's heels again clicked on her way to the chair, where she sat.

"Thanks, mouse," Tayo said, followed by a weak laugh.

"What are you talking about, Tayo?" said Lee.

We are born with the ability to lose our minds at any time from something as simple as that, aren't we?

"There are many ways for a man to lose his mind," Tayo said with his eyes closed. "Some are welcomed completely. We seek them."

Lee stared at him for a few seconds, then looked at Anna and Daria. They both shrugged.

"I'm getting something to eat," Daria said as she stood. "There's leftovers, and we have time."

While she walked toward the kitchen, Tayo inhaled very slowly and gradually expanded his chest. When her steps had ceased, he let it all leak back out. Lee looked down on him, shaking her head.

Another squeak came from behind a wall, then more scratching from behind another.

"This is a damn nut house," Daria said with a loud scoff from the kitchen.

"It is truly that," said Anna. "It is also very dark. Tayo, do you have a flashlight?"

"I don't want any light."

"We can let you remain in the dark if you wish."

"In the cabinet above the sink," he said.

"I'll get it," said Daria.

I'm grateful to have functioning ears. No, I would never attack her. Well, maybe if my neck hadn't just been snapped . . .

Daria returned with the flashlight, which she pointed all around as she handed out food to whoever wanted it.

"Last donut," she said to Alessa, who accepted it without getting up.

She remained near the wall and ate quietly, even though something squeaked behind her. She glanced back, then got up on the couch and sat up on the top, resting her boots on the seat cushions.

After everyone had finished eating, Tayo said, "Please, we don't need the light anymore."

"Tayo," said Anna, "it is less frightening in here with light."

"I fear that it only angers what's lurking in there."

Daria switched it off without comment, and they sat and waited in Tayo's dark, quiet apartment.

*   *   *

At the sound of rapid knocking on the door, everyone except Tayo flinched and looked around the room and at each other.

"That was not a squeak," said Anna.

"Mom, it's just someone at the door. Probably Lin, don't you think?"

"You are probably right, Daria."

No one moved.

"Mom, go on. Check it out."

"Very well."

She handed Ozzy to Daria and left for the door. She only stood near it and didn't open it. They all heard voices on the other side.

"Mom, are you going to let them in?"

"Daria, shh. We do not have any idea who—"

The door swung in slowly, letting inside a strip of sunlight that illuminated Alessa where she sat, high on the couch.

"Anyone home?" Lin said as she leaned into the room.

"Oh, it is you," Anna said, still standing behind the door. She leaned around it, saw Lin, and said, "We are in shock, and we fear every sight and sound."

"That's why the lights are out? You're too afraid of what you might see?"

"No, Lin. The electricity has left. We think whatever is in the wall is causing damage there."

"This still sounds crazy. You know that, right?"

"It is surely crazy, yet we are living it. This would never happen in Russia. Soon, I will take—"

"Yeah, right. I know. Let us in, okay?"

Anna took a step and opened the door farther. Lin walked in first, and Gabriel and Gloriana followed her. Tayo tipped his head to the side to see who had come with Lin.

I hear Lin's voice, and that other hair is unmistakable—that's surely Gabriel. But who is that? Is that breathtaking vision the owner of the voice on the phone?

Anna watched as Lin looked her up and down, then scoffed loudly and turned to look around. She stopped to focus on Alessa, who looked back calmly.

"Nice," said Lin. "Anna, is there a flashlight in here?"

"Daria found one, but Tayo pleaded that it be left off."

"Why?"

"I do not know, but I did not debate," Anna said as she slowly closed the door, darkening the room further.

"Daria," Lin said, "I know you're in here somewhere. Get that flashlight going, okay?"

Anna stifled her laugh as the bright light shined into Lin's face. Lin held up a hand to block it.

"That's great, Daria," she said. "Really helpful. Point that at Tayo a second, will you?"

"Only if you say—"

"Don't."

Anna held her breath as her heart pounded.

"I don't need to see you to teach you a lesson you'll never forget."

The beam of light moved to the floor, where Tayo lay on his back, with Lee sitting next to him.

I am the focus of everyone's attention now? Of course, I am. I'm the living disaster that has drawn together this mismatched group.

"Tayo," she said, "are you okay?"

"Yes. For the moment, Lin."

"Hi," said Lee. "Just so you know, I'm exhausted. I'm keeping up with the damage, but it isn't easy."

"You're still amazing, Lee. Lee Ternity—that's you. Daria, keep that light on. Maybe point it at the ceiling, okay?"

Daria turned the beam upward, and the flashlight illuminated the white plaster, brightening the room enough for everyone to see.

"Everyone's okay?"

"Lee repaired me, and Daria needed no attention," said Anna.

Lin must know if she is to help. Why would I not trust with her my true feelings? I'm already a spectacle, and my words won't increase that by much.

"My neck has been restored," said Tayo, "but I choose to remain still, Lin. I suspect some critical part of my anatomy will explode soon. It's very likely that I might grow a second head, and an additional one after that wouldn't surprise any of my other heads at that point. If the Hunter were to invade my digestive system, I fear that—"

"Whoa. Hold up, okay? Let's take things as they are right now. You said there are symbols missing from your back."

"Yes. By my count—which is a formidable task when one is being annihilated, I can assure you—there are now five that have left my body with no corresponding calamity."

The number is really four, Lin. I cashed in one for my butter knife murder. Oh, I've earned that meager lie.

"And you think they're in the walls? Doing what?"

Does she comprehend what I might consider likely to happen? She dares to even ask?

"You wish for me to engage my imagination?"

It might sever my spine completely, but I must take that risk. I must look upon Lin—she might be my only hope.

Tayo cackled with his head raised off of the floor, his eyes open wide. Daria pointed the beam at his face.

"The ceiling, Daria, okay?" said Lin. "I don't think the man needs a spotlight right now."

"I surely do not," Tayo said and dropped his head onto the hard floor.

"We have a plan," said Lin, "but first, let's all just listen."

Good idea. We can all hear the exact moment when I'm eviscerated and neatly diced and chunks are used to paint obscenities on the walls.

Anna had moved back to the corner, where she stood with Daria by her side. She watched Lin looking around, studying Alessa for a moment before glancing at the other walls.

Come on, mouse. Don't be shy! Reveal yourself!

A squeal and three scratching sounds came from the wall separating Tayo's modest living room from his kitchen. That wall lit up from the flashlight.

"I really don't want to have to tell you again," said Lin.

The ceiling lit up again.

"Was that it?" said Lin. "That mousy kind of sound?"

Does everyone find laughter irresistible as they're about to be slaughtered? Is it just me?

Tayo laughed and said, "A mouse? There isn't a hint of hope that that's a mouse. Not an iota of optimism, or even a microscopic molecule of—"

"Okay, okay," said Lin. "Let's listen some more."

What is the sound of a silent axe burrowing into a madman's back? Will we hear that soon? I wager it's a squishy sound.

Twenty seconds of silence passed, then Gloriana said, "I believe that was only a mouse."

Who is that woman? She is stunningly beautiful and even in the dim light, her eyes fascinate me. What color are they? But if she thinks that's a mouse, I fear she's as insane as me!

"It was NOT a mouse!" said Tayo. "Lin, I know what it will do to me next. It will move my eyes inside my intestines. I will have to watch as—"

Loud screeching came from the wall behind Alessa, but she barely took a look over her shoulder before again looking into the room.

Gabriel leaned close to Lin and said, "Lin, Tayo can't hang on much longer."

It did hang me for a while, though, with the electrical cable. No, Gabriel, I can't do that for very long. Would you like me to try?

"I don't recommend we try to wait for what lurks in the wall to make an appearance."

"You might be right," said Lin. "Hey, Gabby, isn't this bizarre enough that you can, you know, help out?"

What is this crazy talk now? Things must be bizarre, to a high enough level, before Gabriel will help?

"No. I am truly sorry, Lin. My mission is to safeguard you, and that involves me acting like anyone else."

You're only acting?

"You can't use,"—everyone watched Lin pause and look at all the curious faces around her—"any special talents?"

Who or what is Gabriel? If I survive, which I surely won't, will I dare to inquire?

"No. Lancaster Wolfe was different. He was evil. This Hunter is not."

"Not evil," Tayo said and allowed his head to roll to one side

No, it is the essence of goodness. Anything that wields an axe and launches attacks from under a man's skin is of inestimable goodness.

His chest heaved with his silent cackling.

"Fine," Lin said.

Lin pointed toward the door, urging Gabriel and Gloriana to wait there, then she turned toward Alessa. She only nodded, and Lin spun around to face Anna and Daria, causing Anna's heart to skip a beat. She pointed a finger at her daughter, and Anna wasn't surprised to see the beam of light shaking.

"Keep that light where it is, and keep that dog of yours out of the way."

Daria nodded, and Lin said, "Wait. Point that at your hair."

She did.

"No. Come on. Don't be stupid. The other side."

She moved the light, and Lin chuckled at the thick black hair that Lee had restored.

"Nice work," Lin said, looking down at Lee.

Lin looked back up.

"Daria, we're done with your hair."

Daria pointed the beam up again, adding light to the room. Lin walked over and stood beside Tayo.

I feel that someone should soon be throwing dirt on me as I lie here, relieved to be dead. What are you doing, Lin? Will you be the first with a shovel?

In a clear, confident voice, Lin said, "Tayo, I wish to take from you that which has invaded you."

Screeching and scratching erupted from every wall. The light on the ceiling danced around, and Tayo began to wail.

Oh, that did it! You have only angered my back. My guests can dig a grave for me, or they can wait until garbage day, or they can—

"Oh, here we go," said Lin.

All eyes saw everything in the room reflect the green light that was spewing from Lin's eyes.

Chapter 30 – These Damned Souls

Right after Lin's blazing green eyes switched off, Tayo watched her collapse to lie beside him. In the flashlight's direct beam, he flopped his head in her direction, then he looked up at the ceiling.

That really didn't help much, Lin! Thanks for visiting, though, and then taking a nap.

"Easy come, easy go!" he said and shook his head slowly as it rested on the hardwood floor.

Lee reached over his chest, grabbed Lin's arm, and shook her. But that only caused Lin's head to tip sideways.

"Lin, what happened?" she said. "Are you alright?"

Gloriana walked over and stood on Tayo's other side, looking down on them.

She is so near. That helps in a hopeless, belated way, but it's an acceptable way to die: an axe for my back and a dream for my eyes.

"It has taken her to a place I know all too well, Gabriel," she said, still looking down. "My time is nearing its end, whether from natural forces or from Lin's promise."

Lin has promised to end your life? If we die at the same time, will we travel together?

"I will go and assist if I can."

Go where? Assist how? Are they as mad as I?

"How?" said Gabriel. "You still have that kind of power?"

"No, I have only strong intent. I will display it like a tasty morsel in a trap. That Hunter has tried for centuries to destroy me. It will rejoice at the opportunity to take me again."

Oh, you are a madwoman, aren't you? You wish to tempt the one who swings the axe?

"Will you be able to return?" Gabriel said.

Gloriana looked up to hold Gabriel's gaze and said, "Am I meant to?"

How many of us will die today in this tiny apartment?

Tayo watched Gabriel nod silently and when Gloriana crumpled to the floor, he felt Lee jerk her hand free and get out of her way.

"I can't really help them, can I?" said Lee.

"No, not this time," said Gabriel.

That's truly a shame. Perhaps you should try harder to rid me of this curse, then?

"What was she talking about?" said Lee. "Where are they?"

Gabriel said, "I believe she's in the fight, Lee. The Hunter has indeed taken her. They're in a place where it is at its strongest."

In my walls?

"Is Lin going to be alright?"

"She's very strong. I believe she will."

Gabriel turned to face Anna, who had an arm around Daria, who held Ozzy.

"Daria is your name?" Gabriel said, holding one hand up to block the light, "Lin's idea for the flashlight was wise, don't you think?"

"Oh yeah, I just . . . with all the stuff going on . . ."

The room brightened when she pointed the beam up again.

Gabriel turned toward the couch to face Alessa.

"None of this surprises or scares you, does it?"

She is an odd one, but I will bet what's left of my skeleton that she's as—

"This is hopeful," she said, looking calmly at Gabriel, "and it's nothing I need to fear. Do you?"

If she is not afraid, then likely neither is Gabriel. Fine. I'm afraid enough for all of us.

Tayo looked up to watch Gabriel only smile back at the girl.

* * *

Daria squeezed closer to her mother as a loud squeak broke loose from the wall behind the couch, followed by rough scratching that circled the room, traveling from floor to ceiling as it vibrated everything hanging from the walls.

Anna stared in disbelief at Alessa, still seated on the couch back, without any change of expression and calmly looking at Gabriel.

"Mr. Gabriel," said Anna, her voice shaking, "we really must go, Daria and I. Ozzy too. This crazy story must come to an end."

I would leave too. The mouse, I hope, would remain.

Gabriel offered another smile at Alessa, then turned to face Anna.

"I won't stop you. But after all we've been through, wouldn't you like to see what happens next? Aren't you curious?"

Anna shook her head and said, "No, I am not at all. I do not know why, but you ring louder alarms than even Lin. You are too calm as a giant mouse attacks us all."

"Mouse!" said Tayo, still lying on the floor.

Anna looked at Alessa and said, "As are you. Do you not hear the scratch and squeak all around you?"

"Mom," Daria said, almost in her mother's ear, "don't start pissing off the creepy kid too. Let's just—"

"Your hearts are good," said Alessa, pausing and freezing Anna and Daria as they stared at her. "Your souls are safe."

Who is this child, speaking of souls?

Anna tried to speak for several seconds, but she only managed to move her lips. Then, she said, "There are things in the walls that are about to kill us all, and you sit on that furniture like you are eating ice cream in a park. Who are you people?"

Alessa offered a calm smile and said, "You do know that something will eventually end your life, don't you?"

Oh my.

Daria took short steps, trying to keep her heels quiet, and peeked over her mother's shoulder.

"Mom," she said, her voice trembling, "let's get the hell out of here. She's creepy as hell, and these people—"

"People!" Tayo said, followed by a weak cackle.

All eyes looked down on him as he lay there grinning.

I didn't bring up "people." She said it. It's an invitation to tell her my views. What do I think? Here's what I think!

"Do *not* be afraid of people. What inhabits the simple walls of the simple home of a simple man who's simply insane? Oh, yeah, go ahead and fear *that!*"

With Lee still holding his arm, he closed his eyes and laughed quietly just as frantic squeaking erupted from the wall across the room. Lee looked at the wall, and Anna and Daria, who were near, closed their eyes.

"Gabriel," said Lee, "it's all over the place in here. Any advice?"

Gabriel said, "My hope is that Lin, or Lin and Gloriana together, can finish their task quickly. The wall won't resist it much longer."

Ah, her name is Gloriana. Hello, Gloriana. Goodbye, Gloriana. I'm dead.

"Why can it not break through these flimsy walls?" Anna said as her daughter nodded from behind her. "I have seen it do just that. It made a mess, and we wanted to clean it, but—"

"Mom," said Daria. "Lin was right—forget about cleaning, alright?"

"I do not mean these walls," Gabriel said, pointing all around the room and looking at each of them in turn.

What walls, then, Gabriel?

Gabriel ended by looking down at Tayo, who'd picked up his head and grinned while he gazed at Gabriel.

Gabriel pointed down at him and said, "He is the wall."

I am the wall?

Daria whispered to Anna, "What the hell is Gabriel talking about?"

I understand. My dedication. My love of humanity. I am a broken wall, but yes, a wall. If I survive.

"I do not know. He appears more as a floor, does he not?"

Daria shook her head and scoffed as they both watched the grinning man on the floor.

* * *

"There's no safe place in this nut house!" Daria said in a loud whisper from behind Anna, where she stood holding Ozzy.

Every wall in Tayo's apartment housed unknown things that were scratching and squeaking. Lee stayed near Tayo on the floor, holding one of his hands. She tried to understand what he said, but he mostly rolled his head from side to side and muttered words like "explosions" and "dismemberment."

Lin still lay on one side of him and Gloriana on the other. Gabriel watched quietly, then turned to Alessa, who was still seated high on the couch.

Gabriel said, "You have a message, don't you?"

Of course. Why not? Nothing needs to actually make sense.

Alessa nodded.

"I have a message, and I have a mission."

The squeaking lessened, but the scratching kept going.

With a tilted head and a kind smile, Gabriel said, "I think it might be listening."

I know that's funny, but I cannot laugh, Gabriel.

Alessa managed a barely noticeable smile.

"We can start with the message, if you'd like," Gabriel said. "It's more of an explanation, isn't it?"

"Yes."

From her place on the floor, holding Tayo's hand, Lee looked up at her daughter with a confused frown.

"About the Hunter?" said Gabriel.

"Yes. 'It' is really 'they.'"

More than one mouse? Okay, we are now making some sense.

"I have suspected as much."

"I haven't," said Lee. "Lessa, baby, what are you talking about?"

Alessa looked down at her without a smile and said, "If I seem odd, Mom, it's because I am not like so many others. I'm more . . . like Gabriel."

How could that be?

"She's just creepy, Mom," Daria whispered.

"Daria, not now. I fear any one of them might slaughter us."

Lee stared at her daughter but didn't speak and after a few seconds, Alessa turned to Gabriel and said, "I believe you understand this already, Gabriel, so this message is for everyone else here. And Lin too."

"Not Gloriana?"

"No."

Why not her too?

"Tell Lin that what she calls the Hunter is a vast collection of damned souls. They have earned their places in Hell, and they have been given a job, one which they embrace because they have no other purpose left. Their work is to devour the living. They hunt in packs."

"It" is really "they," and they are attacking me and killing me? They are certainly devouring me. I can barely think in words anymore.

"I would too," said Daria quietly.

"Shh."

"It lessens their pain and suffering but only by a small amount. Still, they have nothing else, so they pursue their work with a desperate enthusiasm."

Gabriel nodded and said, "This Hunter, this particular entity, was a collection of forty damned souls?"

"Yes."

"Lin and Gloriana are battling—"

"A different one. There are too many to count."

"I bet Wolfe is a damned soul," Anna said after turning her head toward Daria.

"Benson, too, I bet."

Anna stared at her with eyebrows perked up.

"You know, because he's dead too."

Anna shook her head and turned to the room again.

Alessa was looking at the floor and shaking her head slowly, and Gabriel said, "Yes, it is very much a waste of souls."

Alessa looked back up.

"Some from Tayo have launched themselves, causing havoc for him, then returning to Hell. Others wait in the walls, not understanding their actions or having any plan but still, they are attempting to find some solution."

Anna and Daria looked all around the room as the scratching continued.

"And others remain embedded in Tayo," she said.

Yes, they are . . . embedded . . . and I . . . I can't . . .

"And your mission?" said Gabriel.

"First, to stop the attack from those that remain. They can't return on their own until they act as their lot compels them."

"That's likely to destroy Tayo. We believed it could be vanquished here, and that would help free mankind from the disease and destruction that they bring."

Alessa shook her head, kept gazing at Gabriel, and said, "That's not the plan. This world isn't meant to be easy. Even if it were, don't we all want to return to God eventually?"

Gabriel nodded and looked down at Tayo.

"Yes. These damned souls are what send us home."

"Yes, Gabriel."

The scratching increased, and the squeaking started up again. Daria compressed Ozzy as she squeezed closer against her mother.

"Perhaps we could talk more about this when you're done," said Gabriel. "It might be best if you fulfill your mission sooner rather than later."

The child gazed down at Tayo, studying him intently before speaking.

"I agree. Mom, can we see Tayo's back?"

"Sure."

Lee grabbed Tayo's shoulders and with one strong snap like he was a tablecloth, she lifted and rotated him to face down, carefully holding his head so that it wouldn't clunk on the floor.

"Mom," Daria whispered, "did you see that?"

"How was that a possible thing, Daria?"

He'd never resisted, and he continued to cackle softly. Lee pulled his shirt up to reveal twenty-four symbols that still remained lodged in his skin.

"God, they're moving," said Lee. "Whatever's in there is moving around."

The squeaking inside the walls increased, as did the scratching.

"It's okay, Mom. They'll be gone soon."

* * *

"What will you do?" said Gabriel.

"I will not let these souls harm anyone else."

Tayo's soundless laughter shook him, and Lee still held his hand. Anna and Daria cowered in the corner, and Alessa stood by Tayo and looked down at his back.

Gabriel glanced up at the ceiling, then at Daria.

"Daria, try switching off that light."

Daria clicked off the flashlight and when the bright spot on the ceiling left, the room remained lit.

Anna said softly, "What the—"

"Mom, don't say another word. I want to survive this, alright?"

Alessa stood near Tayo, glowing and lighting the room. Her clothing appeared almost white, not their actual darker colors, and she seemed to be reflecting light off of herself that came to her from every direction.

Everyone watched as she leaned over to look straight down on the symbols that lingered in Tayo's back. Her brightness increased. All squeaking and scratching stopped completely when she spoke.

"Any one of you could have killed this man," she said, "yet you did not. It's not because you knew that I would arrive."

The only movement in the room was from Tayo's rapid, shallow breaths.

"You also knew that you could have set yourselves free to rampage across the Earth if only you had ended his life. Still, you didn't."

She paused but never looked away from the symbols on his back.

"You have suffered so long that you can't even form the question anymore."

She gave Gabriel a look, and she got a smile and nod in return. She looked around at all of the walls, then she focused again on Tayo's affliction.

"So, I will answer the question that you have given up all hope of even asking."

* * *

Anna held up her hand to block some of the light coming from Alessa, and Daria buried her face in her mom's hair. Ozzy peeked around Anna to study the scene with unblinking eyes.

Lee watched only Tayo as she held both of his hands; he said nothing, just whimpered and shook. Gabriel still smiled at Alessa, who continued to light the room as she addressed Tayo's back.

"You," she said, "and those that have acted and returned to Hell,"—Alessa held both of her palms over Tayo's back—"have all chosen good despite your lot. Know that there is mercy in creation, and there is hope, even for you that have none."

She paused as her radiance flared.

"You forty are forgiven. Go to God."

In a completely brightened room, Anna turned away from the sight, embracing Daria and blocking even Ozzy's view. None of them could see what would happen, but they did hear it.

They heard Tayo laugh at regular intervals and each time, the scratching and squeaking in the walls increased. Twenty-four times,

Tayo laughed like a madman while the mice filled the walls to the point of bursting.

Finally, Tayo laughed no more, and the walls were completely silent. Anna, Daria, and Ozzy all turned to see and with the constant illumination from Alessa, they saw the smooth skin of Tayo's back, with no sign of any symbols. His back moved gently with his deep, relaxed breaths.

Lee looked up to smile at Alessa just as her sublime light left her, plunging the room into darkness.

From somewhere in the dark, Gabriel said, "Daria, would you mind?"

She fumbled it around before finding the switch, and the flashlight beam found the ceiling, lighting the room again.

Lee stood near Tayo with Alessa in her arms, unconscious. Only Lin still lay beside Tayo on the floor—Gloriana had vanished.

"She collapsed," said Lee, "but I caught her. Is she going to be alright, Gabriel? Should I try to heal her, or what?"

"There's no need. She will be—"

Gabriel fell silent at seeing Lin dragging her hand across her face then coughing. She sat up and looked around while brushing blond hair over her shoulders.

"Lin, I'm glad to see you back," said Gabriel. "You were safer than you thought. We all were, thanks to Alessa."

"I'm glad to be back. What happened to the Hunter?"

"Alessa took care of that," said Gabriel.

"She killed it? How? Who is she?"

"She's a very special being, Lin. No, she didn't destroy them."

"'Them?' Okay, then, where are they?"

"She brought them a message of forgiveness."

Lin turned toward Lee, who only shrugged back at her.

"We figured something must have happened to her, Lee. Do you remember that talk we had?"

"Oh, yeah. She was just beginning her life inside me when I found that power of mine, the one that healed me."

"Healed you and a lot of other people. Is she going to be okay?"

"Like anyone could know," said Lee, and she looked back at her daughter in her arms.

"Gloriana won't be joining us," Lin said to Gabriel. "She's lost there."

"Yes, she departed a moment ago. That might have been her final act with the last of her strength: she took her physical form with her."

"Is that possible?"

Gabriel smiled and shrugged.

"What isn't, Lin?"

Anna and Daria exchanged a quick look, then watched as Gabriel helped Lin to her feet.

"Gabby, she wasn't completely bad," said Lin. "She spent what strength she had left protecting me. She created the tower, the ocean, sky, and sun. She could have used that power to keep herself insulated for a while."

"Very few are completely bad, Lin."

"I think Benson is," Daria whispered with a grin.

"That might be a real truth," Anna whispered with a sigh.

Gabriel continued: "It seems she had a reason to want you to live."

"She did say she wanted to diminish my life. Even at the very end, that's what she said."

"I believe you will find out how eventually."

"She said some other things too. Things I almost don't dare to think about. I need to ask you about that later."

"There will be time for that."

"Lee," said Lin, "I guess your work here is done. You're heading back to Jacksonville?"

"Yep. Back to a normal life," she said, then laughed. "I hope we meet up again sometime, Lin, maybe for fun instead of whatever all this was."

"I look forward to it."

"Maybe with another bottle of wine."

"Oh, that's for sure."

When Lin had turned toward their corner, with no trace of a smile, Anna squeezed Daria's hand more tightly.

"Can you guess what I'm going to say?"

They continued to stare.

"No? You've heard it before. It's simple: forget everything you've seen the last couple of days. Get back to your lives. Go to Russia. I don't ever, ever want to see any of you again."

"We are mostly happy you have not destroyed us, Lin," said Anna. "You are very generous. We will go."

Anna led the way, stepping around Tayo, still facedown on the floor, and guided her daughter, who didn't attempt to control the sound of her heels on the floor, to the door. She pulled it in, gestured for Daria to take Ozzy out onto the porch, then turned to face the room.

Before Anna could speak, Daria took a step back into the open doorway, made a square with her fingers and spied Lin through the opening, winked, and hurried down the steps.

"God, she never stops, does she?"

"You might be right about her, Lin."

"That's for sure."

Anna took a last look at Lin's short skirt and heels and gave her own skirt a quick tug.

"I will not forget everything about you. I will continue to remember your sense of fashion. That is one thing about you that is not frightening. But I do not wish to see you again. Goodbye."

She rushed out and slammed the door.

*　*　*

"So, that should be the last we see of them, right, Mom?"

Daria had picked up Ozzy from his investigations along the sidewalk, and they both stood on the frozen sidewalk in matching short skirts and heels.

325

"Here, Daria," Anna said and handed her her coat. "I ignored the terror and gathered these for us. I am glad. It is cold."

They both put on their coats and began walking toward the car.

"I hope you are right about those people never again being near us."

"Not in Russia, though, right?" said Daria.

"It is even colder there on most days."

"Cold isn't always a bad thing, Mom."

Anna looked at her daughter, who was grinning at her.

"Oh, you are thinking about—"

Daria nodded and said, "If nothing else, he should see how we're dressed. What do you think might happen then?"

"Daria, we have no time to spend on such things. Do you not wish to be farther away?"

"Oh, you're making sense: Lin could come out here any second. Yeah, let's get the hell out of here."

* * *

Lin watched the door slam shut, sighed, and said, "I feel better already. Gabby, we should get out to the car and head home. Do you feel like cooking when we get back? I'll even eat those hotcakes of yours if that's what you want."

The first I hear after that ordeal is that Lin will eat hotcakes? I feel I could almost laugh about it, though.

"Yes, I'll cook. And yes, I always want the hotcakes."

Lin walked to the door with Gabriel, and she turned and said, "Tayo, you're going to be fine. You've served humanity in an impossible way like probably no one ever has before. Take a vacation. Go somewhere warm and relax."

Will I lie near a pool, feeling that my neck is still snapped? It still wouldn't surprise my head to have a companion head.

In a low, weak voice, Tayo said, "Thank you, Lin. If I willfully shield myself from all recent recollections, a recovery of some type seems possible. I'll try."

"I'll stay with him awhile," said Lee. "I might even give him a tune-up, just to be sure."

Lin smiled and said, "That's a great idea, Lee Ternity. Until we meet again."

Lin stepped outside with Gabriel and shut the door, which woke up Alessa, so Lee set her on her feet.

"Are you okay, Baby?"

"Yeah, Mom."

"You sure?"

Alessa only nodded, then climbed up to her seat high on the couch back. Lee smiled at her and looked down at Tayo.

"I was serious about that tune-up, Tayo. Or did we get everything? I mean, for sure, your neck is okay, right?"

"It was when I picked my head up several times."

He picked it up and set it back down on the floor.

"I believe your repair work was successful. Thanks again, Lee."

"Hey, it's nothing. Maybe you should just lie there awhile, though."

He sighed deeply and said, "Yes, that would be wise."

His phone rang in his pocket, and he took it out and answered it. "Hello?"

Lee and Alessa watched as Tayo waited and listened. After a few seconds, he ended the call and put it back.

"The symbols are gone, but at least one assassin remains. I believe he will attempt to murder me to murder even my memory of those murderous symbols."

Chapter 31 – I'll Arrive Sunday

"You were serious?" said Lee. "How many people are trying to kill you?"

"Lee," Tayo said, shaking his head and looking up from the floor, "each time someone attempted to murder me, it was preceded by a call such as that. It seems they wish to verify that I'm home and not waste a trip."

Lee stood with one hand in a pocket of her jeans, wearing her black leather jacket, her black hair hanging far down her back. She'd left her mirrored sunglasses on top of her head, and she held Alessa's hand.

"What do you mean, 'each time?' Tayo, how many times has someone showed up to kill you?"

"Only twice. This would be the third. But there was another, I believe, who never made it inside."

"Someone stopped him, I'm assuming?"

"Yes, but this new one will surely attempt to gain access."

"Maybe it was a wrong number?"

"Are you asking me to believe that I'm living a life full of good fortune?"

Alessa pulled her hand free and took two steps from the door to look down on Tayo.

"You're okay? You're still okay?" she said.

"Only because I know your mother," he said, looking up into her calm eyes. "And you. Without you two, I would surely be taken away with the trash."

"I'm glad you know us, then."

Tayo stared for a moment, then showed his own weak smile. He nodded.

"Yes. Yes, Alessa, you're right. I truly am fortunate."

He turned his head to look at Lee.

"Your daughter is very wise. Before you leave, can you tell me what just happened?"

"You don't remember?"

"Only that I lay here in agony and fear. Somehow, that turned into laughter. Just laughter, Lee. How did that occur?"

"Lessa, baby," said Lee, "maybe you should tell him?"

She looked up at her mother and said, "I don't remember, Mom. I heard the funny noises. I heard Tayo laughing. That's all."

"Really, that's it? That's all you remember?"

She nodded and said, "Maybe I'm not supposed to remember?"

She held her mother's steady gaze, again resembling a photo of a cute girl with a warm hood turned up. Lee shook her head after a few seconds and looked back at Tayo.

"I'll try to tell you what I saw someday, Tayo. Right now, I need to eat."

"I'm hungry, too, Mom. Not just donuts, okay?"

"Sure, Lessa. We'll stop at a nice restaurant. Tayo, are you sure you don't need us to hang around awhile?"

"I'm fairly sure. I plan to enlist the aid of Benson again. Although he's become a sinister type, I can't dispute his effectiveness. In fact, I believe he'll be eager to help."

"Well, alright, then. Lessa, let's go."

She slid her sunglasses down and pulled the door in.

"Call if you need me, Tayo. Us, I mean," she said, tipping her head toward her daughter.

"I'd welcome you here again anytime, but I'd hope that it's only for your company."

"You got it," Lee said and led her daughter outside, closing the door behind her.

* * *

Finally, I can speak with Jenny without a mouse or an axe terrorizing me. I might have just enough time before the next assassination attempt.

Tayo chuckled to himself as he stood and stretched his arms out to his sides. His smile fled when he rushed to the door and bolted it. He leaned his back against it and let out a deep breath.

Oh, finally, my back is a normal back again. Jenny can wait. It'll be therapeutic even to look upon a back without grotesque symbols.

Still leaning against the door, he looked beyond the couch at his broken hand mirror and the one that had hung on the wall.

Only the one above my dresser now. Why did I not shatter that one as well?

He walked into the bedroom, turned his back to the mirror, and lifted his shirt. Not able to get a clear view and the reassurance he felt sure that that would bring, he took out his phone. Holding it to face the reflection of his back, he snapped a photo.

What will I do if there's even one symbol left? Even if it's small, could that not command a hefty axe and a vindictive mouse?

He let out a slow breath as he held the phone up, a finger poised to tap and open the picture he'd just taken.

Tayo, you're silly. You might not remember the details, but you do know what Alessa is. You don't know how—and perhaps no one can—but you know what. Look at your back.

His finger waited. He watched the phone shaking.

Tayo, they're all gone. You need only confirm that. Alessa wouldn't have bungled her actions to such a degree. Look, you weak, scared man!

The phone rang and vibrated, and he almost dropped it. After jumbling it around, he was able to see that the caller was Jenny. He tapped to answer.

* * *

Seated and buckled in, with the engine running and the car warming up, Lee looked over at Alessa, who had just flipped back her hood.

"Lessa, you really don't remember what happened? Or did you just not want to talk about it?"

"I'm not lying, Mom."

Lee laughed and said, "Yeah, I do know that. Well, maybe it'll come back to you someday."

"It will. I think I know when."

"When, Lessa?"

"When everyone forgets. When no one asks me."

Lee dropped her glasses down along her nose and stared at her daughter. She only looked back, not moving and not even blinking.

"If someone asks, I'll probably have to forget again."

She'd become a photograph.

"I don't even know what to think about you, Baby."

Alessa shook her head twice and said, "That's okay. Do you love me, Mom?"

"Baby, I sure do."

Alessa smiled, checked her seat belt, and looked out through the windshield.

After five seconds of silent gazing, Lee wiped at her eyes, pushed her glasses up, and put the car in drive.

"Let's eat."

"Not just donuts, Mom."

"No, Lessa. Not *just*."

She didn't look when Alessa let escape a soft giggle, but she did smile and wipe at each eye with one finger.

*　　*　　*

Anna's car had barely begun to warm by the time they'd arrived and stopped in front of their apartment building. She put it in park and switched off the engine.

"Daria, Tayo and his home are things from nightmares. Are we finally done with him?"

"Mom, it's not like Tayo was an actual nightmare himself. He just kind of had one attached to him. That sure was damn scary, though."

"Have you considered how many frighteningly unusual people were in that room at one time?"

"Well, Lin, for sure. Her pal, Gabriel, too. Who exactly is Gabriel?"

"I no longer wish to even know. Lee is another. How does she attach feet and hair and heal things?"

"Voodoo, I'd say."

"Not in front of Lin, you will not."

"Nope. That kid was creepy, and I'll never know what happened. Somehow, she fixed Tayo's back? Creepy *and* damn strange."

"I cannot disagree, but, Daria, must you swear so often?"

"No, I don't have to. I want to. I bet you do too. Go on, Mom. Do some swearing. You've earned it."

Anna cleared her throat while trying to pull her skirt down, but it was too short and had climbed up her thighs from sitting.

Daria said, "No, stop that."

"What?"

"You should be hiking it up. Even Lin thought so."

"I think she was mostly trying to terrify me. She was successful."

"I don't know, Mom. Maybe it was just good fashion advice?"

"Do you really believe so?"

"Yep. Benson would tell you the same thing."

Anna giggled softly and said, "Yes, he probably would. That damn dead guy."

"Good, Mom! Yes, he sure is a damn dead guy. Wait till he sees us dressed the same. He'll go crazy."

"Oh, Daria, I think he is already crazy. We must display our matching wardrobe for him?"

"Even a damn dead guy deserves a sexy treat."

"I am a sexy treat?" Anna said with a smile.

"I like that! Yep, you sure are."

"As are you, Daria. Maybe we should see about dressing in shorter skirts."

"Wow, Mom. I think Benson is having a bad influence on you. I like it."

"Yes, well, he is definitely a bad man."

"And you like that? I know I do. I get more bad every time I'm around him."

"It was the same with Lancaster Wolfe, Daria. He, too, was a bad man."

"So, you two really did—"

"Several times. He had a magnetism to him."

"You know, I can't remember why I thought he was creepy back then. I think I'd kind of like having him around again."

"Well, he is dead and gone."

"Unlike Benson, who's dead and still around."

"That is funny, Daria, but maybe true. Damn dead man."

Daria grinned, took out her phone, and started tapping a message. She sent it and put her phone away.

"We should go inside. What did you say to him?"

"Told him he's hot."

"You are silly, Daria. You know that he is very cold."

*　*　*

"Jenny, I'm so happy that you called. How are you?"

"I'm doing well. Things have settled down here, after the murder of Samuel. The police are investigating, and I heard that they believe it was a robbery that escalated."

"It's a sad way for a good man to go."

Will that be the end of the attacks in Nigeria?

"Yes, Tayo, but enough of that. We'll pray for his soul, but we must move on with life. I have big news for you."

Tayo stood in the doorway between his living room and kitchen, frowning at the sight of blood stains where Benson had killed his attacker.

Murder is a messy pastime.

He scoffed and shook his head at the sight of his couch. The plastic tablecloth was bunched up and sloppy, and he knew he'd at least need to straighten that out.

Has the blood beneath that covering been given a chance to evaporate? Probably not. It is still a soggy sponge from my surgery.

"What is the news, Jenny? Did you land that modeling assignment you'd auditioned for?"

"Yes, I did!"

"Congratulations! This is the one, I believe, that will launch your—"

"But, Tayo, that's not the biggest news. I bought a plane ticket."

"You're traveling? To where?"

"To Baltimore, you silly man! I'll arrive Sunday!"

It's Friday, and the garbage collectors will empty that container in the alley on Saturday. That couch must be in it! It cannot wait for next week!

"Jenny, that's wonderful news!" Tayo said as he slid his back down the wall until he rested on his haunches. "Tell me what time you arrive, and I'll pick you up."

With a hand covering his face and his head shaking, Tayo's brain raced in a chaotic pattern around obstacles covered in blood.

Chapter 32 – Finished On Earth

"What'll you have, fella?"

Benson looked up from the bar and held the bartender's steady gaze.

"Whiskey would be good."

The man nodded and just as he turned to fill the order, Benson said, "Microwave it for a few seconds too."

"You serious?"

Benson smiled and said, "Room temperature isn't cutting it for me."

The man grinned, curling up one side of his thick mustache.

"Baltimore, huh? Too damn cold."

"Yep."

Benson heard the oven bell and a few seconds later, the warmed drink sat in front of him.

"Not used to the cold? Bet you're from somewhere else."

"I've been everywhere. But soon, I won't be moving again. I'm never going to leave Baltimore."

The man nodded, and Benson added, "Not alive, anyway."

After squinting at him for a few seconds, he wiped his hands on his jeans, turned, and shuffled toward another customer.

Benson took a sip and turned his head when a man to his left said, "I've never tried that—getting a drink warmed up like that. Is it good?"

He leaned forward, looking past the man, and saw that he sat with a young woman, who was also waiting for his answer. He shook his head, finished his drink, then gave his thought on the topic.

"It'd be easier to just microwave me, don't you think?"

They stared. Benson gave them time to speak, but they didn't. "Where can a man find a microwave oven that big, huh?"

* * *

Back inside their apartment, Anna and Daria hung their coats in the closet. Anna closed the door, leaned her back against it, and leaked out a loud sigh.

"It is good to be home. It is still early, but that is enough for one day already."

Daria was walking toward the kitchen, and she stopped before getting there.

"Yeah, I'd say so. Hey, how come I never wanted to dress like this before?"

"You did like your camouflage dress. Even your jeans and boots."

"I still do but not like this. Besides, that dress isn't short enough for me. Not anymore."

"Call Lin Finity. She can make the adjustments for you."

"No way. Hope to never see her or any of the rest of them ever again."

"Well, we probably will not."

She looked down at her daughter's skirt, stockings, and heels, and said, "She was right about fashion things, though. That is a good look."

"I didn't even think of it then, back at Tayo's. But, Mom, good thing it was dark in there, don't you think? What if she would have seen us both dressed like this?"

"She would have believed we were provoking her. Yes, we might have been slaughtered like livestock if it was not so dark."

"Oh, that's a good word. Yeah, I like that."

"Which of those words do you mean?"

"Provoke. Well, what I mean is that we look provocative."

"Daria, do you mean in some kind of attraction way?"

"Exactly. And we don't just look it. We *are* provocative."

She grinned at her staring mother and added, "*Sexually* provocative."

"Your mind is visiting in different directions these days. Yes, I suppose us dressed as similar could provoke some."

"Like that damn dead Benson, I bet. I never thought like this before he showed up."

"Before he showed up and *before* you killed him?"

Daria laughed and said, "Yep. Exactly. How about some vodka?"

"It is still quite early, Daria. Maybe we—"

"We should have a drink. Yep."

∗   ∗   ∗

"Um," said the stranger at the bar, "yeah, that would sure warm you up. Kill you too."

"Not worried about it," Benson said and held his empty glass out to the barkeep.

He took up his freshly warmed drink in his left hand, drawing the other man's attention while he reached inside his jacket with his right hand. He withdrew the black semi-automatic pistol and laid it on his lap, finger on the trigger, and pointed at the man next to him.

"I'm Benson."

The man looked away from Benson's drink and said, "Sam."

He tipped his head to his left and said, "This is my fiance, Susan."

"Good. Those are good names. Easy to remember when things get crazy."

The man squinted again, looked quickly in the bartender's direction, then back at Benson.

"Um, I'm not sure what—"

"Alright. I'm getting bored. Look what's on my leg. It's looking right back at you and Susie."

Sam froze at the sight of the large bore of the barrel.

"What do you want?"

"Besides a body-size microwave?"

Benson waited, but the man didn't even blink.

"Bad time for a joke. I get that."

Still watching Sam and Susan, Benson finished his drink and set it gently on the bar. With his left hand, he reached for an inside jacket pocket, found a few bills, and dropped them next to the glass.

"Drinks are on me tonight."

Both of them stared.

"That wasn't a joke. Alright, but not really an answer to your question. I want you both to get up and walk out of here slowly. Keep your hands where I can see them, or you'll be like me real quick."

*   *   *

Daria turned the corner into their living room, purposely striking her heels against the wood floor, and found her mother seated on the couch, her legs crossed.

She crossed her arms with the bottle in one hand and two glasses in the other and looked her over.

"Damn, Mom. Showing a lot of leg."

Anna glanced down and smiled.

"Well, if I am a damn treat."

"Yep. You are. Here."

She handed her a glass and sat at the other end of the couch. When Anna extended the glass over, Daria filled it and set the bottle on the table in front of them.

"Cheers," Daria said, and they clinked their glasses.

Each took a sip, but neither set down their glass.

"I could be an alcoholic with little effort, Daria."

"I know. Me too. I think it's just from all the shit we've been through."

"Well, it has been an adventure of some type. It has not all been bad, though."

Daria grinned and said, "Yep. For sure. I can't believe I'm even talking to you about this stuff, but being with Benson was the best sex I ever had."

"Yes, Daria, why are you speaking of such things?"

"You should, too, Mom. What the hell. Think of all that's happened. Tell me: how was it with Benson?"

Anna held her daughter's gaze and peeked at her over the glass as she took another sip.

"Well, Daria, he is certainly cold."

"Yep. Never felt that before. Hey, was Wolfe cold like that?"

Anna let out a short laugh and said, "No, he was an opposite. He had very high temperatures."

"So, I guess we could say that he wasn't a damn dead man like Benson?"

"Well, Daria, he was not dead at that time. He has certainly been killed, though."

"Alright, so Benson was cold. What else?"

Anna scoffed and looked at the glass she held in her lap.

"Oh, I know," said Daria. "That chair. That's it, right?"

"No, Daria, not the chair."

Daria waited with a smile, and finally, Anna smiled and said, "It was being tied to the chair."

"You really did like that, didn't you?"

"Yes. He was cold and bad and so demanding. It all found a way to add up."

"You remember what I told you before, Mom? He's got this weird game that he played with me. I told you about that, right? How he wants me to stab him, right at that time?"

"Yes, you did mention that. It is a difficult thing to understand."

"It was at first but then, I kind of wanted to. It just felt like it'd be something exciting to try."

"Stabbing a dead man, Daria? That is a fun thing?"

"I know it sounds kind of odd, just sitting here on the couch. But, yeah. I'm wondering if I've always wanted to do something like that and somehow, that damn Benson figured it out?"

"How could he figure out a thing like that?"

"I have no idea. I bet it's the same with you, though. He knew you'd like that. Mom, you've probably always liked that, and Benson knew, even if you didn't. He knew it."

"Daria, who is this overpowering dead man? How does he have such influence over us?"

"I don't know, Mom. But I sure can't tell him no. Can you?"

Anna held her daughter's gaze for a long moment, neither smiling, then she said softly, "No."

*   *   *

Benson kept a close eye on the two as he unlocked the front door to his apartment. Sam watched the pocket that contained the gun in Benson's hand, but his other hand gestured for them to enter.

In last, Benson closed and locked the door.

"Don't mind him," he said, pointing the now exposed pistol to the dead assassin slouching in one of the recliners. "If he starts annoying you, let me know. I'll ask him to leave."

Sam and Susan looked from the dead man to Benson and back again.

"Alright, well, here's the deal. First of all, don't worry. I don't plan to kill either of you."

Sam sighed, but Susan didn't make a sound.

Benson tilted his head and looked Susan up and down, then said, "If I have time, I do want some fun, though."

Sam said, "Don't touch her. Look, we have money. Just tell us what—"

Benson held the pistol up, silencing him.

"Things are going well for me. I thought this would all take longer but as it turns out, I won't be needing any money. Not from you and not from Anna either."

"Well, if you don't—"

"Alright, enough talk. Not another word. Both of you, in the bedroom."

He followed them in and directed Susan to stand in the far corner. With his gun close by, Benson tied the man securely to the chair near the door.

"Do I have to gag you?"

"No. No, I won't make any noise. I promise."

He tapped the barrel on Sam's forehead and said, "Well, I'd lie too if I were you."

He wedged in a tight gag.

"Susie, come on. You're in the next room."

Sam started to grunt, and Benson tipped his head to listen, offering him a somber grin. Sam stayed quiet.

Susan walked out first, and Benson followed, pointing her toward the spare room. He pulled the wooden chair to the middle of the room and chuckled when he didn't have to tell her to sit.

Ties were already laid out on the bed, and he paused to smile at the two he'd used with Anna. Then, he wrapped one around each ankle, attaching her to the chair's legs.

He set the gun on the floor and gently pulled her arms around behind her. She started panting, with an occasional high-pitched whimper.

"Shh," he said. "You're going to be fine. You're only my insurance policy."

She quieted down, and he tied her wrists together and to the chair back. Still kneeling, after he'd gagged her, too, he looked around at her chest heaving, stretching her tight t-shirt.

He stood up enough to put his head on her left shoulder, and he said, "Feel how cold."

He touched his cheek to hers, causing her to squirm, but she didn't make any sounds. He looked down at her breasts, rising and falling with each deep breath.

"Well, I'm just about finished on Earth anyway. So, what the hell?"

He reached around with both hands.

Chapter 33 – Two Damn Sexy Treats

"Oh, Daria, I bet that is a reply from Benson."

"Took him long enough," she said and got out her phone.

After reading the message, she typed her own and sent it.

"Well, what did he say?"

"He kept it simple. He said, 'Nope. Dead.'"

"Oh, because you said he was hot. Is he being a comic?"

"Mom, I think he's just being dead. We joke about it but with everything else we've seen, could he really be dead somehow?"

"I do not wish to believe such a thing. We have both had sex with a truly dead man? That would be the most odd thing for us ever."

Daria grinned and nodded her head.

"And we loved it. How about that, Mom?"

Anna tipped back her glass and emptied it.

"Yes, well, we did. We like it even though he is dead?"

"You know what I'm thinking? Maybe we like it *because* he's dead."

Anna squirmed and began pulling the hem of her skirt.

"Mom, you're still going the wrong way. Hey, do this: close your eyes, think about when you were with Benson and his chair, then see if you'd rather pull that skirt up."

"Daria, you are being silly. That would—"

"Try it. I dare you. I bet you'll only feel like undressing and showing off stuff."

"Very well."

Anna closed her eyes and after a few seconds, the beginning of a smile appeared. Daria waited and watched her hand, and she grinned when her mother pulled the skirt up, showing more of her leg while she rubbed at her thigh with her fingertips.

When Anna opened her eyes and pulled back her hand, Daria laughed and said, "Told you. Even just thinking about him, you kind of lose control."

"Because he is dead?"

"Crazy, huh?"

"Yes. Very much. What did you say to his phone?"

"Oh, I just asked him what he was doing. He still has to get rid of that—"

Her phone chimed, and she took it out to read the message.

"Hey, Mom, I'd say just take that skirt off now to save time, get your chair somewhere in front of a mirror, and I'll even tie you up, get you ready for—"

"Daria. That might be practical and possibly fun, but—"

Daria grinned and said, "Which part of it?"

"Well, um . . ."

"Never mind, Mom," Daria said, shaking her head and chuckling. "You don't have to say it."

"What I mean is that it is probably not a good idea. What did he say this time?"

"He said he's coming over. What else?"

* * *

"Well, Susie, those are really nice," Benson said after letting go and standing up. "Bet your skin is nice and warm too. But I have things to take care of. Be here when I get back?"

She only stared at him, her chest rising and falling with quick breaths.

"You know, maybe I do have another minute or two."

He faked reaching for her breasts, and she whined softly, causing him to stop and smile.

"Hey, only joking."

She let out a deep breath.

"Right. I joke at the wrong times. Alright, I can wait till later. You and Sam . . . not a sound. I'll be back quick."

After looking in on Sam, pointing the gun at him for a few seconds while shaking his head slowly, Benson left and locked the door behind him.

* * *

Daria looked up from her phone and said, "Mom, he's out front. He said he wants just me to come out and see him."

"Just to see him?"

"Never know with a dead bad guy. How do I look?"

She stood on her heels and twirled around, then shook back her long black hair.

"You look very good, Daria. A tight sweater is a good thing too."

Daria smiled at her mother while adjusting her breasts with both hands and said, "Go on. Tell me more."

Anna smiled and shook her head, and while looking at Daria's legs, said, "You look like a damn sexy treat."

"Thanks, Mom. That's sweet. You're a sexy treat too."

She blew her a kiss, then walked to the closet, put on her coat, and stood by the door.

"I really have no idea what's going to happen to me next."

"And it is obvious that you like that, Daria."

"You do, too, Mom. No need to admit it."

* * *

After Daria had tapped on the tinted glass, Benson clicked to unlock the passenger door, and she got in.

"Hey, Benson. What's going on?"

"Oh, nothing special. Just another Friday. How about with you?"

"Things were crazy at Tayo's place before. I can't even explain what happened. But it seems like the worst is over."

"Good. I do hope he survives. He's a good man."

"He should, now that all of that is done."

"You look good."

"My mom just said I looked like a damn sexy treat. How about that, huh?"

"She's right. What did you say to her?"

"I told her that she looked like a damn sexy treat too."

"Good. You both are."

"We never talked like that before. It's just lately that—"

"Best not to overthink things. Just let things play out."

"I believe you're right about that," she said and smiled at him.

"I like that you feel you can tell each other stuff like that too."

"That's not weird?"

"Could be weirder."

"Wouldn't even surprise me at this point."

"Perfect. Can't stop thinking about that knife, huh?"

"Yeah. My mom's thinking about being tied to a chair too. How about that?"

"Living can be a surprise sometimes."

She laughed and said, "For a dead guy, you seem to have things figured out."

* * *

"Ozzy, come away from the door. Come up on the couch and keep company by me."

Anna still sat with her legs crossed at one end of the couch, and Ozzy jumped up and sat at the other. She poured more vodka.

"I do not understand all that is happening, Ozzy. I am not connected to things anymore. Does that make sense to you?"

Ozzy tipped his head and held her gaze.

"Even if we forgot about Tayo and Lin and all of them. Just the feelings that are around now. And Daria dressing like Lin now too. She really does look good, does she not?"

The dog only stared.

"She does look sexually provocative, does she not?"

Ozzy panted.

"I believe you have agreed. We say silly things to each other too. We have never done things like that before. Is it all because of Benson?"

He didn't respond.

"That damn dead Benson. It is his fault. You know, Ozzy, I still wonder what things were happening in your sister's bedroom. I almost went in there to enjoy Benson too. But that is not a good idea, is it?"

Ozzy laid himself down and looked up at her.

"Are you taking time to consider that?"

He stared at her, his eyes blinking.

"I could not sleep after that, Ozzy. My imagination was taking me to many interesting places."

She took a drink and lowered the glass back to her lap. With her other hand, she took the hem of her skirt and worked it each way, higher up each time, until most of her leg was exposed.

"Maybe Lin has been right all along. A shorter skirt is always better. Daria's too. Hers should be very short."

The dog began panting again.

"Yes, you agree. Ozzy, if I had gone into that room, I wager I would not have worn any skirt at all. Not Daria either. All because of that dead man. He would do as he wished with two damn sexy treats, would he not?"

She laughed toward the dog, then tipped the glass all the way back.

"It is fun imagining with the vodka but of course, nothing like that will never happen. Oops, I meant 'ever.'"

* * *

"Before I forget . . . here."

He held out the knife that he'd used to kill and that she'd handled while naked with him. She took it by its handle.

"Any special reason?" she said while sliding the side of the blade over her thigh.

"You never know when you might need a backup plan."

"The gun's pretty good backup."

"Best to be sure. Feel like kissing a dead man?"

"Just kissing?"

"No time for anything else. We'll make up for it. Bet on it."

"Hope so."

She leaned over and kissed for a few seconds, then she got up on the seat and turned herself around, leaning between him and the steering wheel.

"Nice. Who are you?"

"I am Anna, alone with the dead man and wishing for more than a kiss."

After rubbing her behind and the backs of her legs for a few seconds, he reached up and felt around above the visor. He'd left something special there, just enough to do what he needed. With the tip of his index finger, he rubbed around on it.

"Mm," she said, tipping her head back to take a breath. "Cold lips. Anything else cold need attention?"

"Only this," he said, then he touched her lips with his middle finger, looking into her eyes the entire time.

When she opened her mouth, he gave her the index finger and the special mixture it carried.

"That's kind of sexy," he said, and she grinned and nodded with her lips tight around his finger.

When her eyes started to close, he pulled it out and spun her back around in her seat.

"Sleepy time."

*　*　*

There is no one I can call to help remove that couch except for Anna. Perhaps Daria would be a good assistant too. Lee has done enough already, and Lin is too far away.

He tapped Anna's name on his phone and waited, staring at the couch.

"Tayo. Are you okay? What is going on?"

"Anna, don't be alarmed. I do have a problem, but it's mostly an issue of logistics."

"What is wrong?"

"Jenny is coming in from Lagos on Sunday. Anna, that couch must be nowhere around."

"When do the people take those things away?"

"Early tomorrow. We must put it in the container today. If I hadn't been attacked in such tortuous ways, I might have the strength on my own. But so many parts of my—"

"Tayo, you do not need to attempt more explanation. I will bring Daria. She is not inside at the moment, but I expect her soon."

"Thank, Anna. I believe that between the three of us, we can make short work of it."

"Well, I agree. I will be there as soon as I can. With Daria. Ozzy too."

"Thank you."

I'll still have much explaining to do, but which might have a more believable explanation: that my new couch was supposed to be delivered but was late, or that I cut myself shaving, while seated there, sending gallons of blood into the cushions?

He sighed and turned toward the kitchen, and his eyes rested on his finger box.

If only all evidence were so easy to remove.

*   *   *

"Sleep, Princess," Benson said as he reached for her purse.

He opened it up, saw what he wanted, and said, "Good girl. Never leave home without it."

After wedging the knife in, he set the purse down and got busy with Daria's pistol. As if he'd done it a thousand times, he quickly disassembled it enough to remove the striker, then he put it all back together.

With the gun again secured in her purse, he set it down next to her. He started to brush her hair aside, and her head tipped toward the window.

"Don't worry, sweet Daria. Wolfe has this all planned out."

She didn't answer.

"Nothing to say, huh? Well, since you're out cold for a while longer, and since I'm finally going to be on my way soon, why the hell not?"

The engine ran, hot air blew from the dash, keeping the interior warm, and Benson whistled while he peeled up Daria's sweater.

* * *

I never did finish inspecting my back. I must do that. If there's any horror still residing there, I cannot place my back into the refuse stream to keep Jenny from seeing it.

Tayo took out his phone and again hesitated before opening the photo he'd taken earlier.

There is no squeaking or scratching. The axe has left me alone. I expect to see only skin. I believe I will see only skin.

He tapped, the photo opened, and he stared with a big smile, seeing the perfect, smooth skin of his back, without a single abnormality.

Thank you, Alessa, for whatever miracle you managed. If you hadn't, I'd surely be either dead or in a straitjacket by now. Possibly both. Thank you, Lee. Without your unexplainable abilities, my body would be a wasteland of damage.

He put the phone away.

Thank you, Lin, too. Though this has been a nightmare of the highest order, the faith that you placed in me is too much for me to comprehend. I will strive always to be as good of a man as you believe I am.

* * *

"Ozzy, Tayo did not say that we should hurry, but I will. We should hurry. Where is your sister?"

The dog pawed at Anna's skirt, and she quickly tugged it down and stood.

"That is a good idea. I will send her a text."

* * *

Benson picked up Daria's phone with one hand and enjoyed her with the other. He read the text, which said, "Daria, we must leave. Tayo needs help with something."

He grinned and said, "Perfect."

He typed, "Just another minute."

After putting her phone away, he enjoyed himself for five more minutes before buttoning her up. He tapped her cheeks lightly, and she mumbled and shook her head until she woke up completely.

"What? Did I fall asleep?"

"You smell like vodka, Anna."

She smiled and said, "I am Anna, and I adore vodka."

"Your mom wants you for something. Since you were snoozing, I replied for you."

"I will check that message when I am on the inside."

"Good, Anna."

Chapter 34 – This Time

Daria slammed the door behind her and before taking off her coat, she smiled at her mother, still seated on the couch and holding a half-full glass.

"See? Told you I wouldn't be out there long."

Anna grinned and said, "Were you also named Anna in that car?"

"Yep," Daria said with her own grin. "I was Anna that adores vodka. And look what I see as soon as I walk back in: another Anna with vodka."

She got her coat hung up in the closet and turned back to the room.

"Well, you should think of keeping the coat out of there. We must go help Tayo with things."

"Oh hell, not more crap in the walls, I hope."

"No, I believe the odd child cured him of that. His couch is his affliction this time. It must be removed so that his Jenny from Nigeria will not see it when she visits."

Daria looked down at her skirt, pointed a toe out to study her high heel, then looked at her mother, dressed the same way.

"Not like this, Mom. Jeans and a sweatshirt for that kind of work."

"Well, Daria, I would prefer to—"

"No, Mom. You're not going to supervise while Tayo and I do all the heavy lifting. Look, you have some jeans that are tight, don't you?"

Anna nodded and said, "Not tight enough, though. I wish to always be—"

"A sexy treat?"

Anna smiled and nodded.

"You will be. Come on. Let's go help that madman."

"And his giant mouse?"
"That's funny, Mom. No. No damn mouse."

* * *

"Alright, Sam," Benson said to the tied-up man in the bedroom. "You and I are going to take a little trip. No Susie, in case you're wondering."

Sam looked around the room while Benson untied him but didn't say anything. He'd seen the pistol in Benson's hand.

"Susie is staying here. Insurance. A guarantee that you'll cooperate."

With his ankles free, Sam stood and rubbed his wrists.

"Fine. I'll do whatever you want. Just so Susan doesn't get hurt."

"She'll be fine. Oh, and if you somehow managed to stop me, don't ask me how, but I rigged up a dead man's switch. Boom goes the apartment. With Susie."

Sam sighed and shook his head.

"Let's get this over with."

Benson winked and said, "That's a good attitude, Sam."

* * *

Both Kelginas, one holding Ozzy, walked up the frozen steps to Tayo's apartment. They wore jeans and sweatshirts and hiking boots.

"This is not the best look, Daria."

"Not like you have anyone to impress. We're here to work anyway, remember?"

"Well, I have never wished to be a furniture delivery person."

"It's just a damn couch. It'll take a few minutes, that's all. Should we knock?"

"He is expectant of us. We can walk in."

As they entered, Tayo was at the door to greet them.

"Anna. And Daria. Thank you for coming."

"Ozzy is here too," Anna said and waved one of his paws.

"Yes, he is. He will be a big help."

"You guys are weird," Daria said with a smirk and pushed her way inside. "So, Tayo, are we keeping the plastic on it?"

"I believe we should. It might delay the rats from their feast."

"Ew," Daria said with a frown. "Or mice. Let's just do this."

She and Anna dumped their coats and other things on the chair and stood next to it, studying their task.

"Tayo," said Anna, "maybe Daria and I can lift one end. Where are we taking it?"

"There's a back door that leads to the alley. We won't have far to carry it."

* * *

Benson put his car in park, and he and Sam watched the door close behind Anna and Daria.

"Show time. Here."

He held out a long knife, and Sam took it. Benson grinned while the man touched the blade near the point, then bent it to each side.

"A fake knife? What's going on?"

"Oh, you need to act as if it's real. Besides those two women that went inside, there's a man in there that you need to kill."

"With this?"

"Kinda sucks, huh?"

"I don't understand."

"Here's the deal: it's kind of a joke. You need to do your best acting when you get in there. Don't be too quick about it either. Stand inside and tell the man you're there to kill him."

"Not a funny joke."

"No, I guess not. Oh, and tell him he knows too much and for that, you've been sent to kill him."

Sam let out a deep sigh, staring at Tayo's door.

"For your darling Susie. Remember that."

"Just go in there, tell him he knows too much, then pretend I'm trying to kill him? With this fake knife?"

"Wild, huh?"

Sam turned to stare at Benson and after a few seconds, Benson turned toward Sam.

"And don't knock."

* * *

"Well, we should begin," Anna said, looking at the couch, then at Tayo.

"We can take it to the door," Tayo said while scratching his chin, "then we can first be sure there are no witnesses before proceeding."

"You're becoming a master criminal," Daria said with a smirk. "Good for you."

Tayo squinted at her for a few seconds, then stood near his end of the couch.

"Come on, Mom. The sooner we get this done, the sooner—"

The door flew open, banging into the closet door, and Sam stepped inside, a very realistic knife in his hand. While looking around the room, he reached behind to close the door.

Projecting his voice like he was on a stage, he said, while looking at Tayo, "You know too much, so I have come to kill you."

"The assassin!" said Tayo. "You do not have to do this."

Daria slowly reached for her purse.

"Oh, but I do!"

She pulled her gun and held it at her side. Anna still held Ozzy, who was growling softly but not trying to escape her arms.

Tayo stared through his black glasses, his dreadlocks hanging still as he didn't move a muscle.

"Please, put your knife down."

Sam hesitated for a moment, then lunged, holding the knife high in the air. Tayo reacted quickly and held his wrist just as Daria leveled her weapon and squeezed the trigger.

"Damn it," she said and threw it onto the chair.

She reached back into her purse and took out Benson's knife. Sam was too focused on Tayo, trying to pretend stab him, and Daria came up behind him.

Turning to see her mother for a second, she saw Anna about to scream and shaking her head from side to side.

Daria winked at her, turned back to the struggling pair, and plunged the point into Sam's back and through his heart. He dropped to the floor and a second later, Tayo let go of his wrist.

He stared at the assassin, then he gaped at Daria and the bloody knife in her hand.

"Daria, you have saved my life."

"I did, didn't I?" she said with a grin, looking down on the bleeding body.

"Daria," said Anna, "how could you do that? You killed him."

She turned to Anna and said, "It was pretty easy, really. Had to save Tayo, right?"

"Yes, well, you did that."

Anna still stared at her daughter, who had turned back to Tayo.

"So. Got another tablecloth?"

Tayo shook his head, looking at her with his eyes stretched wide open.

"Trash day is tomorrow. Plan's the same."

She turned to see her mother still staring with her mouth hanging open. She waited until she'd closed her mouth, looked down at the dead man on Tayo's floor, and began to offer the slightest of grins.

"Be honest, Mom. Pretty exciting, huh?"

She looked up at her daughter. A moment later, she nodded.

"Yes, well, we do have excitement in our lives."

"Yep. Bet I looked good doing that, too, huh?"

Anna's grin expanded, and she said, "I would not have guessed. Yes, you did look like a true professional."

Tayo looked from mother to daughter with his eyebrows way up above his eyeglasses.

"Should have been wearing my skirt and heels. An even shorter skirt. Maybe even lingerie. How sexy would that have been?"

Tayo covered his mouth with one hand, still looking from Anna to Daria and back.

"Try to imagine that, Mom."

Anna gave Daria an unhurried study down, then up. She sighed.

"Very sexy, Daria. I believe even the dead man would agree."

Tayo looked down at Sam, lying motionless in an expanding red puddle. Anna saw the look on his face.

"Not that dead man, Tayo," she said.

Daria said, "Benson. *That* dead man."

* * *

After the Kelginas had left, Tayo stood and stared at the hardwood floor and the blood he'd have to clean up before Jenny arrived.

I should be an expert at blood removal by now. Three men have died in my home: one in my kitchen, by my own hand; one just inside the door, thanks to Benson; and a third near the couch, killed by Daria with a noticeable level of glee and wishing she'd been dressed sexy for it.

His phone rang, and he smiled at the caller ID.

"Jenny, I was just thinking about you!"

* * *

Benson watched as Anna and Daria left Tayo's apartment. He let out a deep sigh, started his car, and left for his apartment.

"It's just you and me now, Susie."

* * *

"Daria," Anna said, glancing away from the road while driving them home, "there is blood on your hand."

"Yep. Not much, though. I need to remember that next time."

"Next time? And remember what?"

"They die too quick with a stab to the heart."

"And what next time do you speak of?"

Daria grinned, looked out her window, and said, "Just saying."

A half a minute of quiet driving followed.

"I'm calling the shower first. It's been a busy day so far, hasn't it?"

"Yes, it truly has. I will call second. I believe we might actually be done with a good deal of problems."

"Just one left. And he's coming over for dinner."

"No, Daria, we are not cooking for that—"

"Nope, we sure aren't. No dinner—he's coming over for us."

"You are speaking of teamwork again?"

She turned to see Daria grinning at her, then looked back at the approaching road.

"Is that really what dead Benson wants?"

"I'm afraid so, Mom. You can try to tell him no, but—"

"Yes, I should make an effort to tell him that, should I not?"

* * *

Lancaster Wolfe had just left Lin Finity's driveway in her hometown in Pennsylvania. His car had been demolished by some force that he couldn't describe, so he'd left it there, in pieces, leaking out every fluid. It was a cold walk, but he didn't care. He'd salvaged his pitcher of martinis and stopped often to take a drink.

He took out his phone, tapped it a few times, and held it to his ear.

"Benson here. So, you did make it back."

"Surprised? I know I am. Somehow, it all worked out. How's the plan going?"

"I had to improvise and pick my own fool to get killed by Daria."

"Good. And did she do it?"

"I didn't see her cross that line, but I'm sure she did. She came back out, but he didn't. Now, I just need to push Anna across too."

"Good work, Benson. I have big plans for those two but only if they're completely under my control. Like a couple of hot pets."

Benson grinned and piloted his car toward his apartment.

He said, "They are definitely that. I invited myself over later."

"Will both be there?"

"Yep. The thing is, will Anna join Daria and me in the bedroom? That's the question."

"If you've been following the plan, she will. When I brought you back, that whole process gave you something extra. Made you more persuasive. I don't think Anna could make herself say no."

"I think you're right about that. They're mostly under control already. If Anna opens the door and walks into that room, I have no doubt that things will wrap up just the way you want."

"Yes. Yes, they will. Then, I'll be done with you, and your soul will be free to finally leave. Kind of agonizing being held back, I bet."

"It does kind of hurt. Being cold sucks too."

"Hey, that's just the way it works. You'll be fine."

"I've done some bad things since you brought me back. I'm worried that—"

"None of that counts on your official record. Technically, you've been possessed. Still are. And since you never gave your consent, you're free to go ahead and give into it. When you're gone this time, your record will be fine."

"Seriously? Because there's this Susie babe tied to a chair in my apartment. I'm heading there now, and I—"

"And you should do whatever the hell you feel like doing. Really, Benson, it won't matter for you. You've got a perfect excuse."

Benson smiled and said, "Nice working with you, Wolfe."

"Ditto. And Benson, I'll know if the plan works."

"You can tell if I'm gone?"

"Yeah. How weird is that? Now, get those Kelgina women ready for me. They better be wearing short skirts, too, when I see them."

"When the plan is done, Boss, they'll never want to wear anything else. I think they're already competing on who can wear the shortest one."

Wolfe laughed and said, "I like it! Nice knowing you, Benson."

Benson laughed and said, "Go to Hell."

"I just left!"

Chapter 35 – That Damn Lin Finity

Still hot from her shower, Daria picked through her mother's closet and got dressed before joining her in the living room. Anna had just set down her empty glass.

"Daria, you have invaded my closet again. That is one of my shortest skirts."

"Yep, but I left the shortest one for you. How's it look?"

"With those high heels, you look very good. You have attractive legs."

"And I'm sure showing a lot of them. Look, Benson will be here soon. If you're going to take a shower . . ."

"Yes, I must. I was a furniture mover for some time today."

"Dead body mover too."

"Yes, well, things like that do happen."

"Damn right, Mom."

Daria's phone chimed, and she grinned at seeing the caller.

Anna reached for the bottle and said, "Do not tell me. That cold, dead Benson?"

"Yep. He's pretty funny sometimes."

"What did he say?"

"He wants to do a sleepover."

"It has been a day for lunatics, Daria. Nothing else I can do will surprise me. It started with Tayo being attacked by his very own back."

"Yeah, then Lin did something, and that other lady disappeared somehow, then that creepy kid—"

"How does someone illuminate a room like that? And what did she do to Tayo?"

Daria poured more for herself, and Anna held out her glass for a refill.

"Who knows? Creepy kid."

"Anyway, we will possibly never know what any of that could be. As if that was not perplexing and horrifying enough, then we—"

"Yeah, I know. I had to kill that guy before he killed Tayo, then we—"

"It was only a phony type of knife, though."

"We didn't know that, Mom. Looked real. Don't know what kind of loser assassin would use that. Anyway, then we wrapped him up in old sheets and blankets, then—"

"We put him out with the bloody couch and other rubbish. Yes, I know. That might be a common thing to Tayo these days but not to me. It was not the most pleasant of things."

"Oh, I don't know. I thought it was all kind of fun."

Anna stared, slowly shaking her head, and Daria grinned and raised her eyebrows a few times.

"Even with the stabbing, Daria?"

"Hell, yeah. Felt damn sexy. Not like you were going to do it either."

"I know. I stood in the corner, only shocked. But someone had to protect Ozzy."

Daria scoffed and shook her head.

"Well, the main thing is that Tayo should be safe now. Oh, and don't forget: Benson has that weird game where he wants me to stab him in the heart too."

"With that same knife?"

"Yep, the real one. That thing's been damn busy."

"Daria, what is that game about?"

"Who knows? I just might take him up on it, though."

"You would stab him in cold blood?"

"That's funny, Mom. Think about what you just said."

Anna laughed once and said, "Oh, because he is dead. Yes, that is rather comical. But, Daria, you would just walk up to him and stab?"

"No, that's not it. He really did say during sex. When I'm about to climax—that's when."

Anna gasped and looked at her daughter, who had a bit of a smirk.

"Daria, do you believe that would be amusing in some way?"

"Oh, I don't know. Yeah, maybe. Might add to the whole experience. I think I'm going to try it."

"No, Daria, that is not something to joke about."

"Right now, it does sound crazy. But when I'm almost there, and I'm holding that knife? Hmm . . . it's a wild time, Mom. I feel like absolutely anything could happen then."

"Well, perhaps the sex makes you insane? Still, it sounds bad."

"Oh, yeah? Maybe when you're there, you'd feel that way too."

"Well, Daria, I am sure we will never know that outcome."

"Alright, fine. So, I'm going to tell him to come over. You can go to bed early and dream of Russia or something."

Anna looked across the room, then turned back to Daria.

"Or I dream of that chair."

Daria smiled and said, "Oh yeah, you and that chair. That's kind of hot. He never told you to stab him, though?"

"No, he did not."

"Guess he likes me better," Daria said with a chuckle.

"Well, that may be. Or he sees you as being closer to a murderer. You did become one in Tayo's apartment."

"No, not really. I was only saving Tayo."

"That is the story to keep. Yes. Oh, fine, Daria. Invite the dead man over. We will see what happens."

"Teamwork. That's what he wants to happen."

She held her mom's steady gaze.

"Oh, I do not think so, Daria."

Daria nodded and gave her a grin.

"Just turn that doorknob. That's all."

Anna took a deep breath and looked down at her drink.

"Good. You're thinking about it."

Anna looked at the ceiling for several seconds, then her lips curled into a smile before she looked at her daughter and shrugged.

"We will see. He is rather persuasive."

*   *   *

Daria paused to listen to the shower running before opening the front door.

"Turned the heat up for you. Just the way you like it."

"Thanks, Anna."

"Oh, that is the right name. I do sometimes forget that fact."

He grinned and walked in, and Daria closed the door and took his coat. He tilted his head and listened.

"She's in the shower?"

"Yes, all of her skin is likely soaking wet by now."

"Thanks—I'm imagining that."

"We could go see."

Benson grinned and said, "Would be a sight. Let's wait."

He looked her up and down, and his eyes stayed down.

"Bare legs are good. Really sexy."

"I am a sexy Russian woman. Is the skirt of a short enough nature?"

He shook his head and looked back into her eyes before reaching around her waist with one arm. With his free hand, he brushed back her long black hair.

"Well, let me see."

The hand around her waist dropped down and found its way up under the skirt.

"That'll do. I like that. Nothing lacy this time."

She closed her eyes, and their lips met, his cold and hers quite warm. After a minute of kissing, while Benson continued to explore with both hands, he broke free.

"Haven't seen that bedroom of yours in such a long time."

"Come with me. I have things I wish to display."

* * *

Anna turned off the shower and killed the fan just in time to hear Daria's heels on the floor outside the bathroom, moving toward her bedroom. And another set of footsteps close behind.

Oh, the dead man is here already! And they are already going to Daria's bedroom?

She dried herself off quickly and looked at the clothing she'd hung on the door hook. A glance toward the floor showed her heels waiting too.

Well, it is only like a game for me, and I will not go in that room. But for fun, because I only pretend, I will not bother with underwear. It is only to feel sexy.

She pulled up the tight, short skirt and slipped her feet into the shoes. She looked in the mirror while buttoning up her blouse, not bothering with her bra either.

Looking into her own eyes, she watched a grin appear as she remembered that she'd liked being called a sexy treat. It didn't matter that it was her daughter who'd said it.

After giving her hair a few strokes with the brush, she took in a deep breath and let it out quickly, opened the door, and felt the equally hot air of her apartment wash over her.

* * *

"Close the door," he said, "but don't lock it."

They stood inside the dimly lit room, both looking at the bed.

"That is Anna's bed," she said with a smile.

"And that?" he said, tipping his head toward the nightstand.

"Oh, that is just Anna's knife. It is a good thing to have nearby."

"Yep."

He peeled his t-shirt up and off and tossed it aside. Then, he turned and embraced her again.

"Kiss me. Kiss my cold lips and let's get you undressed."

She did, and he began tugging her skirt down over her hips. When he leaned back and smiled, she began unbuttoning her blouse. He took his time, but she hurried and threw it aside just as her skirt dropped down around her ankles.

He took a step back and said, "Well, damn. Look at you. Just heels, huh? You looking for trouble, Anna?"

She pulled her legs up one after the other and nudged the skirt off to the side.

"Yes, of course. I am made to serve for just such troubles, am I not?"

"Damn right."

She stooped down and rocked forward onto her knees, then reached for his buckle.

"I am now looking for trouble. Tell me when I am getting warm."

She opened the belt and began with the zipper.

"Yep, you're getting warm. But I'm done with that."

*   *   *

Anna looked at her daughter's closed bedroom door, shook her head twice with a frown, and still walked up to it. With an ear against the door, she could hear them talking.

"Ah, that's good, Anna. Cold, isn't it?"

He is calling her Anna again!

"Yes. I have learned to like it."

What is cold? What is going on in there?

"Good, 'cause I like you on your knees. Especially without your skirt."

"Or my blouse."

You are naked and on your knees already? Daria, that did not take long! And now I do know what is cold.

Anna imagined the scene and without a conscious thought, her hands began pulling up on her skirt.

"Right, you sure lost that quick. Magnificent view from up here."

Yes, I believe that would be quite a view. I have never yet seen such a view as that. I would see many views if I were in there.

"I like giving you any view you want. I bet I look like a sexy treat, do I not?"

"You're a damn sexy treat. You need to get busy, though."

She did quiet down just now. All I need to do is turn the doorknob and walk in. That would not be such a bad thing, would it? Then, I would see all that is going on in there.

"Hey, someone's outside your door."

"Yes. Shall we try to guess who?"

"I know who."

I know who too!

"She'll be in any second now. Watch."

I think the dead man is right.

Anna grinned and reached for the doorknob, resting her hand on it.

"She can't help herself. I bet she'd like watching what you're doing right now."

Would I?

She tested it and found that it was unlocked, but it squealed softly in the quiet hallway.

How can I actually ponder going in there myself? My daughter is naked with a man, and the correct thing is to leave them alone. But I want to be touched too.

"Alright, that's always a good start."

Anna heard bed springs compressing and tried to imagine what was happening.

"Alright, I'm ready for you, Anna. What do I always tell you?"

"Mm . . . have a seat. Yes, I sure will. Anna likes that way of sitting."

This Anna would like that seat too.

She heard more rustling of blankets and creaking and with that noise, she took the chance of turning the knob all the way. She pushed the door, and it opened just enough that she could see inside, but she couldn't see the bed.

"There you go. That's good, Anna. See if you can warm that up."

"I do love trying."

I would surely try too. I would love to try. We would both try.

The bed springs continued a slow, steady squeaking.

I will only look. I have no plan to do more than that.

Anna opened the door wider and peeked around to see Daria naked except for her heels, straddling Benson on the bed. He held her waist with both hands, guiding her up and down while she looked up at the ceiling, her long hair swaying behind her.

That is a stunning thing to see. To see an actual sight is so more powerful than the imagining of it. There is a good feeling even from watching that. You know, I cannot make myself even care anymore.

She walked over toward the bed and at the sound of her heels on the wood floor, both Daria and Benson turned their heads and smiled, but neither of them stopped.

I did think of walking quietly. But I did not want to. I announced my presence in a good way, did I not?

"Well, look who's here," said Benson.

"I could not stop myself," said Anna.

"I know," said Benson. "Damnedest thing."

"I would give you a turn, Anna," said Daria, "but this feels too damn good. Maybe in a while."

Even she calls me Anna now. Of course.

"Still," Benson said to Anna, "get yourself ready. We'll both watch."

Anna looked first at Benson's calm smile, then at her daughter, who said, "Yes, we sure will. We will watch closely."

"By 'ready,' I mean naked."

He glanced at Daria.

"Isn't that right?"

Daria grinned and said, "Yes, we are both required to be naked. You cannot say no, can you?"

Anna sighed and began unbuttoning her blouse.

"No, I cannot."

She pulled it open, baring her breasts, and it surprised her that it didn't feel at all odd to have those two pairs of eyes on them. She knew that they looked good. She paused to look at the eyes gazing at her.

She dropped her blouse behind her, and Benson said, "Good start. Very nice, right?" he said, turning to glance at Daria.

"Yes, they are quite a sight."

"The skirt too," he said.

Yes, of course. I will hope to not need that very, very soon.

Seconds later, Anna had wiggled out of it and stood naked, wearing only her heels, close enough that her thighs touched the soft blankets.

"Oh, look at that. Another one with nothing but heels."

Anna didn't notice that she'd picked her right knee up and rested it on the bed.

"You know you want to kiss me," said Benson. "Now more than ever."

Is he always right? Perhaps. Yes, I must surely do that, or find something else to do, or lose my mind.

Anna didn't hesitate. She climbed up to kneel close to him, leaned over, holding her hair back with one hand, and pressed her lips to his.

What would I have done if not kiss the dead man? I did have several ideas.

She didn't stop even when she heard Daria say, "Teamwork. Yes."

She is right—it has somehow happened. We are now naked and performing as a team for the dead man.

Benson said, "Mm . . . that was sweet. You're a good kisser, Anna."

He glanced up at Daria and said, "Did you know that?"

Daria laughed softly and said, "No, but I would imagine so."

"I bet," he said, then looked at Anna and said, "Sit behind me. Up close. On your knees."

"Yes, that is a good idea," said Daria.

She shuffled around until she sat back on her heels, one knee on each side of his head, unable to get any closer, and he reached back with both hands, touching her everywhere that he could reach.

"That is so very hot, Anna," said Daria as she watched his hands. "The dead man is touching you everywhere, is he not?"

She will always call me Anna? Or only the times we are in bed? Why did I think 'times?'

"Yes, he is," said Anna.

What will I call her? I cannot even care about that anymore either. I know the answer.

"Yes, he is touching me very well, Anna."

"That is correct," said Daria. "I am Anna."

That does not even feel like an odd thing. Has she always been Anna too?

"I think I really am what you said," said Anna.

Daria grinned with her eyes mostly closed, still bouncing on Benson, and said, "Yes, you are a damn sexy treat."

"As are you. We are both naked sexy treats."

"It is good when we are a team?" said Daria.

"I am learning that it is good. Yes."

Daria's gentle bouncing and the thorough fondling of Anna continued in the quiet room until Benson spoke.

"I do remember what you like, Anna."

"I do, too, Anna," said Daria. "This time, I will see it."

Oh, do you both mean the tying of my wrists? Yes, I cannot lie—I do like that, and the dead man knew. I wish that right now too.

Anna reached both arms straight out over Benson's chest, squeezing her breasts together and drawing a stare from her daughter, and he stopped touching her with one hand to pull a tie out from under the blanket.

"Just for you," he said.

Anna's last thoughts of turning back left her when she felt only an odd thrill that he'd handed the tie to the other Anna. She looked up to see her gazing back, keeping up her steady motions, with only a slight grin.

She didn't pull back her hands.

*   *   *

"You have already landed, Jenny? How?"

"Flights got switched, Tayo, and I wanted to surprise you. I'm taking a cab and can get to your apartment very quickly. I'll be seeing you again after so long!"

370

"Yes, that's amazing," he said, staring down at the blood stains. "I'm glad you called. I'll just do some quick tidying up."

"Oh, the cab just pulled up. I gotta go. See you soon!"

"Yes, I can't wait."

Tayo put the phone away, and his black eyes darted around the room. After remembering that he had a small runner near the back door, he hurried to get it.

*   *   *

Just as Daria touched the tie to her mother's wrists, with her holding her palms together as if praying, Benson said, "Wait a sec."

Daria stopped, with the soft cloth resting on Anna's wrists.

My own daughter is binding me for Benson's enjoyment? Yes, she is, and it only seems oddly exciting. I should wonder why, but I do not.

She felt him tip his head against her thigh, toward the nightstand, and he said, "Get that. Give it to her."

Anna looked back into Daria's eyes and saw an excited spark. She glanced down first to see Daria's left hand on her thigh to prop herself up, then she followed her right hand toward the nightstand. She'd never freed herself from Benson as she retrieved the long knife.

Oh, she said Benson liked to play a game with a knife. Now, it seems that I will play this game too. It is a very shiny knife.

Daria wedged the handle between her mother's hands, point down, and she got a solid grasp on it with her fingers laced.

"Ah," said Benson. "That's better. Now, tie her up tight. Around her hands too."

"I will do as you say, of course. I will tie up Anna very tightly."

This is certainly odd, but it does cause some tempting excitement too. My hands will be tied as I hold a sharp knife. It feels good in my hands. I like that I cannot drop it even if I wished to. But I do not.

She watched as Daria wrapped the tie around her wrists and her hands, then finished with a tight knot.

"Shall I tie up Anna in any other ways?" said Daria.

"Ooh, that sounds fun. Not this time."

"Next time, then?"

"If you insist."

Daria grinned while holding both of her hands around Anna's and moved the knife until the point was over Benson's heart.

"There," she said. "We are ready for a very good form of teamwork."

Anna looked up from the knife to her daughter to see her only nodding.

I do not know about this, Daria. I mean, Anna—it makes no sense to keep calling that woman a different name.

She shook her head in response, but she made no effort to move the knife away.

I cannot explain this, but Anna was correct: this is an unusual but exciting game. We are all so close to tragedy, and we are all naked in bed too.

She looked back down when she felt Benson's hands end their playful exploring. He rested his hands on her forearms. Then, she saw Daria's hands rest atop his.

Looking up again, she met Daria's steady gaze. And Anna couldn't be sure, but it appeared that her daughter blew her a kiss, then grinned.

I do not know for sure, but did I just pucker my lips in response? Since I am not sure, I would like to do it again.

* * *

Tayo had just finished placing the narrow carpet over the red streaks and puddles from Daria's stabbing of his most recent assassin, and he stood back to admire his own ingenuity.

Oh, but all it would take is a modest kick or dragging of a foot, and my heinous sins will be discovered.

He surmised that it was close enough to the wall that he could put a heavy cabinet nearby, pinning down one edge and concealing the carnage from earlier. He pivoted it across the room and into its place, sighed with relief, then felt his panic race to its highest possible level as insane squeaking and scratching erupted from every wall.

No, it cannot be!

He dropped to his knees and covered his ears.

The very odd girl who is really a photograph and something else brought the remedy, didn't she? Didn't she rid my home of the giant mouse?

The sounds became deafening. He leaned over to rest his forehead on the rug covering the blood, still holding a hand over each ear.

Is my back again infested? How long before the axe strikes? This time, I will surely grow at least one more head and after that, my eyes will be—

Every sound stopped abruptly, and Tayo remained hunched over, breathing rapidly and tapping his head against the floor.

No axe? The mouse is gone? What new madness is this?

* * *

Still looking into her daughter's eyes, she heard Benson say, "You're getting close, aren't you?"

She watched as Daria said, speaking slowly and in a monotone, "Mm-hmm. I am so goddamn close."

Yes, the other Anna is certainly close. That is how she would look. I like that look on her face.

Anna felt a pressure on her forearms, so she looked down and saw the same arrangement: she held the knife over Benson's heart, unable to let it go from being tied to it, Benson's hands pressed against her forearms, and Daria's were still above his.

But which of you is pushing down? One of you wishes to drive that blade into his heart? Or is it both of you?

"I like you being that close. You've really lost all control, haven't you?"

"Oh, hell yeah," Daria said in almost a whisper.

"Never felt that good before, did it?"

"Mm-mm. Not even close. Damn."

Anna, I wish that I felt that too. Wait. What is that? Oddly, I feel that I might get there, too, even without that damn dead man touching me.

"No turning back?" he said.

"No way. Hell, this is the sweetest ever."

"Yep."

I cannot hold this knife up much longer! But I am beginning to not care. I am starting to believe that I will have the same pleasure as Anna if I do not resist any longer. Both of us. Together. Would that be strange or just better?

* * *

Tayo bolted to his feet at the wild scratching and thumping on his back door.

Would the mouse need to be invited in now? No, Tayo, that is crazy. It is likely not the axe either. That must be Jenny. But why is she in the alley?

After one final examination of the rug, he walked to the door and reached for the handle.

* * *

"Lean closer together, you two," Benson said with a chuckle. "Get a good luck into each other's eyes. This is a big goddamn deal."

I believe it will be the biggest "deal" I have ever felt! It is building like an explosion. I do not know how that can be, but I am glad I will have no choice in the matter. I need only stop resisting. It would feel so sweet to give in.

She looked into her daughter's eyes, so close that she could see nothing else. When Daria started taking quicker, deeper breaths, so did she.

Oh, how can this be possible? How can it be this good without even Benson's touch? I am so close too. I am about to fall into more ecstasy than I ever thought possible.

"Do it," said Benson. "No going back for either of you. You won't believe how good it feels."

He is so damn right. And I love that look in Anna's eyes! Do my eyes show the same?

From Daria's steady bouncing, their noses rubbed together once as they grinned and stared into each other's eyes.

"Wish I'd be around to see what you two do next. But I got a flight to catch."

She is Anna. I see in her eyes that she is truly Anna. Am I still Anna too? Have we become a mirror for each other?

She felt the hands, whether Benson's, or the other Anna's, or both, pulling down more forcefully. And when she heard the other Anna moan and saw her eyes close, she closed her own too.

I do not know who we are anymore. There is only this feeling I cannot resist. The two of us, both called Anna, about to fall off a cliff. I am already falling and cannot be blamed for anything I do . . .

The first massive wave had just begun to sweep her away and when she couldn't remember any reason for not letting the knife drop into his chest, she relaxed and let the point plunge in. Her reward was a rapture that allowed nothing but ravenous hunger and wanton abandon.

Yes, Benson would enjoy the sight now.

She felt no more pressure pulling down on her arms.

I will finish it on my own. I can do nothing but give us the pleasure we both crave.

She gave the blade a hard push and when it could go in no farther, a mindless, sweet waterfall of ecstasy carried them both away from any world she'd ever known, her own crazed moaning mixing with the other Anna's, with only a steamy, Godless night as their witness as they sank deeper and deeper.

* * *

Tayo smoothed down his shirt, checked one last time to be sure that he didn't carry any blood splattering, and planned his first words to Jenny.

It has been so long since we've been together. Should I speak? Or should I just embrace her? I will let the moment decide.

He pulled open the door, lost his smile, and stared at his impatient visitor.

"Who are you, then?" he said as the cold Baltimore air swirled and puffed heavy snowflakes into his apartment.

*   *   *

Although each wave of pleasure seemed to be binding her with a dark, sinister chain, Anna welcomed them all and wished for more. Every link of every chain was a wonderfully sweet secret impossible to ever resist again.

Gradually, she began to perceive the world again, remembering that she was naked in her daughter's bed. She wished that she could view the scene as the tingling snaked and slithered itself through every part of her, reluctant to let her go. She felt Daria back away from her.

Oh, Hell, that was amazing. I do not even care what it took to feel that.

She opened her eyes and saw that Daria had sat back, still atop Benson. She looked down at the knife, tied into her grasp, its blade embedded to its hilt in Benson's chest but no blood anywhere.

His unblinking eyes stared up at her. She leaned to the left, and they didn't follow. To the right, the same thing. She looked up at her daughter.

"He is more dead than usual," said Anna.

"That was absolutely amazing. You felt it, too, right? Your own plus mine?"

Anna sighed and said, "Yes. I have never felt anything like that."

She looked back at the knife and said, "I do not even wish to let go. There are still many tingles to be enjoyed."

She closed her eyes, shuddered, and let out a slow breath.

"Same here," said Daria. "He's deader than ever, and still . . ."

Anna studied her daughter, naked, with a thin sheen of sweat, and still gyrating softly on Benson.

"Daria," she said with a smile, "I must say: you are quite the damn sexy treat."

She saw Daria glance down over her, still sitting back on her heels behind Benson, also naked and with beads of sweat everywhere.

"You, too, Mom. You are a damn sexy naked Russian treat."

"More so now. After that."

They grinned at each other until Daria's phone rang on the nightstand.

"I cannot get it. The knife and I are one."

"Yep. That's what did it. Secret ingredient."

She stretched over to get the phone, then resumed her easy rhythm on Benson. A glance at the calling number caused a squint, and she looked back at her mother and shrugged.

"Put in on speaker. Lay it on the dead man's chest."

"Nice touch."

She tapped it a few times and set it down, almost touching Anna's tied wrists. With their eyes still not completely open as the pleasure hadn't yet let them go, they looked at each other and waited.

"Anna Andreyevna Kelgina! Never thought you'd hear from me again, huh?"

"That is you?" Anna said with a grin toward her daughter. "How can that be?"

"Who knows? Can't explain any of it. Say, I bet you're sinfully naked, aren't you?"

"Yes, I am happy to say that I am completely without clothing."

"And that hot daughter of yours?"

"I'm right here. Wolfe, right? Lancaster Wolfe?"

"Oh, hell yeah. You know what I think? I think you're stripped, too, Daria. Am I right?"

"Hell, I sure am."

"Perfect. Get used to it—that's what a team effort looks like. I'd bet you both have already learned to like it. Kind of feels right?"

They looked at each other and smiled.

Anna said, "I believe that is a real truth."

"We're a couple of sexy treats, Wolfe."

"You always were. You just didn't know it until now. Damn, I love it when things come together."

Anna nodded at her daughter, who grinned and said, "Uh, yeah. Me too. Turns out, it's even better that way."

"Alright, we have work to do, and Hell is on our side this time. Sounds pretty good to you two?"

"It sure as Hell does," said Daria.

"Good. Unquestioning cooperation has its rewards. Here's the first reward, a little secret: One of you, give that knife a little bounce."

Daria placed her hands over Anna's, which still held the knife in Benson's chest. She leaned forward, and they looked into each other's eyes again. She gave the knife a push, and Anna gasped.

Oh, what was that? We are not done yet, the other Anna and I?

"Oh," Anna said, "that was . . . with that knife . . ."

I should return the favor, should I not? Anna would feel that too?

Anna gave the knife a hard shove downward, and Daria smiled and tipped her head back before she again leaned in toward her mother.

"See? See what I mean? You already don't remember which of you is which, do you?"

They gazed into each other's eyes, close from Daria leaning forward.

"I sure as Hell don't," said Daria.

"She could be anyone. And me," said Anna.

"Perfect pleasure, right?"

They each gave the knife more playful pushes, sending the other a reverberating spike each time.

"You two? Everything alright?"

We have no desire to speak, Anna and I. Only this knife. Only how it feels each time.

"Oh, I get it," Wolfe said through the phone. "Alright, just keep going. You have no reason to stop. And guess what? It just keeps on building. See where you end up. Time to lose your minds, girls."

The call ended, and they didn't notice.

Anna gave it a push, then Daria, then Anna again, each finding that even a gentle touch on the knife sent the other higher up on a mountain, and eventually, they'd fall off together into bottomless rapture.

Anna shivered, took a deep breath, and said, "Do not stop, Anna."

Daria grinned with her eyes half-closed and said, "No way in Hell."

"Yes," Anna said with a noticeable shiver. "We are together on our way."

* * *

Bright eyes looked up at Tayo.

"You're not from the neighborhood. Wait. You're not even a dog, are you?"

Before he could back away, there was a lunge, and Tayo lay on his back, arms nonthreatening and spread to each side, with two heavy paws pressing on his chest. Some snow shook off onto his warm skin and quickly melted.

You're not even from America, are you, my new friend?

The head tipped, and big eyes looked into Tayo's.

Running would likely cause a chase—if I could get up—and there's nowhere for me to go. How can your eyes look familiar? Do I know you?

What had started as a low snarl evolved into a softer look. Tayo felt the wet snout touch his lips then back away.

What was that? A kiss? And is that a smile I see now?

A low squeak came from the wall to Tayo's right. Both heads turned, then again focused on each other.

Two louder squeaks came from his left. Together, they gazed at the silent wall but only for a few seconds.

Will I ever be free of the mouse?

The intense eyes stared, and Tayo heard relaxed panting.

If I am to be either ripped to death or kissed to death, I might as well try to be friendly. Your large ears are endearing whether I live or die.

He reached up with both hands and gently patted the coarse fur on both sides.

"You really are smiling, aren't you?"

A cacophony of raging squeaks erupted from every wall and before Tayo could close his eyes and cover his ears, he saw a pair of caramel eyes roll up high, and his guest snarled, gently dug in its claws, and leapt to his right.

Oh God, no! This cannot be!

When the uproar had reached a deafening level, it died a sudden death. Tayo listened, but he didn't open his eyes.

This is a madhouse, and I belong here. You and me, little mouse. But where is my new friend?

He turned his head to the right and gasped. Not daring to take his eyes off of the sight, he stood and gazed at the chair in his living room.

If this is a new instance of insanity for me to endure, no mouse will ever hear me complain.

Curled up on her side on the chair lay a dark-skinned woman, with her knees near her chest and her arms wrapped around them. Her head lay on the chair's arm, her eyes were closed, and her wild dark hair cascaded far over the side, some slipping along the floor before settling as if she'd been dropped there.

She wore nothing, and Tayo stared, frozen in place, gazing at a woman he'd seen but had never actually met. She opened her tired caramel eyes and smiled.

"You?" he said.

She blinked slowly and smiled, but her head still rested on the soft fabric.

"How? How could—"

He heard something plop on the floor and snapped his head to face the front door. Snow blew in all around a slender figure standing there, next to a travel bag, the inrushing wind whipping her thick black hair forward.

"Jenny!"

"What is *this*, Tayo?" Jenny said, staring toward the chair. "This is that damn Lin Finity?"

"No, this is—"

"She has five seconds to leave, Tayo. No time to even get dressed!"

Tayo turned to look at his unexpected guest. Jenny did too. She sat up, stretched her arms to each side, without a smidgen of modesty, and smiled first at Tayo, then at Jenny.

"I am here?" she said, looked around, then focused again on Tayo with a calm smile. "Then, here I shall remain."

Enjoy The Story?

Thank you for reading! Please consider leaving a review and/or a rating at your favorite bookseller or with your favorite book club. Help your fellow readers meet Lin Finity and the Fringes Of Infinity series!

For more about Edward Allen Karr and his books, visit:

www.LakesideLetters.com

And follow him at:

Facebook: EdwardAllenKarr

Instagram: Edward_Allen_Karr

About The Author

Edward Allen Karr was born, raised, and continues to reside in Ohio, USA. His adult life has followed a meandering path, ranging from working an automotive assembly line to designing space flight hardware. And through all of it, he's seen that life is a captivating and ultimately unexplainable endeavor. His writing seeks to add a splash of wonder to a world already awash in it.

*　　*　　*

Lin Finity returns for more magic, romance, and intrigue in:

Lin Finity And The Torrents Of Gold
Fringes Of Infinity Book Six

www.LakesideLetters.com